MR. DOOLEY AT HIS BEST

FINLEY PETER DUNNE

MR. DOOLEY
AT HIS BEST

EDITED BY
ELMER ELLIS

WITH FOREWORD BY
FRANKLIN P. ADAMS

ARCHON BOOKS
1969

SBN: 208 00687 7
LIBRARY OF CONGRESS CATALOG CARD NUMBER: 68-8016
PRINTED IN THE UNITED STATES OF AMERICA

To

The Hennessys of the World
Who Suffer and are Silent

CONTENTS

FOREWORD BY FRANKLIN P. ADAMS

IF MY MOTHER could have realized that I would some day be writing a foreword to a "Mr. Dooley" book, she would have considered me a combination of Aladdin and Shakespere. Even to have known him was a greater honor than she thought I would ever have. But it is even harder for me to realize that I could be writing this; and when Mr. Dunne called me by my first name, which was at our first meeting, I went home on air; my hero, our household hero, had accepted me.

That was one day at the old Waldorf-Astoria bar, and T. A. Daly, at that time editor of *The Catholic Standard and Times*, introduced us. After an hour, "I have to hurry back," Dunne said, "to write a piece tonight." "When do you have to get it in?" I asked naïvely, for I was on the *Evening Mail* staff, and my idea of imminence was a column due in an hour. "Last Thursday," said Pete.

Dunne was an artist. I use the word jealously. He revered the art of saying things perfectly; he hated slovenliness of thought and expression. That, perhaps, is why he had so acute an appreciation of Ring Lardner, an artist comparable to Dunne. And both were cursed, or blessed, with such lofty ideals of writing that almost never were they satisfied with their product; yet I know of no prose writers who could boast—though neither ever did—of so negligible a percentage of second-rateness.

There is nothing to be said here about the origin of the Dooley articles; Finley Peter Dunne's own story in this book telling how they began in Chicago in 1893 is enough. That was the Chicago of the World's Fair; and Dunne was a newspaperman twenty-six years of age, already a veteran reporter of eight years standing. He became a reporter for the *Tribune;* then he went to the *Evening Post,* where the first "Mr. Dooley" piece appeared in August, 1893; in 1897 he became editor of the *Journal,* wherein they were printed until 1900, when he decided to come east.

And still for four or five years "Mr. Dooley" continued to appear weekly, syndicated in the newspapers by R. H. Russell. *Collier's Weekly* then published him with illustrations by C. D. Gibson. I met Dunne in the fall of 1907, when he, as one of the editors of the *American Magazine,* was writing a monthly department, "In the Interpreter's House." It was an editorial article on current matters. It was written in undialect and beautiful English, and though like most other writers he hated work of any kind, the medium of plain English was a relief to him after years of the dialect grind.

It may be that the interest in Irish dialect had waned. For in the nineties of "Mr. Dooley's" wide popularity, the country was full of first and second generation Irish; the fathers of the boys I played with, John Finerty, Harry McCormick, and John Tait, were born in Ireland. And the stage was full of Irishmen; every vaudeville house had one or two Irish acts on its bill; the Russell Brothers, John W. Kelly, Bobby Gaylor, Johnny Ray, Ferguson and Mack, Maggie Cline, and Johnny Carroll; there were still echoes of Harrigan and Hart; and the tenor voices of Chauncey Olcott and Andrew Mack, in Irish plays written for them, were heard in the land. Every burlesque show had its Irish comedian.

Nobody who knew Dunne failed to be impressed; nor did I ever know anybody who came in contact with him, from the Chicago reporters and others who worked with him, to the young men and women he met in Bermuda in 1933, who wasn't full of respect for his erudition and wisdom, and bowled over by his charm. Even though to that young Bermuda crowd he was a nice elderly gentleman who had done something in a literary way, back along about the Battle of Shiloh.

About the time the "Dooley" sketches first appeared in the *Evening Post,* the *Chicago Record* printed a daily column called "Stories of the Streets and of the Town." This was the work of George Ade, and in that column he wrote his first "Fable in Slang." Let Mr. Ade remember Dunne:

"When I arrived in Chicago in 1890, Pete Dunne, although still quite young, was a star reporter on the *Herald.* Even his newspaper stories showed a careful and precious use of words, and his witticisms were crystal clear and models of brevity. When I first met him I was properly awed, because he gave the impression of being informed, wise, vested with authority, superior, cynical, and controversial. Early in the nineties the Whitechapel Club was organized, which is still remembered as a collection of harum-scarum irresponsibles who scorned the

conventions and shared an abiding enthusiasm for al-
coholic liquors. It was more than that. It was really a
round-up of interesting intellectuals whose opinions and
doctrinal beliefs were far in advance of the Chicago en-
vironment of that time, although they have since come
into favor and received governmental endorsement. Not
all of what they stood for will ever be approved by popular vote, because they were irreligious and probably might
have been classified as agnostics. They had such scathing
contempt for the self-seeking political bosses and the
stuffed shirts of the millionaire aristocracy of their own
town, and such a hatred for the tyranny of wealth, that
they probably might have been called socialists, with a
leaning toward outright anarchy. Certainly they believed
that many of the so-called "anarchists," convicted for en-
couraging the Haymarket massacre, had been "framed"
by courts and prosecutors who had been urged to extreme
severity by the panicky millionaires. Many of them had
been behind the scenes and their radical opinions were
fortified by the unpublished stories which they knew so
well but never had been permitted to write.

"Among other members of the Club, besides Pete and
me, were Hermann, the magician, John T. McCutcheon,
Senator Billy Mason, T. E. Powers, Wallace Rice,
Charlie Seymour and Brand Whitlock.

"Pete's stuff ran for a year or two before it began to
attract general attention. Just as 'Dooley' began to court
public favor, I broke out with my early 'Fables in Slang'
and so it happened that Pete and I began our syndicating, under the management of R. H. Russell of New

York, just about the same time. Both of us began to collect important money for the first time. We kept up the syndicating until the demand began to ease off a little, and we were tired of the routine.

"The 'Dooley' sketches were caustic and witty editorials written in the Irish dialect. I don't think Pete ever took them very seriously or agreed with the public that they were more deserving of attention than his chaste and correct editorials done in dignified English. He was like me in that popularity was thrust upon him, and he was marked for all time as a specialist in the production of a certain freak sort of 'humor.' I am sure that none of us ever regarded his output as 'humor,' but merely truth concealed in sugar-coated idiom and dialect. Pete was a positive character with a most engaging personality. He had a smile that was positively radiant. He was a remarkable person, with a vast understanding and an x-ray intelligence, and our friendship will always be one of my prized memories."

The expression of that social consciousness as articulated in the "Dooley" sketches, would never have been printed unless they had been written in dialect. For editors, fearful of calling names, feel that the advertisers and the politicians and the social leaders—money, politics, and social ambition being the Achilles heels of editors and publishers—are journalism's sacred cows. But if pretense and hypocrisy are attacked by the office clown, especially in dialect, the crooks and the shammers think that it is All in Fun. And when the Dunnes and the Lardners die, the papers print editorials saying that there was no malice in their writing and no bitterness in their humor. Few popular writers ever wrote more maliciously and bitterly than Lardner and Dunne. They resented injustice, they loathed sham, and they hated the selfish stupidity that went with them.

Anger, and a warm sympathy for the underprivileged underlay almost all the "Dooley" sketches. They may be divided, roughly, into two classes: those that might, but for a name or two, have been written yesterday; and those that are important only as bits of the American life of the day. Most of them, on the surface, are dated; many of them are outworn—almost museum pieces.

Yet to read them all again brings back to me countless memories of whole episodes and trends of political, social, and literary history. And while they summon vividly Chicago local affairs of the nineties, and this about Tiddy Rosenfelt and that about Willum Jennings Bryan, you can substitute current names in such pieces and it will astonish you to see how many of the sketches are true of today. Essays like "The Crusade Against Vice." "The Supreme Court's Decisions" is sound philosophy; the Dreyfus case articles are sane and burning criticism of conditions that might arise anywhere, in any nation where the prejudgment of biased power affects the liberty of its citizens.

For me to praise "Mr. Dooley" seems absurd; I would as soon endorse a sunrise. But there are many who never have read Finley Peter Dunne's acute essays on American life. To them I should like to make a house-to-house canvass, on a satisfaction-guaranteed-or-money-refunded basis. To Dunneophiles this book will be a joy.

Once Mr. Dunne was speaking of some current authors, writers of photographic dialogue. "They are wonderful," he said, "but they don't make anything up." And that was Peter Dunne's writing religion: To Make Things Up. And the things he made up were great things.

INTRODUCTION BY THE AUTHOR

IN DEARBORN STREET near the *Chicago Tribune* office Mr. James McGarry kept public house. Mr. McGarry, born in the County Roscommon, had lived long in Chicago and both by reason of his natural qualities and his position as presiding officer of what he called "the best club in town, not exclusive mind ye but refined," had an acquaintance amounting to intimacy with nearly everybody worth knowing in politics, on the bench, at the bar, in trade, on the stage or in journalism. Especially in journalism. I have no hesitation in saying that most of the local copy for the *Tribune* and much for the *Herald* and *News* was written in McGarry's back room. He was a stout, rosy-faced, blue-eyed man of sententious speech. He carried himself with dignity as became a personage who was not alone the friend and host of the most brilliant newspaper writers of that period but their counsellor and banker as well. He seldom spoke. "I was," he used to say, "intended be nature to listen not to talk." One of the gayest of our crowd was a reporter who could quote Shakespere for any event or occasion. Leaning easily against the bar he would parry every argument with an apposite line from the poet. This scholar one night found himself financially embarrassed and asked Mr. McGarry for the loan of five dollars until pay day. Mr. McGarry turned slowly to the cash register, rang up "no sale," took five one-dollar bills out of the damper, laid them in front of his young friend and said, "Tommy, what does Shakespere say about borryin' an' lendin'?"

There was a feeling on the staff that Robert Patterson, our editor in chief, and about the most competent one I ever worked under, hired only writers who were customers of James McGarry and only city editors who were not. This may have been true, for "R. W." himself liked a drink now and then—generally now—had a delicate understanding of good writing, and knew that good writers, unlike executives who must be made to toe the line, were not to be held down to strict shop rules. He pampered the young fellows, who wrote to his taste often at the expense of the working classes on the paper.

McGarry kept a watchful eye on his flock and intimated that if it had not been for his "infloonce" with the owner of the *Tribune* all of us would long ago have been out of work.

"Joe was in last night," he would say, wiping the bar and throwing the cloth nonchalantly under it.

"Joe who?"

" 'Joe who,' says ye. Joe who, is it? Well, I'll tell ye. It was the cagy little man in the blue Prince Albert coat that stuffs your envelope every Monday, me good fellow. Joe Medill it was. He drops in every now an' then for a quick one on his way home and we discuss this an' that. He was going into the back room but I steered him off be asking him to have one on the house. It's a good thing I did too, for if he'd gone back he'd've see the whole *Thribune* staff shooting craps with Johnny Wilkie over in the office tearin' his hair waiting for your copy."

Strange to say, I never saw Mr. Medill there.

One day when I had left the *Tribune* and had gone to work on the *Evening Post* under a great managing editor, Cornelius McAuliff, I dropped into McGarry's for a drink. Jay Gould had died that day and Mr. McGarry passed some quaint remarks on this celebrated financier's career. I thought they were funny enough to quote, and I put them into a little piece for the Sunday *Post,* the evening paper's sickly child which soon died of lack of nourishment from advertisers. I attributed them to a mythical "Col. McNeery."

Afterwards, while I was writing editorials for the *Post,* we became engaged in a bitter fight with the crooks in the city council. McAuliff and I were both hot municipal reformers but our publisher wasn't so eager. He was nervous about libel suits and loans at banks that were interested in the franchises for sale in the council. It occurred to me that while it might be dangerous to call an alderman a thief in English no one could sue if a comic Irishman denounced the statesman as a thief. So I revived Col. McNeery and used him to bludgeon the bribe-taking members of the council. I think the articles were effective. The crooks were ridiculed by their friends who delighted in reading these articles aloud in public places, and, as they were nearly all natural Irish comedians, doing it well. If I had written the same thing in English I would inevitably have been pistolled or slugged, as other critics were. But my victims did not dare to complain. They felt bound to smile and treat these highly libellous articles as mere humorous skits. "I had a good laugh over that one

Saturday," Johnny Powers would say. "But why don't
you take a crack at Mann, or Judah or Madden. (Three
highly respectable representatives of big business.) Ye
notice they always vote with us when we need them." So
I did, and was treated with sour looks from the author
of the Mann Act (in later days) but received heartfelt
thanks from the Hon. John Powers and his fellow suf-
ferers.

I was going on well and enjoying myself until one after-
noon when I happened in at Jim McGarry's. My friend
scarcely spoke to me. I tried various topics of conversation. He would have none of them. Suddenly he shook his
finger under my nose.

"You can't put printer's ink on me with impunity," he
cried.

"But, Jim, what have I done?"

"I'll see ye'er boss, young man. I'll see Jawn R.," he
said and turned away.

Sure enough, the next day I had a visit from John R.
Walsh, the banker who owned the *Chicago Herald* and
the *Evening Post*. I knew him well and liked him, even
if he was a pirate, over-punished through President
Taft's malignant hatred of him. Walsh said he had a
favor to ask of me. I knew at once what it was.

"Jim McGarry has been to see you," I said.

"That's it," said my Boss. "You know the old fellow is
broken up over those McNeery articles. His friends are
laughing at him. Can't you change the name?"

Of course I could and would. I called my character
Martin Dooley and placed him in a modest bar room in

Archer Avenue. It was one of the four old plank roads
that once ran from the little city of Chicago to the neigh-
boring farms and vegetable gardens. The name had been
corrupted (or improved if you like) into Archey Road
by the old-fashioned Irish people who lived there. No one
could mistake this humble tapster for the stately liquor
merchant and friend of the arts in Dearborn Street. Our
friendship was at once revived and it continued until Mr.
McGarry was gathered to his fathers.

I went on writing the articles every week from 1893.
My readers at first were mostly newspaper men who kept
my head from swelling by occasionally apply icy fraternal
criticism. After a while, in Chicago and Boston where
General Taylor reprinted his lectures, Mr. Dooley built
up a considerable following among the laity. I recall that
Eugene Field, who was "reading" for a Chicago publisher, was one of the first to suggest making a book of
Dooley's sayings. I wouldn't let him do it. My ambition
lay in another direction. I wanted to be a great publisher.
In time I became a publisher. But I never heard the ad-
jective great applied in my case.

It was not until the war with Spain was declared that
Dooley gained what was, to the author more than anyone
else, an amazing popularity. I have always attributed this
to the possibility that the articles reflected the feeling of
the public about this queer war. It was a feeling made up
of contempt for the foe with quite a distinct apprehension
that perhaps our fighting establishment was as stupid as
our politicians and as unprepared for war. It was. But
fortunately for us the Spaniards were far stupider and

were unprepared too. It is humiliating to recall the spasm of craven fear that spread across the nation when a lying report was circulated that Dewey had been beaten at Manila Bay. Then came Ed Harden's flash from Hong Kong to the *Chicago Tribune,* the scoop of the century, telling of the complete annihilation of the Spanish fleet. Within a few weeks the wretched Spanish navy at Santiago de Cuba came out to be slaughtered. The old ladies of New England emerged from their cellars and the public gave full rein to the comic relief and laughed at Alger and Shafter and the Chicago packers and the absurd heroes of the "opera bouffe war." It was great fun for all —that is, for all who weren't wounded, or whose sons or brothers weren't killed, or who, having successfully invaded Cuba, were not thoroughly routed and slain like flies, at Montauk Point, Suffolk County, State of New York, U. S. A. The Spanish General Incompetence they could beat. But the relentless General Incompetence of their own army was too much for them.

It was to this mood that Mr. Dooley responded. It is still a cause for gratitude on the part of its author that his harmless jokes were so well received, and that, incidentally, they helped to puncture and deflate some of the humbug and sham and cowardice and false pretense that are as inevitable companions of war as lice and pneumococci and taxes.

F. P. D.

January 1, 1936.

INTRODUCING MR. DOOLEY

"I am Dooley, ye say, but ye're on'y a casual obsarver. Ye don't care annythin' about me details. Ye look at me with a gin'ral eye. Nawthin' that happens to me really hurts ye. Ye say, 'I'll go over to see Dooley,' sometimes, but more often ye say, 'I'll go over to Dooley's.' I'm a house to ye, wan iv a thousand that look like a row iv model wurrukin'men's cottages. I'm a post to hitch ye'er silences to. I'm always about th' same to ye. But to me I'm a millyon Dooleys an' all iv thim sthrangers to ME. I niver know which wan iv thim is comin' in. I'm like a hotel keeper with on'y wan bed an' a millyon guests, who come wan at a time an' tumble each other out. I set up late at night an' pass th' bottle with a gay an' careless Dooley that hasn't a sorrow in th' wurruld, an' suddenly I look up an' see settin' acrost fr'm me a gloomy wretch that fires th' dhrink out iv th' window an' chases me to bed. I'm just gettin' used to him whin another Dooley comes in, a cross, cantankerous, crazy fellow that insists on eatin' breakfast with me. An' so it goes. I know more about mesilf than annybody knows an' I know nawthin'. Though I'd make a map fr'm mem'ry an' gossip iv anny other man, f'r mesilf I'm still uncharted."

ARCHEY ROAD

♣　♣　♣

Archey Road stretches back for many miles from
the heart of an ugly city to the cabbage gardens that gave
the maker of the seal his opportunity to call the city "urbs
in horto." Somewhere between the two—that is to say,
forninst th' gas-house and beyant Healey's slough and
not far from the polis station—lives Martin Dooley, doctor
of philosophy.

There was a time when Archey Road was purely Irish.
But the Huns, turned back from the Adriatic and the
stock-yards and overrunning Archey Road, have nearly
exhausted the original population—not driven them out
as they drove out less vigorous races, with thick clubs
and short spears, but edged them out with the more biting
weapons of modern civilization—overworked and under-
eaten them into more languid surroundings remote from
the tanks of the gas-house and the blast furnaces of the
rolling-mill.

But Mr. Dooley remains, and enough remain with him
to save the Archey Road. In this community you can hear
all the various accents of Ireland, from the awkward
brogue of the "far-downer" to the mild and aisy Eliza-
bethan English of the southern Irishman, and all the
exquisite variations to be heard between Armagh and

Bantry Bay, with the difference that would naturally arise from substituting cinders and sulphuretted hydrogen for soft misty air and peat smoke. Here also you can see the wakes and christenings, the marriages and funerals, and the other fêtes of the ol' counthry somewhat modified and darkened by American usage. The Banshee has been heard many times in Archey Road. On the eve of All Saints' Day it is well known that here alone the pookies play thricks in cabbage gardens. In 1893 it was reported that Malachi Dempsey was called "by the other people," and disappeared west of the tracks, and never came back.

A simple people! "Simple, says ye!" remarked Mr. Dooley. "Simple like th' air or th' deep sea. Not complicated like a watch that stops whin th' shoot iv clothes ye got it with wears out. Whin Father Butler wr-rote a book he niver finished, he said simplicity was not wearin' all ye had on ye'er shirt-front, like a tin-horn gambler with his di'mon' stud. An' 'tis so."

The barbarians around them are moderately but firmly governed, encouraged to passionate votings for the ruling race, but restrained from the immoral pursuit of office.

The most generous, thoughful, honest, and chaste people in the world are these friends of Mr. Dooley,—knowing and innocent; moral, but giving no heed at all to patented political moralities.

Among them lives and prospers the traveller, archæologist, historian, social observer, saloon-keeper, economist, and philosopher, who has not been out of the ward for twenty-five years "but twict." He reads the newspapers with solemn care, heartily hates them, and accepts all they print for the sake of drowning Hennessy's rising protests against his logic. From the cool heights of life in the Archey Road, uninterrupted by the jarring noises of crickets and cows, he observes the passing show, and meditates thereon. His impressions are transferred to the desensitized plate of Mr. Hennessy's mind, where they can do no harm.

"There's no betther place to see what's goin' on thin the Ar-rchey Road," says Mr. Dooley. "Whin th' ilicthric cars is hummin' down th' sthreet an' th' blast goin' sthrong at th' mills, th' noise is that gr-reat ye can't think."

He is opulent in good advice, as becomes a man of his station; for he has mastered most of the obstacles in a business career, and by leading a prudent and temperate life has established himself so well that he owns his own house and furnitûre, and is only slightly behind on his license. It would be indelicate to give statistics as to his age. Mr. Hennessy says he was a "grown man whin th' pikes was out in forty-eight, an' I was hedge-high, an' I'm near fifty-five." Mr. Dooley says Mr. Hennessy is eighty. He closes discussion on his own age with the remark, "I'm old enough to know betther." He has served his country with distinction. His conduct of the important office of captain of his precinct (1873–75) was highly commended, and there was some talk of nominating him for alderman. At the expiration of his term he was personally thanked by the Hon. M. McGee, at one time a member of the central committee. But the activity of public life was unsuited to a man of Mr. Dooley's tastes;

and, while he continues to view the political situation always with interest and sometimes with alarm, he has resolutely declined to leave the bar for the forum. His early experience gave him wisdom in discussing public affairs. "Polytics," he says, "ain't bean bag. 'Tis a man's game; an' women, childher, an' pro-hybitionists'd do well to keep out iv it." Again he remarks, "As Shakespere says, 'Ol' men f'r th' council, young men f'r th' ward.' "

1898   F. P. D.

In some cases the sketches have been remodelled and care has been taken to correct typographical blunders, except where they seemed to improve the text. In this connection the writer must offer his profound gratitude to the industrious typographer, who often makes two jokes grow where only one grew before, and has added generously to the distress of amateur elocutionists.

1900   F. P. D.

NEW YEAR'S RESOLUTIONS

☘ ☘ ☘

MR. HENNESSY looked out at the rain dripping
down in Archey Road, and sighed, "A-ha, 'tis a bad spell
iv weather we're havin'."

"Faith, it is," said Mr. Dooley, "or else we mind it more
thin we did. I can't remimber wan day fr'm another. Whin
I was young, I niver thought iv rain or snow, cold or heat.
But now th' heat stings an' th' cold wrenches me bones;
an', if I go out in th' rain with less on me thin a ton iv
rubber, I'll pay dear f'r it in achin' j'ints, so I will. That's
what old age means; an' now another year has been put on
to what we had befure, an' we're expected to be gay. 'Ring
out th' old,' says a guy at th' Brothers' School. 'Ring out
th' old, ring in th' new,' he says. 'Ring out th' false, ring
in th' thrue,' says he. It's a pretty sintimint, Hinnissy; but
how ar-re we goin' to do it? Nawthin'd please me bether
thin to turn me back on th' wicked an' ingloryous past,
rayform me life, an' live at peace with th' wurruld to th'
end iv me days. But how th' divvle can I do it? As th'
fellow says, 'Can th' leopard change his spots,' or can't he?

"You know Dorsey, iv coorse, th' cross-eyed May-o
man that come to this counthry about wan day in advance
iv a warrant f'r sheep-stealin'? Ye know what he done to
me, tellin' people I was caught in me cellar poorin' wather

into a bar'l? Well, last night says I to mesilf, thinkin' iv
Dorsey, I says: 'I swear that henceforth I'll keep me
temper with me fellow-men. I'll not let anger or jealousy
get th' betther iv me,' I says. 'I'll lave off all me old feuds;
an' if I meet me inimy goin' down th' sthreet, I'll go up an'
shake him be th' hand, if I'm sure he hasn't a brick in th'
other hand.' Oh, I was mighty compliminthry to mesilf. I
set be th' stove dhrinkin' hot wans, an' ivry wan I dhrunk
made me more iv a pote. 'Tis th' way with th' stuff. Whin
I'm in dhrink, I have manny a fine thought; an', if I
wasn't too comfortable to go an' look f'r th' ink-bottle, I
cud write pomes that'd make Shakespere an' Mike Scanlan think they were wur-rkin' on a dredge. 'Why,' says I,
'carry into th' new year th' hathreds iv th' old?' I says.
'Let th' dead past bury its dead,' says I. 'Tur-rn ye'er
lamps up to th' blue sky,' I says. (It was rainin' like th'
divvle, an' th' hour was midnight; but I give no heed to
that, bein' comfortable with th' hot wans.) An' I wint to
th' dure, an', whin Mike Duffy come by on number wan
hundherd an' five, ringin' th' gong iv th' ca-ar, I hollered
to him: 'Ring out th' old, ring in th' new.' 'Go back into
ye'er stall,' he says, 'an' wring ye'ersilf out,' he says.
'Ye'er wet through,' he says.

"Whin I woke up this mornin', th' pothry had all disappeared, an' I begun to think th' las' hot wan I took had
somethin' wrong with it. Besides, th' lumbago was grip-
pin' me till I cud hardly put wan foot befure th' other.
But I remimbered me promises to mesilf, an' wint out on
th' sthreet, intindin' to wish ivry wan a 'Happy New
Year,' an' hopin' in me hear-rt that th' first wan I wished

it to'd tell me to go to th' divvle, so I cud hit him in th' eye.
I hadn't gone half a block befure I spied Dorsey acrost
th' sthreet. I picked up a half a brick an' put it in me
pocket, an' Dorsey done th' same. Thin we wint up to
each other. 'A Happy New Year,' says I. 'Th' same to
you,' says he, 'an' manny iv thim,' he says. 'Ye have a
brick in ye'er hand,' says I. 'I was thinkin' iv givin' ye a
New Year's gift,' says he. 'Th' same to you, an' manny
iv thim,' says I, fondlin' me own ammunition. ' 'Tis even
all around,' says he. 'It is,' says I. 'I was thinkin' las' night
I'd give up me gredge again ye,' says he. 'I had th' same
thought mesilf,' says I. 'But, since I seen ye'er face,' he
says, 'I've con-cluded that I'd be more comfortable hatin'
ye thin havin' ye f'r a frind,' says he. 'Ye're a man iv taste,'
says I. An' we backed away fr'm each other. He's a Tip,
an' can throw a stone like a rifleman; an', Hinnissy, I'm
somethin' iv an amachoor shot with a half-brick mesilf.

"Well, I've been thinkin' it over, an' I've argied it
out that life'd not be worth livin' if we didn't keep our
inimies. I can have all th' frinds I need. Anny man can
that keeps a liquor sthore. But a rale sthrong inimy, specially a May-o inimy—wan that hates ye ha-ard, an' that
ye'd take th' coat off yer back to do a bad tur-rn to—is a
luxury that I can't go without in me ol' days. Dorsey is
th' right sort. I can't go by his house without bein' in fear
he'll spill th' chimbly down on me head; an', whin he
passes my place, he walks in th' middle iv th' sthreet, an'
crosses himsilf. I'll swear off on annything but Dorsey.
He's a good man, an' I despise him. Here's long life to
him."

A WINTER NIGHT

♣ ♣ ♣

Any of the Archey Road cars that got out of the barns at all were pulled by teams of four horses, and the snow hung over the shoulders of the drivers' big bearskin coats like the eaves of an old-fashioned house on the blizzard night. There was hardly a soul in the road from the red bridge, west, when Mr. McKenna got laboriously off the platform of his car and made for the sign of somebody's celebrated Milwaukee beer over Mr. Dooley's tavern. Mr. Dooley, being a man of sentiment, arranges his drinks to conform with the weather. Now anybody who knows anything at all knows that a drop of "J.J." and a whisper (subdued) of hot water and a lump of sugar and lemon peel (if you care for lemon peel) and nutmeg (if you are a "jood") is a drink calculated to tune a man's heart to the song of the wind slapping a beer-sign upside down and the snow drifting in under the door. Mr. Dooley was drinking this mixture behind his big stove when Mr. McKenna came in.

"Bad night, Jawn," said Mr. Dooley.

"It is that," said Mr. McKenna.

"Blowin' an' stormin', yes," said Mr. Dooley. "There hasn' been a can in tonight but wan, an' that was a pop bottle. Is the snow-ploughs out, I dinnaw?"

"They are," said Mr. McKenna.

"I suppose Doherty is dhrivin'," said Mr. Dooley. "He's a good dhriver. They do say he do be wan iv the best dhrivers on th' road. I've heerd that th' prisident is dead gawn on him. He's me cousin. Ye can't tell much about what a man 'll be fr'm what th' kid is. That there Doherty was th' worst omadhon iv a boy that iver I knowed. He niver cud larn his a-ah-bee, abs. But see what he made iv himsilf! Th' best dhriver on th' road; an', by dad, 'tis not twinty to wan he won't be stharter befure he dies. 'Tis in th' fam'ly to make their names. There niver was anny fam'ly in th' ol' counthry that turned out more priests than th' Dooleys. By gar, I believe we hol' th' champeenship iv th' wurruld. At M'nooth th' profissor that called th' roll got so fr'm namin' th' Dooley la-ads that he came near bein' tur-rned down on th' cha-arge that he was whistlin' at vespers. His mouth, d'ye mind, took that there shape fr'm sayin' 'Dooley,' 'Dooley,' that he'd looked as if he was whistlin'. D'ye mind? Dear, oh dear, 'tis th' divvle's own fam'ly f'r religion."

Mr. McKenna was about to make a jeering remark to the effect that the alleged piety of the Dooley family had not penetrated to the Archey Road representative, when a person, evidently of wayfaring habits, entered and asked for alms. Mr. Dooley arose, and, picking a half-dollar from the till, handed it to the visitor with great unconcern. The departure of the wayfarer with profuse thanks was followed by a space of silence.

"Well, Jawn," said Mr. Dooley.

"What did you give the hobo?" asked Mr. McKenna.

"Half a dollar," said Mr. Dooley.

"And what for?"

"Binivolence," said Mr. Dooley, with a seraphic smile.

"Well," said Mr. McKenna, "I should say that was benevolence."

"Well," said Mr. Dooley, " 'tis a bad night out, an' th' poor divvle looked that mis'rable it brought th' tears to me eyes, an'——"

"But," said Mr. McKenna, "that ain't any reason why you should give half a dollar to every tramp who comes in."

"Jawn," said Mr. Dooley, "I know th' ma-an. He spinds all his money at Schneider's, down th' block."

"What of that?" asked Mr. McKenna.

"Oh, nawthin'," said Mr. Dooley, "on'y I hope Herman won't thry to bite that there coin. If he does——"

A BACHELOR'S LIFE

"A man with a face that looks as if some wan had thrown it at him in anger nearly always marries befure he is old enough to vote. He feels he has to an' he cultivates what Hogan calls th' graces. How often do ye hear about a fellow that he is very plain but has a beautiful nature. Ye bet he has. If he hadn't an' didn't always keep it in th' show-case where all th' wurruld cud see he'd be lynched be th' Society f'r Municipal Improvement. But it's diff'rent with us comely bachelors. Bein' very beautiful, we can afford to be haughty an' peevish. . . . Th' best lookin' iv us niver get marrid at all."

SHAUGHNESSY

♣ ♣ ♣

"Jawn," said Mr. Dooley in the course of the conversation, "whin ye come to think iv it, th' heroes iv th' wurruld—an' be thim I mean th' lads that've buckled on th' gloves' an' gone out to do th' best they cud—they ain't in it with th' quite people nayether you nor me hears tell iv fr'm wan end iv th' year to another."

"I believe it," said Mr. McKenna; "for my mother told me so."

"Sure," said Mr. Dooley, "I know it is an old story. Th' wurruld's been full iv it fr'm th' beginnin'; an' 'll be full iv it till, as Father Kelly says, th' pay-roll's closed. But I was thinkin' more iv it th' other night thin iver befure, whin I wint to see Shaughnessy marry off his on'y daughter. You know Shaughnessy,—a quite man that come into th' road befure th' fire. He wurruked f'r Larkin, th' conthractor, f'r near twenty years without skip or break, an' seen th' fam'ly grow up be candle-light. Th' oldest boy was intinded f'r a priest. 'Tis a poor fam'ly that hasn't some wan that's bein' iddycated f'r the priesthood while all th' rest wear thimsilves to skeletons f'r him, an' call him Father Jawn 'r Father Mike whin he comes home wanst a year, light-hearted an' free, to eat with thim.

"Shaughnessy's lad wint wrong in his lungs, an' they fought death f'r him f'r five years, sindin' him out to th' West an' havin' masses said f'r him; an', poor divvle, he kept comin' back cross an' crool, with th' fire in his cheeks, till wan day he laid down, an' says he: 'Pah,' he says, 'I'm goin' to give up,' he says. 'An' I on'y ask that ye'll have th' mass sung over me be some man besides Father Kelly,' he says. An' he wint, an' Shaughnessy come clumpin' down th' aisle like a man in a thrance.

"Well, th' nex' wan was a girl, an' she didn't die; but, th' less said, th' sooner mended. Thin they was Terrence, a big, bould, curly-headed lad that cocked his hat at anny man—or woman f'r th' matter iv that—an' that bruk th' back iv a polisman an' swum to th' crib, an' was champeen iv th' South Side at hand ball. An' he wint. Thin th' good woman passed away. An' th' twins they growed to be th' prettiest pair that wint to first communion; an' wan night they was a light in th' window of Shaughnessy's house till three in th' mornin'. I raymimber it; f'r I had quite a crowd iv Willum Joyce's men in, an' we wondhered at it, an' wint home whin th' lamp in Shaughnessy's window was blown out.

"They was th' wan girl left—Theresa, a big, clean-lookin' child that I see grow up fr'm hello to good avnin'. She thought on'y iv th' ol' man, an' he leaned on her as if she was a crutch. She was out to meet him in th' evnin'; an' in th' mornin' he, th' simple ol' man, 'd stop to blow a kiss at her an' wave his dinner-pail, lookin' up an' down th' r-road to see that no wan was watchin' him.

"I dinnaw what possessed th' young Donahue, fr'm th'

Nineteenth. I niver thought much iv him, a stuck-up, aisy-come la-ad that niver had annything but a civil wurrud, an' is prisident iv th' sodality. But he came in, an' married Theresa Shaughnessy las' Thursdah night. Th' ol' man took on twinty years, but he was as brave as a gin'ral iv th' army. He cracked jokes an' he made speeches; an' he took th' pipes fr'm under th' elbow iv Hogan, th' blind-man, an' played 'Th' Wind that shakes th' Barley' till ye'd have wore ye'er leg to a smoke f'r wantin' to dance. Thin he wint to th' dure with th' two iv thim; an' says he, 'Well,' he says, 'Jim, be good to her,' he says, an' shook hands with her through th' carredge window.

"Him an' me sat a long time smokin' across th' stove. Fin'lly, says I, 'Well,' I says, "I must be movin'.' 'What's th' hurry?' says he. 'I've got to go,' says I. 'Wait a mo-ment,' says he. 'Theresa 'll'— He stopped right there f'r a minyit, holdin' to th' back iv th' chair. 'Well,' says he, 'if ye've got to go, ye must,' he says. 'I'll show ye out,' he says. An' he come with me to th' dure, holdin' th' lamp over his head. I looked back at him as I wint by; an' he was settin' be th' stove, with his elbows on his knees an' th' empty pipe between his teeth."

MR. DOOLEY REMEMBERS

"But Hinnissy, th' past always looks betther thin it was. It's only pleasant because it isn't here."

A FAMILY REUNION

♣ ♣ ♣

"WHY AREN'T you out attending the reunion of the Dooley family?" Mr. McKenna asked the philosopher.

"Thim's no rel-ations to me," Mr. Dooley answered. "Thim's farmer Dooleys. No wan iv our fam'ly iver lived in th' counthry. We live in th' city, where they burn gas an' have a polis foorce to get on to. We're no farmers, divvle th' bit. We belong to th' industhreel classes. Thim must be th' Fermanagh Dooleys, a poor lot, Jawn, an' always on good terms with th' landlord, bad ciss to thim, says I. We're from Roscommon. They'se a Dooley family in Wexford an' wan near Ballybone that belonged to th' constabulary. I met him but wanst. 'Twas at an iviction; an', though he didn't know me, I inthrajooced mesilf be landin' him back iv th' ear with a bouldher th' size iv ye'er two fists together. He didn't know me aftherwards, ayether.

"We niver had but wan reunion iv th' Dooley fam'ly, an' that was tin years ago. Me Cousin Felix's boy Aloysius—him that aftherwards wint to New York an' got a good job dhrivin' a carredge f'r th' captain iv a polis station—he was full iv pothry an' things; an' he come around wan night, an' says he, 'D'ye know,' he says,

19

' 'twud be th' hite iv a good thing f'r th' Dooleys to have a reunion,' he says. 'We ought to come together,' he says, 'an' show the people iv this ward,' he says, 'how sthrong we are,' he says. 'Ye might do it betther, me buck,' says I, 'shovellin' slag at th' mills,' I says. 'But annyhow, if ye'er mind's set on it, go ahead,' I says, 'an' I'll attind to havin' th' polis there,' I says, 'f'r I have a dhrag at th' station.'

"Well, he sint out letthers to all th' Roscommon Dooleys; an' on a Saturdah night we come together in a rinted hall an' held th' reunion. 'Twas great sport f'r a while. Some iv us hadn't spoke frindly to each other f'r twinty years, an' we set around an' tol' stories iv Roscommon an' its green fields, an' th' stirabout pot that was niver filled, an' th' blue sky overhead an' th' boggy ground undherfoot. 'Which Dooley was it that hamsthrung th' cows?' 'Mike Dooley's Pat.' 'Naw such thing: 'twas Pat Dooley's Mike. I mane Pat Dooley's Mike's Pat.' F'r 'tis with us as with th' rest iv our people. Ye take th' Dutchman: he has as manny names to give to his childher as they'se nails in his boots, but an Irishman has th' pick iv on'y a few. I knowed a man be th' name iv Clancy,—a man fr'm Kildare. He had fifteen childher; an', whin th' las' come, he says, 'Dooley, d'ye happen to know anny saints?' 'None iv thim thrades here,' says I. 'Why?' says I. 'They'se a new kid at th' house,' he says; 'an', be me troth, I've run out iv all th' saints I knew, an', if somewan don't come to me assistance, I'll have to turn th' child out on th' wurruld without th' rag iv a name to his back,' he says.

"But I was tellin' ye about th' reunion. They was lashins

iv dhrink an' story-tellin', an' Felix's boy Aloysius histed
a banner he had made with 'Dooley Aboo' painted on it.
But, afther th' night got along, some iv us begun to
raymimber that most iv us hadn't been frinds f'r long.
Mrs. Morgan Dooley, she that was Molly Dooley befure
she married Morgan, she turns to me, an' says she, ' 'Tis
sthrange they let in that Hogan woman,' she says—that
Hogan woman, Jawn, bein' th' wife iv her husband's
brother. She heerd her say it, an' she says, 'I'd have ye to
undherstand that no wan iver come out iv Roscommon
that cud hold up their heads with th' Hogans,' she says.
' 'Tis not f'r th' likes iv ye to slandher a fam'ly that's iv
th' landed gintry iv Ireland, an' f'r two pins I'd hit ye a
poke in th' eye,' she says. If it hadn't been f'r me bein'
between thim, they'd have been trouble; f'r they was good
frinds wanst. What is it th' good book says about a
woman scorned? Faith, I've forgotten.

"Thin me uncle Mike come in, as rough a man as iver
laid hands on a polisman. Felix Dooley was makin' a
speech on th' vartues iv th' fam'ly. 'Th' Dooleys,' says he,
'can stand befure all th' wurruld, an' no man can say
ought agin ayether their honor or their integrity,' says
he. 'Th' man that's throwin' that at ye,' says me uncle
Mike, 'stole a saw fr'm me in th' year sivinty-five.' Felix
paid no attintion to me uncle Mike, but wint on, 'We point
proudly to th' motto, "Dooley aboo—Dooley f'river."'
'Th' saw aboo,' says me uncle Mike. 'Th' Dooleys,' says
Felix, 'stood beside Red Hugh O'Neill; an', whin he cut
aff his hand—' 'He didn't cut it off with anny wan else's
saw,' says me uncle Mike. 'They'se an old sayin',' wint on

Felix. 'An' ol' saw,' says me uncle Mike. 'But 'twas new whin ye stole it.'

" 'Now look here,' says Aloysius, 'this thing has gone far enough. 'Tis an outrage that this here man shud come here f'r to insult th' head iv th' fam'ly.' 'Th' head iv what fam'ly?' says Morgan Dooley, jumpin' up as hot as fire. 'I'm th' head iv th' fam'ly,' he says, 'be right iv histhry.' 'Ye're an ol' cow,' says me uncle Mike. 'Th' back iv me hand an' th' sowl iv me fut to all iv ye,' he says. 'I quit ye,' he says. 'Ye're all livin' here undher assumed names'; an' he wint out, followed be Morgan Dooley with a chair in each hand.

"Well, they wasn't two Dooleys in th' hall'd speak whin th' meetin' broke up; an' th' Lord knows, but I don't to this day, who's th' head iv th' Dooley fam'ly. All I know is that I had wan th' nex' mornin'.' "

MARRIAGE

"Ye know a lot about marredge," said Mr. Hennessy.

"I do," said Mr. Dooley.

"Ye was niver marrid?"

"No," said Mr. Dooley. "No, I say, givin' three cheers. I know about marredge th' way an asthronomer knows about th' stars. I'm studyin' it through me glass all th' time."

"Ye're an asthronomer," said Mr. Hennessy, "but," he added, tapping himself lightly on the chest, "I'm a star."

"Go home," said Mr. Dooley crossly, "befure th' mornin' comes to put ye out."

KEEPING LENT

♣ ♣ ♣

Mr. McKenna had observed Mr. Dooley in the act of spinning a long, thin spoon in a compound which reeked pleasantly and smelt of the humming water of commerce; and he laughed and mocked at the philosopher.

"Ah-ha," he said, "that's th' way you keep Lent, is it? Two weeks from Ash Wednesday, and you tanking up."

Mr. Dooley went on deliberately to finish the experiment, leisurely dusting the surface with nutmeg and tasting the product before setting down the glass daintily. Then he folded his apron, and lay back in ample luxury while he began: "Jawn, th' holy season iv Lent was sent to us f'r to teach us th' weakness iv th' human flesh. Man proposes, an' th' Lord disposes, as Hinnissy says.

"I mind as well as though it was yesterday th' struggle iv me father f'r to keep Lent. He began to talk it a month befure th' time. 'On Ash Winsdah,' he'd say, 'I'll go in f'r a rale season iv fast an' abstinince,' he'd say. An' sure enough, whin Ash Winsdah come round at midnight, he'd take a long dhraw at his pipe an' knock th' ashes out slowly agin his heel, an' thin put th' dhudeen up behind th' clock. 'There,' says he, 'there ye stay till Easter morn,' he says. Ash Winsdah he talked iv nawthin' but th' pipe. ''Tis exthrordinney how aisy it is f'r to lave off,' he says. 'All

23

ye need is will power,' he says. 'I dinnaw that I'll iver put a pipe in me mouth again. 'Tis a bad habit, smokin' is,' he says; 'an' it costs money. A man's betther off without it. I find I dig twict as well,' he says; 'an', as f'r cuttin' turf, they'se not me like in th' parish since I left off th' pipe,' he says.

"Well, th' nex' day an' th' nex' day he talked th' same way; but Fridah he was sour, an' looked up at th' clock where th' pipe was. Saturdah me mother, thinkin' to be plazin' to him, says: 'Terrence,' she says, 'ye're iver so much betther without th' tobacco,' she says. 'I'm glad to find you don't need it. Ye'll save money,' she says. 'Be quite, woman,' says he. 'Dear, oh dear,' he says, 'I'd like a pull at th' clay,' he says. 'Whin Easter comes, plaze Gawd, I'll smoke mesilf black an' blue in th' face,' he says.

"That was th' beginnin' iv th' downfall. Choosdah he was settin' in front iv th' fire with a pipe in his mouth. 'Why, Terrence,' says me mother, 'ye're smokin' again.' 'I'm not,' says he: ' 'tis a dhry smoke,' he says; ' 'tisn't lighted,' he says. Wan week afther th' swear-off he came fr'm th' field with th' pipe in his face, an' him puffin' away like a chimbly. 'Terrence,' says me mother, 'it isn't Easter morn.' 'Ah-ho,' says he, 'I know it,' he says; 'but,' he says, 'what th' divvle do I care?' he says. 'I wanted f'r to find out whether it had th' masthery over me; an',' he says, 'I've proved that it hasn't,' he says. 'But what's th' good iv swearin' off, if ye don't break it?' he says. 'An' annyhow,' he says, 'I glory in me shame.'

"Now, Jawn," Mr. Dooley went on, "I've got what

Hogan calls a theery, an' it's this: that what's thrue iv
wan man's thrue iv all men. I'm me father's son a'most
to th' hour an' day. Put me in th' County Roscommon
forty year ago, an' I'd done what he'd done. Put him on
th' Ar-rchey Road, an' he'd be deliverin' ye a lecture on
th' sin iv thinkin' ye're able to overcome th' pride iv th'
flesh, as Father Kelly says. Two weeks ago I looked
with contimpt on Hinnissy f'r an' because he'd not even
promise to fast an' obstain fr'm croquet durin' Lent. To-
night you see me mixin' me toddy without th' shadow iv
remorse about me. I'm proud iv it. An' why not? I was
histin' in me first wan whin th' soggarth come down fr'm
a sick call, an' looked in at me. 'In Lent?' he says, half-
laughin' out in thim quare eyes iv his. 'Yes,' said I. 'Well,'
he says, 'I'm not authorized to say this be th' propaganda,'
he says, 'an' 'tis no part iv th' directions f'r Lent,' he says;
'but,' he says, 'I'll tell ye this, Martin,' he says, 'that
they'se more ways than wan iv keepin' th' season,' he says.
'I've knowed thim that starved th' stomach to feast th'
evil temper,' he says. 'They'se a little priest down be th'
Ninth Ward that niver was known to keep a fast day; but
Lent or Christmas tide, day in an' day out, he goes to th'
hospital where they put th' people that has th' small-pox.
Starvation don't always mean salvation. If it did,' he says,
'they'd have to insure th' pavemint in wan place, an'
they'd be money to burn in another. Not,' he says, 'that I
want ye to undherstand that I look kindly on th' sin
iv——'
   " ' 'Tis a cold night out,' says I.

" 'Well,' he says, th' dear man, 'ye may. On'y,' he says, ' 'tis Lent.'

" 'Yes,' says I.

" 'Well, thin,' he says, 'by ye'er lave I'll take but half a lump iv sugar in mine,' he says."

ST. PATRICK'S DAY

"If there's wan thing that St. Patrick did f'r Ireland that I like betther thin annything else," said Mr. Dooley, " 'tis th' day he fixed f'r his birthday. . . . Bein' an injanius man as well as holy, an' well read in th' calendar, he named a day that was sure to fall somewheres in th' middle iv Lent. . . . About the end iv th' first month I begin to feel that I'm too healthy an' far betther thin anny man ought to be in this sinful wurruld. . . . I begin readin' up relijous books to see whether th' rewards is akel to me heeroyic sacrifices. An' I'm almost ready to offer to thrade in a couple iv millyon years f'r wan pipe full iv kinnikinnick whin th' corner iv me eye catches th' date on th' top iv a pa-aper. It's on'y two days to Pathrick's Day an' a dauntless man can stick it out. But, dear me, th' sixteenth iv March is a long day. It's th' longest day in th' year. Haythen asthronomers say it ain't but I know betther. An' be th' same token th' siventeenth is th' shortest. It's like a dhream. It don't last more thin a minyit but a millyon things can happen in it. Annyhow it comes ar-round at last. Many iv me frinds goes out to meet it. Not me, mind ye. But ye can bet I'm standin' on th' dure step waitin' f'r it with me pipe in me hand."

GOLD–SEEKING

♧ ♧ ♧

"WELL, SIR," said Mr. Hennessy, "that Alaska sure is the gr-reat place. I thought 'twas nawthin' but an iceberg with a few seals roostin' on it, an' wan or two hundherd Ohio politicians that can't be killed on account iv th' threaty iv Pawrs. But here they tell me that 'tis fairly smothered in goold. A man stubs his toe on th' ground, an' lifts th' top off iv a goold mine. Ye go to bed at night, an' ye wake up with goold fillin' in ye'er teeth."

"Yes," said Mr. Dooley, "Clancy's son was in here this mornin', an' he says a frind iv his wint to sleep out in th' open wan night an' whin he got up his pants assayed four ounces iv goold to th' pound, an' his whiskers panned out as much as thirty dollars net."

"If I was a young man an' not tied down here," said Mr. Hennessy, "I'd go there: I wud so."

"I wud not," said Mr. Dooley. "Whin I was a young man in th' ol' counthry, we heerd th' same story about all America. We used to set be th' tur-rf fire o' nights, kickin' our bare legs on th' flure an' wishin' we was in New York, where all ye had to do was to hold ye'er hat an' th' goold guineas'd dhrop into it. An' whin I got to be a man, I come over here with a ham and a bag iv oatmeal, as sure

27

that I'd dhrive me own ca-ar as I was that me name was Martin Dooley. An' that was a cinch.

"But, faith, whin I'd been here a week, I seen that there was nawthin' but mud undher th' pavement—I larned that be means iv a pick-axe at tin shillin's th' day—an' that, though there was plenty iv goold, thim that had it were froze to it; an' I come west, still lookin' f'r mines. Th' on'y mine I sthruck at Pittsburgh was a hole f'r sewer pipe. I made it. Siven shillin's th' day. Smaller thin New York, but th' livin' was cheaper, with Mon'gahela rye at five a throw, put ye'er hand around th' glass.

"I was still dreamin' goold, an' I wint down to Saint Looey. Th' nearest I come to a fortune there was findin' a quarther on th' sthreet as I leaned over th' dashboord iv a car to whack th' off mule. Whin I got to Chicago, I looked around f'r the goold mine. They was Injuns here thin. But they wasn't anny mines I cud see. They was mud to be shovelled an' dhrays to be dhruv an' beats to be walked. I choose th' dhray; f'r I was niver cut out f'r a copper, an' I'd had me fill iv excavatin'. An' I dhruv th' dhray till I wint into business.

"Me experyence with goold minin' is it's always in th' nex' county. If I was to go to Alaska, they'd tell me iv th' finds in Seeberya. So I think I'll stay here. I'm a silver man, annyhow; an' I'm contint if I can see goold wanst a year, whin some prominent citizen smiles over his newspaper. I'm thinkin' that ivry man has a goold mine undher his own dure-step or in his neighbor's pocket at th' farthest."

"Well, annyhow," said Mr. Hennessy, "I'd like to kick

up th' sod, an' find a ton iv goold undher me fut."

"What wud ye do if ye found it?" demanded Mr. Dooley.

"I—I dinnaw," said Mr. Hennessy, whose dreaming had not gone this far. Then, recovering himself, he exclaimed with great enthusiasm, "I'd throw up me job an' —an' live like a prince."

"I tell ye what ye'd do," said Mr. Dooley. "Ye'd come back here an' sthrut up an' down th' sthreet with ye'er thumbs in ye'er armpits; an' ye'd dhrink too much, an' ride in sthreet ca-ars. Thin ye'd buy foldin' beds an' piannies, an' start a reel estate office. Ye'd be fooled a good deal an' lose a lot iv ye'er money, an' thin ye'd tighten up. Ye'd be in a cold fear night an' day that ye'd lose ye'er fortune. Ye'd wake up in th' middle iv th' night, dhreamin' that ye was back at th' gas-house with ye'er money gone. Ye'd be prisidint iv a charitable society. Ye'd have to wear ye'er shoes in th' house, an' ye'er wife'd have ye around to rayciptions an' dances. Ye'd move to Mitchigan Avnoo, an' ye'd hire a coachman that'd laugh at ye. Ye'er boys'd be joods an' ashamed iv ye, an' ye'd support ye'er daughters' husbands. Ye'd rackrint ye'er tinants an' lie about ye'er taxes. Ye'd go back to Ireland on a visit, an' put on airs with ye'er cousin Mike. Ye'd be a mane, closefisted, onscrupulous ol' curmudgeon; an' whin ye'd die, it'd take half ye'er fortune f'r rayqueems to put ye r-right. I don't want ye iver to speak to me whin ye get rich, Hinnissy."

"I won't," said Mr. Hennessy.

MACHINERY

The "man down Pinnsylvanya" was George F. Baer, President of the Philadelphia and Reading Railroad. In answer to an appeal for help to settle the coal strike he had replied, "The rights and interests of the laboring man will be protected and cared for—not by the labor agitators, but by the Christian men to whom God in His infinite wisdom has given the control of the property interests of the country . . ."

♣ ♣ ♣

Mr. Dooley was reading from a paper. " 'We live,' he says, 'in an age iv wondhers. Niver befure in th' histhry iv th' wurruld has such pro-gress been made.'

"Thrue wurruds an' often spoken. Even in me time things has changed. Whin I was a la-ad Long Jawn Wintworth cud lean his elbows on th' highest buildin' in this town. It took two months to come here fr'm Pittsburgh on a limited raft an' a stage coach that run fr'm La Salle to Mrs. Murphy's hotel. They wasn't anny tillygraft that I can raymimber an' th' sthreet car was pulled be a mule an' dhruv be an engineer be th' name iv Mulligan. We thought we was a pro-grissive people. Ye bet we did. But look at us today. I go be Casey's house tonight an' there it is a fine storey-an'-a-half frame house with Casey settin' on th' dure shtep dhrinkin' out iv a pail. I go be Casey's house to-morrah an' it's a hole in th' groun'. I rayturn to Casey's house on Thursdah an' it's a fifty-eight storey buildin' with a morgedge onto it an' they're thinkin' iv takin' it down an' replacin' it with a modhren sthructure. Th' shoes that Corrigan th' cobbler wanst wurruked on f'r a week, hammerin' away like a wood pecker, is now tossed out be th' dozens fr'm th' mouth iv a masheen. A cow goes lowin' softly in to Armours an' comes out glue, beef, gelatine, fertylizer, celooloid, joolry, sofy cushions, hair restorer, washin' sody, soap, lithrachoor an' bed springs so quick that while aft she's still cow, for'ard she may be annything fr'm buttons to Pannyma hats. I can go fr'm Chicago to New York in twinty hours, but I don't have to, thank th' Lord. Thirty years ago we thought 'twas marvelous to be able to tillygraft a man in Saint Joe an' get an answer that night. Now, be wireless tillygraft, ye can get an answer befure ye sind th' tillygram if they ain't careful. Me frind Macroni has done that. Be manes iv his wondher iv science a man on a ship in mid-ocean can sind a tillygram to a man on shore, if he has a confid'rate on board. That's all he needs. Be mechanical science an' thrust in th' op'rator annywan can set on th' shore iv Noofoundland an' chat with a frind in th' County Kerry. . . .

"What's it done f'r th' wurruld? says ye. It's done ivrything. It's give us fast ships an' an autymatic hist f'r th' hod, an' small flats an' a taste iv solder in th' peaches. If annybody says th' wurruld ain't betther off thin it was, tell him that a masheen has been invinted that makes honey out iv pethrolyum. If he asts ye why they ain't anny Shakesperes today, say: 'No, but we no longer make sausages be hand.' . . .

"I sometimes wondher whether pro-gress is anny more thin a kind iv a shift. It's like a merry-go-round. We get up on a speckled wooden horse an' th' mechanical pianny plays a chune an' away we go, hollerin'. We think we're thravellin' like th' divvle but th' man that doesn't care about merry-go-rounds knows that we will come back where we were. We get out dizzy an' sick an' lay on th' grass an' gasp: 'Where am I? Is this th' meelin-yum?' An' he says: 'No, 'tis Ar-rchey Road.' Father Kelly says th' Agyptians done things we cudden't do an' th' Romans put up sky-scrapers an' aven th' Chinks had tillyphones an' phony-grafts.

"I've been up to th' top iv th' very highest buildin' in town, Hinnissy, an' I wasn't anny nearer Hivin thin if I was in th' sthreet. Th' stars was as far away as iver. An' down beneath is a lot iv us runnin' an' lapin' an' jumpin' about, pushin' each other over, haulin' little sthrips iv ir'n to pile up in little buildin's that ar-re called sky-scrapers but not be th' sky; wurrukin' night an' day to make a masheen that'll carry us fr'm wan jack-rabbit colony to another an' yellin', 'Pro-gress!' Pro-gress, oho! I can see th' stars winkin' at each other an' sayin': 'Ain't they funny! Don't they think they're playin' hell!' . . ."

"What d'ye think iv th' man down in Pinnsylvanya who says th' Lord an' him is partners in a coal mine?" asked Mr. Hennessy, who wanted to change the subject.

"Has he divided th' profits?" asked Mr. Dooley.

MR. DOOLEY
FOLLOWS THE FLAG

*what Hogan calls wan iv th' mute, ingloryous heroes
"This war, Hinnissy, has been a gr-reat sthrain on
me. To think iv th' suffrin' I've endured! F'r weeks I
lay awake at nights fearin' that th' Spanish ar-rma-
dillo'd lave the Cape Verde Islands, where it wasn't,
an' take th' thrain out here, an' hur-rl death an'
desthruction into me little store. Day be day th' pitiless
exthries come out an' beat down on me. Ye hear iv
Teddy Rosenfelt plungin' into ambuscades an' Sicrety
iv Wars; but d'ye hear iv Martin Dooley, th' man
behind th' guns, four thousan' miles behind thim, an'
willin' to be further? They ar-re no bokays f'r me. I'm
iv th' war; an' not so dam mute, ayther. Some day,
Hinnissy, justice'll be done me, an' th' likes iv me;
an', whin th' story iv a gr-reat battle is written, they'll
print th' kilt, th' wounded, th' missin', an' th' seryously
disturbed. An' thim that have bore thimsilves well an'
bravely an' paid th' taxes an' faced th' deadly newspa-
apers without flinchin' 'll be advanced six pints an'
given a chanst to tur-rn jack f'r th' game. But me
wurruk ain't over jus' because Mack has inded th'
war an' Teddy Rosenfelt is comin' home
to bite th' Sicrety iv War."*

WAR PREPARATIONS

The opera bouffe character of certain aspects of the Spanish-American War in 1898 furnished Mr. Dooley with subjects for comment that increased his circle of admirers enormously.

The confusion of organizing an army was more than evident in the newspapers of the day. The two chief concentration camps were at Chickamauga Park and Tampa. The fondness of the commanding general, Nelson A. Miles, for public statements and gold braid was often noted. When he left Washington to "take the field" at Tampa, he was accompanied by Mrs. Miles, a daughter, and a son.

♣ ♣ ♣

"WELL," MR. HENNESSY asked, "how goes th' war?"

"Splendid, thank ye," said Mr. Dooley. "Fine, fine. It makes me hear-rt throb with pride that I'm a citizen iv th' Sixth Wa-ard."

"Has th' ar-rmy started f'r Cubia yet?"

"Wan ar-rmy, says ye? Twinty! Las' Choosdah an advance ar-rmy iv wan hundherd an' twinty thousand men landed fr'm th' *Gussie*, with tin thousand cannons hurlin' projick-tyles weighin' eight hundherd pounds sivinteen miles. Winsdah night a second ar-rmy iv injineers, miners, plumbers, an' lawn tinnis experts, numberin' in all four hundherd an' eighty thousand men, ar-rmed with death-dealin' canned goods, was hurried to Havana to storm th' city.

"Thursdah mornin' three thousand full rigimints iv

35

r-rough r-riders swum their hor-rses acrost to Matoonzas, an' afther a spirited battle captured th' Rainy Christiny golf links, two up an' hell to play, an' will hold thim again all comers. Th' same afthernoon th' reg'lar cavalry, consistin' iv four hundherd an' eight thousan' well-mounted men, was loaded aboord th' tug *Lucy J.,* and departed on their earned iv death amidst th' cheers iv eight millyon sojers left behind at Chickamaha. These cav'lry'll cooperate with Commodore Schlow; an' whin he desthroys th' Spanish fleet, as he does ivry Sundah an' holy day except in Lent, an' finds out where they ar-re an' destroys thim, afther batterin' down th' forts where they ar-re con-cealed so that he can't see thim, but thinks they ar-re on their way f'r to fight Cousin George Dooley, th' cav'-lry will make a dash back to Tampa, where Gin'ral Miles is preparin' to desthroy th' Spanish at wan blow—an' he's th' boy to blow.

"Th' gin'ral arrived th' other day, fully prepared f'r th' bloody wurruk iv war. He had his intire fam'ly with him. He r-rode recklessly into camp, mounted on a superb specyal ca-ar. As himsilf an' Uncle Mike Miles, an' Cousin Hennery Miles, an' Master Miles, aged eight years, dismounted fr'm th' specyal train, they were received with wild cheers be eight millyon iv th' bravest sojers that iver give up their lives f'r their counthry. Th' press cinsorship is so pow'rful that no news is allowed to go out; but I have it fr'm th' specyal corryspondint iv Mesilf, Clancy th' Butcher, Mike Casey, an' th' City Directhry that Gin'ral Miles instantly repaired himsilf to th' hotel, where he made his plans f'r cr-rushin' th' Spanyards at wan blow. He will equip th' ar-rmy with blow-guns at wanst. His uniforms ar-re comin' down in specyal steel protected bullyon trains fr'm th' mint, where they've been kept f'r a year. He has ordhered out th' gold resarve f'r to equip his staff, numberin' eight thousan' men, manny iv whom ar-re clubmen; an', as soon as he can have his pitchers took, he will cr-rush th' Spanish with wan blow. Th' pur-pose iv th' gin'ral is to permit no delay. Decisive action is demanded be th' people. An', whin th' hot air masheens has been sint to th' front, Gin'ral Miles will strike wan blow that'll be th' damdest blow since th' year iv th' big wind in Ireland.

"Iv coorse, they'se dissinsions in th' cabinet; but they don't amount to nawthin'. Th' Sicrety iv War is in favor iv sawin' th' Spanish ar-rmy into two-be-four joists. Th' Sicrety iv th' Threeasury has a scheme f'r roonin' thim be lindin' thim money. Th' Sicrety iv th' Navy wants to sue thim befure th' Mattsachusetts Supreme Coort. I've heerd that th' President is arrangin' a knee dhrill, with th' idee iv prayin' th' villyans to th' divvil. But these diff'rences don't count. We're all wan people, an' we look to Gin'ral Miles to desthroy th' Spanish with wan blow. Whin it comes, trees will be lifted out be th' roots. Morro Castle'll cave in, an' th' air'll be full iv Spanish whiskers. A long blow, a sthrong blow, an' a blow all together."

"We're a gr-reat people," said Mr. Hennessy, earnestly.

"We ar-re," said Mr. Dooley. "We ar-re that. An' th' best iv it is, we know we ar-re."

MULES AND OTHERS

The newspapers of June 17, 1898, reported that three thousand army mules had stampeded through the camp at Tampa, Florida, the night before, and forced many a nightshirt-clad recruit into the treetops for safety. General R. A. Alger, politician from Michigan, was the Secretary of War. "Mack," of course, was President McKinley. Admiral W. T. Sampson was in command of the Atlantic fleet.

♣ ♣ ♣

"I SEE," said Mr. Dooley, "th' first gr-reat land battle iv th' war has been fought."

"Where was that?" demanded Mr. Hennessy, in great excitement. "Lord save us, but where was that?"

"Th' Alger gyards," said Mr. Dooley, "bruk fr'm th' corral where they had thim tied up, atin' thistles, an' med a desp'rate charge on th' camp at Tampa. They dayscinded like a whur-rl-wind, dhrivin' th' astonished throops befure thim, an' thin charged back again, completin' their earned iv desthruction. At th' las' account th' brave sojers was climbin' threes an' tillygraft poles, an' a rig'mint iv mules was kickin' th' pink silk linin' out iv th' officers' quarters. Th' gallant mules was led be a most courageous jackass, an' 'tis undhersthud that me frind Mack will appint him a brigadier-gin'ral jus' as soon as he can find out who his father is. 'Tis too bad he'll have no childher to perpituate th' fame iv him. He wint through

th' camp at th' head iv his throops iv mules without castin'
a shoe. He's th' biggest jackass in Tampa to-day, not
exciptin' th' cinsor; an' I doubt if they'se a bigger wan in
Wash'n'ton, though I cud name a few that cud thry a race
with him. Annyhow, they'll know how to reward him.
They know a jackass whin they see wan, an' they see a
good manny in that peaceful city.

"Th' charge iv Tampa'll go into histhry as th' first land
action iv th' war. An', be th' way, Hinnissy, if this here
sociable is f'r to go on at th' prisint rate, I'm sthrong to
ar-rm th' wild ar-rmy mules an' th' unbridled jackasses iv
th' pe-rary an' give thim a chanst to set Cubia free. Up to
this time th' on'y hero kilt on th' Spanish side was a
jackass that poked an ear above th' batthries at Matoonzas
f'r to hear what was goin' on. 'Behold,' says Sampson, 'th'
insolince iv th' foe,' he says. 'For-rm in line iv battle, an'
hur-rl death an' desthruction at yon Castilyan gin'ral.'
'Wait,' says an officer. 'It may be wan iv our own men. It
looks like th' Sicrety iv'—'Hush!' says th' commander. 'It
can't be an American jackass, or he'd speak,' he says.
'Fire on him.' Shot afther shot fell round th' inthrepid
ass; but he remained firm till th' dinnymite boat
Vesoovyus fired three hundherd an' forty thousand pounds
iv gum cotton at him, an' the poor crather was smothered
to death. Now, says I, give these Tampa mules a chanst,
an' we'll have no need iv wastin' ammun-ni-tion. Properly
led, they'd go fr'm wan end iv Cubia to th' other, kickin'
th' excelsior out iv ivry stuffed Spanish gin'ral fr'm
Bahoohoo Hoondoo at Sandago de Cubia. They'd be no
loss iv life. Th' sojers who haven't gone away cud come

home an' get cured iv th' measles an' th' whoopin'-cough an' the cholera infantum befure th' public schools open in th' fall, an' iverything wud be peaceful an' quiet an' prosp'rous. Th' officers in th' field at prisint is well qualified f'r command iv th' new ar-rmy; an', if they'd put blinders on th' mules, they wudden't be scared back be wan iv thim Spanish fleets that a jackass sees whin he's been up all night, secretly stuffing himsilf with silo. They'd give wan hew-haw, an' follow their leaders through th' hear-rt iv th' inimy's counthry. But give thim th' wurrud to git ap, an' they'd ate their thistles undher th' guns iv some ol' Morro Castle befure night.

"Ye don't see th' diff'rence, says ye. They ain't anny in th' leaders. As efficient a lot iv mules as iver exposed their ears. Th' throuble is with th' rank an' file. They're men. What's needed to carry on this war as it goes to-day is an ar-rmy iv jacks an' mules. Whin ye say to a man, 'Git ap, whoa, gee, back up, get alang!' he don't know what ye're dhrivin' at or to. But a mule hears th' ordhers with a melancholy smile, dhroops his ears, an' follows his war-rm, moist breath. Th' ordhers fr'm Washin'ton is perfectly comprehinsible to a jackass, but they don't mane annything to a poor, foolish man. No human bein', Hinnissy, can undherstand what the divvle use it was to sink a ship that cost two hundherd thousan' dollars an' was worth at laste eighty dollars in Sandago Harbor, if we have to keep fourteen ships outside to prevint five Spanish ships fr'm sailin'. Th' poor, tired human mind don't tumble, Hinnissy, to th' raison f'r landin' four hundherd marines at Guanotommy to clear th' forests, whin Havana is livin'

free on hot tamales an' ice-cream. Th' mind iv a Demos-
theens or a Tim Hogan would be crippled thryin' to figure
out why throops ar-re sint out fr'm Tampa an' thin ordhered back through a speakin' chube, while wan iv th'
new brigadeer-gin'rals has his hands manicured an' says
good-by to his nurse. But it ought to be as plain to th'
mule that hears it as it is to th' jackasses that gets it up.
What we need, Hinnissy, is a perfect undherstandin' between th' ar-rmy an' th' administhration. We need what
Hogan calls th' esphrite th' corpse, an' we'll on'y have it
whin th' mules begins to move."

"I shud think," said Mr. Hennessy, "now that th'
jackasses has begun to be onaisy——"

"We ought to be afraid th' Cabinet an' th' Board iv
Sthrateejy 'll be stampeded?" Mr. Dooley interrupted.
"Niver fear. They're too near th' fodder."

ARMY APPOINTMENTS

"Well, sir," said Mr. Dooley, "I didn't vote f'r Mack,
but I'm with him now. I had me doubts whether he was th'
gr-reatest military janius iv th' cinchry, but they'se no
question about it. We go into this war, if we iver do go
into it, with th' most fash'nable ar-rmy that iver creased
its pants. 'Twill be a daily hint fr'm Paris to th' crool
foe. . . . Th' ar-rmy'll be followed by specyal corre-
spondints fr'm Butthrick's Pattherns an' Harper's Bazar;
an', if our brave boys don't gore an' pleat th' inimy, 'twill
be because th' inimy'll be r-rude enough to shoot in anny
kind iv clothes they find on th' chair whin they wake
up."

COUSIN GEORGE

The first news of Dewey's victory in Manila Harbor came to the United States from Spanish sources. It was some time before the arrival of the Admiral's official report because of a cut cable. During this period, there was considerable suspense in the United States over just what had happened to the Americans after the naval battle. Mark Hanna, Senator from Ohio and close associate of President McKinley, was the personification of the big business man in politics.

⚘ ⚘ ⚘

"WELL," said Mr. Hennessy, in tones of chastened joy: "Dewey didn't do a thing to thim. I hope th' poor la-ad ain't cooped up there in Minneapolis."

"Niver fear," said Mr. Dooley, calmly. "Cousin George is all r-right."

"Cousin George?" Mr. Hennessy exclaimed.

"Sure," said Mr. Dooley. "Dewey or Dooley, 'tis all th' same. We dhrop a letter here an' there, except th' haitches —we niver dhrop thim,—but we're th' same breed iv fightin' men. Georgy has th' thraits iv th' fam'ly. Me uncle Mike, that was a handy man, was tol' wanst he'd be sint to hell f'r his manny sins, an' he desarved it; f'r, lavin' out th' wan sin iv runnin' away fr'm annywan, he was booked f'r ivrything from murdher to missin' mass. 'Well,' he says, 'anny place I can get into,' he says, 'I can get out iv,' he says. 'Ye bet on that,' he says.

"So it is with Cousin George. He knew th' way in, an' it's th' same way out. He didn't go in be th' fam'ly inthrance, sneakin' along with th' can undher his coat. He left Ding Dong, or whativer 'tis ye call it, an' says he, 'Thank Gawd,' he says, 'I'm where no man can give me his idees iv how to r-run a quiltin' party, an' call it war,' he says. An' so he sint a man down in a divin' shute, an' cut th' cables, so's Mack cudden't chat with him. Thin he prances up to th' Spanish forts, an' hands thim a few oranges. Tosses thim out like a man throwin' handbills f'r a circus. 'Take that,' he says, 'an' raymimber th' Maine,' he says. An' he goes into th' harbor, where Admiral What-th'-'ell is, an', says he, 'Surrinder,' he says. 'Niver,' says th' Dago. 'Well,' says Cousin George, 'I'll just have to push ye ar-round,' he says. An' he tosses a few slugs at th' Spanyards. Th' Spanish admiral shoots at him with a bow an' arrow, an' goes over an' writes a cable. 'This mornin' we was attackted,' he says. 'An',' he says, 'we fought the inimy with great courage,' he says. 'Our victhry is com-plete,' he says. 'We have lost ivrything we had,' he says. 'Th' threacherous foe,' he says, 'afther destroyin' us, sought refuge behind a mud-scow,' he says; 'but nawthin' daunted us. What boats we cudden't r-run ashore we surrindered,' he says. 'I cannot write no more,' he says, 'as me coat-tails are afire,' he says; 'an' I am bravely but rapidly leapin' fr'm wan vessel to another, followed be me valiant crew with a fire-engine,' he says. 'If I can save me coat-tails,' he says, 'they'll be no kick comin',' he says. 'Long live Spain, long live mesilf.'

"Well, sir, in twenty-eight minyits be th' clock Dewey

he had all th' Spanish boats sunk, an' that there harbor lookin' like a Spanish stew. Thin he r-run down th' bay, an' handed a few war-rm wans into th' town. He set it on fire, an' thin wint ashore to war-rm his poor hands an' feet. It chills th' blood not to have annything to do f'r an hour or more."

"Thin why don't he write somethin'?" Mr. Hennessy demanded.

"Write?" echoed Mr. Dooley. "Write? Why shud he write? D'ye think Cousin George ain't got nawthin' to do but to set down with a fountain pen, an' write: 'Dear Mack—At 8 o'clock I begun a peaceful blockade iv this town. Ye can see th' pieces ivrywhere. I hope ye're injyin' th' same gr-reat blessin'. So no more at prisint. Fr'm ye'ers thruly, George Dooley.' He ain't that kind. 'Tis a nice day, an' he's there smokin' a good tin-cint see-gar, an' throwin' dice f'r th' dhrinks. He don't care whether we know what he's done or not. I'll bet ye, whin we come to find out about him, we'll hear he's ilicted himself king iv th' Ph'lippeen Islands. Dooley th' Wanst. He'll be settin' up there undher a pa'm-three with naygurs fannin' him an' a dhrop iv licker in th' hollow iv his ar-rm, an' hootchy-kootchy girls dancin' befure him, an' ivry tin or twinty minyits some wan bringin' a prisoner in. 'Who's this?' says King Dooley. 'A Spanish gin'ral,' says th' copper. 'Give him a typewriter an' set him to wurruk,' says th' king. 'On with th' dance,' he says. An' afther awhile, whin he gits tired iv th' game, he'll write home an' say he's got th' islands; an' he'll tur-rn thim over to th' gover'mint an' go back to his ship, an' Mark Hanna'll

organize th' Ph'lippeen Islands Jute an' Cider Comp'ny, an'
th' rivolutchinists'll wish they hadn't. That's what'll happen. Mark me wurrud."

PRAYERS FOR VICTORY

"It looks to me," said Mr. Dooley, "as though me frind
Mack'd got tired iv th' Sthrateejy Board, an' was goin' to
lave th' war to th' men in black."

"How's that?" asked Mr. Hennessy, who was at best
but a clouded view of public affairs.

"Well," said Mr. Dooley, "while th' sthrateejans have
been wearin' out their jeans on cracker-boxes in Wash-
'n'ton, they'se been goin' on th' mos' deadly conflict iver
heerd tell iv between th' pow'rful preachin' navies in th'
two counthries. . . ."

"What d'ye think about it?" asked Mr. Hennessy.

"Well," said Mr. Dooley, "I dinnaw jus' what to think
iv it. Me own idee is that war is not a matther iv prayers
so much as a matther iv punchin'; an' th' on'y place a
prayer book stops a bullet is in th' story books. . . ."

"That's th' way I look at it," said Mr. Hennessy.
"When 'tis an aven thing in th' prayin', may th' best
man win."

"Ye're r-right, Hinnissy," said Mr. Dooley, warmly.
"Ye're r-right. An' th' best man will win."

STRATEGY

General Maximo Gomez was the commander of the Cuban troops in rebellion against Spain. Richard Harding Davis, the novelist, was a colorful war correspondent considerably in the news himself. "Pat Mountjoy" was Mr. Dooley's translation of Patricio Montojo y Pasaron, the admiral who commanded the Spanish naval forces at Manila.

♣   ♣   ♣

"A STRATEEJAN," SAID Mr. Dooley, in response to Mr. Hennessy's request for information, "is a champeen checker-player. Whin th' war broke out, me frind Mack wint to me frind Hanna, an' says he, 'What,' he says, 'what can we do to cr-rush th' haughty power iv Spain,' he says, 'an' br-ring this hateful war to a early conclusion?' he says. 'Mobilize th' checker-players,' says Hanna. An' fr'm all cor-rners iv th' counthry they've gone to Washin'ton, where they're called th' Sthrateejy Board.

"Day an' night they set in a room with a checker-board on th' end iv a flour bar'l, an' study problems iv th' navy. At night Mack dhrops in. 'Well, boys,' says he, 'how goes th' battle?' he says. 'Gloryous,' says th' Sthrateejy Board. 'Two more moves, an' we'll be in th' king row.' 'Ah,' says Mack, 'this is too good to be thrue,' he says. 'In but a few brief minyits th' dhrinks'll be on Spain,' he says. 'Have ye anny plans f'r Sampson's fleet?' he says. 'Where is it?' says th' Sthrateejy Board. 'I dinnaw,' says Mack. 'Good,' says th' Sthrateejy Board. 'Where's th' Spanish fleet?' says they. 'Bombardin' Boston, at Cadiz, in San June de Matzoon, sighted near th' gashouse be our special correspondint, copyright, 1898, be Mike O'Toole.' 'A sthrong position,' says th' Sthrateejy Board. 'Undoubtedly, th' fleet is headed south to attack and seize Armour's glue facthory. Ordher Sampson to sail north as fast as he can, an' lay in a supply iv ice. Th' summer's comin' on. Insthruct Schley to put on all steam, an' thin put it off again, an' call us up be telephone. R-rush eighty-three millyon throops an' four mules to Tampa, to Mobile, to Chickenmaha, to Coney Island, to Ireland, to th' divvle, an' r-rush thim back again. Don't r-rush thim. Ordher Sampson to pick up th' cable at Lincoln Par-rk, an' run into th' bar-rn. Is th' balloon corpse r-ready? It is? Thin don't sind it up. Sind it up. Have th' Mulligan Gyards co-op'rate with Gomez, an' tell him to cut away his whiskers. They've got tangled in th' riggin'. We need yellow-fever throops. Have ye anny yellow fever in th' house? Give it to twinty thousand three hundherd men, an' sind thim afther Gov'nor Tanner. Teddy Rosenfelt's r-rough r-riders ar-re downstairs, havin' their uniforms pressed. Ordher thim to th' goluf links at wanst. They must be no indecision. Where's Richard Harding Davis? On th' bridge iv th' *New York?* Tur-rn th' bridge. Seize Gin'ral Miles' uniform. We must strengthen th' gold resarve. Where's th' *Gussie?* Runnin' off to Cubia with wan hundherd men an' ar-rms, iv coorse. Oh, war is a dhreadful thing. It's ye'er move, Claude,' says th' Sthrateejy Board.

"An' so it goes on; an' day by day we r-read th' tur-rble

story iv our brave sthrateejans sacrificin' their time on th' altar iv their counthry, as Hogan says. Little we thought, whin we wint into this war, iv th' horrors it wud bring. Little we though iv th' mothers at home weepin' f'r their brave boys down at Washin'ton hur-rtin' their poor eyes over a checker-board. Little we thought iv these devoted men, as Hogan says, with achin' heads, plannin' to sind three hundherd thousand millyon men an' a carload iv beans to their fate at Tampa, Fla. But some wan must be sacrificed, as Hogan says. An' these poor fellows in Washin'ton with their r-red eyes an' their tired backs will be an example to future ginerations, as Hogan says, iv how an American sojer can face his jooty whin he has to, an' how he can't whin he hasn't to."

"Dewey ain't a sthrateejan?" inquired Mr. Hennessy.

"No," said Mr. Dooley. "Cousin George is a good man, an' I'm very fond iv him—more be raison iv his doin' that May-o bosthoon Pat Mountjoy, but he has low tastes. We niver cud make a sthrateejan iv him. They'se a kind iv a vulgar fightin' sthrain in him that makes him want to go out an' slug somewan wanst a month. I'm glad he ain't in Washin'ton. Th' chances ar-re he'd go to th' Sthrateejy Board and pull its hair."

THE DESTRUCTION OF
CERVERA'S FLEET

*The destruction of Admiral Cervera's fleet by the United
States Navy was followed by another battle between the
friends of the American naval officers Sampson and Schley
over which commander deserved the credit for the victory.
In fact, the controversy began in the telegraphed reports
of the battle. Advocates of Sampson had not hesitated to
accuse Schley of cowardice, and Speaker T. B. Reed's remark represented the opinion of many.—"I don't see what
the row between these two naval heroes is about. As far as
I can see one of them wasn't in the fight at all and the other
was doing his damnedest to get out of it." The publication
of Volume III of Edgar S.* Maclay's History of the
United States Navy, *which gave an extremely anti-Schley
account of the battle of Santiago, was the occasion for the
second part of Mr. Dooley's comment. Among the ships
engaged in the battle was J. P. Morgan's former yacht*
Corsair, *converted and renamed the* Gloucester. *The names
of the Spanish ships mentioned were:* Cristóbal Colón,
Vizcaya, Almirante Oquendo. *"Fighting Bob" Evans,
commander of the* Iowa, *was among other things noted for
his explicit language.*

"**Y**E'VE GOT things mixed up," said Mr. Dooley. "I
get th' news sthraight. 'Twas this way. Th' Spanish fleet
was bottled up in Sandago Harbor, an' they dhrew th' cork.
That's a joke. I see it in th' pa-apers. Th' gallant boys iv
th' navy was settin' out on th' deck, defindin' their coun-

thry an' dhrawin' three ca-ards apiece, whin th' Spanish admiral con-cluded 'twud be better f'r him to be desthroyed on th' ragin' sea, him bein' a sailor, thin to have his fleet captured be cav'lry. Annyhow, he was willin' to take a chance; an' he says to his sailors: 'Spanyards,' he says, 'Castiles,' he says, 'we have et th' las' bed-tick,' he says; 'an', if we stay here much longer,' he says, 'I'll have to have a steak off th' armor plate fried f'r ye," he says. 'Lave us go out where we can have a r-run f'r our money,' he says. An' away they wint. I'll say this much f'r him, he's a brave man, a dam brave man. I don't like a Spanyard no more than ye do, Hinnissy. I niver see wan. But, if this here man was a—was a Zulu, I'd say he was a brave man. If I was aboord wan iv thim yachts that was convarted, I'd go to this here Cervera, an' I'd say: 'Manuel,' I'd say, 'ye're all right, me boy. Ye ought to go to a doctor an' have ye'er eyes re-set, but ye're a good fellow. Go downstairs,' I'd say, 'into th' basemint iv th' ship,' I'd say, 'an' open th' cupboard jus' nex' to th' head iv th' bed, an' find th' bottle marked "Floridy Wather," an' threat ye'ersilf kindly.' That's what I'd say to Cervera. He's all right.

"Well, whin our boys see th' Spanish fleet comin' out iv th' harbor, they gathered on th' deck an' sang th' naytional anthem, 'They'll be a hot time in th' ol' town tonight.' A lift-nant come up to where Admiral Sampson was settin' playin' sivin up with Admiral Schley. 'Bill,' he says, 'th' Spanish fleet is comin' out,' he says. 'What talk have ye?' says Sampson. 'Sind out some row-boats an' a yacht, an' desthroy thim. Clubs is thrumps,' he says, and he wint on playin'. Th' Spanish fleet was attackted on all sides be our br-rave la-ads, nobly assisted be th' dispatch boats iv the newspapers. Wan by wan they was desthroyed. Three battleships attackted th' convarted yacht *Gloucester*. Th' *Gloucester* used to be owned be Pierpont Morgan; but 'twas convarted, an' is now leadin' a dacint life. Th' *Gloucester* sunk thim all, th' *Christobell Comma*, the *Viscera*, an' th' *Admiral O'Quinn*. It thin wint up to two Spanish torpedo boats an' giv thim wan punch, an' away they wint. Be this time th' sojers had heerd of th' victhry, an' they gathered on th' shore, singin' th' naytional anthem, 'They'll be a hot time in th' ol' town to-night, me babby.' Th' gloryous ol' chune, to which Washington an' Grant an' Lincoln marched, was took up be th' sailors on th' ships, an' Admiral Cervera r-run wan iv his boats ashore, an' jumped into th' sea. At last accounts th' followin' dispatches had been received: 'To Willum McKinley: Congratulations on ye'er noble victhry. (Signed) Willum McKinley.' 'To Russell A. Alger: Ye done splendid. (Signed) Russell A. Alger.' 'To James Wilson, Sicrety iv Agriculture: This is a gr-reat day f'r Ioway. Ar-re ye much hur-rted? (Signed) James Wilson.' . . .

"An' now it's Schley's turn. I knew it was comin' to Schley an' here it comes. Ye used to think he was a gran' man, that whin ol' Cervera come out iv th' harbor at Sandago called out 'Come on, boys,' an' plunged into th' Spanish fleet an' rayjooced it to scrap-iron. That's what ye thought, an' that's what I thought, an' we were wrong. We were wrong, Hinnissy. I've been r-readin' a thrue histhry iv th' campaign be wan iv th' gr-reatest historyians now employed as a clerk in th' supply stores iv th' Brooklyn navy yard. Like mesilf, he's a fireside vethran iv th' war. He's a mimber iv th' Martin Dooley Post No. 1, Definders iv th' Hearth. He's th' boy f'r ye. If iver he beats his sugar scoop into a soord, ye'll think ol' Farragut was a lady cook on a lumber barge. Says th' historyian: 'Th' conduck iv Schley durin' th' campaign was such as to bring th' bright blush iv shame to ivry man on th' pay roll iv our beloved counthry. 'Tis well known that whin ordhered be th' gallant Jawn D. Long to lave Hampton Roads, he thried to jump overboord an' swim ashore. He was chloryformed an' kep' undher hatches till th' ship was off th' coast iv Floridy. Whin he come to, he fainted at th' sight iv a Spanish ditchnry an' whin a midshipman wint by with a box iv Castile soap, he fell on th' deck writhin' in fear an' exclaimed: "Th' war is over. I'm shot." Off Cyenfoogoose, he see a starvin' reconcenthrado on th' shore an' cried out: "There's Cervera. Tell him to come on boord an' accept me soord." He was knocked down be a belayin' pin in th' hands iv th' gunner's mate an' carried to Sandago. Whin th' catiff wretch an' cow'rd see brave Cervera comin' out iv th' harbor, he r-run up th' signal: "Cease firin'. I'm a prisoner." Owin' to th' profanity iv dauntless Bob Ivans, which was arisin' in a dark purple column at th' time, Cervera cud not see this recreent message an' attimpted to r-run away. Th' American admiral followed him like th' cow'rd that he was, describin' a loop that I'd dhraw f'r ye if th' head bookkeeper'd lind me a pincil an' rammin' th' *Ioway,* th' *Matsachoosetts* an' th *Oregon.* His face was r-red with fear an' he cried in a voice that cud be heard th' lenth iv th' ship: "He don't see th' signal. I've surrindered, Cervera. I'm done. I quit. I'm all in. Come an' take me soord an' cut off me buttons. Boys, fire a few iv thim eight-inch shells an' atthract his attintion. That was a good wan. Give him some more. R-run alongside an' ram him if nicissry. Rake him fore an' aft. There goes his biler. Now, perhaps he'll take notice. Great hivins, we're lost! He's sinkin' befure we can surrinder. Get out me divin' shoot, boy, an' I'll go afther him an' capitulate. Oh, war is a tur-rble thing!" I have attimpted to be fair with Admiral Schley. If I'm not, it's his own fault an' mine. I can on'y add that 'tis th' opinyion iv all th' boys in th' store that he ought to be hanged, drawn, quarthered, burnt at th' stake an' biled in oil as a catiff, cow'rd an' thraitor. 'Tis a good thing f'r th' United States that me frind Sampson come back at th' r-right moment an' with a few well-directed wurruds to a tillygraft operator, secured th' victhry. Ol' Loop-th'-loops was found lyin' head first in a coal bunker an' whin pulled out be th' legs exclaimed, "Emanuel, don't shoot me. I'm a Spanish spy in disgeese." '

"So they've arristed Schley. As soon as th' book come out th' Sicrety iv th' Navy issued a warrant again him, chargin' him with victhry an' he's goin' to have to stand thrile f'r it. I don't know what th' punishment is, but 'tis somethin' hard f'r th' offinse is onus'l. They're sure to bounce him an' maybe they'll give his job to Cervera. As far as I can see, Hinnissy, an' I cud see as far as me fellow vithran Maclay an' some nine hundherd miles farther, Emanuel is th' on'y wan that come out iv that battle with honor. Whin Schley was thryin' to give up th' ship, or was alongside it on a stagin' makin' dents in th' armor plate with a pick-axe, Sampson was off writin' letters to himsilf an' Bob Ivans was locked in a connin' tower with a life priserver buckled around his waist. Noble ol' Cervera done nawthin' to disgrace his flag. He los' his ships an' his men an' his biler an' ivrything except his ripytation. He saved that be bein' a good swimmer an' not bein' an officer iv th' United States Navy."

"I shud think Schley'd thry an' prove an allybi," Mr. Hennessy suggested pleasantly.

"He can't," said Mr. Dooley. "His frind Sampson's got that."

OUR CUBIAN ALLIES

"The trouble is the Cubians don't undherstand our civilization. Over here freedom means hard wurruk. . . . Ye can't make a Cubian undherstand that freedom means th' same thing as a pinitinchry sintince. Whin we thry to get him to wurruk, he'll say: 'Why shud I? I haven't committed anny crime.' That's goin' to be th' throuble. Th' first thing we know we'll have another war in Cubia whin we begin disthributin' good jobs, twelve hours a day, wan sivinty-five. Th' Cubians ain't civilized in our way. I sometimes think I've got a touch iv Cubian blood in me own veins."

GENERAL MILES'S MOONLIGHT
EXCURSION

Immediately following the capture of Santiago by the troops under Shafter's command, General Miles led a force to occupy Puerto Rico. The people in that island not only failed to resist but welcomed the troops. In the meantime, the American newspapers had published a round robin from Shafter's officers, urging that the army in Cuba be returned to the United States. The frequent reference in Spanish papers to "Yankee pigs" explains the pork chop decoration.

♣ ♣ ♣

"DEAR, OH, dear," said Mr. Dooley, "I'd give five dollars—an' I'd kill a man f'r three—if I was out iv this Sixth Wa-ard to-night, an' down with Gin'ral Miles' gran' picnic an' moonlight excursion in Porther Ricky. 'Tis no comfort in bein' a cow'rd whin ye think iv thim br-rave la-ads facin' death be suffication in bokays an' dyin' iv waltzin' with th' pretty girls iv Porther Ricky.

"I dinnaw whether Gin-ral Miles picked out th' job or whether 'twas picked out f'r him. But, annyhow, whin he got to Sandago de Cubia an' looked ar-round him, he says to his frind Gin'ral Shafter, 'Gin'ral,' says he, 'ye have done well so far,' he says. ' 'Tis not f'r me to take th' lorls fr'm th' steamin' brow iv a thrue hero,' he says. 'I lave ye here,' he says, 'f'r to complete th' victhry ye have so nobly begun,' he says. 'F'r you,' he says, 'th' wallop in th'

55

eye fr'm th' newspaper rayporther, th' r-round robing, an' th' sunsthroke,' he says, 'f'r me th' hardship iv th' battle field, th' late dinner, th' theayter party, an' th' sickenin' polky,' he says. 'Gather,' he says, 'th' fruits iv ye'er bravery,' he says. 'Return,' he says, 'to ye'er native land, an' receive anny gratichood th' Sicrety iv War can spare fr'm his own fam'ly,' he says. 'F'r me,' he says, 'there is no way but f'r to tur-rn me back upon this festive scene,' he says, 'an' go where jooty calls me,' he says. 'Ordherly,' he says, 'put a bottle on th' ice, an' see that me goold pants that I wear with th' pale blue vest with th' di'mon buttons is irned out,' he says. An' with a haggard face he walked aboord th' excursion steamer, an' wint away.

"I'd hate to tell ye iv th' thriles iv th' expedition, Hinnissy. Whin th' picnic got as far as Punch [Ponce], on th' southern coast iv Porther Ricky, Gin'ral Miles gazes out, an' says he, 'This looks like a good place to hang th' hammicks, an' have lunch,' says he. 'Forward, brave men,' says he, 'where ye see me di'mon's sparkle,' says he. 'Forward, an' plant th' crokay ar-rches iv our beloved counthry,' he says. An' in they wint, like inthrepid warryors that they ar-re. On th' beach they was met be a diligation fr'm th' town of Punch, con-sistin' iv th' mayor, th' common council, th' polis an' fire departments, th' Gr-rand Ar-rmy iv th' Raypublic, an' prominent citizens in carredges. Gin'ral Miles, makin' a hasty tielet, advanced onflinchingly to meet thim. 'Gintlemen,' says he, 'what can I do f'r ye?' he says. 'We come,' says th' chairman iv th' comity, 'f'r to offer ye,' he says; 'th' r-run iv th' town,' he says. 'We have held out,' he says, 'as long as we cud,' he says. 'But,' he says, 'they'se a limit to human endurance,' he says. 'We can withstand ye no longer,' he says. 'We surrinder. Take us prisoners, an' rayceive us into ye'er gloryous an' well-fed raypublic,' he says. 'Br-rave men,' says Gin'ral Miles, 'I congratulate ye,' he says, 'on th' heeroism iv yer definse,' he says. 'Ye stuck manfully to yer colors, whativer they ar-re,' he says. 'I on'y wondher that ye waited f'r me to come befure surrindhrin,' he says. 'I welcome ye into th' Union,' he says. 'I don't know how th' Union'll feel about it, but that's no business iv mine,' he says. 'Ye will get ye'er wur-rkin-cards fr'm th' walkin' diligate,' he says; 'an' ye'll be entitled,' he says, 'to pay ye'er share iv th' taxes an' to live awhile an' die whin ye get r-ready,' he says, 'jus' th' same as if ye was bor-rn at home,' he says. 'I don' know th' names iv ye; but I'll call ye all Casey, f'r short,' he says. 'Put ye'er bokays in th' hammick,' he says, 'an return to Punch,' he says; 'an' freeze somethin' f'r me,' he says, 'f'r me thrawt is parched with th' labors iv th' day,' he says. Th' r-rest iv th' avenin' was spint in dancin', music, an' boat-r-ridin'; an' an inj'yable time was had.

"Th' nex' day th' army moved on Punch; an' Gin'ral Miles marched into th' ill-fated city, preceded be flowergirls sthrewin' r-roses an' geranyums befure him. In th' afthernoon they was a lawn tinnis party, an' at night th' gin'ral attinded a banket at th' Gran' Palace Hotel. At midnight he was serenaded be th' Raymimber th' Maine Banjo an' Mandolin Club. Th' entire popylace attinded, with pork chops in their button-holes to show their pathritism. Th' nex' day, afther breakfastin' with Mayor

Casey, he set out on his weary march over th' r-rough, flower-strewn paths f'r San Joon. He has been in gr-reat purl fr'm a witherin' fire iv bokays, an' he has met an' overpowered some iv th' mos' savage orators in Porther Ricky; but, whin I las' heerd iv him, he had pitched his tents an' ice-cream freezers near the inimy's wall, an' was grajully silencin' thim with proclamations."

"They'll kill him with kindness if he don't look out," said Mr. Hennessy.

"I dinnaw about that," said Mr. Dooley, "but I know this, that there's th' makin' iv gr-reat statesmen in Porther Ricky. A proud people that can switch as quick as thim la-ads have nawthin' to larn in th' way iv what Hogan calls th' signs iv gover'mint, even fr'm th' Supreme Court."

THE END OF THE WAR

"An' so th' war is over?" asked Mr. Hennessy.

"On'y part iv it," said Mr. Dooley. "Th' part that ye see in th' pitcher pa-apers is over, but th' tax collector will continyoo his part iv th' war with relentless fury. Cav'lry charges are not th' on'y wans in a rale war."

THE PHILIPPINES

The disposition of the Philippines was the subject of many an editorial after the news of Dewey's victory, with opinion divided between retaining them and making some other arrangement for their government. The description of the Islands was aimed at the quality of information supplied by the newspapers.

♧ ♧ ♧

"I KNOW WHAT I'd do if I was Mack," said Mr. Hennessy. "I'd hist a flag over th' Ph'lippeens, an' I'd take in th' whole lot iv thim."

"An' yet," said Mr. Dooley, " 'tis not more thin two months since ye larned whether they were islands or canned goods. Ye'er back yard is so small that ye'er cow can't turn r-round without buttin' th' wood-shed off th' premises, an' ye wudden't go out to th' stock yards without takin' out a policy on yer life. Suppose ye was standin' at th' corner iv State Sthreet an' Ar-rchey Road, wud ye know what car to take to get to th' Ph'lippeens? If yer son Packy was to ask ye where th' Ph'lippeens is, cud ye give him anny good idea whether they was in Rooshia or jus' west iv th' thracks?"

"Mebbe I cudden't," said Mr. Hennessy, haughtily, "but I'm f'r takin' thim in, annyhow."

"So might I be," said Mr. Dooley, "if I cud on'y get me mind on it. Wan if the worst things about this here war is th' way it's makin' puzzles f'r our poor, tired heads. Whin I wint into it, I thought all I'd have to do was to set up here behind th' bar with a good tin-cint see-gar in me teeth, an' toss dinnymite bombs into th' hated city iv Havana. But look at me now. Th' war is still goin' on; an' ivry night, when I'm countin' up th' cash, I'm askin' mesilf will I annex Cubia or lave it to the Cubians? Will I take Porther Ricky or put it by? An' what shud I do with th' Ph'lippeens? Oh, what shud I do with thim? I can't annex thim because I don't know where they ar-re. I can't let go iv thim because some wan else'll take thim if I do. They are eight thousan' iv thim islands, with a population iv wan hundherd millyon naked savages; an' me bedroom's crowded now with me an' th' bed. How can I take thim in, an' how on earth am I goin' to cover th' nakedness iv thim savages with me wan shoot iv clothes? An' yet 'twud break me heart to think iv givin' people I niver see or heerd tell iv back to other people I don't know. An', if I don't take thim, Schwartzmeister down th' sthreet, that has half me thrade already, will grab thim sure.

"It ain't that I'm afraid iv not doin' th' r-right thing in th' end, Hinnissy. Some mornin' I'll wake up an' know jus' what to do, an' that I'll do. But 'tis th' annoyance in th' mane time. I've been r-readin' about th' counthry. 'Tis over beyant ye'er left shoulder whin ye're facin' east. Jus' throw ye'er thumb back, an' ye have it as ac'rate as anny man in town. 'Tis farther thin Boohlgahrya an' not so far as Blewchoochoo. It's near Chiny, an' it's not so near; an', if a man was to bore a well through fr'm Goshen, Indianny, he might sthrike it, an' thin again he might not. It's a poverty-sthricken counthry, full iv goold an' precious stones, where th' people can pick dinner off th' threes an' ar-re starvin' because they have no step-ladders. Th' inhabitants is mostly naygurs an' Chinnymen, peaceful, industhrus, an' law-abidin', but savage an' bloodthirsty in their methods. They wear no clothes ex-cept what they have on, an' each woman has five hus-bands an' each man has five wives. Th' r-rest goes into th' discard, th' same as here. Th' islands has been ownded be Spain since befure th' fire; an' she's threated thim so well they're now up in ar-rms again her, except a majority iv thim which is thurly loyal. Th' natives seldom fight, but whin they get mad at wan another they r-run-a-muck. Whin a man r-runs-a-muck, sometimes they hang him an' sometimes they discharge him an' hire a new motorman. Th' women ar-re beautiful, with languishin' black eyes, an' they smoke see-gars, but ar-re hurried an' incomplete in their dhress. I see a pitcher iv wan th' other day with nawthin' on her but a basket of cocoanuts an' a hoop-skirt. They're no prudes. We import juke, hemp, cigar wrap-pers, sugar, an' fairy tales fr'm th' Ph'lippeens, an' ex-port six-inch shells an' th' like. Iv late th' Ph'lippeens has awaked to th' fact that they're behind th' times, an' has received much American amminition in their midst. They say th' Spanyards is all tore up about it.

"I larned all this fr'm th' papers, an' I know 'tis sthraight. An' yet, Hinnissy, I dinnaw what to do about th' Ph'lippeens. An' I'm all alone in th' wurruld. Ivrybody else has made up his mind. Ye ask anny con-ducthor on Ar-rchy Road, an' he'll tell ye. Ye can find out fr'm th' paper; an', if ye really want to know, all ye have to do is to ask a prom'nent citizen who can mow all th' lawn he owns with a safety razor. But I don't know."

"Hang on to thim," said Mr. Hennessy, stoutly. "What we've got we must hold."

"Well," said Mr. Dooley, "if I was Mack, I'd lave it to George. I'd say: 'George,' I'd say, 'if ye're f'r hangin' on, hang on it is. If ye say, lave go, I dhrop thim.' 'Twas George won thim with th' shells, an' th' question's up to him."

THE PHILIPPINE PEACE

"'Tis sthrange we don't hear much talk about th' Ph'lippeens," said Mr. Hennessy.

"Ye ought to go to Boston," said Mr. Dooley. "They talk about it there in their sleep. Th' raison it's not discussed annywhere else is that ivrything is perfectly quiet there. We don't talk about Ohio or Ioway or anny iv our other possissions because they'se nawthin' doin' in thim parts. . . ."

"But sure they might do something f'r thim," said Mr. Hennessy.

"They will," said Mr. Dooley. "They'll give thim a measure iv freedom."

"But whin?"

"Whin they'll sthand still long enough to be measured," said Mr. Dooley.

EXPANSION

The Filipinos under Aguinaldo's leadership did not take kindly to American rule, and that seems to have influenced the opinion of Mr. Hennessy. Andrew Carnegie's steel company had been accused of supplying armor plate to the navy that had blow holes in it. Nevertheless, the steel maker had come out of the war a vigorous anti-imperialist. Commissary-General C. P. Eagan had gained notoriety by appearing before a board of inquiry and reading a paper filled with filthy abuse of General Miles.

"Well," said Mr. Dooley, "we've got 'em."
"Again," said Mr. Hennessy, with a faint attempt at a joke.
"Never mind," said Mr. Dooley. "We've got th' Ph'lippeens. . . ."

♣ ♣ ♣

"WHIN WE plant what Hogan calls th' starry banner iv Freedom in th' Ph'lippeens," said Mr. Dooley, "an' give th' sacred blessin' iv liberty to the poor, downtrodden people iv thim unfortunate isles—damn thim!— we'll larn thim a lesson."

"Sure," said Mr. Hennessy, sadly, "we have a thing or two to larn oursilves."

"But it isn't f'r thim to larn us," said Mr. Dooley. " 'Tis not f'r thim wretched an' degraded crathers, without a mind or a shirt iv their own, f'r to give lessons in politeness an' liberty to a nation that mannyfacthers more dhressed beef than anny other imperyal nation in th'

wurruld. We say to thim: 'Naygurs,' we say, 'poor, disso-
lute, uncovered wretches,' says we, 'whin th' crool hand iv
Spain forged man'cles f'r ye'er limbs, as Hogan says, who
was it crossed th' say an' sthruck off th' comealongs? We
did—by dad, we did. An' now, ye mis'rable, childish-minded
apes, we propose f'r to larn ye th' uses iv liberty. In ivry
city in this unfair land we will erect schoolhouses an'
packin' houses an' houses iv correction; an' we'll larn ye
our language, because 'tis aisier to larn ye ours than to larn
oursilves yours. An' we'll give ye clothes, if ye pay f'r
thim; an', if ye don't ye can go without. An', whin ye're
hungry, ye can go to th' morgue—we mane th' resth'rant—
an' ate a good square meal iv ar-rmy beef. An' we'll sind th'
gr-reat Gin'ral Eagan over f'r to larn ye etiquette, an'
Andhrew Carnegie to larn ye pathritism with blow-holes
into it, an' Gin'ral Alger to larn ye to hould onto a job;
an', whin ye've become edycated an' have all th' blessin's
iv civilization that we don't want, that'll count ye one.
We can't give ye anny votes, because we haven't more
thin enough to go round now; but we'll threat ye th' way
a father shud threat his childher if we have to break ivry
bone in ye'er bodies. So come to our ar-rms,' says we.

"But, glory be, 'tis more like a rasslin' match than a
father's embrace. Up gets this little monkey iv an
Aggynaldoo, an' says he, 'Not for us,' he says. 'We thank
ye kindly; but we believe,' he says, 'in pathronizin' home
industhries,' he says. 'An',' he says, 'I have on hand,' he
says, 'an' f'r sale,' he says, 'a very superyor brand iv
home-made liberty, like ye'er mother used to make,' he
says. ' 'Tis a long way fr'm ye'er plant to here,' he says,
'an' be th' time a cargo iv liberty,' he says, 'got out here

an' was handled be th' middlemen,' he says, 'it might spoil,' he says. 'We don't want anny col' storage or embalmed liberty,' he says. 'What we want an' what th' ol' reliable house iv Aggynaldoo,' he says, 'supplies to th' thrade,' he says, 'is fr-resh liberty r-right off th' far-rm,' he says. 'I can't do annything with ye'er proposition,' he says. 'I can't give up,' he says, 'th' rights f'r which f'r five years I've fought an' bled ivry wan I cud reach,' he says. 'Onless,' he says, 'ye'd feel like buyin' out th' whole business,' he says. 'I'm a pathrite,' he says; 'but I'm no bigot,' he says.

"An' there it stands, Hinnissy, with th' indulgent parent kneelin' on th' stomach iv his adopted child, while a dillygation fr'm Boston bastes him with an umbrella. There it stands, an' how will it come out I dinnaw. I'm not much iv an expansionist mesilf. F'r th' las' tin years I've been thryin' to decide whether 'twud be good policy an' thrue to me thraditions to make this here bar two or three feet longer, an manny's th' night I've laid awake tryin' to puzzle it out. But I don't know what to do with th' Ph'lippeens anny more thin I did las' summer, befure I heerd tell iv thim. We can't give thim to anny wan without makin' th' wan that gets thim feel th' way Doherty felt to Clancy whin Clancy med a frindly call an' give Doherty's childher th' measles. We can't sell thim, we can't ate thim, an' we can't throw thim into th' alley whin no wan is lookin'. An' 'twud be a disgrace f'r to lave befure we've pounded these frindless an' ongrateful people into insinsibility. So I suppose, Hinnissy, we'll have to stay an' do th' best we can, an' lave Andhrew Carnegie secede fr'm th' Union. They'se wan consolation; an' that is, if th'

American people can govern thimsilves, they can govern annything that walks."

" 'Twill cost a power iv money," said Mr. Hennessy, the prudent.

"Expand, ixpind," said Mr. Dooley. "That's a joke, an' I med it."

GOVERNOR TAFT'S REPORT

"Th' Ph'lippeens," says Guv'nor Taft, "is wan or more iv th' beautiful jools in th' diadem iv our fair nation. Formerly our fair nation didn't care f'r jools, but done up her hair with side combs, but she's been abroad some since an' she come back with beautiful reddish goolden hair that a tiara looks well in an' that is betther f'r havin' a tiara. She is not as young as she was. Th' simple home-lovin' maiden that our fathers knew has disappeared an' in her place we find a Columbya, gintlemen, with ma-churer charms, a knowledge iv Europeen customs an' not averse to a cigareet. So we have pinned in her fair hair a diadem that sets off her beauty to advantage an' holds on th' front iv th' hair, an' th' mos' lovely pearl in this ornymint is thim sunny little isles iv th' Passyfic. . . . They raise unknown quantities iv produce, none iv which forchinitly can come into this counthry. All th' riches iv Cathay, all th' wealth iv Ind, as Hogan says, wud look like a second morgedge on an Apache wickeyup compared with th' untold an' almost unmintionable products iv that gloryous domain. Me business kept me in Manila or I wud tell ye what they are. Besides some iv our lile sub-jects is gettin' to be good shots an' I didn't go down there f'r that purpose."

WAR AND WAR MAKERS

With war on against the Filipinos the dispatches of General E. S. Otis became the chief news from that region. A short time later news of the Boer War began to crowd that from the Philippines out of the headlines. Joseph Chamberlain was the leading British imperialist statesman, and Paul Kruger was President of the Boer Republic.

"Do ye think th' United States is enthusyastic f'r Boers?" asked the innocent Hennessy.
"It was," said Mr. Dooley, "but in th' las' few weeks it's had so many things to think iv. Th' enthusyasm iv this counthry, Hinnissy, always makes me think iv a bonfire on an ice-floe. It burns bright so long as ye feed it, an' it looks good, but it don't take hold, somehow, on th' ice."

♧ ♧ ♧

"I TELL YE, Hinnissy," said Mr. Dooley, "ye can't do th' English-speakin' people. Oursilves an' th' hands acrost th' sea ar-re rapidly teachin' th' benighted Lutheryan an' other haythin that as a race we're onvincible an' oncatchable. Th' Anglo-Saxon race meetin's now goin' on in th' Ph'lippeens an' South Africa ought to convince annywan that, give us a fair start an' we can bate th' wurruld to a tillygraft office.

"Th' war our cousins be Sir Thomas Lipton is prosecutin', as Hogan says, again' th' foul but accrate Boers is doin' more thin that. It's givin' us a common war lithrachoor. I wudden't believe at first whin I r-read th' dispatches in th' pa-apers that me frind Gin'ral Otis wasn't in South Africa. It was on'y whin I see another chapter iv his justly cillybrated seeryal story, intitled 'Th' Capture iv Porac' that I knew he had an imitator in th' mother counthry. An' be hivins, I like th' English la-ad's style almost as well as our own gr-reat artist's. Mebbe 'tis, as th' pa-apers say, that Otis has writ himsilf out. Annyhow th' las' chapter isn't thrillin'. He says: 'To-day th' ar-rmy undher my command fell upon th' inimy with gr-reat slaughter an' seized th' important town of Porac which I have mintioned befure, but,' he says, 'we ar-re fortunately now safe in Manila.' Ye see he doesn't keep up th' intherest to th' end. Th' English pote does betther."

" 'Las' night at eight o'clock,' he says, 'we found our slendher but inthrepid ar-rmy surrounded be wan hundhred thousan' Boers,' he says. 'We attackted thim with gr-reat fury,' he says, 'pursuin' thim up th' almost inaccessible mountain side an' capturin' eight guns which we didn't want so we give thim back to thim with siveral iv our own,' he says. 'Th' Irish rig'mints,' he says, 'th' Kerry Rifles, th' Land Leaguers' Own, an' th' Dublin Pets, commanded be th' pop'lar Irish sojer Gin'ral Sir Ponsonby Tompkins wint into battle singin' their well-known naytional anthem: "Mrs. Innery Awkins is a fust-class name!" Th' Boers retreated,' he says, 'pursued be th' Davitt Terrors who cut their way through th' fugitives with awful slaughter,' he says. 'They have now,' he says, 'pinethrated as far as Pretoria,' he says, 'th' officers arrivin' in first-class carredges an' th' men in thrucks,' he says, 'an' ar-re camped in th' bettin' shed where they ar-re afforded ivry attintion be th' vanquished inimy,' he says. 'As f'r us,' he says, 'we decided afther th' victhry to light out f'r Ladysmith!' he says. 'Th' inimy had similar intintions,' he says, 'but their skill has been vastly overrated,' he says. 'We bate thim,' he says, 'we bate thim be thirty miles,' he says. That's where we're sthrong, Hinnissy. We may get licked on th' battle field, we may be climbin' threes in th' Ph'lippeens with arrows stickin' in us like quills, as Hogan says, into th' fretful porcupine or we may be doin' a mile in five minyits flat down th' pike that leads to Cape Town pursued be th' less fleet but more ignorant Boers peltin' us with guns full iv goold an' bibles, but in th' pages iv histhry that our childhren read we niver turned back on e'er an inimy. We make our own gloryous pages on th' battlefield, in th' camp an' in th' cab'net meetin'.''

"Well, 'tis all r-right f'r ye to be jokin'," said Mr. Hennessy, "but there's manny a brave fellow down there that it's no joke to."

"Thrue f'r ye," said Mr. Dooley, "an' that's why I wisht it cud be fixed up so's th' men that starts th' wars could do th' fightin'. Th' throuble is that all th' prelimin'ries is arranged be matchmakers an' all they'se left f'r fighters is to do th' murdherin'. A man's got a good job at home an' he wants to make it sthronger. How can he do it? Be throwin' out someone that's got an akelly good job down th' sthreet. Now he don't go over as I wud an' say, 'Here Schwartzmeister (or Kruger as th' case may be), I don't like ye'er appearance, ye made a monkey iv me in argymint befure th' neighborhood an' if ye continyue

in business ye'll hurt me thrade, so here goes to move ye
into th' sthreet!' Not that la-ad. He gets a crowd around
him an' says he: 'Kruger (or Schwartzmeister as th' case
may be) is no good. To begin with he's a Dutchman. If
that ain't enough he's a cantin', hymn singin' murdhrous
wretch that wudden't lave wan iv our counthrymen ate a
square meal if he had his way. I'll give ye all two dollars
a week if ye'll go over an' desthroy him.' An' th' other
la-ad, what does he do? He calls in th' neighbors an' says
he: 'Dooley is sindin' down a gang iv savages to murdher
me. Do ye lave ye'er wurruk an' ye'er families an' rally
ar-round me an' where ye see me plug hat wave do ye go
in th' other direction,' he says, 'an' slay th' brutal inimy,'
he says. An' off goes th' sojers an' they meet a lot iv la-ads
that looks like thimsilves an' makes sounds that's more
or less human an' ates out iv plates an' they swap smokin'
tobacco an' sing songs together an' th' next day they're
up early jabbing holes in each other with baynits. An'
whin its all over they'se me an' Chamberlain at home
victoryous an' Kruger an' Schwartzmeister at home
akelly victoryous. An' they make me prime minister or
aldherman but whin I want a man to put in me coal I
don't take wan with a wooden leg.

"I'll niver go down again to see sojers off to th' war.
But ye'll see me at th' depot with a brass band whin th'
men that causes wars starts f'r th' scene iv carnage. Whin
Congress goes forth to th' sun-kissed an' rain jooled isles
iv th' Passyfic no more heartier cheer will be heard thin
th' wan or two that rises fr'm th' bosom iv Martin
Dooley. Says I, give thim th' chanst to make histhry an'

lave th' young men come home an' make car wheels. If Chamberlain likes war so much 'tis him that ought to be down there in South Africa peltin' over th' road with ol' Kruger chasin' him with a hoe. Th' man that likes fightin' ought to be willin' to turn in an' spell his fellow-counthrymen himsilf. An' I'd even go this far an' say that if Mack wants to subjoo th' damn Ph'lippeens——"

"Ye're a thraitor," said Mr. Hennessy.

"I know it," said Mr. Dooley, complacently.

"Ye're an anti-expansionist."

"If ye say that agin," cried Mr. Dooley, angrily, "I'll smash in ye'er head."

AMERICAN DIPLOMACY

Gov'nor Taft [of the Philippines] has been in Rome showin' th' wurruld how successful, sthraightforward, downright, outspoken, manly, frank, fourteen ounces to th' pound American business da'lings can be again th' worn-out di-plomacy iv th' Papal Coort. Whin last heerd fr'm, this astoot an' able man, backed up be th' advice iv Elihoo Root iv York state, was makin' his way tow'rd Manila on foot, an' siv'ral mimbers iv th' Colledge iv Cardinals was heerd to regret that American statesmen were so thin they cudden't find annything to fit thim in his trunk."

THE SUPREME COURT'S
DECISIONS

The Republican victory in the election of 1900 determined that a policy of retaining the new territories acquired in the peace treaty with Spain would be followed for a time at least. This created the legal problem of keeping the new possessions outside of the area to which the Constitution extended so that tariffs could be levied on their products imported into the United States. The issue was broader than this, for if the Constitution followed the flag as most Democrats insisted, the Bill of Rights would increase the difficulty of governing dependencies. Consequently, the decision that the Constitution did not follow the flag was a victory for expansion. The Supreme Court, in coming to this decision in a series of cases in 1901, must have set a record for lack of agreement among the judges. In one decision there were five judges supporting the conclusion for reasons that were expressed in three different opinions. The minority of four was able to express its dissent in two opinions.

"I SEE," SAID Mr. Dooley, "th' Supreme Coort has decided th' Constitution don't follow th' flag."

"Who said it did?" asked Mr. Hennessy.

"Some wan," said Mr. Dooley. "It happened a long time ago an' I don't raymimber clearly how it come up, but some fellow said that ivrywhere th' Constitution wint, th' flag was sure to go. 'I don't believe wan wurrud iv it,'

says th' other fellow. 'Ye can't make me think th' Constitution is goin' thrapezin' around ivrywhere a young lift-
nant in th' ar-rmy takes it into his head to stick a flag
pole. It's too old. It's a home-stayin' Constitution with a
blue coat with brass buttons onto it, an' it walks with a
goold-headed cane. It's old an' it's feeble an' it prefers to
set on th' front stoop an' amuse th' childher. It wudden't
last a minyit in thim thropical climes. 'Twud get a pain
in th' fourteenth amindmint an' die befure th' doctors cud
get ar-round to cut it out. No, sir, we'll keep it with us,
an' threat it tenderly without too much hard wurruk,
an' whin it plays out entirely we'll give it dacint buryal
an' incorp'rate oursilves under th' laws iv Noo Jarsey.
That's what we'll do,' says he. 'But,' says th' other, 'if it
wants to thravel, why not lave it?' 'But it don't want to.'
'I say it does.' 'How'll we find out?' 'We'll ask th' Supreme
Coort. They'll know what's good f'r it.'

"So it wint up to th' Supreme Coort. They'se wan thing
about th' Supreme Coort, if ye lave annything to thim, ye
lave it to thim. Ye don't get a check that entitles ye to
call f'r it in an hour. The Supreme Coort iv th' United
States ain't in anny hurry about catchin' th' mails. It
don't have to make th' las' car. I'd back th' Aujitoroom
again it anny day f'r a foot race. If ye're lookin' f'r a
game iv quick decisions an' base hits, ye've got to hire
another empire. It niver gives a decision till th' crowd
has dispersed an' th' players have packed their bats in th'
bags an' started f'r home.

"F'r awhile ivrybody watched to see what th' Supreme
Coort wud do. I knew mesilf I felt I cudden't make an-

other move in th' game till I heerd fr'm thim. Buildin' op'rations was suspinded an' we sthud wringin' our hands outside th' dure waitin' f'r information fr'm th' bedside. 'What 're they doin' now?' 'They just put th' argymints iv larned counsel in th' ice box an' th' chief justice is in a corner writin' a pome. Brown J. an' Harlan J. is discussin' th' condition iv th' Roman Empire befure th' fire. Th' r-rest iv th' Coort is considherin' th' question iv whether they ought or ought not to wear ruchin' on their skirts an' hopin' crinoline won't come in again. No decision today!' An' so it wint f'r days, an' weeks an' months. Th' men that had argyied that th' Constitution ought to shadow th' flag to all th' tough resorts on th' Passyfic coast an' th' men that argyied that th' flag was so lively that no constitution cud follow it an' survive, they died or lost their jobs or wint back to Salem an' were f'rgotten. Expansionists contracted an' anti-expansionists blew up an' little childher was born into th' wurruld an' grew to manhood an' niver heerd iv Porther Ricky except whin some wan got a job there. I'd about made up me mind to thry an' put th' thing out iv me thoughts an' go back to wurruk when I woke up wan mornin' an' see be th' pa-aper that th' Supreme Coort had warned th' Constitution to lave th' flag alone an' tind to its own business.

"That's what th' pa-aper says, but I've r-read over th' decision an' I don't see annything iv th' kind there. They'se not a wurrud about th' flag an' not enough to tire ye about th' Constitution. 'Tis a matther iv limons, Hinnissy, that th' Supreme Coort has been settin' on f'r this gineration—a cargo iv limons sint fr'm Porther Ricky to

some Eyetalian in Philydelphy. Th' decision was r-read
by Brown J., him bein' th' las' justice to make up his mind,
an' ex-officio, as Hogan says, th' first to speak, afther a
crool an' bitther contest. Says Brown J.: 'Th' question
here is wan iv such gr-reat importance that we've been
sthrugglin' over it iver since ye see us las' an' on'y come
to a decision (Fuller C. J., Gray J., Harlan J., Shiras J.,
McKenna J., White J., Brewer J., an' Peckham J. dissentin' fr'm me an' each other) because iv th' hot
weather comin' on. Wash'n'ton is a dhreadful place in
summer (Fuller C. J. dissentin'). Th' whole fabric iv
our government is threatened, th' lives iv our people an'
th' progress iv civilization put to th' bad. Men ar-re excited. But why? We ar-re not. (Harlan J., "I am." Fuller
C. J. dissentin', but not f'r th' same reason.) This thing
must be settled wan way or th' other undher that dear
ol' Constitution be varchue iv which we are here an' ye
ar-re there an' Congress is out West practicin' law. Now
what does th' Constitution say? We'll look it up thoroughly whin we get through with this case (th' rest iv th'
Coort dissentin'). In th' manetime we must be governed
be th' ordnances iv th' Khan iv Beloochistan, th' laws iv
Hinnery th' Eighth, th' opinyon iv Justice iv th' Peace
Oscar Larson in th' case iv th' township iv Red Wing
varsus Petersen, an' th' Dhred Scott decision. What do
they say about limons? Nawthin' at all. Again we take th'
Dhred Scott decision. This is wan iv th' worst I iver
r-read. If I cudden't write a betther wan with blindhers on,
I'd leap off th' bench. This horrible fluke iv a decision
throws a gr-reat, an almost dazzlin' light on th' case. I

will turn it off. (McKenna J. concurs, but thinks it ought to be blowed out.) But where was I? I must put on me specs. Oh, about th' limons. Well, th' decision iv th' Coort (th' others dissentin') is as follows: First, that th' Disthrict iv Columbya is a state; second, that it is not; third, that New York is a state; fourth, that it is a crown colony; fifth, that all states ar-re states an' all territories ar-re territories in th' eyes iv other powers, but Gawd knows what they ar-re at home. In th' case iv Hogan varsus Mullins, th' decision is he must paper th' barn. (Hinnery VIII, sixteen, six, four, eleven.) In Wiggins varsus et al. th' cow belonged. (Louis XIV, 90 in rem.) In E. P. Vigore varsus Ad Lib., the custody iv th' childher. I'll now fall back a furlong or two in me chair, while me larned but misguided collagues r-read th' Histhry iv Iceland to show ye how wrong I am. But mind ye, what I've said goes. I let thim talk because it exercises their throats, but ye've heerd all th' decision on this limon case that'll get into th' fourth reader.' A voice fr'm th' audjeence, 'Do I get me money back?' Brown J.: 'Who ar-re ye?' Th' Voice: 'Th' man that ownded th' limons.' Brown J.: 'I don't know.' (Gray J., White J., dissentin' an' th' r-rest iv th' birds concurrin' but f'r entirely diff'rent reasons.)

"An' there ye have th' decision, Hinnissy, that's shaken th' intellicts iv th' nation to their very foundations, or will if they thry to read it. 'Tis all r-right. Look it over some time. 'Tis fine spoort if ye don't care f'r checkers. Some say it laves th' flag up in th' air an' some say that's where it laves th' Constitution. Annyhow, something's in th' air. But there's wan thing I'm sure about."

"What's that?" asked Mr. Hennessy.

"That is," said Mr. Dooley, "no matther whether th' Constitution follows th' flag or not, th' Supreme Coort follows th' iliction returns."

A SPEECH BY PRESIDENT McKINLEY

"Th' proceedin's was opened with a prayer that Providence might r-remain undher th' protection iv th' administration . . . Mack r-rose up in a perfect hur-cane iv applause, an' says he, 'Gintlemen,' he says, 'an' fellow-heroes. . . . We cannot tur-rn back,' he says, 'th' hands iv th' clock that, even as I speak,' he says, 'is r-rushin' through th' hear-rts iv men,' he says, 'dashin' its spray again th' star iv liberty an' hope, an' no north, no south, no east, no west, but a steady purpose to do th' best we can, considerin' all th' circumstances iv th' case,' he says. 'I hope I have made th' matther clear to ye,' he says, 'an', with these few remarks,' he says, 'I will tur-rn th' job over to destiny,' he says, 'which is sure to lead us iver on an' on, an' back an' forth, a united an' happy people, livin',' he says, 'undher an administration that, thanks to our worthy Prisident an' his cap'ble an' earnest advisers, is second to none,' he says."

MR. DOOLEY ON
NATIONAL POLITICS

*"An' a man wudden't think iv runnin' f'r prisident
onless he cud prove he'd been raised on a farm. I
doubt if Woodrow Wilson iver wud've been ilicted
if th' rumor hadn't gone out that Princeton was an
agaraculchural colledge, which has always
been th' believ iv th' pupils at New
Haven an' Cambridge."*

PLATFORM MAKING

*The Democratic Convention of 1900, under Bryan's leader-
ship and against the wishes of the eastern faction in the
party, definitely re-endorsed the platform of 1896, includ-
ing its free silver proposal. However, it declared imperial-
ism to be the "paramount issue."*

♩ ♩ ♩

"T HAT STHRIKES me as a gran' platform," said Mr.
Hennessy. "I'm with it fr'm start to finish."

"Sure ye are," said Mr. Dooley, "an' so ye'd be if it begun: 'We denounce Terence Hinnissy iv th' Sixth Ward
iv Chicago as a thraitor to his country, an inimy iv civilization, an' a poor thing.' Ye'd say: 'While there are wan
or two things that might be omitted, th' platform as a
whole is a statesmanlike docymint, an' wan that appeals
to th' intelligince iv American manhood.' That's what ye'd
say, an' that's what all th' likes iv ye'd say. An' whin
iliction day comes 'round th' on'y question ye'll ast ye'ersilf is: 'Am I with Mack or am I with Billy Bryan?' An'
accordin'ly ye'll vote.

" 'Tis always th' same way, an' all platforms is alike. I
mind wanst whin I was an alter-nate to th' county convintion—'twas whin I was a power in polytics an' th'
on'y man that cud do annything with th' Bohemian vote—
I was settin' here wan night with a pen an' a pot iv ink
befure me, thryin' to compose th' platform f'r th' nex'

day, f'r I was a lithry man in a way, d'ye mind, an' I knew th' la-ads'd want a few crimps put in th' Raypublicans in a ginteel style, an' 'd be sure to call on me f'r to do it. Well, I'd got as far down as th' tariff an' was thryin' f'r to express me opinyon without swearin', whin who shud come in but Lafferty, that was sicrety iv McMahon, that was th' Main Guy in thim days, but aftherward thrun down on account iv him mixin' up between th' Rorkes an' th' Dorseys. Th' Main Guy Down Town said he wudden't have no throuble in th' ward, an' he declared McMahon out. McMahon had too much money annyhow. If he'd kept on, dollar bills'd have been extinct outside iv his house. But he was a sthrong man in thim days an' much liked.

"Annyhow, Lafferty, that was his sicrety, come in, an' says he: 'What are ye doin' there?' says he. 'Step soft,' says I; 'I am at wurruk,' I says. 'Ye shudden't do lithry wurruk on an empty stomach,' says he. 'I do nawthin' on an empty stomach but eat,' says I. 'I've had me supper,' I says. 'Go 'way,' says I, 'till I finish th' platform,' I says. 'What's th' platform?' says he. 'F'r th' county con-vintion,' says I.

"Well, sir, he set down on a chair, an' I thought th' man was goin' to die right there on th' premises with laughter. 'Whin ye get through with ye'er barkin',' says I, 'I'll throuble ye to tell me what ye may be doin' it f'r,' I says. 'I see nawthin' amusin' here but ye'er prisince,' I says, 'an' that's not a divvle iv a lot funnier than a wooden leg,' I says, f'r I was mad. Afther awhile he come to, an' says he: 'Ye don't raally think,' says he, 'that ye'll get a chanct to spring that platform,' he says. 'I do,' says I.

'Why,' he says, 'the platform has been adopted,' he says. 'Whin?' says I. 'Befure ye were born,' says he. 'In th' reign iv Bildad th' first,' says he—he was a larned man, was Lafferty, though a dhrinkin' man. All sicreties iv polyticians not in office is dhrinkin' men, Hinnissy. 'I've got th' copy iv it here in me pocket,' he says. 'Th' boss give it to me to bring it up to date,' he says. 'They was no sthrike last year an' we've got to put a sthrike plank in th' platform or put th' prisident iv th' Lumber Shover's union on th' county board, an',' he says, 'they ain't room,' he says.

" 'Why,' says Lafferty, 'ye ought to know th' histhry iv platforms,' he says. An' he give it to me, an' I'll give it to ye. Years ago, Hinnissy, manny years ago, they was a race between th' Dimmycrats an' th' Raypublicans f'r to see which shud have a choice iv principles. Th' Dimmy-crats lost. I dinnaw why. Mebbe they stopped to take a dhrink. Annyhow, they lost. Th' Raypublicans come up an' they choose th' 'we commind' principles, an' they was nawthin' left f'r the Dimmycrats but th' 'we denounce an' deplores.' I dinnaw how it come about, but th' Dimmycrats didn't like th' way th' thing shtud, an' so they fixed it up between thim that whichiver won at th' iliction shud com-mind an' congratulate, an' thim that lost shud denounce an' deplore. An' so it's been, on'y th' Dimmycrats has had so little chanct f'r to do annything but denounce an' de-plore that they've almost lost th' use iv th' other wurruds.

"Mack sets back in Wash'n'ton an' writes a platform f'r th' comity on risolutions to compose th' week afther. He's got a good job—forty-nine ninety-two, sixty-six a month— an' 'tis up to him to feel good. 'I—I mean we,' he says, 'congratulate th' counthry on th' matchless statesmanship, onshrinkin' courage, steady devotion to duty an' principle iv that gallant an' hon'rable leader, mesilf,' he says to his sicrety. 'Take that,' he says, 'an' elaborate it,' he says. 'Ye'll find a ditchnry on th' shelf near th' dure,' he says, 'if ye don't think I've put what I give ye sthrong enough,' he says. 'I always was,' he says, 'too retirin' f'r me own good,' he says. 'Spin out th' r-rest,' he says, 'to make about six thousan' wurruds,' he says, 'but be sure don't write annything too hot about th' Boer war or th' Ph'lippeens or Chiny, or th' tariff, or th' goold question, or our relations with England, or th' civil sarvice,' he says. ' 'Tis a foolish man,' he says, 'that throws a hunk iv coal fr'm his own window at th' dhriver iv a brick wagon,' he says.

"But with Billy Bryan 'tis diff'rent. He's out in Lincoln, Neebrasky, far fr'm home, an' he says to himsilf: 'Me throat is hoarse, an' I'll exercise me other fac'lties,' he says. 'I'll write a platform,' he says. An' he sets down to a typewriter, an' denounces an' deplores till th' hired man blows th' dinner horn. Whin he can denounce an' deplore no longer he views with alarm an' declares with indignation. An' he sinds it down to Kansas City, where th' cot beds come fr'm."

"Oh, ye're always pitchin' into some wan," said Mr. Hennessy. "I bet ye Willum Jennings Bryan niver see th' platform befure it wint in. He's too good a man."

"He is all iv that," said Mr. Dooley. "But ye bet he knows th' rale platform f'r him is: 'Look at th' bad breaks Mack's made,' an' Mack's platform is: 'Ye'd get worse if ye had Billy Bryan.' An' it depinds on whether most iv th' voters ar-re tired out or on'y a little tired who's ilicted. All excipt you, Hinnissy. Ye'll vote f'r Bryan?"

"I will," said Mr. Hennessy.

"Well," said Mr. Dooley, "d'ye know, I suspicted ye might."

THE DEMOCRATIC PARTY

"Man an' boy I've seen th' Dimmycratic party hangin' to th' ropes a score iv times. I've seen it dead an' burrid an' th' Raypublicans kindly buildin' a monymint f'r it an' preparin' to spind their declinin' days in th' custom house. I've gone to sleep nights wondhrin' where I'd throw away me vote afther this an' whin I woke up there was that crazy-headed ol' loon iv a party with its hair sthreamin' in its eyes, an' an axe in its hand, chasin' Raypublicans into th' tall grass. 'Tis niver so good as whin 'tis broke, whin rayspictable people speak iv it in whispers, an' whin it has no leaders an' on'y wan principel, to go in an' take it away fr'm th' other fellows. Something will turn up, ye bet, Hinnissy. Th' Raypublican party may die iv over-feedin' or all th' leaders pump out so much ile they won't feel like leadin'. An' annyhow they'se always wan ray iv light ahead. We're sure to have hard times. An' whin th' la-ads that ar-re baskin' in th' sunshine iv prosperity with Andhrew Carnaygie an' Pierpont Morgan an' me frind Jawn D. finds that th' sunshine has been turned off an' their fellow-baskers has relieved thim iv what they had in th' dark, we'll take thim boys be th' hand an' say: 'Come over with ye'er own kind. Th' Raypublican party broke ye, but now that ye'er down we'll not turn a cold shoulder to ye. Come in an' we'll keep ye—broke.' "

THE TARIFF

During the campaign of 1908, Taft had promised a revision of the tariff downward. The resulting Payne-Aldrich law was far from a downward revision, and became one of the causes of the secession of the Progressives in 1912.

"How glad I am to know that Congress has adjourned after rejoocin' th' tariff to a level where th' poorest are within its reach."

"WELL, SIR, 'tis a gr-r-rand wurruk thim Sinitors an' Congressmen are doin' in Wash'n'ton. Me heart bleeds f'r th' poor fellows, steamin' away undher th' majestic tin dome iv th' capitol thryin' to rejooce th' tariff to a weight where it can stand on th' same platform with me frind big Bill without endangerin' his life. Th' likes iv ye wud want to see th' tariff rejooced with a jack plane or an ice pick. But th' tariff has been a good frind to some iv thim boys an' it's a frind iv frinds iv some iv th' others an' they don't intend to be rough with it. A little gentle massage to rejooce th' most prom'nent prochooberances is all that is nicissry. Whiniver they rub too hard an' th' tariff begins to groan, Sinitor Aldhrich says: 'Go a little asier there, boys. He's very tender in some iv thim sched-ules. P'raps we'd betther stop f'r th' day an' give him a little nourishment to build him up,' he says. An' th' last I

heerd about it, th' tariff was far fr'm bein' th' wan an'
emacyated crather ye'd like to see comin' out iv th' Sinit
chamber. It won't have to be helped onto ye'er back an' ye
won't notice anny reduction in its weight. No, sir, I shudden't be surprised if it was heartier thin iver.

"Me congressman sint me a copy iv th' tariff bill th'
other day. He's a fine fellow, that congressman iv mine.
He looks afther me inthrests well. He knows what a
gr-reat reader I am. I don't care what I read. So he sint
me a copy iv th' tariff bill an' I've been studyin' it f'r a
week. 'Tis a good piece iv summer lithrachoor. 'Tis full iv
action an' romance. I haven't read annything to akel it
since I used to get th' Deadwood Dick series.

"I'm in favor iv havin' it read on th' Foorth iv July
instead iv th' Declaration iv Indypindance. It gives ye some
idee iv th' kind iv gloryous governmint we're livin' undher, to see our fair Columbia puttin' her brave young
arms out an' defindin' th' products iv our soil fr'm steel
rails to porous plasthers, hooks an' eyes, artyficial horse
hair an' bone casings, which comes undher th' head iv
clothin' an' I suppose is a polite name f'r pantaloons.

"Iv coorse, low people like ye, Hinnissy, will kick because it's goin' to cost ye more to indulge ye'er taste in
ennervatin' luxuries. D'ye know Sinitor Aldhrich? Ye
don't? I'm surprised to hear it. He knows ye. Why, he all
but mentions ye'er name in two or three places. He does
so. 'Tis as if he said: 'This here vulgar plutycrat, Hinnissy, is turnin' th' heads iv our young men with his
garish display. Befure this, counthries have perished because iv th' ostintation iv th' arrystocracy. We must pre-

sarve th' ideels iv American simplicity. We'll show this vulgar upstart that he can't humilyate his fellow citizens be goin' around dhressed up like an Asyatic fav'rite iv th' Impror Neero, be Hivens. How will we get at him?' says he. 'We'll put a tax iv sixty per cént. on ready made clothin' costin' less thin ten dollars a suit. That'll teach him to squander money wrung fr'm Jawn D. Rockyfellar in th' Roo dilly Pay. We'll go further thin that. We'll put a tax iv forty per cent. on knitted undherwear costin' less thin a dollar twenty-five a dozen. We'll make a specyal assault on woolen socks an' cowhide shoes. We'll make an example iv this here pampered babe iv fortune,' says he. . . .

"Ye'd think th' way such as ye talk that ivrything is taxed. It ain't so. 'Tis an insult to th' pathritism iv Congress to say so. Th' Republican party, with a good deal iv assistance fr'm th' pathriotic Dimmycrats, has been thrue to its promises. Look at th' free list, if ye don't believe it. Practically ivrything nicissry to existence comes in free. What, f'r example, says ye? I'll look. Here it is. Curling stones. There, I told ye. Curling stones are free. Ye'll be able to buy all ye'll need this summer f'r practically nawthin'. No more will ladies comin' into this counthry have to conceal curling stones in their stockin's to avoid th' iniquitous customs. . . .

"What other nicissities, says ye? Well, there's sea moss. That's a good thing. Ivry poor man will apprecyate havin' sea moss to stir in his tea. Newspapers, nuts, an' nux vomica ar-re free. Ye can take th' London *Times* now. But that ain't all by anny means. They've removed th' jooty on pulu. I didn't think they'd go that far, but in spite iv th' protests iv th' pulu foundhries iv Sheboygan they ruthlessly sthruck it fr'm th' list iv jootyable articles. Ye know what pulu is, iv coorse, an' I'm sure ye'll be glad to know that this refreshin' bev'rage or soap is on th' free list. Sinitor Root in behalf iv th' pulu growers iv New York objicted, but Sinitor Aldhrich was firm. 'No, sir,' he says, 'we must not tax annything that enters into th' daily life iv th' poor,' he says. 'While not a dhrinkin' man mesilf, I am no bigot, an' I wud not deny anny artisan his scuttle iv pulu,' he says. So pulu was put on th' free list, an' iv coorse zapper an' alazarin had to go on, too, as it is on'y be addin' thim to pulu that ye can make axle-grease. . . .

"Yes, sir, canary bur-rd seed is free. What else? Lookin' down th' list I see that divvy-divvy is free also. This was let in as a compliment to Sinitor Aldhrich. It's his motto. Be th' inthraduction iv this harmless dhrug into th' discussion he's been able to get a bill through that's satisfacthry to ivrywan. But I am surprised to see that spunk is on th' free list. Is our spunk industhree dead? Is there no pathrite to demand that we be proticted against th' pauper spunk iv Europe? Maybe me frind Willum Taft had it put on th' free list. I see in a pa-aper th' other day that what was needed at th' White House was a little more spunk. But does he have to import it fr'm abroad, I ask ye? Isn't there enough American spunk?

"Well, sir, there are a few iv th' things that are on th' free list. But there are others, mind ye. Here's some iv

thim: Apatite, hog bristle, wurruks iv art more thin
twinty years old, kelp, marshmallows, life boats, silk worm
eggs, stilts, skeletons, turtles, an' leeches. Th' new tariff
bill puts these familyar commodyties within th' reach iv
all. But there's a bigger surprise waitin' for ye. What
d'ye think ends th' free list? I'll give ye twinty chances an'
ye'll niver guess. Blankets? No. Sugar? Wrong. Flannel
shirts? Thry to be a little practical, Hinnissy. Sinitor
Aldhrich ain't no majician. Well, I might as well tell ye
if ye're sure ye'er heart is sthrong an' ye can stand a
joyful surprise. Ar-re ye ready? Well, thin, joss sticks an'
opyum f'r smokin' ar-re on th' free list! . . .

"Th' tariff bill wudden't be complete without that there
item. But it ought to read: 'Opyum f'r smokin' while
readin' th' tariff bill.' Ye can take this sterlin' piece iv
lithrachoor to a bunk with ye an' light a ball iv hop. Befure
ye smoke up p'raps ye can't see where th' tariff has been
rejooced. But afther ye've had a long dhraw it all becomes
clear to ye. Ye'er worries about th' childhren's shoes disappear an' ye see ye'ersilf floatin' over a purple sea iv
alazarin, in ye'er private yacht, lulled be th' London
Times, surrounded be wurruks iv art more thin twinty
years old, atin' marshmallows an' canary bur-rd seed,
while th' turtles an' leeches frisk on th' binnacle.

"Well, sir, if nobody else has read th' debates on th'
tariff bill, I have. An' I'll tell ye, Hinnissy, that no such
orathry has been heerd in Congress since Dan'l Webster's
day, if thin. . . .

"Says th' sinitor fr'm Louisyanny: 'Louisyanny, th'
proudest jool in th' dyadim iv our fair land, remains thrue

to th' honored teachin's iv our leaders. Th' protictive tariff
is an abomynation. It is crushin' out th' lives iv our people.
An' wan iv th' worst parts iv this divvlish injine iv tyranny is th' tariff on lathes. Fellow sinitors, as long,' he
says, 'as I can stand, as long as nature will sustain me in
me protest, while wan dhrop iv pathriotic blood surges
through me heart, I will raise me voice agin a tariff on
lathes, onless,' he says, 'this dhread implymint iv oppres-
syon is akelly used,' he says, 'to protict th' bland an' beautiful molasses iv th' state iv me birth,' he says.

"'I am heartily in sympathy with th' sinitor fr'm
Louisyanny,' says th' sinitor fr'm Virginya. 'I loathe th'
tariff. Fr'm me arliest days I was brought up to look on
it with pizenous hathred. At manny a con-vintion ye cud
hear me whoopin' again it. But if there is such a lot iv
this monsthrous iniquity passin' around, don't Virginya
get none? How about th' mother iv prisidents? Ain't she
goin' to have a grab at annything? Gintlemen, I do not
ask, I demand rights f'r me commonwealth. I will talk
here ontil July fourth, nineteen hundhred an' eighty-two,
agin th' proposed hellish tax on feather beds onless somethin' is done f'r th' tamarack bark iv old Virginya.'

"A sinitor: 'What's it used f'r?'

"Th' sinitor fr'm Virginya: 'I do not quite know. It is
ayether a cure f'r th' hives or enthers largely into th'
mannyfacture iv carpet slippers. But there's a frind iv
mine, a lile Virginyan, who makes it an' he needs th'
money.'

"'Th' argymints iv th' sinitor fr'm Virginya are onan-
swerable,' says Sinitor Aldhrich. 'Wud it be agreeable to

me Dimmycratic collague to put both feather beds an' his
what's-ye-call-it in th' same item?'

"'In such circumstances,' says th' sinitor fr'm Virginya, 'I wud be foorced to waive me almost insane prej-
udice agin th' hellish docthrines iv th' distinguished sinitor fr'm Rhode Island,' says he.

"An' so it goes, Hinnissy. Niver a sordid wurrud, mind
ye, but ivrything done on th' fine old principle iv give an'
take."

"Well," said Mr. Hennessy, "what diff'rence does it
make? Th' foreigner pays th' tax, annyhow."

"He does," said Mr. Dooley, "if he ain't turned back at
Castle Garden."

PARTY CLAIMS

"Ivry year men crawl out iv th' hospitals, where they've
been since last iliction day, to vote th' Raypublican ticket
in Mississippi. There's no record iv it, but it's a fact.
Today th' Dimmycrats will on'y concede Vermont, Maine,
an' Pennsylvania to th' Raypublicans, an' th' Raypublicans concede Texas, Allybammy an' Mississippi to th'
Dimmycrats. But it's arly yet. Wait awhile. Th' wurruk
iv th' campaign has not begun. . . . About th' middle iv
October th' Raypublican who concedes Texas to th' Dimmycrats will be dhrummed out iv th' party as a thraitor,
an' ye'll hear that th' Dimmycratic party in Maine is so
cheered be th' prospects that his frinds can't keep him
sober."

1924

The oil scandals of the Harding Administration became public shortly before the beginning of the 1924 campaign. "Billy Mack" is, of course, William G. McAdoo.

♣ ♣ ♣

"A<small>M</small> I <small>GOIN'</small> to th' Dimmycrat convintion?" said Mr. Dooley. "Ye can bet I am, I'm goin' if I have to hitch onto a freight. In th' first place I want to have a look at th' great an' wicked me-thropolus. I haven't see that vain, corrupt, but fascinatin' Babylon since I thramped acrost it on me way to fame an' fortune in th' goolden West. I don't think New York is as bad as it's painted be Bill White an' Hinnery Allen, but I sincerely hope it is. 'Twud be a turr'ble disappintment to me to spind me good money an' find mesilf landed in a varchous, hard-workin' community like th' wan I've been livin' in these manny years. If New York expicts to live up to its repytation among us austere, but curyous Westhern Dimmycrats it'd betther begin to put on its paint an' bob its hair at wanst. If Vice ain't dazzlin' an' rampant whin I get there I'll take th' next train back. An' thin there's th' convintion. Iv all th' circuses, 15-round bouts or endurance contests that Tex Rickard iver managed this will be th' noblest. It's goin' to be a gr-reat episode in th' life iv a quite Chicago merchant, who has no divarsions but bein' stuck up ivry week or two be a gunman. An' they do say,

with all our boastin', there's ten gunmen in New York
to wan in Chicago.

"That goes to show us Dimmycrats ought niver to
despair iv a good time. Not that Dimmycrats, Hinnissy,
as a rule, are iv a repinin' nature. To be a Dimmycrat a
man must be as hopeful as an investor in a policy ticket. A
few months ago I looked f'r a monotonous convintion an'
a teejous campaign. Th' cards were shuffled an' marked.
We wud hold a four-card heart flush; we wud bet it like
th' cheerful souls we are; on iliction day we'd draw th'
customary two spot iv clubs. Uncle Cal wud set in th'
White House in front iv th' fire with his slippers on
broadcastin' bedtime stories an' old New England sayin's
f'r the voters. Billy Mack wud tear around th' counthry
denouncin' railroad comp'nies fr'm th' back platform iv a
private car an' that's all there be to it. Th' votes wud be
counted be a quarther to eight an' at half-past I'd be
undher th' comforter befure th' band began to insult me
ears with 'Marchin' Thro' Georgia.'

"But, thank th' Lord f'r th' gin'rous open-handed ile
men, that's all changed f'r th' betther an' th' sunshine has
begun to break through th' clouds f'r our grand ol' party.
I niver see a campaign open, as Hogan says, under more
fav'rable or more disagreeable auspices. Scandal that
wanst was resarved f'r th' mornin' iv iliction day is in
full bloom at this minyit, an' th' bad language that we
used to save up f'r October is now freely exchanged
whereiver thoughtful men gather together. Th' intelligint
ilictors are already layin' in their store iv hard coal, brick
bats an' cabbageheads to greet th' candydates whin they
appear on th' hustings. Befure Siptimber dawns I look to

be gettin' a little sense into Larkin's head be hammerin' it with a thransparency while he feebly retorts be thryin' to set fire to me with a karosene torch. Th' intilligent American voter ain't goin' to set around th' radio listenin' to solemn wurrds iv wisdom this year. Polyticks was niver meant f'r th' home annyhow. All us voters iver gets fr'm it is a chance to go out nights an' frolic, an' th' fellow that thries to appeal to our reason will have about as much of an aujeence as a lecturer on th' League iv Nations at a chicken fight. Be th' look iv things there'll be no home life f'r Uncle Cal this comin' Fall. Befure th' punkins're on th' vine he'll have to put on his linen duster an' circylate amongst th' inhabitants tellin' thim what he thinks iv his opponent, which ain't much.

"What will our platform be like? How do I know? I don't care. No wan iver reads a platform but th' boy that wrote it. Th' Dimmycrat platform this year will be wan sintince: 'We pint with pride to th' rottenness iv th' Ray-publicans.' We're goin' to appeal on their record. 'Tis a wise policy. I heerd it first fr'm th' lips iv our sainted leader, Willum O'Brien. A fellow be th' name iv Flan-nigan was runnin' again him f'r alderman. 'Willum,' says I to th' gr-reat man, f'r we were very intimate, mind ye, in thim days an' I've often held his hat whin he was rollin' on th' flure in a discussion iv some important public ques-tion, 'Willum,' says I, 'ar-re ye goin' to stand on ye'er record?' 'I shud think not,' says he. 'I might fall through. I'm goin' to stand on Flannigan's. What's more,' he says, 'I'm goin' to jump on it,' he says. . . .

"I'd like to go down to th' convintion," said Mr. Hen-nessy. 'How long d'ye think it will last?'"

"That depinds on how much self-resthraint New York shows," said Mr. Dooley. "I figure that about th' end iv th' first week th' gr-reat, gin'rous, warmhearted methropolus will say: 'Th' boys have been away fr'm home long enough. They've had a good time. Their show is funny, but th' action dhrags. Let's break 'em tonight.' An' th' nex' day we'll pull th' name iv our standard bearer out iv a hat an' go home on th' brake beams."

VOTING

"That frind iv ye'ers, Dugan, is an intilligent man," said Mr. Dooley. "All he needs is an index an' a few illusthrations to make him a bicyclopedja iv useless information."

"Well," said Mr. Hennessy, judiciously, "he ain't no Socrates an' he ain't no answers-to-questions column; but he's a good man that goes to his jooty, an' as handy with a pick as some people are with a cocktail spoon. What's he been doin' again' ye?"

"Nawthin'," said Mr. Dooley, "but he was in here Choosday. 'Did ye vote?' says I. 'I did,' says he. 'Which wan iv th' distinguished bunko steerers got ye'er invalu-'ble suffrage?' says I. 'I didn't have none with me,' says he, 'but I voted f'r Charter Haitch,' says he. 'I've been with him in six ilictions,' says he, 'an' he's a good man,' he says. 'D'ye think ye're votin' f'r th' best?' says I. 'Why, man alive,' says I, 'Charter Haitch was assassinated three years ago,' I says. 'Was he?' says Dugan. 'Ah, well, he's lived that down be this time. He was a good man,' he says."

MR. DOOLEY ON
THEODORE ROOSEVELT

*"Th' capital iv th' nation has raymoved to Eyesther
Bay, a city on th' north shore iv Long Island, with
a population iv three millyion clams, an' a number iv
mosquitos with pianola attachments an' steel rams.
There, day by day, th' head iv th' nation thransacts
th' nation's business as follows: four A.M., a plunge
into th' salt, salt sea an' a swim iv twenty miles;
five A.M., horse-back ride, th' prisidint insthructin'
his two sons, aged two and four rayspictively, to
jump th' first Methodist church without knockin' off
th' shingles; six A.M. rassles with a thrained grizzly
bear; sivin A.M., breakfast; eight A.M., Indyan clubs;
nine A.M., boxes with Sharkey; tin A.M., bates th'
tinnis champeen; iliven A.M., rayceives a band iv
rough riders an' person'lly supervises th' sindin' iv
th' ambylance to look afther th' injured in th' village; noon, dinner with Sharkey, Oscar Featherstone,
th' champeen roller-skater iv Harvard, '98, Pro-fissor
McGlue, th' archyologist, Lord Dum de Dum, Mike
Kehoe, Immanuel Kant Gumbo, th' naygro pote,
Horrible Hank, th' bad lands scout, Sinitor Lodge,
Lucy Emerson Tick, th' writer on female sufferage,
Mud-in-th'-Eye, th' chief iv th' Ogallas, Gin'ral
Powell Clayton, th' Mexican mine expert, four rough
riders with their spurs on, th' Ambassadure iv France
an' th' Cinquovasti fam'ly, jugglers. Th' conversa-*

tion, we larn fr'm wan iv th' guests who's our spoortin'
iditor, was jined in be th' prisidint an' dealt with art,
boxin', lithrachoor, horse-breakin', science, shootin',
polytics, how to kill a mountain line, di-plomacy,
lobbing, pothry, th' pivot blow, rayform, an' th' campaign in Cubia. Whin our rayporther was dhriven off
th' premises be wan iv th' rough riders, th' head iv th'
nation was tachin' Lord Dum de Dum an' Sicrety
Hay how to do a handspring, an' th' other guests was
scattered about th' lawn, boxin', rasslin', swingin' on
th' thrapeze, ridin' th' buckin' bronco an' shootin'
at th' naygro pote f'r th' dhrinks—in short
enjyin' an ideel day in th' counthry."

A BOOK REVIEW

*In the land attack upon Santiago, the Rough Riders, under
the command of Theodore Roosevelt, had played a signifi-
cant part. Not long after the war was over, Roosevelt wrote
a history of the regiment which he and Leonard Wood had
raised and commanded. Mr. Dooley's review brought the
consolation from Senator Lodge that such a notice indi-
cated that Roosevelt had "advanced far on the high road to
fame." Roosevelt replied ruefully, "How he does get at any
joint in the harness." To F. P. Dunne he wrote, "I regret to
state that my family and intimate friends are delighted with
your review of my book."*

☙ ☙ ☙

"WELL SIR," said Mr. Dooley, "I jus' got hold iv a
book, Hinnissy, that suits me up to th' handle, a gran'
book, th' grandest iver seen. Ye know I'm not much
throubled be lithrachoor, havin' manny worries iv me
own, but I'm not prejudiced agin books. I am not. Whin
a rale good book comes along I'm as quick as anny wan
to say it isn't so bad, an' this here book is fine. I tell ye 'tis
fine."

"What is it?" Mr. Hennessy asked languidly.

" 'Tis 'Th' Biography iv a Hero be Wan Who Knows.'
'Tis 'Th' Darin' Exploits iv a Brave Man be an Actual
Eye Witness.' 'Tis 'Th' Account iv th' Desthruction iv
Spanish Power in th' Ant Hills,' as it fell fr'm th' lips iv
Tiddy Rosenfelt an' was took down be his own hands. Ye

99

see 'twas this way, Hinnissy, as I r-read th' book. Whin
Tiddy was blowed up in th' harbor iv Havana he instantly
con-cluded they must be war. He debated th' question long
an' earnestly an' fin'lly passed a jint resolution declarin'
war. So far so good. But there was no wan to carry it on.
What shud he do? I will lave th' janial author tell th' story
in his own wurruds.

" 'Th' sicrety iv war had offered me,' he says, 'th' command of a rig'mint,' he says, 'but I cud not consint to remain in Tampa while perhaps less audacious heroes was
at th' front,' he says. 'Besides,' he says, 'I felt I was in-
competent f'r to command a rig'mint raised be another,'
he says. 'I determined to raise wan iv me own,' he says.
'I selected fr'm me acquaintances in th' West,' he says,
'men that had thravelled with me acrost th' desert an' th'
storm-wreathed mountain,' he says, 'sharin' me burdens
an' at times confrontin' perils almost as gr-reat as anny
that beset me path,' he says. 'Together we had faced th'·
turrors iv th' large but vilent West,' he says, 'an' these
brave men had seen me with me trusty rifle shootin' down
th' buffalo, th' elk, th' moose, th' grizzly bear, th' mountain goat,' he says, 'th' silver man, an' other ferocious
beasts iv thim parts,' he says. 'An they niver flinched,' he
says. 'In a few days I had thim perfectly tamed,' he says,
'an' ready to go annywhere I led,' he says. 'On th' thrans-
port goin' to Cubia,' he says, 'I wud stand beside wan iv
these r-rough men threatin' him as an akel, which he was
in ivrything but birth, education, rank, an' courage, an'
together we wud look up at th' admirable stars iv that
tolerable southern sky an' quote th' Bible fr'm Walt Whit-

man,' he says. 'Honest, loyal, thrue-hearted la-ads, how kind I was to thim,' he says.

" 'We had no sooner landed in Cubia than it become nicissry f'r me to take command iv th' ar-rmy which I did at wanst. A number of days was spint be me in recon-noitring, attinded on'y be me brave an' fluent body guard, Richard Harding Davis. I discovered that th' inimy was heavily inthrenched on th' top iv San Joon hill immejiately in front iv me. At this time it become apparent that I was handicapped by th' prisence iv th' ar-rmy,' he says. 'Wan day whin I was about to charge a block house sturdily definded by an ar-rmy corps undher Gin'ral Tamale, th' brave Castile that I aftherwards killed with a small ink-eraser that I always carry, I r-ran into th' entire military force iv th' United States lying on its stomach. 'If ye won't fight,' says I, 'let me go through,' I says. 'Who ar-re ye?' says they. 'Colonel Rosenfelt,' says I. 'Oh, excuse me,' says the gin'ral in command (if me mimry serves me thrue it was Miles) r-risin' to his knees an' salutin'. This showed me 'twud be impossible f'r to carry th' war to a successful con-clusion unless I was free, so I sint th' ar-rmy home an' attackted San Joon hill. Ar-rmed on'y with a small thirty-two which I used in th' West to shoot th' fleet prairie dog, I climbed that precipitous ascent in th' face iv th' most gallin' fire I iver knew or heerd iv. But I had a few r-rounds iv gall mesilf an' what cared I? I dashed madly on cheerin' as I wint. Th' Spanish throops was dhrawn up in a long line in th' formation known among military men as a long line. I fired at th' man nearest to me an' I knew be th' expression iv his face that th' trusty bullet wint home. It passed through his frame, he fell, an' wan little home in far-off Catalonia was made happy be th' thought that their riprisintative had been kilt be th' future governor iv New York. Th' bullet sped on its mad flight an' passed through th' intire line fin'lly imbeddin' itself in th' abdomen iv th' Ar-rch-bishop iv Santago eight miles away. This ended th' war.'

" 'They has been some discussion as to who was th' first man to r-reach th' summit iv San Joon hill. I will not attempt to dispute th' merits iv th' manny gallant sojers, statesmen, corryspondints, an' kinetoscope men who claim th' distinction. They ar-re all brave men an' if they wish to wear me laurels they may. I have so manny annyhow that it keeps me broke havin' thim blocked an' irned. But I will say f'r th' binifit iv posterity that I was th' on'y man I see. An' I had a tillyscope.'

"I have thried, Hinnissy," Mr. Dooley continued, "to give you a fair idee iv th' contints iv this remarkable book, but what I've tol' ye is on'y what Hogan calls an outline iv th' principal pints. Ye'll have to r-read th' book ye'ersilf to get a thrue conciption. I haven't time f'r to tell ye th' wurruk Tiddy did in ar-rmin' an' equippin' himsilf, how he fed himsilf, how he steadied himsilf in battle an' en-couraged himsilf with a few well-chosen wurruds whin th' sky was darkest. Ye'll have to take a squint into th' book ye'ersilf to larn thim things."

"I won't do it," said Mr. Hennessy. "I think Tiddy Rosenfelt is all r-right an' if he wants to blow his hor-rn lave him do it."

"Thrue f'r ye," said Mr. Dooley, "an' if his valliant

deeds didn't get into this book 'twud be a long time befure
they appeared in Shafter's histhry iv th' war. No man
that bears a gredge agin himsilf" iver be governor iv
a state. An' if Tiddy done it all he ought to say so an' re-
lieve th' suspinse. But if I was him I'd call th' book 'Alone
in Cubia.' "

ROOSEVELT AND TAFT

"It looks to me as though Tiddy was thryin' in a bunch
iv green motormen to see whether they could run th' car
th' way he wants it run. . . . An' now he's thryin' out
Taft. Look at thim comin' up th' sthreet. Taft knows th'
brakes well but he ain't very familyar with th' power. 'Go
ahead,' says Rosenfelt. 'Don't stop here. Pass that banker
by. He's on'y wan fare. There's a crowd iv people at th'
nex' corner. Stop f'r thim an' give thim time to get
aboord. Now start th' car with a jump so they'll know something is goin' on. Go fast by Wall Sthreet an' ring th'
gong, but stop an' let thim get aboord whin they're out iv
breath. Who's that ol' lady standin' in th' middle iv th'
sthreet wavin' an umbrelly? Oh, be Hivens, 'tis th' Constitution. Give her a good bump. No, she got out iv th'
way. Ye'd iv nailed her if ye hadn't twisted th' brake.
What ailed ye? Well, niver mind; we may get her comin'
back."

SWEARING

The speech satirized below is a reference to President Roosevelt's first message to Congress.

"I'd like to tell me frind Tiddy that they'se a sthrenuse life an' a sthrenuseless life."

♣ ♣ ♣

"DID YE see what th' Prisidint said to th' throlley man that bumped him?" asked Mr. Dooley.

"I did not," said Mr. Hennessy. "What was it?"

"I can't tell ye till I get mad," said Mr. Dooley. "Lave us go into ixicutive sission. Whisper. That was it. Ha, ha. He give it to him sthraight. A good, honest, American blankety-blank. Rale language like father used to make whin he hit his thumb with th' hammer. No 'With ye'er lave' or 'By ye'er lave,' but a dacint 'Damn ye, sir,' an' a little more f'r th' sake iv imphasis.

"What else wud ye have him do? 'Twas nayether th' time nor th' occasion, as th' candydate said whin they ast him where he got his money, 'twas nayether th' time nor th' occasion f'r wurruds that wud be well rayceived at Chautauqua. A throlley car had pushed him an' diplomatic relations was suspinded. He was up on top iv a bus, hurryin' fr'm speech to speech an' thinkin' what to say next. 'Th' thrusts,' says he to himsilf, 'are heejous mon-

sthers built up be th' inlightened intherprise iv th' men
that have done so much to advance progress in our beloved counthry,' he says. 'On wan hand I wud stamp thim
undher fut; on th' other hand not so fast. What I want
more thin th' bustin' iv th' thrusts is to see me fellow
counthrymen happy an' continted. I wudden't have thim
hate th' thrusts. Th' haggard face, th' droopin' eye, th'
pallid complexion that marks th' inimy iv thrusts is not
to me taste. Lave us be merry about it an' jovyal an' affectionate. Lave us laugh an' sing th' octopus out iv existence.
Betther blue but smilin' lips anny time thin a full coal
scuttle an' a sour heart. As Hogan says, a happy peas-
anthry is th' hope iv th' state. So lave us warble ti-lire-a-
lay——' Jus' thin Euclid Aristophanes Madden on th'
quarther deck iv th' throlley car give a twisht to his brake
an' th' chief ixicutive iv th' nation wint up in th' air with
th' song on his lips. He wint up forty, some say, fifty feet.
Sicrety Cortilloo says three hundherd an' fifty. Annyhow
whin he come down he landed nachrally on his feet.

"Now, Hinnissy, no matther what a man may've been
wan minyit befure he was hit be a throlley car, a minyit
afther he's on'y a man. Th' throlley car plays no fav'rites.
It bounces th' high an' th' low alike. It tears th' exalted
fr'm their throne an' ilivates th' lowly. So whin th' prisidint got back to the earth he wasn't prisidint anny longer
but Tiddy Rosenfelt, 180 pounds iv a man. An' he done
accordin'ly. If it'd been Willum Jennings Bryan, he'd've
ast th' throlley engineer was he a mimber iv th' Union. If
he cud show a wurrukin' card he was entitled to bump
anny wan. At worst Willum Jennings Bryan wud've writ-

ten an article about him in th' *Commoner,* or if he felt unusually vindicative, maybe he'd sind it to him through th' mails. Whin Sicrety Cortilloo come to fr'm a dhream that he'd jus' rayfused a favor to Sinitor Tillman, he hauled out a little note book an' got ready to take down something that cud be put on th' thransparencies two years fr'm now—something like—'No power on earth can stop American business entherprise.' But nawthin' that will iver be printed in th' first reader dhropped fr'm th' lips iv th' chief ixicutive. With two jumps he was in th' throlley man's hair an' spoke as follows— No, I won't say it again. But I'll tell ye this much, a barn-boss that was standin' by an' heerd it, said he niver befure regretted his father hadn't sint him to Harvard.

"We know what Wash'n'ton said to his gin'rals an' what Grant said to Lee an' what Cleveland said to himsilf. They're in th' books. But engraved in th' hearts iv his counthrymen is what Rosenfelt said to th' throlley man. 'Twas good because 'twas so nachral. Most iv th' sayin's I've read in books sounds as though they was made be a patent inkybator. They go with a high hat an' a white tie. Ye can hear th' noise iv th' phonygraft. But this here jim of emotion an' thought come sthraight fr'm th' heart an' wint right to th' heart. That's wan reason I think a lot iv us likes Tiddy Rosenfelt that wudden't iver be suspicted iv votin' f'r him. Whin he does anny talkin'—which he sometimes does—he talks at th' man in front iv him. Ye don't hear him hollerin' at posterity. Posterity don't begin to vote till afther th' polls close. So whin he wished to convey to th' throlley man th' sintiments iv his bosom, he done it in wurruds suited to th' crisis, as Hogan wud say. They do say his remarks singed th' hair off th' head iv th' unforchnit man.

"I don't believe in profanity, Hinnissy—not as a reg'lar thing. But it has its uses an' its place. . . .

"I niver knew Father Kelly to swear but wanst. 'Twas a little wan, Hinnissy. Dhropped fr'm th' lips iv a polisman it wud've sounded like a 'thank ye kindly.' But, be Hivins, whin I heerd it I thought th' roof wud fall down on th' head iv Scanlan that he was thryin' to show th' evil iv his ways. Melia Murdher, but it was gran'! They was more varchue in that wan damn thin in a fastin' prayer. Scanlan wint to wurruk th' nex' day an' he hasn't tasted a dhrop since.

"But th' best thing bout a little judicyous swearin' is that it keeps th' temper. 'Twas intinded as a compromise between runnin' away an' fightin'. Befure it was invinted they was on'y th' two ways out iv an argymint."

"But I've heerd ye say a man was swearin' mad," said Mr. Hennessy.

"He wasn't fightin' mad, thin," said Mr. Dooley.

"Oh, well," said Mr. Hennessy, "we are as th' Lord made us."

"No," said Mr. Dooley, "lave us be fair. Lave us take some iv th' blame oursilves."

MR. DOOLEY IN POLITICS
AND OUT

" 'Tis as much as a man's life is worth these days,"
said Mr. Dooley, "to have a vote. Look here," he continued, diving under the bar and producing a roll of
paper. "Here's th' pitchers iv candydates I pulled
down fr'm th' windy, an' jus' knowin' they're here
makes me that nervous f'r th' contints iv th' cash
dhrawer I'm afraid to tur-rn me back f'r a minyit.
I'm goin' to throw thim out in th' back yard.

"All heroes, too, Hinnissy. They'se Mike O'Toole,
th' hero iv Sandago, that near lost his life be dhrink
on his way to th' arm'ry, an' had to be sint home without lavin' th' city. There's Turror Teddy Mangan, th'
night man at Flaher-ty's, that loaded th' men that
loaded th' guns that kilt th' mules at Matoonzas.
There's Hero O'Brien, that wud've inlisted if he
hadn't been too old, an' th' contractin' business in
such good shape. There's Bill Cory, that come near
losin' his life at a cinematograph iv th' battle iv Manila. They're all here, bedad, r-ready to sarve their
counthry to th' bitter end, an' to r-rush, voucher
in hand, to th' city treasurer's office at
a minyit's notice."

TIMES PAST

" 'Tis manny years since I took an active part in that
agrable game beyond stickin' up th' lithygrafts iv both th'
distinguished lithygrafters that was r-runnin' f'r office in
me front window."

♣ ♣ ♣

Mr. Dooley scrutinized Mr. McKenna sharply:
"Ye've been out ilictin' some man, Jawn, an' ye needn't
deny it. I seen it th' minyit ye come in. Ye'er hat's dinted,
an' ye have ye'er necktie over ye'er ear; an' I see be ye'er
hand ye've hit a Dutchman. Jawn, ye know no more about
polyticks thin a mimber iv this here Civic Featheration.
Didn't ye have a beer bottle or an ice-pick? Ayether iv
thim is good, though, whin I was a young man an' precinct
captain an' intherested in th' welfare iv th' counthry, I
found a couplin' pin in a stockin' about as handy as annything.

"Thim days is over, though, Jawn, an' between us polyticks don't intherest me no more. They ain't no liveliness in
thim. Whin Andy Duggan r-run f'r aldherman against
Schwartzmeister, th' big Dutchman—I was precinct captain then, Jawn—there was an iliction f'r ye. 'Twas on our
precinct they relied to ilict Duggan; f'r the Dutch was
sthrong down be th' thrack, an' Schwartzmeister had a
band out playin' 'Th' Watch on th' Rhine.' Well, sir, we
opened th' polls at six o'clock, an' there was tin Schwartzmeister men there to protect his intherests. At sivin

o'clock there was only three, an' wan iv thim was goin' up
th' sthreet with Hinnissy kickin' at him. At eight o'clock,
be dad, there was on'y wan; an' he was sittin' on th' roof
iv Gavin's blacksmith shop, an' th' la-ads was thryin' to
borrow a laddher fr'm th' injine-house f'r to get at him.
'Twas thruck eighteen; an' Hogan, that was captain,
wudden't let thim have it. Not ye'er Hogan, Jawn, but th'
meanest fireman in Bridgeport. He got kilt aftherwards.
He wudden't let th' la-ads have a laddher, an' th' Dutchman stayed up there; an', whin there was nawthin' to do,
we wint over an' thrun bricks at him. 'Twas gr-reat sport.

"About four in th' afthernoon Schwartzmeister's band
come up Ar-rchey Road, playin' 'Th' Watch on th' Rhine.'
Whin it got near Gavin's, big Peter Nolan tuk a runnin'
jump, an' landed feet first in th' big bass dhrum. Th' man
with th' dhrum walloped him over th' head with th'
dhrumstick, an' Dorsey Quinn wint over an' tuk a slide
trombone away fr'm th' musician an' clubbed th' bass
dhrum man with it. Thin we all wint over, an' ye niver see
th' like in ye'er born days. Th' las' I see iv th' band it was
goin' down th' road towards th' slough with a mob behind
it, an' all th' polis foorce fr'm Deerin' Sthreet afther th'
mob. Th' la-ads collected th' horns an th' dhrums, an' that
started th' Ar-rchey Road brass band. Little Mike Doyle
larned to play 'Th' Rambler fr'm Clare' beautifully on
what they call a pickle-e-o befure they sarved a rayplivin
writ on him.

"We cast twinty-wan hundherd votes f'r Duggan, an'
they was on'y five hundherd votes in th' precinct. We'd
cast more, but th' tickets give out. They was tin votes in

th' box f'r Schwartzmeister whin we counted up; an' I felt that mortified I near died, me bein' precinct captain, an' res-sponsible. 'What'll we do with thim? Out th' window,' says I. Just thin Dorsey's nanny-goat that died next year put her head through th' dure. 'Monica,' says Dorsey (he had pretty names for all his goats), 'Monica, are ye hungry,' he says, 'ye poor dear?' Th' goat give him a pleadin' look out iv her big brown eyes. 'Can't I make ye up a nice supper?' says Dorsey. 'Do ye like paper?' he says. 'Would ye like to help desthroy a Dutchman,' he says, 'an' perform a sarvice f'r ye'er counthry?' he says. Thin he wint out in th' next room, an' come back with a bottle iv catsup; an' he poured it on th' Schwartzmeister ballots, an' Monica et thim without winkin'.

"Well, sir, we ilicted Duggan; an' what come iv it? Th' week befure iliction he was in me house ivry night, an' 'twas 'Misther Dooley, this,' an' 'Mr. Dooley, that,' an' 'What'll ye have, boys?' an' 'Niver mind about th' change.' I niver see hide nor hair iv him f'r a week afther iliction. Thin he come with a plug hat on, an' says he: 'Dooley,' he says, 'give me a shell iv beer,' he says: 'give me a shell iv beer,' he says, layin' down a nickel. 'I suppose ye're on th' sub-scription,' he says. 'What for?' says I. 'F'r to buy me a goold star,' says he. With that I eyes him, an' says I: 'Duggan,' I says, 'I knowed ye whin ye didn't have a coat to ye'er back,' I says, 'an' I'll buy no star f'r ye,' I says. 'But I'll tell ye what I'll buy f'r ye,' I says. 'I'll buy rayqueem masses f'r th' raypose iv ye'er sowl, if ye don't duck out iv this in a minyit.' Whin I seen him last, he was back dhrivin' a dhray an' atin' his dinner out iv a tin can."

DRINK AND POLITICS

♧ ♧ ♧

"Sure, it's a sthrange change has come over our polyticks since I was captain iv me precinct. We ar-re fallen, as Hogan says, on iffiminate days. Th' hardy an' gloryous peeryod in th' histhry iv th' republic has passed, an' th' times whin Hinnery Clay an' Dan'l Webster wud sit f'r hours pushin' th' scuttle to an' fro acrost th' table has gone to return no more. Booze an' iloquence has both passed out iv our public life. No longer is th' gr-reat statesman carried to th' platform be loving hands an' lashed to th' railin' where him an' King Alcohol sings a duet on th' splindors iv th' blue sky an' th' onfadin' glories iv th' flag, but afther atin' a pepsin tablet an' sippin' a glass iv light gray limonade he reads to th' assimbled multitchood th' financial repoort iv th' Standard Ile comp'ny f'r th' physical year endin' June first.

"Mind ye, all this was befure me time. In me day I niver knew a gr-reat statesman that dhrank, or if he did he niver landed anny job betther thin clerk in th' weather office. But as Hogan says Shakespere says, they pretinded a vice if they had it not. A polytician was a baten man if th' story wint around that he was sildom seen dhrunk in public. His aim was to create an imprissyon that he was a gay fellow, a jovyal toss pot, that thought

114

nawthin' iv puttin' a gallon iv paint into him durin' an
avenin's intertainment. They had to exercise diplomacy,
d'ye mind, to keep their repytations goin'. Whin Higgins
was runnin' f'r sheriff he always ordhered gin an' I always give him wather. Ye undherstand, don't ye? Ye know
what gin looks like? Well, wather looks like gin. Wan day
Gallagher took up his glass be mistake an' Higgins lost
th' precinct be forty votes. Sinitor O'Brien held a bolder
coorse. He used to dump th' stuff on th' flure whin no
wan was lookin' an' go home with a light foot while I
swept out his constitooents. Yes, sir, I've seen him pour
into th' sawdust quarts an' gallons iv me precious old
Remorse Rye, aged be me own hands on th' premises.

"Th' most onpopylar president we iver had was Ruther-
ford B. Hayes—an' why? Was it because he stole th'
prisidincy away fr'm Sam'l J. Tilden? It was not. Anny
wan wud steal a prisidincy fr'm a Dimmycrat in thim
days an' think th' larceny was pathritism. No, sir, 'twas
because whin people wint up to th' White House they got
nawthin' to dhrink but sparklin' wather, a bivridge, Hinnissy, that is nayether cheerin' nor ineebratin', but gives
ye th' most inconvanient part iv a deebauch, that is th'
hiccups. Fr'm 8 o'clock, whin they set down to dinner, to
8:30, whin th' last southren congressman ran shriekin'
down th' sthreet, this gr-reat but tactless man pumped
his guests full iv imprisoned gas. An' whin his term ex-
pired he wint back where he come fr'm an' I niver heerd
iv him again. Polytickally speakin', d'ye mind, he wint
down, as ye might say, to a wathry grave.

"But it's all changed now. Polyticians no longer come

into me place. I'm glad iv it. I prefer th' thrade iv prosp'rous steel mannyfacthrers like ye'ersilf. It's more reg'-lar. A statesman wud no more be seen goin' into a saloon thin he wud into a meetin' iv th' Anti-Semitic league. Th' imprissyon he thries to give is that th' sight iv a bock beer sign makes him faint with horror, an' that he's stopped atin' bread because there's a certain amount iv alcohol concealed in it. He wishes to brand as a calumy th' statement that his wife uses an alcohol lamp to heat her curlin' irns. Ivry statesman in this broad land is in danger iv gettin' wather-logged because whiniver he sees a possible vote in sight he yells f'r a pitcher iv ice wather an' dumps into himsilf a basin iv that noble flooid that in th' more rugged days iv th' republic was on'y used to put out fires an' sprinkle th' lawn."

STATISTICS

"That's th' beauty about iliction statistics: they're not burdened with annything like facts. All a man wants is a nice room in th' back iv a Chinese laundhry an' a lung full iv opium, an' he can make a monkey out iv th' la-ad that wrote th' arith-metic. He sees majorities grinnin' through th' transom an' roostin' on th' top iv th' bed an' crawlin' up his leg. Here's wan man says Texas will go Raypublican, an' th' on'y states Bryan has sure is Mississippi, Arkansas, an' Hell. Here's another claims Bryan'll carry New Hampshire an' Upper Canada, an' that McKinley won't get wan vote in Canton but his own, an' he won't get that if he hears Bryan make wan speech."

THE CRUSADE AGAINST VICE

*"A rayformer thries to get into office on a flyin' machine.
He succeeds now an' thin, but th' odds are a hundherd to
wan on th' la-ad that tunnels through."*

♣ ♣ ♣

"VICE," SAID Mr. Dooley, "is a creature of such
heejous mien, as Hogan says, that th' more ye see it th'
betther ye like it. I'd be afraid to enther upon a crusade
again vice f'r fear I might prefer it to th' varchous life
iv a rayspictable liquor dealer. But annyhow th' crusade
has started, an' befure manny months I'll be lookin' undher th' table whin I set down to a peaceful game iv
solytaire to see if a polisman in citizens' clothes ain't con-
cealed there.

"Th' city iv New York, Hinnissy, sets th' fashion iv
vice an' starts th' crusade again it. Thin ivrybody else
takes it up. They'se crusades an' crusaders in ivry hamlet
in th' land an' places that is cursed with nawthin' worse
thin pitchin' horseshoes sinds to th' neighborin' big city
f'r a case iv vice to suppress. We're in th' mist iv a crusade now, an' there isn't a polisman in town who isn't
thremblin' f'r his job.

"As a people, Hinnissy, we're th' greatest crusaders
that iver was—f'r a short distance. On a quarther mile
thrack we can crusade at a rate that wud make Hogan's

frind, Godfrey th' Bullion look like a crab. But th' throuble is th' crusade don't last afther th' first sprint. Th' crusaders drops out iv th' procission to take a dhrink or put a little money on th' ace an' be th' time th' end iv th' line iv march is reached th' boss crusader is alone in th' job an' his former followers is hurlin' bricks at him fr'm th' windows iv policy shops. Th' boss crusader always gets th' double cross. If I wanted to sind me good name down to th' ginerations with Cap. Kidd an' Jesse James I'd lead a movement f'r th' suppression iv vice. I wud so.

"Ye see, Hinnissy, 'tis this way: th' la-ads ilicted to office an' put on th' polis foorce is in need iv a little loose change, an' th' on'y way they can get it is to be negotyatin' with vice. Tammany can't raise anny money on th' churches; it won't do f'r thim to raid a gints' furnishin' sthore f'r keepin' disorderly neckties in th' window. They've got to get th' money where it's comin' to thim an' 'tis on'y comin' to thim where th' law an' vile human nature has a sthrangle holt on each other. A polisman goes afther vice as an officer iv th' law an' comes away as a philosopher. Th' theery iv mesilf, Hogan, Croker, an' other larned men is that vice whin it's broke is a crime an' whin it's got a bank account is a necessity an' a luxury.

"Well, th' la-ads goes on usin' th' revised statues as a sandbag an' by an' by th' captain iv th' polis station gets to a pint where his steam yacht bumps into a canoe iv th' prisidint iv th' Standard Ile Comp'ny an' thin there's th' divvle to pay. It's been a dull summer annyhow an' people ar-re lookin' f'r a change an' a little diversion, an' somebody who doesn't raymimber what happened to th' last

man that led a crusade again vice, gets up an', says he:
'This here city is a verytable Sodom an' it must be cleaned
out,' an' ivrybody takes a broom at it. Th' churches ap-
pints comities an' so does th' Stock Exchange an' th'
Brewers' Society an' afther awhile other organizations
jumps into th' fray, as Hogan says. Witnesses is sum-
moned befure th' comity iv th' Amalgamated Union iv
Shell Wurrukers, th' S'ciety f'r th' Privintion iv Good
Money, th' Ancient Ordher iv Send Men, th' Knights iv
th' Round Table with th' slit in th' centhre; an' Spike
McGlue th' burglar examines thim on vice they have met
an' what ought to be done tow'rd keepin' th' polis in
nights. Thin th' man that objects to canary bur-rds in
windows, sthreet-music, vivysection, profanity, expensive
fun'rals, open sthreet cars an' other vices, takes a hand
an' ye can hear him as well as th' others. Vice is th' on'y
thing talked iv at th' church socyables an' th' mothers'
meetin's; 'tis raysolved be th' Insomnya Club that now's
th' time to make a flyin' wedge again th' divvlish hurdy
gurdy an' meetin's are called to burn th' polis in ile f'r not
arrestin' th' criminals who sell vigitables at th' top iv their
lungs. Some wan invints an anti-vice cocktail. Lectures is
delivered to small bodies iv preachers on how to detect
vice so that no wan can palm off countherfeit vice on
thim an' make thim think 'tis good. Th' polis becomes
active an' whin th' polis is active 'tis a good time f'r dacint
men to wear marredge certy-ficates outside iv their coats.
Hanyous monsthers is nailed in th' act iv histin' in a shell
iv beer in a German Garden; husbands waits in th' polis
station to be r-ready to bail out their wives whin they're

arrested f'r shoppin' afther four o'clock; an' there's more
joy over wan sinner rayturned to th' station thin f'r ninety
an' nine that 've rayformed.

"Th' boss crusader is havin' th' time iv his life all th'
while. His pitcher is in th' papers ivry mornin' an' his
sermons is a directhry iv places iv amusement. He says
to himsilf 'I am improvin' th' wurruld an' me name will
go down to th' ginerations as th' greatest vice buster iv
th' cinchry. Whin I get through they won't be enough
crime left in this city to amuse a sthranger fr'm Hannybal
Missoury f'r twinty minyits,' he says. That's where he's
wrong. Afther awhile people gets tired iv th' pastime.
They want somewhere to go nights. Most people ain't
vicious, Hinnissy, an' it takes vice to hunt vice. That accounts f'r polismen. Besides th' horse show or th' football
games or something else excitin' divarts their attintion an'
wan day th' boss crusader finds that he's alone in Sodom.
'Vice ain't so bad afther all. I notice business was betther
whin 'twas rampant,' says wan la-ad. 'Sure ye're right,'
says another. 'I haven't sold a single pink shirt since that
man Parkers closed th' faro games,' says he. 'Th' theay-
tre business ain't what it was whin they was more vice,'
says another. 'This ain't no Connecticut village,' he says.
'An' 'tis no use thryin' to inthrajooce soomchury ligisla-
tion in this impeeryal American city,' he says, 'where people come pursooed be th' sheriff fr'm ivry corner iv th'
wurruld,' he says. 'Ye can't make laws f'r this community
that wud suit a New England village,' he says, 'where,' he
says, 'th' people ar-re too uncivilized to be immoral,' he
says. 'Vice,' he says, 'goes a long way tow'rd makin' life

bearable,' he says. 'A little vice now an' thin is relished be th' best iv men,' he says. 'Who's this Parkers, annyhow, intherferin' with th' liberty iv th' individooal, an',' he says, 'makin' it hard to rent houses on th' side sthreets,' he says. 'I bet ye if ye invistigate ye'll find that he's no betther thin he shud be himsilf,' he says. An' th' best Parkers gets out iv it is to be able to escape fr'm town in a wig an' false whiskers. Thin th' captain iv th' polis that's been a spindin' his vacation in th' disthrict where a man has to be a Rocky Mountain sheep to be a polisman, returns to his old place, puts up his hat on th' rack an' says, 'Garrity, if annybody calls ye can tell him to put it in an anvelope an' leave it in me box. An' if ye've got a good man handy I wisht ye'd sind him over an' have him punch th' bishop's head. His grace is gettin' too gay.'

"An' there ye ar-re, Hinnissy. Th' crusade is over an' vice is rampant again. I'm afraid, me la-ad, that th' frinds iv vice is too sthrong in this wurruld iv sin f'r th' frinds iv varchue. Th' good man, th' crusader, on'y wurruks at th' crusade wanst in five years, an' on'y whin he has time to spare fr'm his other joóties. 'Tis a pastime f'r him. But th' definse iv vice is a business with th' other la-ad an' he nails away at it, week days an' Sundays, holy days an' fish days, mornin', noon an' night."

"They ought to hang some iv thim polyticians," said Mr. Hennessy angrily.

"Well," said Mr. Dooley, "I don't know. I don't expict to gather calla lillies in Hogan's turnip patch. Why shud I expict to pick bunches iv spotless statesmen fr'm th' gradooation class iv th' house iv correction?"

ORATORY IN POLITICS

♣ ♣ ♣

"I MIND TH' first time Willum J. O'Brien r-run f'r office, th' Raypublicans an' th' Indypindants an' th' So- cialists an' th' Prohybitionist (he's dead now, his name was Larkin) nommynated a young man be th' name iv Dorgan that was in th' law business in Halsted Sthreet, near Cologne, to r-run again him. Smith O'Brien Dorgan was his name, an' he was wan iv th' most iloquint young la-ads that iver made a speakin' thrumpet iv his face. He cud holler like th' empire iv a base-ball game; an', whin he delivered th' sintimints iv his hear-rt ye'd think he was thryin' to confide thim to a man on top iv a high buildin'. He was prisidint iv th' lithry club at th' church; an' Father Kelly tol' me that, th' day afther he won th' debate on th' pen an' th' soord in favor iv th' pen, they had to hire a carpenter to mend th' windows, they'd sagged so. They called him th' boy or-rator iv Healey's slough.

"He planned th' campaign himsilf. 'I'll not re-sort,' says he, 'to th' ordin'ry methods,' he says. 'Th' thing to do,' he says, 'is to prisint th' issues iv th' day to th' voters,' he says. 'I'll burn up ivry precin't in th' ward with me iloquince,' he says. An' he bought a long black coat, an' wint out to spread th' light.

"He talked ivrywhere. Th' people jammed Finucane's Hall, an' he tol' thim th' time had come f'r th' masses to r-rise. 'Raymimber,' says he, 'th' idees iv Novimb'r,' he says. 'Raymimber Demosthens an' Cicero an' Oak Park,' he says. 'Raymimber th' thraditions iv ye'er fathers, iv Wash'n'ton an' Jefferson an' Andhrew Jackson an' John L. Sullivan,' he says. 'Ye shall not, Billy O'Brien,' he says, 'crucify th' voters iv th' Sixth Ward on th' double cross,' he says. He spoke to a meetin' in Deerin' Sthreet in th' same wurruds. He had th' sthreet-car stopped while he coughed up reemarks about th' Constitution until th' bar-rn boss sint down an' threatened to discharge Mike Dwyer that was dhrivin' wan hundherd an' eight in thim days, though thransferred to Wintworth Avnoo later on. He made speeches to polismin in th' squadroom an' to good la-ads hoistin' mud out iv th' dhraw at th' red bridge. People'd be settin' quite in th' back room playin' forty-fives whin Smith O'Brien Dorgan'd burst in, an' addhress thim on th' issues iv th' day.

"Now all this time Bill O'Brien was campaignin' in his own way. He niver med wan speech. No wan knew whether he was f'r a tariff or again wan, or whether he sthud be Jefferson or was knockin' him, or whether he had th' inthrests iv th' toilin' masses at hear-rt or whether he wint to mass at all, at all. But he got th' superintindint iv th' rollin'-mills with him; an' he put three or four good fam'lies to wurruk in th' gas-house, where he knew th' main guy, an' he made reg-lar calls on th' bar-rn boss iv th' sthreet-ca-ars. He wint to th' picnics, an' hired th' or-chesthry f'r th' dances, an' voted himsilf th' most pop'-lar man at th' church fair at an expinse iv at laste five hundherd dollars. No wan that come near him wanted f'r money. He had headquarthers in ivry saloon fr'm wan end iv th' ward to th' other. All th' pa-apers printed his pitcher, an' sthud by him as th' frind iv th' poor.

"Well, people liked to hear Dorgan at first, but afther a few months they got onaisy. He had a way iv breakin' into festive gatherin's that was enough to thry a saint. He delayed wan prize fight two hours, encouragin' th' voters prisint to stand be their principles, while th' principals sat shiverin' in their cor-rners until th' polis r-run him out. It got so that men'd bound into alleys whin he come up th' sthreet. People in th' liquor business rayfused to let him come into their places. His fam'ly et in th' coal-shed f'r fear iv his speeches at supper. He wint on talkin', and Willum J. O'Brien wint on handin' out th' dough that he got fr'm th' gas company an' con-ciliatin' th' masses; an', whin iliction day come, th' judges an' clerks was all f'r O'Brien, an' Dorgan didn't get votes enough to wad a gun. He sat up near all night in his long coat, makin' speeches to himsilf; but tord mornin' he come over to my place where O'Brien sat with his la-ads. 'Well,' says O'Brien, 'how does it suit ye?' he says. 'It's sthrange,' says Dorgan. 'Not sthrange at all,' says Willum J. O'Brien. 'Whin ye've been in polytics as long as I have, ye'll know,' he says, 'that th' rolyboly is th' gr-reatest or-rator on earth,' he says. 'Th' American nation in th' Sixth Ward is a fine people,' he says. 'They love the eagle,' he says, 'on th' back iv a dollar,' he says. 'Well,' says Dorgan, 'I can't undherstand it,' he says. 'I med as manny as three thousan' speeches,' he says. 'Well,' says Willum J. O'Brien, 'that was my majority,' he says. 'Have a dhrink,' he says."

MR. DOOLEY
LOOKS ABROAD

"But if all thim gr-reat powers, as they say thim-silves, was f'r to attack us, d'ye know what I'd do? I'll tell ye. I'd blockade Armour an' Comp'ny an' th' wheat ilivators iv Minnysoty. F'r Hinnissy, I tell ye, th' hand that rocks th' scales in th' grocery store is th' hand that rules th' wurruld."

THE DECLINE
OF NATIONAL FEELING

"You and me, Hinnissy, has got to bring on this here Anglo-Saxon 'lieance," said Mr. Dooley after the Spanish American War. "An Anglo-Saxon, Hinnissy, is a German that's forgot who was his parents. They're a lot iv thim in this counthry. There must be as manny as two in Boston: they'se wan up in Maine, an' another lives at Bogg's Ferry in New York State, an' dhrives a milk wagon. Mack is an Anglo-Saxon. His folks come fr'm th' County Armagh, an' their naytional Anglo-Saxon hymn is 'O'Donnell Aboo.' Teddy Rosenfelt is another Anglo-Saxon. An' I'm an Anglo-Saxon. I'm wan iv th' hottest Anglo-Saxons that iver come out iv Anglo-Saxony. Th' name iv Dooley has been th' proudest Anglo-Saxon name in th' County Roscommon f'r many years."

♣ ♣ ♣

"WHAT AR-RE ye goin' to do Pathrick's Day?" asked Mr. Hennessy.

"Pathrick's Day?" said Mr. Dooley. "Pathrick's Day? It seems to me I've heard th' name befure. Oh, ye mane th' day th' low Irish that hasn't anny votes cillybrates th' birth iv their naytional saint, who was a Fr-rinchman."

"Ye know what I mane," said Mr. Hennessy, with rising wrath. "Don't ye get gay with me now."

"Well," said Mr. Dooley, "I may cillybrate it an' I

127

may not. I'm thinkin' iv savin' me enthusyasm f'r th'
queen's birthday, whiniver it is that that blessid holiday
comes ar-round. Ye see, Hinnissy, Pathrick's Day is out iv
fashion now. A few years ago ye'd see the Prisidint iv
th' United States marchin' down Pinnsylvania Avnoo,
with th' green scarf iv th' Ancient Ordher on his shoulders an' a shamrock in his hat. Now what is Mack doin'?
He's settin' in his parlor, writin' letthers to th' queen, be
hivins, askin' afther her health. He was fr'm th' north
iv Ireland two years ago, an' not so far north ayether,—
just far enough north f'r to be on good terms with Derry
an' not far enough to be bad frinds with Limerick. He
was raised on butthermilk an' haggis, an' he dhrank his
Irish nate with a dash iv orange bitthers in it. He's
been movin' steadily north since; an', if he keeps on
movin', he'll go r-round th' globe, an' bring up somewhere
in th' south iv England.

"An' Hinnery Cabin Lodge! I used to think that Hinnery would niver die contint till he'd took th' Prince iv
Wales be th' hair iv th' head,—an' 'tis little th' poor
man's got—an' dhrag him fr'm th' tower iv London to
Kilmainham Jail, an' hand him over to th' tindher mer-
cies, as Hogan says, iv Michael Davitt. Thim was th' days
whin ye'd hear Hinnery in th' Sinit, spreadin' fear to th'
hear-rts iv th' British aristocracy. 'Gintlemen,' he says,
'an' fellow-sinitors, th' time has come,' he says, 'whin th'
eagle burrud iv freedom,' he says, 'lavin',' he says, 'its
home in th' mountains,' he says, 'an' circlin',' he says,
'undher th' jool'd hivin,' he says, 'fr'm where,' he says,
'th' Passamaquoddy rushes into Lake Erastus K. Ropes,'
he says, 'to where rowls th' Oregon,' he says, 'fr'm th'

lakes to th' gulf,' he says, 'fr'm th' Atlantic to th' Passific where rowls th' Oregon,' he says, 'an' fr'm ivry American who has th' blood iv his ancesthors' hathred iv tyranny in his veins,—your ancesthors an' mine, Mr. Mc-Adoo,' he says—'there goes up a mute prayer that th' nation as wan man, fr'm Bangor, Maine, to where rowls th' Oregon, that,' he says, 'is full iv salmon, which is later put up in cans, but has th' same inthrest as all others in this question,' he says, 'that,' he says, 'th' descindants iv Wash'n'ton an',' he says, iv Immitt,' he says, 'will jine hands f'r to protect,' he says, 'th' codfisheries again th' Vandal hand iv th' British line,' he says. 'I therefore move ye, Mr. Prisidint, that it is th' sinse iv this house, if anny such there be, that Tay Pay O'Connor is a greater man thin Lord Salisberry,' he says.

"Now where's Hinnery? Where's th' bould Fenian? Where's th' moonlighter? Where's th' pikeman? Faith, he's changed his chune, an' 'tis 'Sthrangers wanst, but brothers now,' with him, an' 'Hands acrost th' sea an' into some wan's pocket,' an' 'Take up th' white man's burden an' hand it to th' coons,' an' 'An open back dure an' a closed fr-ront dure.' 'Tis th' same with all iv thim. They'se me frind Joe Choate. Where'd Joe spind th' night? Whisper, in Windsor Castle, no less, in a nightshirt iv th' Prince iv Wales; an' th' nex' mornin' whin he come downstairs, they tol' him th' rile fam'ly was late risers, but, if he wanted a good time, he cud go down an' look at th' cimit'ry! An' he done it. He went out an' wept over th' grave iv th' Father iv his Counthry. Ye'er man, George Wash'n'ton, Hinnissy, was on'y th' stepfather.

"Well, glory be, th' times has changed since me frind Jawn Finerty come out iv th' House iv Riprisintatives; an', whin some wan ast him what was goin' on, he says, 'Oh, nawthin' at all but some damned American business.' Thim was th' days! . . .

"They'se goin' to be a debate on th' 'lieance at th' ninety-eight picnic at Ogden's gr-rove," said Mr. Hennessy.

"P'r'aps," said Mr. Dooley, sweetly, "ye might like to borry th' loan iv an ice-pick."

THE IRISH

"Well, I didn't intind to get excited over this Pathrick's Day, but somehow or other ivry time it comes ar-round I feel like goin' up on th' roof an' singin' 'O'Donnell Aboo' so all may hear. I don't know why."

"Maybe," said Mr. Hennessy, " 'tis because ye're Irish."

"I hadn't thought iv that," said Mr. Dooley. "P'raps ye're right. It's something I niver have been able to get over. Be this time it's become an incur'ble habit. Annyhow 'tis a good thing to be an Irishman because people think that all an Irishman does is to laugh without a reason an' fight without an objick. But ye an' I, Hinnissy, know these things ar-re on'y our divarsions. It's a good thing to have people size ye up wrong, whin they're got ye'er measure ye're in danger."

"Sometimes I think we boast too much," said Mr. Hennessy.

"Well," said Mr. Dooley, "it's on'y on Pathrick's Day we can hire others to blow our horns f'r us."

THE RISING OF THE SUBJECT RACES

♣ ♣ ♣

"Ye'er frind Simpson was in here a while ago," said Mr. Dooley, "an' he was that mad."

"What ailed him?" asked Mr. Hennessy.

"Well," said Mr. Dooley, "it seems he wint into me frind Hip Lung's laundhry to get his shirt an' it wasn't ready. Followin' what Hogan calls immemoryal usage, he called Hip Lung such names as he cud remimber and thried to dhrag him around th' place be his shinin' braid. But instead iv askin' f'r mercy, as he ought to, Hip Lung swung a flatiron on him an' thin ironed out his spine as he galloped up th' stairs. He come to me f'r advice an' I advised him to see th' American consul. Who's th' American consul in Chicago now? I don't know. But Hogan, who was here at th' time, grabs him be th' hand an' says he: 'I congratulate ye, me boy,' he says. 'Ye have a chance to be wan iv th' first martyrs iv th' white race in th' gr-reat sthruggle that's comin' between thim an' th' smoked or tinted races iv th' wurruld,' he says. 'Ye'll be another Jawn Brown's body or Mrs. O'Leary's cow. Go back an' let th' Chink kill ye an' cinchries hence people will come with wreathes and ate hard-biled eggs on ye'er grave,' he says.

"But Simpson said he did not care to be a martyr. He said he was a retail grocer be pro-fissyon an' Hip Lung was a customer iv his, though he got most iv his vittles fr'm th' taxydermist up th' sthreet an' he thought he'd go around to-morrah an' concilyate him. So he wint away.

"Hogan, d'ye mind, has a theery that it's all been up with us blondes since th' Jap'nese war. Hogan is a prophet. He's wan iv th' gr-reatest prophets I know. A prophet, Hinnissy, is a man that foresees throuble. . . . He cudden't find a goold mine f'r ye but he cud see th' bottom iv wan through three thousand feet iv bullyon. He can peer into th' most blindin' sunshine an' see th' darkness lurkin' behind it. He's predicted ivry war that has happened in our time and eight thousand that haven't happened to happen. If he had his way th' United States navy wud be so big that there wudden't be room f'r a young fellow to row his girl in Union Park. He can see a war cloud where I can't see annything but somebody cookin' his dinner or lightin' his pipe. He'd make th' gr-reat foreign iditor an' he'd be fine f'r th' job f'r he's best late at night.

"Hogan says th' time has come f'r th' subjick races iv th' wurruld to rejooce us fair wans to their own complexion be batin' us black and blue. Up to now 'twas: 'Sam, ye black rascal, tow in thim eggs or I'll throw ye in th' fire. 'Yassir,' says Sam. 'Comin',' he says. 'Twas: 'Wow Chow, while ye'er idly stewin' me cuffs I'll set fire to me unpaid bills.' 'I wud feel repaid be a kick,' says Wow Chow. 'Twas: 'Maharajah Sewar, swing th' fan swifter or I'll have to roll over f'r me dog whip.' 'Hig-

gins Sahib,' says Maharapah Sewar, 'Higgins Sahib, beloved iv Gawd an' Kipling, ye'er punishments ar-re th'
nourishment iv th' faithful. My blood hath served thine
f'r manny ginerations. At laste two. 'Twas thine old man
that blacked me father's eye an' sint me uncle up f'r
eighty days. How will ye'er honor have th' accursed
swine's flesh cooked f'r breakfast in th' mornin' when I'm
through fannin' ye?'

"But now, says Hogan, it's all changed. Iver since th'
Rooshyans were starved out at Port Arthur and Ports-
mouth, th' wurrud has passed around an' ivry naygur
fr'm lemon color to coal is bracin' up. He says they have
aven a system of tilly-graftin' that bates ours be miles.
They have no wires or poles or wathered stock but th'
population is so thick that whin they want to sind wurrud
along th' line all they have to do is f'r wan man to nudge
another an' something that happens in Northern Chiny is
known in Southern Indya befure sunset. And so it passed
through th' undherwurruld that th' color line was not to
be dhrawn anny more, an' Hogan says that almost anny
time he ixpicts to see a black face peerin' through a
window an' in a few years I'll be takin' in laundhry in a
basement instead iv occypyin' me present impeeryal position, an' ye'll be settin' in front iv ye'er cabin home
playin' on a banjo an' watchin' ye'er little pickahinnissies
rollickin' on th' ground an' wondhern' whin th' lynchin'
party'll arrive. . . .

"I don't see what th' subjick races got to kick about,
Hinnissy. We've been awfully good to thim. We sint thim
missionaries to teach thim th' error iv their relligyon an'

nawthin' cud be kinder thin that f'r there's nawthin' people like betther thin to be told that their parents are not be anny means where they thought they were but in a far more crowded an' excitin' locality. An' with th' missionaries we sint sharpshooters that cud pick off a Chinyman beatin' th' conthribution box at five hundherd yards. We put up palashal goluf-coorses in the cimitries an' what was wanst th' tomb iv Hung Chang, th' gr-reat Tartar Impror, rose to th' dignity iv bein' th' bunker guardin' th' fifth green. No Chinyman cud fail to be pleased at seein' a tall Englishman hittin' th' Chinyman's grandfather's coffin with a niblick. We sint explorers up th' Nile who raypoorted that th' Ganzain flows into th' Oboo just above Lake Mazap, a fact that th' naygurs had known f'r a long time. Th' explorer announces that he has changed th' names iv these wather-coorses to Smith, Blifkins an' Winkinson. He wishes to deny th' infamyous story that he iver ate a native alive. But wan soon succumbs to th' customs iv a counthry an' Sir Alfred is no viggytaryan. . . .

"It's no laughin' matther, I tell ye. A subjick race is on'y funny whin it's raaly subjick. About three years ago I stopped laughin' at Jap'nese jokes. Ye have to feel supeeryor to laugh an' I'm gettin' over that feelin'. An' nawthin' makes a man so mad an' so scared as whin something he looked down on as infeeryor tur-rns on him. If a fellow man hits him he hits him back. But if a dog bites him he yells 'mad dog' an' him an' th' neighbors pound th' dog to pieces with clubs. If th' naygurs down South iver got together an' flew at their masters ye'd

hear no more coon songs f'r awhile. It's our conceit
makes us supeeryor. Take it out iv us an' we ar-re about
th' same as th' rest. . . .

"An' I sigh f'r th' good old days befure we become
what Hogan calls a wurruld power. In thim days our fa-
v'rite spoort was playin' solytare, winnin' money fr'm
each other, an' no wan th' worse off. Ivrybody was in-
vious iv us. We didn't care f'r th' big game goin' on in
th' corner. Whin it broke up in a row we said: 'Gintlemen, gintlemen!' an' maybe wint over an' grabbed somebody's stake. But we cudden't stand it anny longer. We
had to give up our simple little game iv patience an' cut
into th' other deal. An' now, be Hivins, we have no peace
iv mind. Wan hand we have wan partner; another hand
he's again us. This minyit th' Jap an' me ar-re playin'
together an' I'm tellin' him what a fine lead that was;
th' next an' he's again me an' askin' me kindly not to
look at his hand. There ar-re no frinds at cards or wurruld
polyticks. Th' deal changes an' what started as a frindly
game iv rob ye'er neighbor winds up with an old ally
catchin' me pullin' an ace out iv me boot an' denouncin'
me."

"Sure thim little fellows wud niver tackle us," said
Mr. Hennessy. "Th' likes iv thim!"

"Well," said Mr. Dooley, " 'tis because they ar-re little
ye've got to be polite to thim. A big man knows he don't
have to fight, but whin a man is little an' knows he's
little an' is thinkin' all th' time he's little an' feels that
ivrybody else is thinkin' he's little, look out f'r him."

THE DREYFUS CASE

The Dreyfus case concerned the railroading of a young Jewish officer to Devil's Island by the high officials of the French Army. When Colonel Picquart disproved the evidence on which the conviction of treason had been secured and fastened it upon Colonel Esterhazy, the Army officials chose to defend their earlier decision and Esterhazy was acquitted. Before his trial the Dreyfus question had become a bitter issue in France, and the affair was followed with only slightly less interest in America. Prominent among those who had become partisans of justice for Dreyfus was the novelist Emile Zola. After Esterhazy's acquittal, Zola published his famous open letter, "J'accuse," for which he too was tried and condemned. To bolster the Army's case with the public, Colonel Henry produced another document implicating Dreyfus. When it was proved that Henry had forged this, he was arrested, and committed suicide, which was the occasion of this essay.

♣   ♣   ♣

"I SEE BE the pa-apers," said Mr. Dooley, "that Col. Hinnery, th' man that sint me frind Cap Dhry-fuss to th' cage, has moved on. I sup-pose they'll give th' Cap a new thrile now."

"I hope they won't," said Mr. Hennessy. "I don't know annything about it, but I think he's guilty. He's a Jew."

"Well," said Mr. Dooley, "ye'er thoughts on this subject is inthrestin', but not conclusive, as Dorsey said to

136

th' Pollack that thought he cud lick him. Ye have a
r-right to ye'er opinyon, an' ye'll hold it annyhow,
whether ye have a r-right to it or not. Like most iv ye'er
fellow-citizens, ye start impartial. Ye don't know annything about th' case. If ye knew annything, ye'd not have
an opinyon wan way or th' other. They'se niver been a
matther come up in my time that th' American people was
so sure about as they ar-re about th' Dhry-fuss case. Th'
Frinch ar-re not so sure, but they'se not a polisman in this
counthry that can't tell ye jus' where Dhry-fuss was whin
th' remains iv th' poor girl was found. That's because th'
thrile was secret. If 'twas an open thrile, an' ye heerd th'
tistimony, an' knew th' language, an' saw th' safe afther
'twas blown open, ye'd be puzzled, an' not care a rush
whether Dhry-fuss was naked in a cage or takin' tay with
his uncle at th' Benny Birth Club.

"I haven't made up me mind whether th' Cap done th'
shootin' or not. He was certainly in th' neighborhood
whin th' fire started, an' th' polis dug up quite a lot iv
lead pipe in his back yard. But it's wan thing to sus-pect
a man iv doin' a job an' another thing to prove that he
didn't. Me frind Zola thinks he's innocint, an' he raised
th' divvle at th' thrile. Whin th' judge come up on th' bench
an' opened th' coort, Zola was settin' down below with
th' lawyers. 'Let us pro-ceed,' says th' impartial an' fair-
minded judge, 'to th' thrile iv th' haynious monsther Cap
Dhry-fuss,' he says. Up jumps Zola, an' says he in
Frinch: 'Jackuse,' he says, which is a hell of a mane
thing to say to anny man. An' they thrun him out.
'Judge,' says th' attorney f'r th' difinse, 'an' gintlemen

iv th' jury,' he says. 'Ye're a liar,' says th' judge.
'Cap, ye're guilty, an' ye know it,' he says. 'Th' decision
iv th' coort is that ye be put in a cage, an' sint to th'
Divvle's own island f'r th' r-rest iv ye'er life,' he says.
'Let us pro-ceed to hearin' th' tisti-mony,' he says. 'Call
all th' witnesses at wanst,' he says, 'an' lave thim have it
out on th' flure,' he says. Be this time Zola has come back;
an' he jumps up, an', says he, 'Jackuse,' he says. An' they
thrun him out.

" 'Befure we go anny farther,' says th' lawyer f'r th'
difinse, 'I wish to sarve notice that, whin this thrile is
over, I intind,' he says, 'to wait outside,' he says, 'an'
hammer th' hon'rable coort into an omelet,' he says.
'With these few remarks I will close,' he says. 'Th' coort,'
says th' judge, 'is always r-ready to defind th' honor iv
France,' he says; 'an', if th' larned counsel will consint,' he says, 'to step up here f'r a minyit,' he says, 'th'
coort'll put a sthrangle hold on him that'll not do him a
bit iv good,' he says. 'Ah!' he says. 'Here's me ol' frind
Pat th' Clam,' he says. 'Pat, what d'ye know about this
case?' he says. 'None iv ye'er business,' says Pat. 'Answered like a man an' a sojer,' says th' coort. 'Jackuse,'
says Zola fr'm th' dureway. An' they thrun him out.
'Call Col. Hinnery,' says th' coort. 'He ray-fuses to answer.' 'Good. Th' case is clear. Cap forged th' will. Th'
coort will now adjourn f'r dools, an' all ladin' officers iv
th' ar-rmy not in disgrace already will assimble in jail,
an' com-mit suicide,' he says. 'Jackuse,' says Zola, an'
started f'r th' woods, pursued be his fellow-editors. He's
off somewhere in a three now hollerin' 'Jackuse' at ivry

wan that passes, sufferin' martyrdom f'r his counthry an' writin' now an' thin about it all.

"That's all I know about Cap Dhry-fuss' case, an' that's all anny man knows. Ye didn't know as much, Hinnissy, till I told ye. I don't know whether Cap stole th' dog or not."

"What's he charged with?" Mr. Hennessy asked, in bewilderment.

"I'll niver tell ye," said Mr. Dooley. "It's too much to ask."

"Well, annyhow," said Mr. Hennessy, "he's guilty, ye can bet on that."

NATIONAL HOUSECLEANING

"An' there ye ar-re, Hinnissy. Th' noise ye hear is not th' first gun iv a rivolution. It's on'y th' people iv th' United States batin' a carpet. Ye object to th' smell? That's nawthin'. We use sthrong disinfectants here. A Frinchman or an Englishman cleans house be sprinklin' th' walls with cologne; we chop a hole in th' flure an' pour in a kag iv chloride iv lime. Both are good ways. It depinds on how long ye intind to live in th' house. What were those shots? That's th' housekeeper killin' a couple iv cockroaches with a Hotchkiss gun. Who is that yellin'? That's our ol' frind High Fi-nance bein' compelled to take his annual bath. Th' housecleanin' season is in full swing, an' there's a good deal iv dust in th' air; but I want to say to thim neighbors iv ours, who're peekin' in an' makin' remarks about th' amount iv rubbish, that over in our part iv th' wurruld we don't sweep things undher th' sofa."

THE HAGUE CONFERENCE

President Roosevelt dispatched the fleet around the world the same year that the Second Hague Conference met. The head of the American delegation to the conference was Joseph H. Choate.

♣ ♣ ♣

"I SEE," SAID Mr. Hennessy, "we're goin' to sind th' navy to th' Passyfic."

"I can't tell," said Mr. Dooley, "whether th' navy is goin' to spend th' rest iv its days protectin' our possessions in th' Oryent or whether it is to remain in th' neighborhood iv Barnstable makin' th' glaziers iv New England rich beyond th' dhreams iv New England avarice, which ar-re hopeful dhreams. Th' Cabinet is divided, th' Sicrety iv th' Navy is divided, th' Prisidint is divided an' th' press is divided. Wan great iditor, fr'm his post iv danger in Paris, has ordhered th' navy to report at San Francisco at four eight next Thursday. Another great iditor livin' in Germany has warned it that it will do so at its peril. Nawthin' is so fine as to see a great modhern journalist unbend fr'm his mighty task iv selectin' fr'm a bunch iv phottygrafts th' prettiest cook iv Flatbush or engineerin' with his great furrowed brain th' Topsy Fizzle compytition to trifle with some light warm-weather subjick like internaytional law or war. But men such as these can do annything.

"But, annyhow, what diff'rence does it make whether th' navy goes to th' Passyfic or not? If it goes at all, it won't be to make war. They've dumped all th' fourteen inch shells into th' sea. Th' ammunition hoists ar-re filled with American beauty roses an' orchids. Th' guns are loaded with confetty. Th' officers dhrink nawthin' sthronger thin vanilla an' sthrawberry mixed. Whin th' tars go ashore they hurry at wanst to th' home iv th' Christyan Indeavor Society or throng th' free libries readin' relligious pothry. Me frind Bob Ivans is goin' to conthribute a series iv articles to th' *Ladies' Home Journal* on croshaying. F'r th' Hague peace conference has abolished war, Hinnissy. Ye've seen th' last war ye'll iver see, me boy.

"Th' Hague conference, Hinnissy, was got up be th' Czar iv Rooshya just befure he moved his army again th' Japs. It was a quiet day at Saint Pethersburg. Th' Prime Minister had just been blown up with dinnymite, th' Czar's uncle had been shot, an' wan iv his cousins was expirin' fr'm a dose iv proosic acid. All was comparative peace. In th' warrum summer's afthernoon th' Czar felt almost dhrousy as he set in his rile palace an' listened to th' low, monotonous drone iv bombs bein' hurled at th' Probojensky guards, an' picked th' broken glass out iv th' dhrink that'd just been brought to him be an aged servitor who was prisidint iv th' Saint Pethersburg lodge iv Pathriotic Assassins. Th' monarch's mind turned to th' subjick iv war an' he says to himsilf: 'What a dhreadful thing it is that such a beautiful wurruld shud be marred be thousands iv innocint men bein' sint out to shoot each other f'r no cause whin they might betther stay at home an' wurruk f'r their rile masthers,' he says. 'I will disguise mesilf as a moojik an' go over to th' tillygraft office an' summon a meetin' iv th' Powers,' he says.

"That's how it come about. All th' Powers sint dilly-gates an' a g-reat manny iv th' weaknesses did so too. They met in Holland an' they have been devotin' all their time since to makin' war impossible in th' future. Th' meetin' was opened with an acrimonyous debate over a resolution offered be a dillygate fr'm Paryguay callin' f'r immeejit disarmamint, which is th' same, Hinnissy, as notifyin' th' Powers to turn in their guns to th' man at th' dure. This was carrid be a very heavy majority. Among those that voted in favor iv it were: Paryguay, Uryguay, Switzerland, Chiny, Bilgium, an' San Marino. Opposed were England, France, Rooshya, Germany, Italy, Austhree, Japan, an' the United States.

"This was regarded be all present as a happy auggry. Th' convintion thin discussed a risolution offered be th' Turkish dillygate abolishin' war altogether. This also was carrid, on'y England, France, Rooshya, Germany, Italy, Austhree, Japan, an' th' United States votin' no.

"This made th' way clear f'r th' discussion iv th' larger question iv how future wars shud be conducted in th' best inthrests iv peace. Th' conference considhered th' possibility iv abolishin' th' mushroom bullet which, entherin' th' inteeryor iv th' inimy not much larger thin a

marble, soon opens its dainty petals an' goes whirlin'
through th' allyminthry canal like a pin-wheel. Th' Chinese dillygate said that he regarded this here insthrumint
iv peace as highly painful. He had an aunt in Pekin, an
estimable lady, unmarried, two hundherd an' fifty years
iv age, who received wan without warnin' durin' th'
gallant riscue iv Pekin fr'm th' foreign legations a few
years ago. He cud speak with feelin' on th' subjick as
th' Chinese army did not use these pro-jictyles but were
armed with bean-shooters.

"Th' English dillygate opposed th' resolution. 'It is,'
says he, 'quite true that these here pellets are in many
cases harmful to th' digestion, but I think it wud be goin'
too far to suggest that they be abolished ontil their
mannyfacther is betther undherstud be th' subjick races,'
he says. 'I suppose wan iv these bullets might throw a
white man off his feed, but we have abundant proof that
whin injicted into a black man they gr-reatly improve
his moral tone. An' afther all, th' improvemint iv th'
moral tone is, gintlemen, a far graver matther thin anny
mere physical question. We know fr'm expeeryence in
South Africa that th' charmin' bullet now undher discussion did much to change conditions in that enlightened an'
juicy part iv his Majesty's domains. Th' darky that happened to stop wan was all th' betther f'r it. He retired
fr'm labor an' give up his squalid an' bigamious life,' he
says. 'I am in favor, howiver, iv restrictin' their use to
encounters with races that we properly considher infeeryor,' he says. Th' dillygate fr'm Sinagambya rose
to a question iv privilege. 'State ye'er question iv privi-

lege,' says th' chairman. 'I wud like to have th' windows open,' says th' dillygate fr'm Sinagambya. 'I feel faint,' he says.

"Th' Hon'rable Joe Choate, dillygate fr'm th' United States, moved that in future wars enlisted men shud not wear ear-rings. Carrid, on'y Italy votin' no.

"Th' conference thin discussed blowin' up th' inimy with dinnymite, poisinin' him, shootin' th' wounded, settin' fire to infants, bilin' prisoners-iv-war in hot lard, an' robbin' graves. Some excitemint was created durin' th' talk be th' dillygate fr'm th' cannybal islands who proposed that prisoners-iv-war be eaten. Th' German dillygate thought that this was carryin' a specyal gift iv wan power too far. It wud give th' cannybal islands a distinct advantage in case iv war, as Europeen sojers were accustomed to horses. Th' English dillygate said that while much cud be said against a practice which personally seemed to him rather unsportsmanlike, still he felt he must reserve th' right iv anny cannybal allies iv Brittanya to go as far as they liked.

"Th' Hon'rable Joe Choate moved that in future wars no military band shud be considered complete without a base-dhrum. Carrid.

"Th' entire South American dillygation said that no nation ought to go to war because another nation wanted to put a bill on th' slate. Th' English dillygate was much incensed. 'Why, gintlemen,' says he, 'if ye deprived us iv th' right to collect debts be killin' th' debtor ye wud take away fr'm war its entire moral purpose. I must ask ye again to cease thinkin' on this subjick in a gross mateeryal way an' considher th' moral side alone,' he says. Th' conference was much moved be this pathetic speech, th' dillygate fr'm France wept softly into his hankerchef, an' th' dillygate fr'm Germany wint over an' forcibly took an open-face goold watch fr'm th' dillygate fr'm Vinzwala.

"Th' Hon'rable Joe Choate moved that in all future wars horses shud be fed with hay wheriver possible. Carrid. . . ."

AN INTERNATIONAL POLICE FORCE

"Be Hivins, Hinnissy, I looked forward to th' day whin, if a king, impror, or czar started a rough-house, th' blue bus wud come clangin' through th' sthreets an' they'd be hauled off to Holland f'r trile. . . . I thought th' coort wud have a kind iv a bridewell built, where they'd sind th' internaytional dhrunks an' disordhlies, an' where ye cud go anny day an' see Willum Hohenzollern cooperin' a bar'l, an' me frind Joe Chamberlain peggin' shoes. . . . But it hasn't come. . . . I want to see th' day whin just as Bill Hohenzollern an' Edward [of England] meets on th' corner an' prepares a raid on a laundhry a big polisman will step out iv a dure an' say: 'I want ye, Bill, an' ye might as well come along quiet.' But I suppose it wud be just th' same thing as it is now in rale life."

"How's that?" asked Mr. Hennessy.

"All th' biggest crooks wud get on th' polis foorce," said Mr. Dooley.

MR. DOOLEY ON HIGH
FINANCE AND OTHER
BUSINESS

☘

"Why is England losin' her supreemacy, Hinnissy?
Because Englishmen get down to their jobs at iliven
o'clock figurin' a goluf scoor on their cuffs an' lave at
a quarther to twelve on a bicycle. We bate thim because 'twas th' habit iv our joynt iv commerce f'r to
be up with th' cock an' down to th' damper befure th'
cashier come; an' in his office all day long in his
shirt sleeves an' settin' on th' safe till th' las' man had
gone. Now, if ye call up wan iv these captains iv industhree at wan o'clock iv a Saturdah afthernoon, th'
office boy answers th' tillyphone. Th' Titan iv Commerce is out in a set iv green an' blue knee breeches,
batin' a hole in a sand pile an' cur-rsin' th' evil fate
that made him a millyonaire whin nature intinded
him f'r a goluf champeen. Ye can't keep ye'er eye on
th' ball an' on th' money at th' same time. Ye've got
to be wan thing or another in this wurruld. I niver
knew a good card player or a great spoortsman
that cud do much iv annything else."

THE BIG FINE

On April 13, 1907, Federal Judge Kenesaw Mountain Landis handed down a decision fining Rockefeller's Standard Oil Company something over twenty-nine million dollars for breaking the federal law against rebating. In the end the corporation paid nothing, as the higher courts set aside the penalty.

❧　❧　❧

"THAT WAS a splendid fine they soaked Jawn D. with," said Mr. Dooley.

"What did they give him?" asked Mr. Hennessy.

"Twinty-nine millyon dollars," said Mr. Dooley.

"Oh, great!" said Mr. Hennessy. "That's a grand fine. It's a gorjous fine. I can't hardly believe it."

"It's thrue, though," said Mr. Dooley. "Twinty-nine millyon dollars. Divvle th' cent less. I can't exactly make out what th' charge was that they arrested him on, but th' gin'ral idee is that Jawn D. was goin' around loaded up to th' guards with Standard Ile, exceedin' th' speed limit in acquirin' money, an' singin' 'A charge to keep I have' till th' neighbors cud stand it no longer. The judge says: 'Ye're an old offender an' I'll have to make an example iv ye. Twinty-nine millyon dollars or fifty-eight millyon days. Call th' next case, Misther Clerk.

"Did he pay th' fine? He did not. Iv coorse he cud if he wanted to. He wuddn't have to pawn annything to get

th' money, ye can bet on that. All he'd have to do would
be to put his hand down in his pocket, skin twenty-nine
millyon dollar bills off iv his roll an' hurl thim at th' clerk.
But he refused to pay as a matter iv principle. 'Twas not
that he needed th' money. He don't care f'r money in th'
passionate way that you an' me do, Hinnissy. Th' likes iv
us are as crazy about a dollar as a man is about his child
whin he has on'y wan. Th' chances are we'll spoil it. But
Jawn D., havin' a large an' growin' fam'ly iv dollars,
takes on'y a kind iv gin'ral inthrest in thim. He's issued
a statement sayin' that he's a custojeen iv money appinted
be himsilf. He looks afther his own money an' th' money
iv other people. He takes it an' puts it where it won't hurt
thim an' they won't spoil it. He's a kind iv a society f'r
th' previntion of croolty to money. If he finds a man mis-
using his money he takes it away fr'm him an' adopts it.
Ivry Saturdah night he lets th' man see it f'r a few hours.
An' he says he's surprised to find that whin, with th'
purest intintions in th' wurruld, he is found thryin' to
coax our little money to his home where it'll find conjanial
surroundings an' have other money to play with, th'
people thry to lynch him an' th' polis arrest him f'r abduction.

"So as a matther iv principle he appealed th' case. An
appeal, Hinnissy, is where ye ask wan coort to show its
contempt f'r another coort. 'Tis sthrange that all th'
pathrites that have wanted to hang Willum Jennings
Bryan an' mesilf f'r not showin' proper respect f'r th'
joodicyary are now showin' their respect f'r th' joodicyary be appealin' fr'm their decisions. Ye'd think Jawn D.

wud bow his head reverentially in th' awful presence iv
Kenesaw Mt. Landis an' sob out: 'Thanks ye'er honor.
This here noble fine fills me with joy. But d'ye think ye
give me enough? If agreeable I'd like to make it an even
thirty millyons.' But he doesn't. He's like mesilf. Him an'
me bows to th' decisions iv th' coorts on'y if they bow
first.

"I have gr-reat respect f'r th' joodicyary, as fine a lot
iv cross an' indignant men as ye'll find annywhere. I have
th' same respect f'r thim as they have f'r each other. But
I niver bow to a decision iv a judge onless, first, it's pleasant to me, an', second, other judges bow to it. Ye can't be
too careful about what decisions ye bow to. A decision
that seems agreeable may turn out like an acquaintance ye
scrape up at a picnic. Ye may be ashamed iv it to-morrah.
Manny's th' time I've bowed to a decree iv a coort on'y to
see it go up gayly to th' Supreme Coort, knock at th' dure
an' be kicked down stairs be an angry old gintleman in
a black silk petticoat. A decree iv th' coort has got to be
pretty vinrable befure I do more thin greet it with a
pleasant smile.

"Me idee was whin I read about Jawn D.'s fine that
he'd settle at wanst, payin' twenty-eight millyon dollars in
millyon dollar bills an' th' other millyon in chicken-feed
like ten thousand dollar bills just to annoy th' clerk. But I
ought to've known betther. Manny's th' time I've bent me
proud neck to a decision iv a coort that lasted no longer
thin it took th' lawyer f'r th' definse to call up another
judge on th' tillyphone. A judge listens to a case f'r days
an' hears, while he's figurin' a possible goluf score on his

blottin' pad, th' argymints iv two or three lawyers that no wan wud dare to offer a judgeship to. Gin'rally speakin', judges are lawyers. They get to be judges because they have what Hogan calls th' joodicyal timp'ramint, which is why annybody gets a job. Th' other kind won't take a job. They'd rather take a chance. Th' judge listens to a case f'r days an' decides it th' way he intinded to. D'ye find th' larned counsel that's just been beat climbin' up on th' bench an' throwin' his arms around th' judge? Ye bet ye don't. He gathers his law books into his arms, gives th' magistrate a look that means, 'There's an iliction next year,' an' runs down th' hall to another judge. Th' other judge hears his kick an' says he: 'I don't know annything about this here case except what ye've whispered to me, but I know me larned collague an' I wuddent thrust him to referee a roller-skatin' contest. Don't pay th' fine till ye hear fr'm me.' Th' on'y wan that bows to th' decision is th' fellow that won, an' pretty soon he sees he's made a mistake, f'r wan day th' other coort comes out an' declares that th' decision of th' lower coort is another argymint in favor iv abolishin' night law schools. . . .

"Well, sir, glory be but times has changed whin they land me gr-reat an' good frind with a fine that's about akel to three millyon dhrunk an' disorderly cases. 'Twud've been cheaper if he'd took to dhrink arly in life. . . ."

"Well," said Mr. Hennessy, " 'tis time they got what was comin' to thim."

"I'll not say ye're wrong," said Mr. Dooley. "I see th' way me frind Jawn D. feels about it. He thinks he's doin' a great sarvice to th' worruld collectin' all th' money in sight. It might remain in incompetint hands if he didn't get it. 'Twud be a shame to lave it where it'd be misthreated. But th' on'y throuble with Jawn is that he don't see how th' other fellow feels about it. As a father iv about thirty dollars I want to bring thim up mesilf in me own foolish way. I may not do what's right be thim. I may be too indulgent with thim. Their home life may not be happy. Perhaps 'tis clear that if they wint to th' Rockyfellar institution f'r th' care iv money they'd be in betther surroundings, but whin Jawn thries to carry thim off I raise a cry iv 'Polis,' a mob iv people that niver had a dollar iv their own, an' niver will have wan, pounce on th' misguided man, th' polis pinch him, an' th' governmint condemns th' institution an' lets out th' inmates an' a good manny iv thim go to th' bad."

"D'ye think he'll iver sarve out his fine?" asked Mr. Hennessy.

"I don't know," said Mr. Dooley. "But if he does, whin he comes out at the end iv a hundhred an fifty-eight thousand years he'll find a great manny changes in men's hats an' th' means iv transportation but not much in annything else. He may find flyin' machines, though it'll be arly f'r thim, but he'll see a good manny people still walkin' to their wurruk."

"Th' wurruld is full iv crooks," said Mr. Hennessy.

"It ain't that bad," said Mr. Dooley. "An', besides, let us thank Hivin they put in part iv their time cheatin' each other."

MAKING A WILL

"If a man is wise, he gets rich an' if he gets rich, he gets foolish, or his wife does. That's what keeps th' money movin' around. . . . Aisy come, lazy do."

♧ ♧ ♧

"I NIVER MADE a will," said Mr. Dooley. "I didn't want to give mesilf a headache thinkin' iv something to put into it. A will iv mine wud be a puny little thing annyhow an' if anny wan thried to file it he'd be lible to be locked up f'r contimpt iv th' probate coort. Besides, I wuddn't like to cause anny onseemly wrangles an' maybe lawsuits among me heirs about who wud pay f'r th' express wagon to carry th' estate to th' city dump. An' annyhow I've always thought that if there's goin' to be ayether cheers or tears at me obsekees they shud spring fr'm th' heart, not fr'm mercinary motives. If anny fellow feels like cillybratin' me departure let him do it out iv his own pocket. Thin I'll know he's sincere. 'Twud grieve me if some wan broke into song at th' news an' a sthranger was to ask: 'Is that wan iv his inimies?' an' th' reply was, 'No, it's wan iv his heirs.'

"So f'r wan reason or another I've niver made a will, but I'll not deny it must be considhrable spoort f'r thim that has th' manes an' th' imagination to injye it. I'm pretty sure I'd bust into tears whin th' lawyers wrote down th' directions f'r somebody else to set in me rockin' chair, an' I can't think iv annything that wud brighten th' wurruld with me out iv it. But that wud be because I wuddn't go at it in th' right way. To be injyeable a will must be at wan an' th' same time a practical joke on th' heirs an' an advertisemint iv the man that made it. Manny a man niver has his own way till he has it through his will. Afther he's dead an' gone, he shoves his hat on th' back iv his head an' stalks up an' down through th' house, sayin, 'I'll show ye who's th' boss here. F'r th' first time in me life, now that I'm dead, I'm goin' to be obeyed.' No wondher that manny meek millyonaires comforts their declinin' years with this amusemint. It is as Hogan says, th' last infirmary f'r their noble minds. It's a chance f'r thim to tache th' fam'ly their proper place, an' blow their own horns without havin' anny wan interrupt th' solo. . . .

"Think iv th' throuble ye can cause an' the insults ye can hurl at ye'er inimies. I often thought 'twud be a fine way iv gettin' aven with a man I didn't like. Supposin' Hogan an' me had a quarrul an' I didn't have time to write a frindly biography about him, or was afraid I might go first. Nawthin' wud be nater thin to put him in me will. 'I hereby cancel all bequests to me frind Terrence Hogan on account iv his bad habits.'

"I bet he'd be sorry I was gone. How he'd wish he cud have me back agin f'r a while.

"I niver see anny wan that entherd into th' spirit iv makin' a will so thurly as our ol' frind Dochney. Ye didn't like him, but I did. I liked him because he was so simple an' sincere. Prudent fellows like ye'ersilf, that spind ye'er lives pilin' up great stores iv good will an' affiction an' a comfortable conscience f'r ye'er old age don't apprecyate a spindthrift like Dochney, who threw all these things away in th' pursuit iv his pleasure, which was makin' money. Ye thought he was a bad man, but I knew him f'r a single-minded, innocint ol' la-ad who niver harmed anny wan excipt f'r gain an' was incapable iv falsehood outside iv business. To those who see him in th' rough battle iv life at home or among his neighbors, he may've seemed hard, but we who knew him in th' quiet seclusyon iv th' bank among his recreations, found another Dochney, a cheerful soul, who always had a smile on his face, wrote little verses to th' promissory notes an' cuddn't keep his feet still whin th' goold coin clatthered on th' counter. If Dochney had wan fault it was he was too sintimental about money. Men like ye ar-re th' ra-ally rapacyous wans. Ye have nawthin' but desire f'r money. Ye don't want to give it a home an' take care iv it. But Dochney had a tender feelin' f'r it. Tears come to his eyes as he watched it grow. He become so attached to it that no wan cud pry it away fr'm him. An' money reciprocated. Iv'ry dollar he had wurruked f'r him. It wint out an' decoyed another dollar an' aven if it come back ladin' nawthin' more thin a little chickenfeed Dochney wasn't cross about it. He wud pat a nickel on th' back an' say: 'Ye're small now, but with a little incouragemint we'll make a big sthrappin' dollar out iv ye yet.'

"Dochney lived to an old age, because as th' pote says, 'There's nawthin' like avarice to keep a man young.' Th'

Spanyards knew that, whin they sarched f'r th' fountain iv perpetchool youth. They'd heerd th' Indyans had money. Annyhow, Dochney's cheeks wore th' bloom iv usury long afther manny philanthropists ar-re lookin' pale. But th' time come whin somethin' in th' eyes iv his financial frinds told him 'twud be betther not to go downtown agin unarmed, an' he retired. He planted his money th' way they do eyesthers an' let it breed, sindin' down wanst a week to haul out enough to sustain life an' puttin' th' rest back in agin.

"But this was no life f'r wan that had been an eyesther pirate in his day, an' Dochney begun to pine. I thried to amuse him. I had th' congressman sind him ivry day th' new currency bill; I cut out th' repoorts wanst a week iv th' bankruptcys in th' United States an' Canady an' wurruked th' cash registher f'r him be th' hour, because he liked th' old refrain. But nawthin' did him anny good ontil Dock O'Leary advised him to alter his will. Th' Dock says he always thries this prescription on aged millyonaires afther th' oxygen fails. Wan mornin' Dochney come in lookin' as cheerful as an advertisemint iv a breakfast food an' jinglin' his key ring in his pocket, f'r he niver carrid annything else to jingle, but made a practice iv exthractin' car fare out iv th' gran'childher's bank with a penknife ivry mornin'.

" 'Ye're lookin' well, me ol' buccaneer,' said I. 'It's feelin' well I am,' says he, fillin' his pocket fr'm th' cheese bowl. 'I've been with me lawyer all mornin' revisin' me will. I find I've left out a good many ol' frinds. Ye haven't a middle inityal to ye'er name, have ye?' 'Give me a glass iv sas-prilly,' he says. Well, sir; though I knew th' crafty ol' pirate, th' thought suddenly lept into me head that maybe his heart or his brain had softened an' he'd put me in th' will. In that fatal sicond I bought two autymobills, a yacht, an' a goold watch an' chain an' shook me ol' frinds, an' whin I come to me sinses he'd gone an' hadn't settled f'r th' sas-prilly.

"Well, th' fun he had afther that. All day long he wint around makin' delicate inquiries about people's circumstances an' in th' mornin' he was downtown puttin' something new in his will. He hadn't been a popylar man. He had cashed in th' affictions iv his neighbors arly in life. An' prejudices ar-re hard to overcome. But grajaly—that is to say, within a week or ten days—people begun to see that a gr-reat injustice had been done to him. He didn't say annythin' about a will. But he had a way iv askin' people did they spell their name with an aitch or a zee an' puttin' it down in a notebook that was very consolin'. His rilitives begun to show a gr-reat inthrest in him an' some iv thim come fr'm as far as San Francisco to cheer his declinin' years an' form vigilance committees to protect him fr'm fortune hunters. He was niver alone, but always had th' most agreeable s'ciety. 'Twas 'Uncle, that's a fine cough ye have; wuddn't ye like to set in this cool draft?' Or 'Cousin Andhrew, tell us that joke ye made las' night. I nearly died laughin' at it, but no wan can tell it like ye'ersilf.'

"He niver took a meal at home. He stopped payin' all bills. He insisted on all babies born in th' ward bein' named afther him. He insulted people an' challenged thim to fight. By an' by th' pa-apers got hold iv him an' always spoke iv him as th' eccenthric philanthropist. Rows if carredges shtud at his dure an' inside iv his house he debated with th' thrustees iv binivolint institutions an' prisidints iv colledges about their plans f'r new buildin's. Wan iv th' ladin' univarsities sint th' glee club down to serenade him. He was ilicted vice prisidint iv Andhrew Carnaygie's peace comity, thrustee iv th' art museem, director in th' Home f'r Wan Eyed Owls, an' L. L. D. in Skowhegan univarsity.

"An' all th' time th' wurruld was talkin' about this gr-reat binifacthor all Mrs. Dochney cud find in her cold heart to say was, 'There's no fool like an ol' fool,' an' wint about her housewurruk an' made poultices f'r him whin he come home fr'm the meetin' iv th' s'ciety f'r pathronizin' th' poor, where they'd give him a cold in th' chest fr'm th' hankerchief salute.

"Well, sir, all times, good an' bad, has got to come to an end, an' wan day Dochney come in to see me. 'I think,' says he, 'I'll go home an' go to bed an' stay there. I've finished me will an' me life is no longer safe fr'm th' binificyants. There's a prisidint iv a colledge comin' to town. He's an eager idjacator, an' as I don't want to die with me boots on I think I won't see him. Here's 5 cints I owe ye f'r th' sas-prilly,' he says. An' he wint away an' I niver set eyes on him agin. He left a will in five lines, givin' all his money to th' good woman, an' sayin' that he thought he'd done enough f'r iv'rybody else by keepin' thim in hopes all these years, which is th' on'y pleasure in life."

"I niver cud undherstand a man like Dochney makin' money," said Mr. Hennessy.

"He made it," said Mr. Dooley, "because he honestly loved it with an innocint affiction. He was thrue to it. Th' reason ye have no money is because ye don't love it f'r itsilf alone. Money won't iver surrinder to such a flirt."

PANICS

"Don't get excited about it, Hinnissy, me boy. Cheer up. 'Twill be all right to-morrah, or th' next day, or some time. 'Tis wan good thing about this here wurruld, that nawthin' lasts long enough to hurt. I have been through manny a panic. I cud handle wan as well as Morgan. Panics cause thimsilves an' take care iv thimsilves. Who do I blame for this wan? Grogan blamed Rosenfelt yesterday; to-day he blames Mulligan; to-morrah he won't blame anny wan an' thin th' panic will be over. I blame no wan, an' I blame ivry wan. All I say to ye is, be brave, be ca'm an' go on shovellin'. So long as there's a Hinnissy in th' wurruld, an' he has a shovel, an' there's something f'r him to shovel, we'll be all right, or pretty near all right."

"Don't ye think Rosenfelt has shaken public confidence?" asked Mr. Hennessy.

"Shaken it," said Mr. Dooley, "I think he give it a good kick just as it jumped off th' roof."

MR. DOOLEY ON ATHLETICS

*"In me younger days 'twas not considhered rayspic-
table f'r to be an athlete. An athlete was always a man
that was not sthrong enough f'r wurruk. Fractions
druv him fr'm school an' th' vagrancy laws
druv him to baseball."*

THE POWER OF LOVE

On St. Patrick's Day, 1897, "Ruby Robert" Fitzsimmons won the world's heavyweight championship from "Gentleman Jim" Corbett, also known as "Pompadour Jim." Corbett held the championship by right of his defeat of John L. Sullivan five years before. In the Fitzsimmons battle at Carson City, Corbett seemed to have a clear advantage until the fourteenth round, when Fitzsimmons delivered the "solar plexus punch" that won the fight and was ever afterwards associated with the great Fitz. The Mrs. Fitzsimmons of that day was the former Rose Julian, a professional acrobat.

♣ ♣ ♣

"'Twas this way," said Mr. Hennessy, sparring at Mr. Dooley. "Fitz led his right light on th' head, thin he stuck his thumb in Corbett's hear-rt, an' that was th' end iv th' fight an' iv Pompydour Jim. I tol' ye how it wud come out. Th' punch over th' hear-rt done th' business."

"Not at all," said Mr. Dooley. "Not at all. 'Twas Mrs. Fitzsimmons done th' business. Did ye see th' pitcher iv that lady? Did ye? Well, 'twud've gone har-rd with th' la-ad if he'd lost th' fight in th' ring. He'd have to lose another at home. I'll bet five dollars that th' first lady iv th' land licks th' champeen without th' aid iv a stove lid. I know it.

"As me good frind, Jawn Sullivan, says, 'tis a great comfort to have little reminders iv home near by whin ye're fightin'. Jawn had none, poor lad; an' that accounts f'r th' way he wint down at last. Th' home infloo-ence is felt in ivry walk iv life. Whin Corbett was poundin' th' first jintleman iv th' land like a man shinglin' a roof, th' first lady iv th' land stood in th' corner, cheerin' on th' bruised an' bleedin' hero. 'Darlin',' she says, 'think iv ye'er home, me love. Think,' she says, 'iv our little child larnin' his caddychism in Rahway, New Jersey,' she says. 'Think iv th' love I bear ye,' she says, 'an' paste him,' she says, 'in th' slats. Don't hit him on th' jaw,' she says. 'He's well thrained there. But tuck ye'er lovin' hooks into his diseased an' achin' ribs,' she says. 'Ah, love!' she says; 'recall thim happy goolden days iv our coortship, whin we walked th' counthry lane in th' light iv th' moon,' she says, 'an hurl ye'er maulies into his hoops,' she says. 'Hit him on th' slats!' An' Fitz looked over his shoulder an' seen her face, an' strange feelin's iv tendherness come over him; an' thinks he to himself: 'What is so good as th' love iv a pure woman? If I don't nail this large man, she'll prob'ly kick in me head.' An' with this sacred sintimint in his heart he wint over an' jolted Corbett wan over th' lathes that retired him to th' home f'r decayed actors.

"'Twas a woman's love that done it, Hinnissy. I'll make a bet with ye that, if th' first lady iv th' land had been in th' ring instead iv th' first gintleman, Corbett wuddn't have lasted wan r-round. I'd like to have such a wife as that. I'd do th' cookin', an' lave th' fightin' to her. There ought to be more like her. Th' throuble with th' race we're bringin' up is that th' fair sect, as Shakespere calls thim, lacks inthrest in their jooty to their husbands. It's th' business iv men to fight, an' th' business iv their wives f'r

to make thim fight. Ye may talk iv th' immyrality iv nailin'
a man on th' jaw, but 'tis in this way on'y that th' wurruld
increases in happiness an' th' race in strenth. Did ye see
annywan th' other day that wasn't askin' to know how th'
fight come out? They might say that they re-garded th'
exhibition as brutal an' disgustin', but divvle a wan iv
thim but was waitin' around th' corner f'r th' rayturns,
an' prayin' f'r wan or th' other iv th' big la-ads. Father
Kelly mentioned th' scrap in his sermon last Sundah. He
said it was a disgraceful an' corruptin' affair, an' he was
ashamed to see th' young men iv th' parish takin' such an
inthrest in it in Lent. But late Winsdah afthernoon he
came bustlin' down th' sthreet. 'Nice day,' he says. It was
poorin' rain. 'Fine,' says I. 'They was no parade today,'
he says. 'No,' says I. 'Too bad,' says he; an' he started to
go. Thin he turned, an' says he: 'Be th' way, how did that
there foul an' outhrajous affray in Carson City come out?'
'Fitz,' says I, in th' fourteenth.' 'Ye don't say,' he says,
dancin' around. 'Good,' he says. 'I told Father Doyle this
mornin' at breakfuss that if that red-headed man iver got
wan punch at th' other lad, I'd bet a new cassock—Oh,
dear!' he says, 'what am I sayin'?' 'Ye're sayin',' says I,
'what nine-tenths iv th' people, laymen an' clargy, are
sayin',' I says. 'Well,' he says, 'I guess ye're right,' he
says. 'Afther all,' he says, 'an' undher all, we're mere
brutes; an' it on'y takes two la-ads more brutal than th'
rest f'r to expose th' sthreak in th' best iv us. Foorce rules
th' wurruld, an' th' churches is empty whin th' blood begins to flow,' he says. 'It's too bad, too bad,' he says. 'Tell
me, was Corbett much hurted?' he says."

FOOTBALL

"Ye see," said Mr. Dooley, "whin 'tis done be la-ads that wurruks at it, an' has no other occupation, it's futball; an', whin it is done in fun an' be way of a joke, it's disordherly conduct, assault an' battery an' rite . . . Down town it's futball; out here it's the Irish killin' each other. Down town th' spectators sees it f'r a dollar apiece; out here it costs the spectator ne'er a cint, but th' players has to pay tin dollars an' costs."

♣   ♣   ♣

"WHIN I WAS a young man," said Mr. Dooley, "an' that was a long time ago—but not so long ago as manny iv me inimies'd like to believe, if I had anny inimies—I played futball, but 'twas not th' futball I see whin th' Brothers school an' th' Saint Aloysius Tigers played las' week on th' pee-raries.

"Whin I was a la-ad, iv a Sundah afthernoon we'd get out in th' field where th' oats'd been cut away, an' we'd choose up sides. Wan cap'n'd pick wan man, an' th' other another. 'I choose Dooley,' 'I choose O'Connor,' 'I choose Dimpsey,' 'I choose Riordan,' an' so on till there was twinty-five or thirty on a side. Thin wan cap'n'd kick th' ball, an' all our side'd r-run at it an' kick it back; an' thin wan iv th' other side'd kick it to us, an' afther awhile th' game'd get so timpischous that all th' la-ads iv both sides'd be in wan pile, kickin' away at wan or th' other or

at th' ball or at th' empire, who was mos'ly a la-ad that
cudden't play an' that come out less able to play thin he
was whin he wint in. An', if anny wan laid hands on th'
ball he was kicked be ivry wan else an' be th' empire. We
played fr'm noon till dark, an' kicked th' ball all th' way
home in th' moonlight.

"That was futball, an' I was a great wan to play it. I'd
think nawthin' iv histin' th' ball two hundherd feet in th'
air, an' wanst I give it such a boost that I stove in th' ribs
iv th' Prowtestant minister—bad luck to him, he was a
kind man—that was lookin' on fr'm a hedge. I was th'
finest player in th' whole county, I was so.

"But this here game that I've been seein' ivry time th'
pagan fistival iv Thanksgivin' comes ar-round, sure it
ain't th' game I played. I seen th' Dorgan la-ad comin' up
th' sthreet yesterdah in his futball clothes—a pair iv mat-
thresses on his legs, a pillow behind, a mask over his nose,
an' a bushel measure iv hair on his head. He was followed
be three men with bottles, Dr. Ryan, an' th' Dorgan
fam'ly. I jined thim. They was a big crowd on th' pee-rary
—a bigger crowd than ye cud get to go f'r to see a prize
fight. Both sides had their frinds that give th' colledge
cries. Says wan crowd: 'Take an ax, an ax, an ax, to
thim. Hooroo, hooroo, hellabaloo. Christyan Bro-others!'
an' th' other says, 'Hit thim, saw thim, gnaw thim, chaw
thim, Saint Alo-ysius!' Well, afther awhile they got down
to wurruk. 'Sivin, eighteen, two, four,' says a la-ad. I've
seen people go mad over figures durin' th' free silver
campaign, but I niver see figures make a man want f'r to
go out an' kill his fellow-men befure. But these here fig-

ures had th' same effect on th' la-ads that a mintion iv Lord Castlereagh'd have on their fathers. Wan la-ad hauled off, an' give a la-ad acrost fr'm him a punch in th' stomach. His frind acrost th' way caught him in th' ear. Th' cinter rush iv th' Saint Aloysiuses took a runnin' jump at th' left lung iv wan iv th' Christyan Brothers, an' wint to th' grass with him. Four Christyan Brothers leaped most crooly at four Saint Aloysiuses, an' rolled thim. Th' cap'n iv th' Saint Aloysiuses he took th' cap'n iv th' Christyan Brothers be th' leg, an' he pounded th' pile with him as I've seen a section hand tamp th' thrack. All this time young Dorgan was standin' back, takin' no hand in th' affray. All iv a suddent he give a cry iv rage, an' jumped feet foremost into th' pile. 'Down!' says th' empire. 'Faith, they are all iv that,' says I, 'Will iver they get up?' 'They will,' says ol' man Dorgan. 'Ye can't stop thim,' says he.

"It took some time f'r to pry thim off. Near ivry man iv th' Saint Aloysiuses was tied in a knot around wan iv th' Christyan Brothers. On'y wan iv thim remained on th' field. He was lyin' face down, with his nose in th' mud. 'He's kilt,' says I. 'I think he is,' says Dorgan, with a merry smile. ' 'Twas my boy Jimmy done it, too,' says he. 'He'll be arrested f'r murdher,' says I. 'He will not,' says he. 'There's on'y wan polisman in town cud take him, an' he's down town doin' th' same f'r somebody,' he says. Well, they carried th' corpse to th' side, an' took th' ball out iv his stomach with a monkey wrinch, an' th' game was rayshumed. 'Sivin, sixteen, eight, ilivin,' says Saint Aloysius; an' young Dorgan started to run down th' field.

They was another young la-ad r-runnin' in fr-ront iv
Dorgan; an', as fast as wan iv th' Christyan Brothers
come up an' got in th' way, this here young Saint Aloysius
grabbed him be th' hair iv th' head an' th' sole·iv th' fut,
an' thrun him over his shoulder. 'What's that la-ad doin'?'
says I. 'Interferin',' says he. 'I shud think he was,' says I,
'an' most impudent,' I says. ' 'Tis such interference as
this,' I says, 'that breaks up fam'lies'; an' I come away.

" 'Tis a noble sport, an' I'm glad to see us Irish ar-re
gettin' into it. Whin we larn it thruly, we'll teach thim
colledge joods fr'm th' pie belt a thrick or two."

"We have already," said Mr. Hennessy. "They'se a
team up in Wisconsin with a la-ad be th' name iv Jeremiah
Riordan f'r cap'n, an' wan named Patsy O'Dea behind
him. They come down here, an' bate th' la-ads fr'm th'
Chicawgo Colledge down be th' Midway."

"Iv coorse, they did," said Mr. Dooley. "Iv coorse they
did. An' they cud bate anny collection iv Baptists that iver
come out iv a tank."

*"Jawn D. didn't mind whin th' pro-fissor in Agyptology
pulled a boner in thranslatin' th' epytaph on King Tut's
tomb; 'Accidents will happen,' said he smilingly, 'in th'
best regylated business.' But he was much humilyated
whin his little Baptists were tumbled be th' followers iv
George Fox on th' futball field. Jawn D. give no money to
th' colledges befure futball was inthrajooced. . . ."*

THE HIGHER BASEBALL

"D'YE IVER go to a baseball game?" asked Mr. Hennessy.

"Not now," said Mr. Dooley. "I haven't got th' intellick f'r it. Whin I was a young fellow nawthin' plazed me betther thin to go out to th' ball grounds, get a good cosy seat in th' sun, take off me collar an' coat an' buy a bottle iv pop, not so much, mind ye, f'r th' refrishment, because I niver was much on pop, as to have something handy to reprove th' empire with whin he give an eeronyous decision. Not only that, me boy, but I was a fine amachure ball-player mesilf. I was first baseman iv th' Prairie Wolves whin we beat th' nine iv Injine Company Five be a scoor iv four hundherd an' eight to three hundherd an' twinty-five. It was very close. Th' game started just afther low mass on a Sundah mornin' an' was called on account iv darkness at th' end iv th' fourth inning. I knocked th' ball over th' fence into Donovan's coal yard no less thin twelve times. All this talk about this here young fellow Baker makes me smile. Whin I was his age I wudden't count annything but home-runs. If it wasn't a home-run I'd say: 'Don't mark it down' an' go back an' have another belt at th' ball. Thim were th' days.

"We usen't to think base-ball was a science. No man

was very good at it that was good at annything else. A
young fellow that had a clear eye in his head an' a sthrong
pair iv legs undher him an' that was onaisy in th' close
atmosphere iv th' school room, an' didn't like th' pro-
fissyon iv plumbing was like as not to join a ball team. He
come home in th' fall with a dimon in his shirt front an'
a pair iv hands on him that looked like th' boughs iv a
three that's been sthruck be lightenin' an' he was th' hero
in th' neighborhood till his dimon melted an' he took to
drivin' a thruck. But 'tis far different nowadays. To be
a ball-player a man has to have a joynt intilleck. Inside
base-ball, th' pa-apers calls it, is so deep that it'd give brain
fever to a pro-fissor iv asthronomy to thry to figure it
out. Each wan iv these here mathymatical janiuses has to
carry a thousand mysteeryous signals in his head an'
they're changed ivry day an' sometimes in th' middle iv
th' game. I'm so sorry f'r th' poor fellows. In th' old days
whin they were through with th' game they'd maybe
sthray over to th' Dutchman's f'r a pint iv beer. Now they
hurry home to their study an' spind th' avnin' poorin'
over books iv allgibera an' thrigynomethry.

"How do I know? Hogan was in here last night with
an article on th' 'Mysthries iv Base-ball.' It's be a larned
man. Here it is: Th' ordhinary observer or lunk-head who
knows nawthin' about base-ball excipt what he larned be
playin' it, has no idee that th' game as played to-day is
wan iv th' most inthricate sciences known to mankind.
In th' first place th' player must have an absolute masthry
iv th' theery iv ballistic motion. This is especially thrue iv
th' pitcher. A most exact knowledge in mathymatics is

required f'r th' position. What is vulgarly known as th' spit-ball on account iv th' homely way in which th' op-'rator procures his effects is in fact a solution iv wan iv th' most inthricate problems in mechanics. Th' purpose iv th' pitcher is to project th' projectyle so that at a pint be-tween his position an' th' batsman th' tindincy to pro-ceed on its way will be countheracted be an impulse to return whence it come. Th' purpose iv th' batsman is, afther judgin' be scientific methods th' probable coorse or thrajecthry iv th' missile to oppose it with sufficyent foorce at th' proper moment an' at th' most efficient point, first to retard its forward movement, thin to correct th' osseyla-tions an' fin'ly to propel it in a direction approximately opposite fr'm its original progress. This, I am informed, is technically known as 'bustin' th' ball on th' nose (or bugle).' In a gr-reat number iv cases which I observed th' experiment iv th' batsman failed an' th' empire was obliged so to declare, th' ball havin' actually crossed th' plate but eluded th' (intended) blow. In other cases where no blow was attimpted or aven meditated I noted that th' empire erred an' in gin'ral I must deplore an astonishin' lack in thrained scientific observation on th' part iv this officyal. He made a number iv grievous blundhers an' I was not surprised to larn fr'm a gintleman who set next to me that he (th' empire) had spint th' arly part iv his life as a fish in the Mammoth Cave iv Kentucky. I thried me best to show me disapproval iv his unscientific an' infamous methods be hittin' him over th' head with me umbrella as he left th' grounds. At th' requist iv th' iditor iv th' magazine I intherviewed Misther Bugs Mulligan th' pitcher iv th' Kangaroos afther th' game. I found th' cillybrated expert in th' rotundy iv th' Grand Palace Hotel where he was settin' with other players polishin' his finger nails. I r-read him my notes on th' game an' he expressed his approval addin' with a show at laste iv enthusyasm: 'Bo, ye have a head like a dhrum.' I requested him to sign th' foregoin' statement but he declined remarkin' that th' last time he wrote his name he sprained his wrist an' was out iv the game f'r a week.

"What'd I be doin' at th' likes iv a game like that? I'd come away with a narvous headache. No, sir, whin I take a day off, I take a day off. I'm not goin' to a base-ball game. I'm goin' to take a bag iv peanuts an' spind an afthernoon at th' chimical labrytory down at th' colledge where there's something goin' on I can undherstand."

"Oh, sure, said Mr. Hennessy, "if 'twas as mysteryous as all that how cud Tom Donahue's boy Petie larn it that was fired fr'm th' Brothers School because he cuddn't add? . . ."

"Annyhow 'tis a gr-rand game, Hinnissy, whether 'tis played th' way th' pro-fissor thinks or th' way Petie larned to play it in th' back yard an' I shuddn't wondher if it's th' way he's still playin'. Th' two gr-reat American spoorts are a good deal alike—polyticks an' baseball. They're both played be pro-fissyonals, th' teams ar-re r-run be fellows that cuddn't throw a base-ball or stuff a ballot-box to save their lives an' ar-re on'y intherested in countin' up th' gate receipts, an' here ar-re we settin' out in th' sun on th' bleachin' boords, payin' our good money f'r th' spoort, hot an' uncomfortable but happy, injying

ivry good play, hootin' ivry bad wan, knowin' nawthin'
about th' inside play an' not carin,' but all jinin' in th'
cry iv 'Kill th' empire.' They're both grand games."

"Speakin' iv polyticks," said Mr. Hennessy, "who
d'ye think'll be ilicted?"

"Afther lookin' th' candydates over," said Mr. Dooley,
"an' studyin' their qualifications carefully I can't thruth-
fully say that I see a prisidintial possibility in sight."

COLLEGE EDUCATION

"Weren't ye in here last year an' I said to ye: 'How's
Aloysius gettin' along? That was a fine oration he made
on l'avin' school about standin' on th' threshold iv th' sea
iv life an' this an' that. What's he goin' to be?' 'Oh, I
don't know,' says ye, 'a colledge profissor, or a lawyer or
something. His head is that full iv larnin' he can't think.
Ivry time he thries to ketch a baseball it bounces off his
nose.'

" 'An' how's that little ruffyan Pathrick Sarsfield Hinnissy? Is he anny brighter thin he was? Can he undherstand wurruds iv wan syllable?' says I. 'Now,' says ye,
'ye're talkin' about th' flower iv th' flock. Ye'll hear fr'm
that boy some day. He ain't much good as a scholar, but
nayther was I whin I was his age. But, by gorry, he can
kick a futball as though he hated it. . . . I don't know
what he intinds to do whin he gets out iv colledge.' 'Ye
needn't bother,' says I. 'He won't get out in ye'er lifetime.
Both th' charackter iv his scholarship an' his futball will
keep him there till his beard is a yard long,' says I."

GOLF

"Wurruk is wurruk if ye're paid to do it an' it's pleasure if ye pay to be allowed to do it."

♣   ♣   ♣

"WELL, SIR," said Mr. Dooley, "I don't want to say annything that wud hurt a frind, but I do think th' authorities ar-re very lax in lavin' Hogan at large, as they ar-re doin'."

"An' what ails Hogan?" Mr. Hennessy asked.

"He's got what th' dock calls a fixed deelusion," said Mr. Dooley. "He thinks he's a goluf player. No, he don't play th' game. Nobody does that. They wurruk at it. But Hogan he slaves at it. He don't think iv annything else. He takes it down to th' wather-office with him in th' mornin', an' he carries it home with him at night an' sleeps with it. If ye go over to his house at this minyit ye'll find him in th' front parlor swingin' a poker an' tellin' th' good woman how he played th' eighth hole. There's nawthin' more excitin' to th' mother iv siven at th' end of a complete wash-day thin to listen to an account iv a bum goluf game fr'm th' lips iv her lifemate. 'Tis almost as absorbin' as th' invintory iv a grocery store. I was over there th' other night, an' he broke three panes iv glass showin' me what he calls a mashie shot, an' he near took an ear off his aunt Bridget practisin' with a war-club that

175

he calls a nibbelick. I wuddn't be harsh with him, but a few months or aven years in a well upholstered cell with a ball an' chain on his leg, might restore him to himself an' make him again th' safe an' bashful husband an' father he wanst was.

"But 'tis a gr-reat game, a gr-rand, jolly, hail-fellow-well-met spoort. With th' exciption maybe iv th' theery iv infant damnation, Scotland has given nawthin' more cheerful to th' wurruld thin th' game iv goluf. Whin 'twas first smuggled into this counthry, I cuddn't make out what 'twas like. I thought whin I first read about it that it was intinded f'r people with a hackin' cough, an' that no wan who was robust enough to play 'Twinty Ques- tions' in a wheel-chair, wud engage in it without a blush. I had it in me mind that 'twas played iv a rainy afther- noon in th' front parlor. Th' two athletes got out their needles an' their embroidery canvas, give a shout iv glee an' flew at it. Th' results was submitted to th' *Ladies Home Journal,* an' me frind Eddie Bok decided who was champeen, an' give him a goold thimble f'r a prize.

"But I know better now. 'Tis a rough an' angry game, full of ondacint remarks an' other manly char- ackteristics, d'ye mind. . . . At th' end iv ivry goluf match th' player loathes himsilf, is not on speakin' terms with th' fellow he played again, cud kill his own caddy an' his op- ponent's, an' hates th' criminal that laid out th' coorse, th' game itsilf, th' Jook iv Argyll, each wan iv his clubs, th' little bur-rd that twittered whin he was shootin', th' pretty wild flowers on th' margin iv th' links, an' each separate spear iv grass on th' puttin'-green. If that Dutch pote that wrote th' 'Hymn iv Hate' wants to write an-other on th' same subjick with a rale punch in it he ought to larn goluf. 'Twuld help him.

"How's it played, says ye? I don't exactly know. I niver studied law. But ye can get th' rules iv th' game in th' public library, in siven volumes edited be th' Lord Chief Justice iv Scotland. If ye have a dispute over th' rules, th' quickest way to get a decision is to hire a lawyer, make a test case, an' carry it to th' Supreme Coort. In a gin'ral way, all I can say about it is that it's a kind iv a game iv ball that ye play with ye'er own worst inimy which is ye'ersilf, an' a man ye don't like goes around with ye an' gloats over ye, an' a little boy follows ye to carry th' clubs an' hide th' ball afther ye've hit it. Th' ball is small, made iv injy rubber an' filled with a pizinous substance, an' if ye hit it a good smash it busts an' puts out ye'er eye. Ye're supposed to smash this little grenade fr'm place to place an' here an' there an' up an' down an' hither an' yon with an enormous insthrument iv wood or iron, ontil in due time ye get to what is called a puttin'-green. There's a little hole with a tin can in it in th' middle iv this place, an' whin ye're within a fut or two iv this hole ye take a small hammer out iv th' bag, an' ye hit th' ball four or five times till it tumbles into th' hole. Thin ye wipe th' cold sweat fr'm ye'er brow, write down '5' on a little card, an' walk away a few feet an' do it all over again.

"So far so good. But that ain't nearly all. ... Ye're told be a frind that ye ought to take a lesson. So ye pick out a bright-faced Scotch lad with a head shaped like a alligator pear an' who can hit th' ball a mile blindfolded an' ye give him what change ye have an' ask him to pint out ye'er faults. He pints out all ye'er wife has told ye about an' manny dark wans besides. I see Hogan takin' a goluf lesson wanst, an' how he iver dared to lift his head agin is more thin I cud undherstand. Afther th' pro-fissyonal has recited th' catalog iv ye'er sins an' vices, an' ye've made an act iv conthrition, he tells ye how to hit th' ball. Ye'd think that ought to be aisy. Just go up an' give it a cuff.

"But it ain't annything like as soft as that. There ar-re forty different things ye have to think iv with each shot, an' if ye do wan iv thim wrong, ye're a lost soul. When ye'er idjication is completed ye go out an' do all th' things he told ye, but nineteen, an' th' ball skips lightly into a pit. Now is ye'er time to escape. If ye lave it lie there, turn ye'er back on it, run to th' parish-house an' ask f'r th' prayers iv th' congregation, it may not be too late. Ye may be saved. Fly, weak an' wretched man, while ye have th' strenth! But if ye delay, if ye step but wan fut into th' thrap, ye're doomed an' on'y th' kindly hand iv death will release ye fr'm a life iv shame. . . .

"Did I iver see th' game played? Faith, I did. Th' other mornin' I see Hogan go out with his kit iv tools. In other games wan bat is enough, but in goluf ye have to own twinty. All th' money that used to go f'r shoes in Hogan's fam'ly now goes f'r goluf-clubs. If he manages to hit th' ball with a club, he tells ye he wuddn't part with that club f'r a hundherd dollars an' asts ye to feel it an' say ain't that a nice club. Whin he misses it he says th' club has gone back on him an' he buys a new wan. He has as manny implymints iv this new thrade iv his as a tinker. He has a hammer to beat th' ball into th' ground with, an' a pick to get it out, an' a little shovel to scrape it fr'm th' sand, an' a little hatchet to knock it into th' hole whin he gets near it. 'Where ar-re ye goin' with th' hardware?' says I. 'Is it to open a safe or build a battleship?' says I. 'I'm goin' to play goluf,' says he angrily. 'This is th' day I hang Larkin's hide on th' fence,' he says.

"So I followed him out to Douglas Park, an' there we met Larkin, who had a bag iv akel size. Hogan used to be champeen caber tosser iv th' ward an' Larkin was a sthructural ir'n-wurruker befure his health give out an' he become a horseshoer, but they groaned undher their burdens. Fortchnitly at that moment two bright little boys iv about eight years stepped up an' relieved thim iv their burden. 'What are these pigmies goin' to do with this here year's output iv th' Gary mills?' says I. 'They're goin' to carry thim,' says Larkin. 'They're caddies,' he says. 'Well,' says I, ' 'tis very nice iv th' little toddlers. Th' young cannot start too arly in helpin' th' aged. But,' I says, 'why don't ye get up on their backs an' have thim carry ye around? A little more weight wuddn't make much difference,' says I. 'Hush up,' says Hogan.

"Th' poor fellow was standin' on what they call th' tee, which is where ye take th' first lick at th' ball. He had a pole in his hand an' was swingin' it at a dandeline an' missin'. Ivinchooly he stepped up to where th' ball roosted on a little pile iv sand, stood with his legs apart like th' statue he calls th' Goloshes iv Rhodes, waggled th' stick in th' air, p'inted it tords th' pole, cried out, 'Stand away,

Larkin, get round behind me, Martin, stop shufflin' there, boy,' an' screamed 'Fore' at a fat old gintleman that was at wurruk in a thrench three city blocks ahead. Thin he hauled off with th' bat, muttherin' to himsilf: 'Eye on th' ball, slow back, keep th' lift arm sthraight, pivot on th' right foot, folly through.' Up crept th' dhread insthrument slow an' cautious an' down it came with a blow that wud've foorced th' Dardanelles. I expicted to see th' ball splintered into a thousan' pieces or disappear into space. But it didn't. It left th' tee ridin' on a piece iv turf th' size iv ye'er hat, floated lazily off to wan side, dhropped, bounced twice, an' nestled in a bush. 'Watch it, boy,' yells Hogan. 'Watch it. Go right to it. Oh,' says he, 'what did I do that was wrong, what *did* I do?' says he, wringin' his hands. 'Ye dhropped ye're right shouldher,' says Larkin. 'Took ye're eye off it,' says Larkin's caddy. 'Toed it,' says an innocint bystander. 'Ye made a mistake thryin' to hit at all. Ye shud've kicked it,' says I. Hogan stood by, his face convulsed with mortyfication ontil Larkin, a man whose Sundah mornin' recreation used to be raisin' a kag iv beer over his head fifty times, give a lunge at th' ball, done a complete spin an' missed it altogether. Thin a wan smile come to Hogan's lips. 'What ar-re ye haw-hawin' about?' says Larkin. They niver spoke again. Most iv th' time they weren't in speakin' distance iv each other. Fr'm time to time they wud meet be chanst on a puttin'-green an' Hogan wud say to himself: 'I'm down in twelve,' an' Larkin wud kick his ball over to th' next tee. So they wint rollickin' on. Hogan spoke to me wanst. He said: 'Dammit, stop coughin'.' Whin I left thim at th' sivinth hole th'

excitemint was at its hite. Larkin' was lookin' f'r his ball
in a geeranyum bush, an' Hogan was choppin' down an
evergreen three with wan iv his little axes. 'Where ar-re
ye goin'?' says he. 'I don't know,' says I, 'but I may dhrop
in at th' morgue an' listen to an inquest,' says I. 'I've got
to spend me holiday someway,' says I.

"I see Hogan th' next day an' asked him why he played.
'Why,' says I, 'd'ye make a joke iv ye'ersilf at ye'er time
iv life, an' ye a man with a family?' says I. 'That's just
it,' says he. 'I do it because iv me time iv life an' me fam'ly
cares,' says he. 'I defy anny man in th' wurruld to get a
bad lie in a bunker an' think iv annything else. He's that
mad all his other sorrows, his debts, his sins, an' his future, disappears,' he says, 'like a summer cloud in a
hur'cane. I'm that onhappy nawthin' bothers me. If a man
come up an' told me me house was afire I'.d not hear him.
I don't know what it is,' says he, 'onless,' he says, 'it's th'
feelin' that ye're bein' persecuted. It's ye'er sinse iv injustice that's stirred up in ye, that makes ye injye a
round,' says he."

"Is th' Prisidint a good goluf player, d'ye know, at
all?" asked Mr. Hennessy after a moment of judicial
silence.

"As a goluf player he cud give Lincoln a sthroke a
hole," said Mr. Dooley.

ATHLETICS FOR WOMEN

♣ ♣ ♣

"WE'RE GETTIN' to be th' gr-reatest spoortin' nation in th' wurruld," said Mr. Hennessy, who had been laboring through pages of athletic intelligence which he could not understand.

"Oh, so we ar-re," said Mr. Dooley. "An' I wondher does it do us anny good. . . ."

"But 'tis good f'r th' women," said Mr. Hennessy.

"Is it, faith?" said Mr. Dooley. "Well, it may be, but it's no good f'r th' woman or f'r th' men. I don't know annything that cud be more demoralizin' thin to be marrid to a woman that cud give me a sthroke a shtick at goluf. 'Tis goin' to be th' roon iv fam'ly life. 'Twill break up th' happy home. I'm a man, we'll say, that's down town fr'm th' arly mornin' bendin' over a ledger an' thryin' to thrap a dollar or two to keep th' landlord fr'm th' dure. I dispise athletes. I see that all th' men that have a metallic rattle whin they get on a movin' sthreet car are pounds overweight an' wud blow up if they jogged around th' corner. Well, I come home at night an' no matther how I've been 'Here-you-d' all day, I feel in me heart that I'm th' big thing there. What makes me feel that way, says ye? 'Tis th' sinse iv physical supeeryority. Me wife is smarter thin I am. She's had nawthin' to do all day but th' house-

182

wurruk an' puttin' in th' coal an' studyin' how she can make me do something I don't want to do that I wud want to do if she didn't want me to do it. She's thrained to th' minyit in havin' her own way. Her mind's clearer, mine bein' full iv bills iv ladin'; she can talk betther an' more frequent; she can throw me fam'ly in me face an' whin har-rd put to it, her starry eyes can gleam with tears that I think ar-re grief, but she knows diff'rent. An' I give in. But I've won, just th' same. F'r down in me heart I'm sayin': 'Susette, if I were not a gintleman that wud scorn to smash a lady, they'd be but wan endin' to this fracas. Th' right to th' pint iv th' jaw, Susette.' I may niver use it, d'ye mind. We may go on livin' together an' me losin' a battle ivry day f'r fifty year. But I always know 'tis there an' th' knowledge makes me a proud an' haughty man. I feel me arm as I go out to lock th' woodshed agin, an' I say to mesilf: 'Oh, woman, if I iver cut loose that awful right.' An' she knows it too. If she didn't she wuddn't waste her tears. Th' sinse of her physical infeeryority makes her weep. She must weep or she must fight. Most anny woman wud rather do battle thin cry, but they know it's no use.

"But now how is it? I go home at night an' I'm met at th' dure be a female joynt. Me wife's th' champeen lady golufess iv th' Ivy Leaf Goluf club; th' finest oarslady on th' canal; a tinnis player that none can raysist without injury. She can ride a horse an' I cuddn't stay on a merry-go-round without clothespins. She can box a good welterweight an' she's got medals f'r th' broad jump. Th' on'y spoorts she isn't good at is cookin' an' washin'. This large lady, a little peevish because she's off her dhrive, meets me at th' dure an' begins issuin' ordhers befure I have me shoes off. 'Tis just th' same as if I was back on th' hoist. She doesn't argy, she doesn't weep. She jus' says 'Say you,' an' I'm off on th' bound. I look her over an' say I to mesilf: 'What's th' good? I cuddn't cross that guard,' an' me reign is ended. I'm back to th' ranks iv th' prolitory.

"It won't do, Hinnissy. It's a blow at good govermint. 'Twill disrupt th' home. Our fathers was r-right. They didn't risk their lives an' limbs be marryin' these female Sharkeys. What they wanted was a lady that they'd find settin' at home whin they arrived tired fr'm th' chase, that played th' harp to thim an' got their wampum away fr'm thim more like a church fair thin like a safe blower. In th' nex' eighty or ninety years if I make up me mind to lave this boistherous life an' settle down, th' lady that I'll rayquist to double me rent an' divide me borrowin' capacity will wear no medals f'r athletic spoorts. F'r, Hinnissy, I'm afraid I cud not love a woman I might lose a fight to."

"I see be th' pa-aper," said Mr. Hennessy, "th' athletic girl is goin' out, what iver that means."

"She had to," said Mr. Dooley, "or we wud."

MR. DOOLEY, LITERARY CRITIC

"Annyhow, th' truth is a tough boss in lithrachoor. He don't pay aven boord wages, an' if ye go to wurruk f'r him ye want to have a job on th' side."

BOOKS

☘ ☘ ☘

"Ivry time I pick up me mornin' paper to see how th' scrap come out at Batthry D," said Mr. Dooley, "th' first thing I r-run acrost is somethin' like this: "A hot an' handsome gift f'r Christmas is Lucy Ann Patzooni's "Jims iv Englewood Thought" '; or 'If ye wud delight th' hear-rt iv yer child, ye'll give him Dr. Harper's monymental histhry iv th' Jewish thribes fr'm Moses to Dhryfuss' or 'Ivrybody is r-readin' Roodyard Kiplin's "Busy Pomes f'r Busy People." ' Th' idee iv givin' books f'r Christmas prisints whin th' stores are full iv tin hor-rns an' dhrums an' boxin' gloves an' choo-choo ca-ars! People must be crazy."

"They ar-re," said Mr. Hennessy. "My house is so full iv books ye cuddn't tur-rn aroun dwithout stumblin' over thim. I found th' life iv an ex-convict, the 'Prisoner iv Zinders,' in me high hat th' other day, where Mary Ann was hidin' it fr'm her sister. Instead iv th' childher fightin' an' skylarkin' in th' evenin', they're settin' around th' table with their noses glued into books. Th' ol' woman doesn't read, but she picks up what's goin' on. 'Tis 'Honoria, did Lor-rd What's-his-name marry th' fair Aminta?' or 'But that Lady Jane was a case.' An' so it goes. There's no injymint in th' house, an' they're usin' me cravats f'r bookmarks."

" 'Tis all wrong," said Mr. Dooley. "They're on'y three books in th' wurruld worth readin'—Shakespere, th' Bible, an' Mike Ahearn's histhry iv Chicago. I have Shakespere on thrust, Father Kelly r-reads th' Bible f'r me, an' I didn't buy Mike Ahearn's histhry because I seen more thin he cud put into it. Books is th' roon iv people, specially novels. Whin I was a young man, th' parish priest used to preach again thim; but nobody knowed what he meant. At that time Willum Joyce had th' on'y library in th' Sixth Wa-ard. Th' mayor give him th' bound volumes iv th' council proceedings, an' they was a very handsome set. Th' on'y books I seen was th' kind that has th' life iv th' pope on th' outside an' a set iv dominos on th' inside. They're good readin'. Nawthin' cud be betther f'r a man whin he's tired out afther a day's wurruk thin to go to his library an' take down wan iv th' gr-reat wurruks iv lithratchoor an' play a game iv dominos f'r th' dhrinks out iv it. Anny other kind iv r-readin', barrin' th' newspapers, which will niver hurt anny onedycated man, is desthructive iv morals.

"I had it out with Father Kelly th' other day in this very matther. He was comin' up fr'm down town with an' ar-rmful iv books f'r prizes at th' school. 'Have ye th' Key to Hivin there?' says I. 'No,' says he, 'th' childher that'll get these books don't need no key. They go in under th' turnstile,' he says, laughin'. 'Have ye th' Lives iv th' Saints, or the Christyan Dooty, or th' Story iv Saint Rose iv Lima?' I says. 'I have not,' says he. 'I have some good story books. I'd rather th' kids'd r-read Charles Dickens than anny iv th' tales iv thim holy men that was burned in ile or et up be lines,' he says. 'It does no good in these degin'rate days to prove that th' best that can come to a man f'r behavin' himsilf is to be cooked in a pot or digisted be a line,' he says. 'Ye're wrong,' says I. 'Beggin' ye'er riv'rince's pardon, ye're wrong,' I says. 'What ar-re ye goin' to do with thim young wans? Ye're goin' to make thim near-sighted an' round-shouldered,' I says. 'Ye're goin' to have thim believe that, if they behave thimsilves an' lead a virchous life, they'll marry rich an' go to Congress. They'll wake up some day, an' find out that gettin' money an' behavin' ye'ersilf don't always go together,' I says. 'Some iv th' wickedest men in th' wur-ruld have marrid rich,' I says. 'Ye're goin' to teach thim that a man doesn't have to use an ax to get along in th' wur-ruld. Ye're goin' to teach thim that a la-ad with a curlin' black mustache an' smokin' a cigareet is always a villyan, whin he's more often a barber with a lar-rge family. Life, says ye! There's no life in a book. If ye want to show thim what life is, tell thim to look around thim. There's more life on a Saturdah night in th' Ar-rchy Road thin in all th' books fr'm Shakespere t oth' rayport iv th' drainage thrustees. No man,' I says, 'iver wrote a book if he had annything to write about, except Shakespere an' Mike Ahearn. Shakespere was all r-right. I niver read anny of his pieces, but they sound good; an' I know Mike Ahearn is all r-right.' "

"What did he say?" asked Mr. Hennessy.

"He took it all r-right," said Mr. Dooley. "He kind o' grinned, an' says he: 'What ye say is thrue, an' it's not thrue,' he says. 'Books is f'r thim that can't injye thim-

silves in anny other way,' he says. 'If ye're in good health,
an' ar-re atin' three squares a day, an' not ayether sad or
very much in love with ye'er lot, but just lookin' on an'
not carin', a'—he said rush—'not carin' a rush, ye don't
need books,' he says. 'But if ye're a down-spirited thing
an' want to get away an' can't, ye need books. 'Tis betther
to be comfortable at home thin to go to th' circus, an' 'tis
betther to go to th' circus thin to r-read anny book. But
'tis betther to r-read a book thin to want to go to th' circus
an' not be able to,' he says. 'Well,' says I, 'whin I was
growin' up, half th' congregation heerd mass with their
prayer books tur-rned upside down, an' they were as pious
as anny. Th' Apostles' Creed niver was as con-vincin' to
me afther I larned to r-read it as it was whin I cuddn't
read it, but believed it.' "

*"But, annyhow, they say that man first begun writin'
whin he had to hammer out his novels an' pomes on a piece
iv rock, an' th' hammer has been th' imblim iv lithrachor
iver since."*

THE POET'S FATE

"What I like about Kipling is that his pomes is right off th' bat, like me con-versations with you, me boy. . . . No col' storage pothry f'r Kipling. Ivrything fr-resh an' up to date. All lays laid this mornin'."

♣ ♣ ♣

"WHO WAS it said he didn't care who made th' laws iv a counthry if he cud on'y write th' pomes?" asked Mr. Dooley.

"I niver heerd," said Mr. Hennessy.

"Well, 'twas some frind iv Hogan's," said Mr. Dooley. "An' th' man was wrong. He was wrong, Hinnissy. I don't want to make th' laws iv th' counthry. I'm doin' pretty well to keep thim that ar-re made now. An' as f'r th' pothry, I'd as lave 'twas wrote be other hands thin mine. I was r-readin' in th' pa-aper th' other day iv a la-ad down in th' midway that says Longfellow that I used to think was a rale good pote—he wrote life is rale, life is earnest, d'ye mind, an' I believe th' same mesilf—Longfellow ought niver to 've left th' plumbin' business an' Milton was about as much iv a pote as Edward Atkinson, an' Shakespere shud be took up f'r obtainin' money be false pretinces.

"Ivrybody has a crack at a pote whin he gets a chanst. There's me frind, Roodyard Kipling. I don't mind tellin' ye he ain't my kind iv a pote. Hogan is more to me taste.

Did ye iver r-read his pomes 'Oh, Star' an' 'Oh, Moon'? Well, that's as far as he iver wint. He goes home at night an' takes off his coat an' sets down with a pencil in his mouth an' writes: 'Oh, Star,' an' 'Oh, Moon,' an' thin he can't think iv annything that wud do justice to thim, so he says, 'Oh, th' divvle,' an' comes over here f'r a dhrink.

"Roodyard Kipling is a diff'rint kind iv a pote. He don't keep pothry f'r style so that he can turn out behind it an' say, 'Boys, what d'ye think iv that f'r high-stheppin' verse?' Comfort an' not display is his motto. Whin he asks what Hogan calls th' Muse f'r to come up an' spind a week with him, he doesn't expict her to set all day in th' hammock on th' front stoop singin' about th' bur-rds. She's got to do th' week's washin', clane th' windows, cook th' meals, chune th' pianny, dust th' furniture, mend th' socks, an' milk th' cow be day, an' be night she's got to set up an' balance th' books iv an empire. Whin this Muse has thrown up her job at Kipling's, she'll be as good a second girl as anny pote wud want to hire. So Roodyard Kipling's pomes is in gr-reat demand. They're warranted not to tear or shrink or r-run in th' wash an' he'll guarantee to fit all sizes an' ages. 'Will ye have wan or two hip pockets in ye'er pome, Mr. Rhodes?' he says. 'Boy, wrap up this package iv self-rising pothry f'r th' Canajeen market. I can do this kind iv a war pome f'r ye f'r eight an' six.' An' so it goes. He's got orders to put th' annyul rayport iv th' Bank iv England, th' crop statistics iv th' Agaricoolchral Departmint an' th' quotations iv th' Stock Exchange in pothry. His pothry will be listed nex' year an' ye can r-read it on a ticker in a

saloon. He had a pome th' other day showin' that th'
English army ought to buy more horses an' mules, f'r as
he pinted out, a horse can r-run fasther thin anny man, no
matther what his record may be. 'Twas a good wurrukin'
pome. I didn't like it as much as th' 'Oh, Star' kind, but,
sure, live an' let live is me motto, an' if a man wants to
insthruct his counthry what it ought to do be playin' his
advice on a harp or doin' a jig, 'tis not f'r me to criticise
him. I don't want to hang Roodyard Kipling because he
had a pome that sounds like a speech be Lyman J. Gage on
th' legal tindher act.

"But 'tis diff'rint with me fellow citizens an' fellow
lithry joynts. A few years ago Roodyard Kipling come
over here an' got pnoomony iv th' lungs an' it looked f'r
a long time as though th' nex' pome he figured in wud
be wrote with a stone mason's chisel. Well, sir, it leaked
out that he had a bad chest an' th' kind-hearted American
public begun to weep into its beer. They was a line iv
tillygraft boys a block long at th' hotel with messages iv
condolence fr'm frinds iv his he niver see or heerd iv,
copies iv th' same havin' been sint to th' local newspaper.
Th' pa-apers was full iv tindher remarks to th' gin'ral
effect that if Kipling died, Lithrachoor wud count th'
cash raygisther, put up th' shutters an' go out into th'
night. Th' articles was accompanied be silictions fr'm his
copyright pomes. Conductors on th' sthreet cars sobbed
at th' mintion iv his name, fatal cocktails was called afther
him, near ivry clergyman in th' counthry side-thracked th'
sermon on vice an' bracketed Kipling with Martin Luther
an' Rockefellar. Down on th' Stock Exchange, sthrong

men cried as they said: 'Poor Kipling. What did he write?'
Th' Amalgamated Browning, Omar Khayyam an' Walt
Whitman Assocyation iv tin workers iv Baraboo, Wis.,
held a meetin' an' raysolved that Civilization wud lose an
eye if Kipling wint, an' it was th' sinse iv th' meetin' that
th' threasurer be insthructed to hire a copy iv his book
an' see if it was as good as they said. Th' sicker he got
th' bigger man he was. Ivry time his timprachoor wint
up, his repytation as a pote advanced tin degrees. Bets
was offered in th' pool rooms five to wan an' no takers
that he cud give Homer an' Shakespere twinty pounds
an' a bating. If he'd gone out, they were goin' to put spectacles an' a fur coat on th' goddess iv liberty an' call it
Kipling.

"Thin he made th' mistake iv his life. He lived. If ye
iver get to be a pote, Hinnissy, don't take any chances on
fame. Cinch it. Jump into th' river. But Roodyard Kipling didn't know. He wint away an' settled down an'
begun to hammer out a few lenths iv jinted pothry to
sind over to his kind frinds in America. An' what did his
kind frinds do? I picked up a pa-aper th' other day. I raymimber 'twas wan that had confissed to me that if annything happened to Kipling, th' iditor wud feel that he
cuddn't go on with his wurruk without a substantial increase in salary. Well, they was an article about a man
that had killed his wife, an' it says: 'Misther So-an'-so, a
well-known an' pop'lar burglar on th' west side, yisterdah was so unforchnit as to sink an ax into Mrs. So-
an'-so. It is believed he acted undher gr-reat provocation.'
Nex' to this piece iv society news was a scholarly article

on Roodyard Kipling. 'We have just been r-readin' a
pome be that confidence op'rator, Roodyard Kipling, an'
if there is a pressman in this buildin' that cuddn't write
a betther wan, we'd feed him to his own press. We do
not see who buys th' wurruks iv this fiend in human
form, but annybody that does ought to be put in a place
where th' green goods men can't get at him. Whin we
recall th' tears we shed whin this miscreent was pretindin'
to be sick, we feel like complainin' to th' polis. If he iver
comes to this counthry agin, we will be wan iv tin thousan' to go out an' lynch him. To think iv th' way this
imposter has been threated an' thin see that young swan
iv Main Street, our own townsman, Higbie L. Duff,
clerkin' in a shoe store, makes us ashamed iv our
counthry.'

"An' there ye ar-re. That's what happens to a pote whin
he's found out an' no pote can escape. Th' Amalgamated
Assocyation iv Baraboo has become th' Society f'r th'
Previntion iv Kipling, th' Stock Exchange is r-readin'
th' *Polis Gazette,* an' ye won't anny more hear Kipling
mintioned in th' pulpit thin ye will th' Bible."

"I don't suppose he cares," said Mr. Hennessy.

"Well, maybe he don't know," said Mr. Dooley. "But it
ought to be a lesson f'r anny young man who thinks iv
goin' into pothry. They'se on'y wan thing f'r a pote to
do: just as they're about to hang th' lorls on his brow
befure they begin to throw th' bricks, he ought to pass
away. Th' nex' best thing is to write his pothry where no
wan can see him an' dhrop it quitely in th' sthreet. Thin
they may blame it on some wan else."

BIOGRAPHY

*"What's fame, afther all, me la-ad? 'Tis apt to be what
some wan writes on ye'er tombstone as annything ye did
f'r ye'ersilf. It takes two to make it, but on'y wan has much
iv a hand. 'Tis not a man's life in wan volume be himsilf,
but his 'Life' in three volumes be wan iv his frinds. . . . A
hundherd years fr'm now Hogan may be as famous as th'
Impror Willum, an' annyhow they'll both be dead an' that's
th' principal ingreejent iv fame."*

⚛   ⚛   ⚛

"**H**OGAN HAS been in here this afthernoon, an I've
heerd more scandal talked thin I iver thought was in the
wurrld."

"Hogan had betther keep quiet," said Mr. Hennessy.
"If he goes circulatin' anny stories about me I'll——"

"Ye needn't worry," said Mr. Dooley. "We didn't con-
discend to talk about annywan iv ye'er infeeryor station.
If ye want to be th' subjick iv our scand'lous discoorse
ye'd betther go out an' make a repytation. No, sir, our
talk was entirely about th' gr-reat an' illusthrees an' it ran
all th' way fr'm Julius Cayzar to Ulysses Grant.

"Dear, oh dear, but they were th' bad lot. Thank
th' Lord nobody knows about me. Thank th' Lord I had
th' good sinse to retire fr'm polyticks whin me repytation had spread as far as Halsted Sthreet. If I'd let it
go a block farther I'd've been sorry f'r it th' rest iv me life
an' some years afther me death.

"I wanted to be famous in thim days, whin I was young an' foolish. 'Twas th' dhream iv me life to have people say as I wint by: 'There goes Dooley, th' gr-reatest states-man iv his age,' an' have thim name babies, sthreets, schools, canal boats, an' five-cent seegars afther me, an' whin I died to have it put in th' books that 'at this critical peeryod in th' history of America there was need iv a man who combined strenth iv charackter with love iv counthry. Such a man was found in Martin Dooley, a prom'nent retail liquor dealer in Ar-rchey Road.'

"That's what I wanted, an' I'm glad I didn't get me wish. If I had, 'tis little attintion to me charackter that th' books iv what Hogan calls bi-ography wud pay, but a good deal to me debts. Though they mintioned th' fact that I resked death f'r me adopted fatherland, they'd make th' more intherestin' story about th' time I almost met it be fallin' down stairs while runnin' away fr'm a polisman. F'r wan page thèy'd print about me love iv counthry, they'd print fifty about me love iv dhrink. . . .

"They niver leave th' ladies out iv these stories iv th' gr-reat. A woman that marries a janius has a fine chance iv her false hair becomin' more immortal thin his gr-reat-est deed. It don't make anny diff'rence if all she knew about her marital hero was that he was a consistent feeder, a sleepy husband, an' indulgent to his childher an' some-times to himsilf, an' that she had to darn his socks. Nearly all th' gr-reat men had something th' matther with their wives. I always thought Mrs. Wash'n'ton, who was th' wife iv th' father iv our counthry, though childless her-silf, was about right. She looks good in th' pitchers, with a shawl ar-round her neck an' a frilled night-cap on her head. But Hogan says she had a tongue sharper thin George's soord, she insulted all his frinds, an' she was much older thin him. As f'r George, he was a case. I wish th' counthry had got itsilf a diff'rent father. A gr-reat moral rellijous counthry like this desarves a betther parent.

"They were all alike. I think iv Bobby Burns as a man that wrote good songs, aven if they were in a bar-brous accint, but Hogan thinks iv him as havin' a load all th' time an' bein' th' scandal iv his parish. I remimber Andhrew Jackson as th' man that licked th' British at New Orleans be throwin' cotton bales at thim, but Hogan remimbers him as a man that cudden't spell an' had a wife who smoked a corncob pipe. I remimber Abraham Lincoln f'r freein' th' slaves, but Hogan remimbers how he used to cut loose yarns that made th' bartinder shake th' stove harder thin it needed. I remimber Grant f'r what he done ar-round Shiloh whin he was young, but Hogan remimbers him f'r what he done ar-round New York whin he was old.

"An' so it goes. Whin a lad with nawthin' else to do starts out to write a bi-ography about a gr-reat man, he don't go to th' war departmint or th' public library. No, sir, he begins to search th' bureau dhrawers, old pigeon-holes, th' records iv th' polis coort, an' th' recollections iv th' hired girl. He likes letters betther thin annything else. He don't care much f'r th' kind beginnin': 'Dear wife, I'm settin' in front iv th' camp fire wearin' th' flannel chest protector ye made me, an' dhreamin' iv ye,'

but if he can find wan beginnin': 'Little Bright Eyes: Th'
old woman has gone to th' counthry,' he's th' happiest
bi-ographer ye cud see in a month's thravel. . . .

"It seems to me, Hinnissy, that this here thing called
bi-ography is a kind iv an offset f'r histhry. Histhry lies
on wan side, an' bi-ography comes along an' makes it
rowl over an' lie on th' other side. Th' historyan says, go
up; th' bi-ographer says, come down among us. I don't
believe ayether iv thim.

"I was talkin' with Father Kelly about it afther Hogan
wint out. 'Were they all so bad, thim men that I've been
brought up to think so gloryous?' says I. 'They were
men,' says Father Kelly. 'Ye mustn't believe all ye hear
about thim, no matther who says it,' says he. 'It's a thrait
iv human nature to pull down th' gr-reat an' sthrong.
Th' hero sthruts through histhry with his chin up in th'
air, his scipter in his hand an' his crown on his head. But
behind him dances a boot-black imitatin' his walk an'
makin' faces at him. Fame invites a man out iv his house
to be crowned f'r his gloryous deeds, an' sarves him with
a warrant f'r batin' his wife. 'Tis not in th' nature iv
things that it shuddn't be so. We'd all perish iv humilya-
tion if th' gr-reat men iv th' wurruld didn't have nachral
low-down thraits. If they don't happen to possess thim, we
make some up f'r thim. We allow no man to tower over us.
Wan way or another we level th' wurruld to our own
height. If we can't reach th' hero's head we cut off his
legs. It always makes me feel aisier about mesilf whin I
r-read how bad Julius Cayzar was. An' it stimylates
compytition. If gr-reatness an' goodness were hand in

hand 'tis small chance anny iv us wud have iv seein' our pitchers in th' pa-apers.'

"An' so it is that the battles ye win, th' pitchers ye paint, th' people ye free, th' childher that disgrace ye, th' false step iv ye'er youth, all go thundherin' down to immortality together. An' afther all, isn't it a good thing? Th' on'y bi-ography I care about is th' one Mulligan th' stone-cutter will chop out f'r me. I like Mulligan's style, f'r he's no flatthrer, an' he has wan model iv biography that he uses f'r old an' young, rich an' poor. He merely writes something to th' gin'ral effect that th' deceased was a wondher, an' lets it go at that."

"Which wud ye rather be, famous or rich?" asked Mr. Hennessy.

"I'd like to be famous," said Mr. Dooley, "an' have money enough to buy off all threatenin' bi-ographers."

PRINTER AND EDITOR

"Afther awhile th' iditor come in an' he swore more thin annybody else. But 'twas aisy to see he'd not larned th' thrade iv printer. He swore with th' enthusyasm an' inacc'racy iv an amachoor, though I mus' say he had his good pints. I wisht I cud raymimber what it was he called th' Czar iv Rooshya f'r dyin' jus' as th' pa-aper was goin' to press. I cud've often used it since. But it's slipped me mind."

HISTORY

"Big Bill" Taft succeeded Roosevelt as President. "Bath House John" was a notoriously corrupt political leader in Chicago.

"I know histhry isn't thrue, Hinnissy, because it ain't like what I see ivry day in Halsted Sthreet. If any wan comes along with a histhry iv Greece or Rome that'll show me th' people fightin', gettin' dhrunk, makin' love, gettin' marrid, owin' th' grocery man an' bein' without hard-coal, I'll believe they was a Greece or Rome, but not befure. Historyans is like doctors. They are always lookin' f'r symptoms. Those iv them that writes about their own times examines th' tongue an' feels th' pulse an' makes a wrong dygnosis. Th' other kind iv histhry is a postmortem examination. It tells ye what a counthry died iv. But I'd like to know what it lived iv."

⚜ ⚜ ⚜

"THERE'S ON'Y wan thing that wud make me allow mesilf to be a hero to th' American people, an' that is it don't last long. A few columns in th' newspaper, a speech in Congress, assault an' batthry be a mob in th' sthreet, a flatthrin' offer fr'm a dime museem, an' thin ye sink back into th' discard an' are not mintioned agin onless ye get into jail, whin ye have a more extended notice thin ye'er crime entitles ye to.

"Oh, as Hogan says, why shud th' spirit iv mortal be proud? Many's th' hero I've known in me day—gin'rals, admirals, polismen, firemen, prize-fighters, pedesthreens, bicycle riders, actors, authors, conkerers iv thirty quails in thirty days, an' where are they now, I'll ask ye? Down in th' coal cellar iv th' Hall iv Fame with th' rest iv us polthroons.

"Histhry will do thim justice, says ye? Ye needn't be too sure about that. Don't make any foolish bets on histhry. Like a good many people that I know, th' Muse iv Histhry, as Hogan wud say, has a long mim'ry but 'tis inaccrate. 'Tis like a cousin iv mine that cud remimber things that happened forty years ago, but they were niver so. A little while ago there was a fellow come over here that wrote a histhry iv Rome. This country, they tell me, is like Rome, an' is goin' to have th' same ending because iv th' large Eyetalyan popylation in both.

"Anyhow, all I know about Rome is what Hogan has told me, an' he was always boostin' up Joolyus Cayzar to me. I got an idee fr'm Hogan's talk that Joolyus Cayzar was a fine man; a little gay, mind ye, with th' ladies, but a fine man. . . . But this profissor iv histhry says Hogan is all wrong. 'Joolyus Cayzar was be no means th' tulip he is pitchered be historyans nearer his time thin mesilf,' says he. 'The further ye get away fr'm anny peeryod th' betther ye can write about it. Ye 're not subjick to interruptions be people that were there. I wud not undertake to write a histhry iv Peorya in nineteen hundherd an' eight, but if ye want th' latest news from Rome two thousand years ago, hand me that fountain pen. Far fr'm bein' a gr-reat man, Joolyus Cayzar was a pretty ordhinry charackter. He was always out f'r th' money. All iv his alleged wars were carrid on to help th' grocery business iv Rome that he was a secret pardner in.

He was a mean, close-fisted man. He done Cicero out of
his house be threatenin' to build a liv'ry stable next dure
to it, an' thin buyin' it cheap, an' his throuble with
Pompey come fr'm sellin' his old chum a horse that he
swore anny child cud dhrive, an' that run away with
Mrs. Pompey in Centhral Park, an' smashed Pompey's
best two-seated chariot. He was killed in a barroom be
Brutus, a worthless fellow that he'd adopted to get hold
iv his money. Th' real hero iv th' peeryod was Marcus
Mephitus Jenks. It was Jenks that th' glory an' grandeur
iv Rome is due to. It was Jenks who won th' battles, Jenks
that rayformed th' almanac, an' Jenks that modeled th'
laws. But Jenks was a modest hero. He had no press
agent. Sthrange to say, I can find no contimpry rifrences
to Jenks but a few vulgar jokes. But he was a great man.
Now that th' clouds iv calumy has rolled away it gives
me great pleasure to say that Jenks, not Cayzar, was th'
boy. . . .'

"An' there ye are, Hinnissy. How do you know what
Histhry is goin' to say about these here stirrin' times that
we're livin' in? A few thousand iv years fr'm now a visitor fr'm New Zealand, as Hogan says, surveyin' th' roons
iv th' Fort Wayne freight house fr'm a broken arch iv
Jackson sthreet bridge, may run acrost a copy iv
th' *Daily Bazoo,* an' write a story iv th' state iv America in nineteen hundherd an' nine: 'Th' principal occy-
pations iv th' people were murdher, divoorce, prize-
fightin', lynching, Marathon racin', abduction, burglary,
an' Salomying. Ivrybody was stealin' annything they cud
lay their hands on. A naygur prize-fighter havin' baten a
white prize-fighter, an almost univarsal demand arose

fr'm all classes f'r th' renowned James J. Jeffries to issue fr'm th' seclusion iv his saloon an' put a head on th' Senegambyan. So intent were th' people on their barbarous pastimes that th' full name iv th' prisidint at th' time has been lost. All th' historyan can find about him is that his name was Teddy, an' that he spint his time shootin' hippy pottymusses in Africa, lavin' th' conthrol iv th' counthry to wealthy malyfactors who had put him into office. He was succeeded be an effyminate charackter, who is now recalled only because he consumed forty opposums (an extinct marsoopyal) in forty consecutive days, an' played a game called bumple-puppy, which consisted in apparently purposely missing a small gutta-perchy ball placed on a pile iv x sand. All that is further known about this charackter is that he was called "Big Bill," an' is said to have weighed four tons. Th' most prominent citizen iv th' decayin' raypublic besides James J. Jeffries was Lydia Pinkham. Ivrywhere was public an' private corruption, low ambitions an' base amusements. But amidst th' riot iv corruption a few points stand out in contemperory lithrachoor to show that there were pure men an' women makin' th' brave battle f'r th' human race. Tens iv thousands iv suffrin' people were cured iv incurable diseases be usin' Befoolim, a remedy enthrusted to th' wurruld be an old Indyan herb doctor an' mannyfacthered an' sold be unknown philanthropists at a dollar a bottle. Millyons iv dollars were given away annually be th' promoters iv mining schemes; an' there arose in th' city iv Chicago, as if to shame his venal surroundings, a pathrite who worked so unselfishly in th' cause iv civic purity that he won th' affectionate surname iv th' "Bath House." ' . . .

"As Hogan says, ivry man is a hero excipt thim that have vallays. If ye black ye'er own shoes, shave ye'ersilf, an' turn on th' water in ye'er own bath ye're a hero, ex-officio, as th' sayin' goes. All me acquaintances are heroes. I niver yet knew a man that hired another man to help him on with his shirt. An' if Congress goes on passin' risolutions thankin' la-ads f'r wurrukin' when there was nawthin' else to do, they'll have to get some new presses in th' govermint printing office. Faith, who ain't a hero amongst us all, all us inexpeeryenced sailors on a ship that's sinking slowly undher our feet, day be day an' year be year? Some ships gets stove in arly an' some late, but they all go down. An' here we are on boord laughin', an' atin', an' quarrlin', an' schemin', an' layin' out a new course ivry hour with ne'er a thought iv sindin' a 'C. Q. D.'"

"Be th' way," said Mr. Hennessy, "ye spoke of vallays. What is a vallay, annyhow? What does he do?"

"A vallay," said Mr. Dooley, "as I undherstand it, is an English gintleman who has arose be conscientious wurruk to th' position iv a boot-jack."

OUR MODERN NEWSPAPERS

"A gr-reat panorama iv life is th' daily press. Here ye can meet kings, imp'rors, an' prisidints, murdhrers, scientists, highway robbers, an' s'ciety leaders; watch dynasties tumble an' heavyweight champeens; see gr-reat cities rocked be earthquakes an' larn to tak th' knife be th' handle, not th' blade whin 'atin' spinach."

MR. DOOLEY ON WOMEN AND THEIR PROBLEMS

❧

"Faith, they're all alike. If it ain't a sthraight stick, it's a crooked wan; an' th' man was niver yet born, if he had a hump on his back as big as a coal-scuttle an' had a face like th' back iv a hack, that cudden't get th' wink iv th' eye fr'm some woman. They're all alike, all alike. Not that I've annything again thim; 'tis thim that divides our sorrows an' doubles our joys, an' sews chiny buttons on our pa-ants an' mends our shirts with blue yarn. But they'll lead a man to desthruction an' back agin, thim same women."

WOMAN SUFFRAGE

"They haven't th' right to vote, but they have th' priv'lege iv controllin' th' man ye ilict. They haven't th' right to make laws, but they have th' priv'lege iv breakin' thim, which is betther. They haven't th' right iv a fair thrile be a jury iv their peers; but they have th' priv'lege iv an unfair thrile be a jury iv their admirin' infeeryors. If I cud fly d'ye think I'd want to walk?"

♣ ♣ ♣

"I SEE BE th' pa-apers that th' ladies in England have got up in their might an' demanded a vote."

"A what?" cried Mr. Hennessy.

"A vote," said Mr. Dooley.

"Th' shameless viragoes," said Mr. Hennessy. . . .

"Why," said Mr. Dooley, "they wuddn't know how to vote. They think it's an aisy job that anny wan can do, but it ain't. It's a man's wurruk, an' a sthrong man's with a sthrong stomach. I don't know annything that requires what Hogan calls th' exercise iv manly vigor more thin votin'. It's th' hardest wurruk I do in th' year. I get up befure daylight an' thramp over to th' Timple iv Freedom, which is also th' office iv a livery stable. Wan iv th' judges has a cold in his head an' closes all th' windows. Another judge has built a roarin' fire in a round stove an' is cookin' red-hots on it. Th' room is lit with candles an' karosene lamps, an' is crowded with pathrites who haven't been to bed. At th' dure are two or three polismen that maybe ye don't care to meet. Dock O'Leary says he don't

know annything that'll exhaust th' air iv a room so quick
as a polisman in his winter unyform. All th' pathrites an',
as th' pa-apers call thim, th' high-priests iv this here
sacred rite, ar-re smokin' th' best seegars that th' token
money iv our counthry can buy.

"In th' pleasant warmth iv th' fire, th' harness on th'
walls glows an' puts out its own peculiar aromy. Th'
owner iv th' sanchooary iv Liberty comes in, shakes up a
bottle iv liniment made iv carbolic acid, pours it into
a cup an' goes out. Wan iv th' domestic attindants iv th'
guests iv th' house walks through fr'm makin' th' beds.
Afther a while th' chief judge, who knows me well,
because he shaves me three times a week, gives me a
contimchous stare, asks me me name an' a number iv
scand'lous questions about me age.

"I'm timpted to make an angry retort, whin I see th'
polisman movin' nearer, so I take me ballot an' wait
me turn in th' booth. They're all occupied be writhin'
freemen, callin' in sthrangled voices f'r somewan to light
th' candle so they'll be sure they ain't votin' th' prohybition ticket. Th' calico sheets over th' front iv th' booths
wave an' ar-re pushed out like th' curtains iv a Pullman
car whin a fat man is dhressin' inside while th' thrain is
goin' r-round a curve. In time a freeman bursts through,
with perspyration poorin' down his nose, hurls his suffrage at th' judge an' staggers out. I plunge in, sharpen
an inch iv lead pencil be rendin' it with me teeth, mutilate
me ballot at th' top iv th' Dimmycratic column, an' run
f'r me life.

"Cud a lady do that, I ask ye? No, sir, 'tis no job f'r
th' fair. It's men's wurruk. Molly Donahue wants a vote,

but though she cud bound Kamachatka as aisily as ye cud this precinct, she ain't qualified f'r it. It's meant f'r gr-reat sturdy American pathrites like Mulkowsky th' Pollacky down th' sthreet. He don't know yet that he ain't votin' f'r th' King iv Poland. He thinks he's still over there pretindin' to be a horse instead iv a free American givin' an imytation iv a steam dhredge.

"On th' first Choosday afther th' first Monday in November an' April a man goes ar-round to his house, wakes him up, leads him down th' sthreet, an' votes him th' way ye'd wather a horse. He don't mind inhalin' th' air iv liberty in a livery stable. But if Molly Donahue wint to vote in a livery stable, th' first thing she'd do wud be to get a broom, sweep up th' flure, open th' windows, disinfect th' booths, take th' harness fr'm th' walls, an' hang up a pitcher iv Niagary be moonlight, chase out th' watchers an' polis, remove th' seegars, make th' judges get a shave, an' p'raps invalydate th' iliction. It's no job f'r her, an' I told her so.

"'We demand a vote,' says she. 'All right,' says I, 'take mine. It's old, but it's trustworthy an' durable. It may look a little th' worse f'r wear fr'm bein' hurled again a Republican majority in this counthry f'r forty years, but it's all right. Take my vote an' use it as ye please,' says I, 'an' I'll get an hour or two exthry sleep iliction day mornin',' says I. 'I've voted so often I'm tired iv it annyhow,' says I. 'But,' says I, 'why shud anny wan so young an' beautiful as ye want to do annything so foolish as to vote?' says I. 'Ain't we intelligent enough?' says she. 'Ye're too intilligent,' says I. 'But intilligence don't give ye a vote.' . . .

"I believe ye're in favor iv it ye'ersilf," said Mr. Hennessy.

"Faith," said Mr. Dooley, "I'm not wan way or th' other. I don't care. What diff'rence does it make? I wudden't mind at all havin' a little soap an' wather, a broom an' a dusther applied to polyticks. It wuddn't do anny gr-reat harm if a man cuddn't be illicited to office onless he kept his hair combed an' blacked his boots an' shaved his chin wanst a month. Annyhow, as Hogan says, I care not who casts th' votes iv me counthry so long as we can hold th' offices. An' there's on'y wan way to keep the women out iv office, an' that's to give thim a vote."

MARRIAGE

"A marrid man gets th' money, Hinnissy, but a bachelor man gets th' sleep. Whin all me marrid frinds is off to wurruk poundin' th' ongrateful sand an' wheelin' th' rebellyous slag, in th' heat iv th' afthernoon, ye can see ye'er onfortchnit bachelor frind perambulatin' up an' down th' shady side iv th' sthreet, with an umbrelly over his head an' a wurrud iv cheer fr'm young an' old to enliven his loneliness."

"But th' childher?" asked Mr. Hennessy slyly.

"Childher!" said Mr. Dooley. "Sure I have th' finest fam'ly in th' city. Without scandal I'm th' father iv ivry child in Ar-rchey Road fr'm end to end."

"An' none iv ye'er own," said Mr. Hennessy.

"I wish to hell, Hinnissy," said Mr. Dooley savagely, "ye'd not lean again that mirror, I don't want to have to tell ye agin."

MR. DOOLEY, EDUCATOR

"Not that I'm bothered about posterity. Let it go its way an' I'll go mine. I don't see anny raison f'r givin' betther sinse to a race iv impydint omadhons that a hundherd years fr'm now will be laughin' at th' funny clothes I wear an' wonderin' how I managed to get around in a clumsy masheen like an airplane."

THE EDUCATION OF THE YOUNG

"If ye had a boy wud ye sind him to colledge?" asked Mr.
Hennessy.
"Well," said Mr. Dooley, "at th' age whin a boy is fit to be
in colledge I wudden't have him around th' house."

⚜ ⚜ ⚜

THE TROUBLED Mr. Hennessy had been telling
Mr. Dooley about the difficulty of making a choice of
schools for Packy Hennessy, who at the age of six was at
the point where the family must decide his career.

" 'Tis a big question," said Mr. Dooley, "an' wan that
seems to be worryin' th' people more thin it used to whin
ivry boy was designed f'r th' priesthood, with a full undherstandin' be his parents that th' chances was in favor
iv a brick yard. Nowadays they talk about th' edycation iv
th' child befure they choose th' name. 'Tis: 'Th' kid talks
in his sleep. 'Tis th' fine lawyer he'll make.' Or, 'Did ye
notice him admirin' that photygraph? He'll be a gr-reat
journalist.' Or, 'Look at him fishin' in Uncle Tim's watch
pocket. We must thrain him f'r a banker.' Or, 'I'm afraid
he'll niver be sthrong enough to wurruk. He must go into
th' church.' Befure he's baptized too, d'ye mind. 'Twill not
be long befure th' time comes whin th' soggarth'll chris-
ten th' infant: 'Judge Pathrick Aloysius Hinnissy, iv th'
Northern District iv Illinye,' or 'Profissor P. Aloysius
Hinnissy, LL.D., S.T.D., P.G.N., iv th' faculty iv Nothre

Dame.' Th' innocent child in his cradle, wondherin' what ails th' mist iv him an' where he got such funny lookin' parents fr'm, has thim to blame that brought him into th' wurruld if he dayvilops into a sicond story man befure he's twinty-wan an' is took up be th' polis. Why don't you lade Packy down to th' occylist an' have him fitted with a pair iv eye-glasses? Why don't ye put goloshes on him, give him a blue umbrelly an' call him a doctor at wanst an' be done with it?

"To my mind, Hinnissy, we're wastin' too much time thinkin' iv th' future iv our young, an' thryin' to larn thim early what they oughtn't to know till they've growed up. We sind th' childher to school as if 'twas a summer garden where they go to be amused instead iv a pini-tinchry where they're sint f'r th' original sin. Whin I was a la-ad I was put at me ah-bee abs, th' first day I set fut in th' school behind th' hedge an' me head was sore inside an' out befure I wint home. Now th' first thing we larn th' future Mark Hannas an' Jawn D. Gateses iv our naytion is waltzin', singin', an' cuttin' pitchers out iv a book. We'd be much betther teachin' thim th' sthrangle hold, f'r that's what they need in life.

"I know what'll happen. Ye'll sind Packy to what th' Germans call a Kindygartin, an' 'tis a good thing f'r Germany, because all a German knows is what some wan tells him, an' his grajation papers is a certy-ficate that he don't need to think annymore. But we've inthrajooced it into this counthry, an' whin I was down seein' if I cud injooce Rafferty, th' Janitor iv th' Isaac Muggs Grammar School, f'r to vote f'r Riordan—an' he's goin' to—I dhropped in on Cassidy's daughter, Mary Ellen, an' see

her kindygartnin'. Th' childher was settin' ar-round on
th' flure an' some was moldin' dachshunds out iv mud an'
wipin' their hands on their hair, an' some was carvin'
figures iv a goat out iv paste-board an' some was singin'
an' some was sleepin' an' a few was dancin' an' wan la-ad
was pullin' another la-ad's hair. 'Why don't ye take th'
coal shovel to that little barbaryan, Mary Ellen?' says I.
'We don't believe in corporeal punishment,' says she.
'School shud be made pleasant f'r th' childher," she says.
'Th' child who's hair is bein' pulled is larnin' patience,'
she says, 'an' th' child that's pullin' th' hair is discoverin'
th' footility iv human indeavor,' says she. 'Well, oh,
well,' says I, 'times has changed since I was a boy,' I
says. 'Put thim through their exercises,' says I. 'Tommy,'
says I, 'spell cat,' I says. 'Go to th' divvle,' says th'
cheerub. 'Very smartly answered,' says Mary Ellen. 'Ye
shud not ask thim to spell,' she says. 'They don't larn that
till they get to colledge,' she says, 'an',' she says, 'sometimes not even thin,' she says. 'An' what do they larn?'
says I. 'Rompin',' she says, 'an' dancin',' she says, 'an' inde-
pindance iv speech, an' beauty songs, an' sweet thoughts,
an' how to make home home-like,' she says. 'Well,'
says I, 'I didn't take anny iv thim things at colledge, so ye
needn't unblanket thim,' I says. 'I won't put thim through
anny exercise to-day,' I says. 'But whisper, Mary Ellen,'
says I, 'Don't ye niver feel like bastin' th' seeraphims?'
'The' teachin's iv Freebull and Pitzotly is conthrary to
that,' she says. 'But I'm goin' to be marrid an' lave th'
school on Choosdah, th' twinty-sicond iv Janooary,' she
says, 'an' on Mondah, th' twinty-first, I'm goin' to ask a
few iv th' little darlin's to th' house an',' she says, 'stew

thim over a slow fire,' she says. Mary Ellen is not a German, Hinnissy.

"Well, afther they have larned in school what they ar-re licked f'r larnin' in th' back yard—that is squashin' mud with their hands—they're conducted up through a channel iv free an' beautiful thought till they're r-ready f'r colledge. Mamma packs a few doylies an' tidies into son's bag, an' some silver to be used in case iv throuble with th' landlord, an' th' la-ad throts off to th' siminary. If he's not sthrong enough to look f'r high honors as a middleweight pugilist he goes into th' thought depart-mint. Th' prisidint takes him into a Turkish room, gives him a cigareet an' says : 'Me dear boy, what special branch iv larnin' wud ye like to have studied f'r ye be our com-pitint profissors ? We have a chair iv Beauty an' wan iv Puns an' wan iv Pothry on th' Changin' Hues iv th' Set-tin' Sun, an' wan on Platonic Love, an' wan on Non-sense Rhymes, an' wan on Sweet Thoughts, an' wan on How Green Grows th' Grass, an' wan on th' Relation iv Ice to th' Greek Idee iv God,' he says. 'This is all ye'll need to equip ye f'r th' perfect life, onless,' he says, 'ye intind bein' a dintist, in which case,' he says, 'we won't think much iv ye, but we have a good school where ye can larn that disgraceful thrade,' he says. An' th' la-ad makes his choice, an' ivry mornin' whin he's up in time he takes a whiff iv hasheesh an' goes off to hear Profissor Maryanna tell him that 'if th' dates iv human knowledge must be rejicted as subjictive, how much more must they be subjicted as rejictive if, as I think, we keep our thoughts fixed upon th' inanity iv th' finite in comparison

with th' onthinkable truth with th' ondivided an' onimagi-
nable reality. Boys, ar-re ye with me?' . . ."

"I don't undherstand a wurrud iv what ye're sayin',"
said Mr. Hennessy.

"No more do I," said Mr. Dooley. "But I believe 'tis as
Father Kelly says: 'Childher shuddn't be sint to school
to larn, but to larn how to larn. I don't care what ye larn
thim so long as 'tis onpleasant to thim.' 'Tis thrainin' they
need, Hinnissy. That's all. I niver cud make use iv what
I larned in colledge about thrigojoomethry an'—an'—
grammar an' th' welts I got on th' skull fr'm th' school-
masther's cane I have niver been able to turn to anny
account in th' business, but 'twas th' bein' there an' havin'
to get things to heart without askin' th' meanin' iv thim
an' goin' to school cold an' comin' home hungry, that
made th' man iv me ye see befure ye."

"That's why th' good woman's throubled about Packy,"
said Hennessy.

"Go home," said Mr. Dooley.

THE DESCENT OF MAN

"There's on'y wan thing I can say in favor iv science."

"What's that?" asked Mr. Hennessy.

"It's give us a good definse f'r our crimes," said Mr.
Dooley. "F'r if we were started th' way th' Bible says we
have wasted our opporchunities an' ought to be in jail;
but if our ancesthors were what this scientist says they
ar-re anny good lawyer cud get us off be pointin' out that
with our bringin' up it's a miracle we ain't cannybals."

MR. CARNEGIE'S GIFT

*The Carnegie Trust for Scottish Universities was created
in 1901 with a ten million dollar endowment. Carnegie had
turned over active control of his steel company the same year
to the United States Steel Corporation which J. P. Morgan
had created as the most powerful corporation in the United
States, with the possible exception of the Standard Oil
Company. John D. Rockefeller, of the latter corporation,
was contributing heavily to the support of the University of
Chicago. Homestead, Pennsylvania, was the location of
one of the Carnegie steel mills, well known to newspaper
readers because of the sanguinary labor troubles there in
1892.*

♧   ♧   ♧

"TIN MILLYON dollars to make th' Scotch a larned
people," said Mr. Dooley.

"Who done that?" asked Mr. Hennessy.

"Andhrew Carnaygie," says Mr. Dooley. "He reaches
down into his pocket where he keeps th' change an' pulls
up tin millyon bawbies, an' says he: 'Boys, take ye'er
fill iv larnin', an' charge it to me,' he says. 'Divvle hang
th' expinse,' he says. 'The' more th' merryer,' he says.
'A short life an' a happy wan,' he says. 'Larn annything
ye like,' he says. 'Name ye'er priference,' he says, 'an'
put it all down to Carnaygie,' he says. . . .

"Th' day whin we millyonaires bought yachts an'
brown stone houses with mansard roofs onto thim an'
were proud iv havin' thim has gone by, Hinnissy. 'Twill

not be long befure none will be so poor as not to own a private yacht, an' th' nex' time a Coxey army starts f'r Wash'n'ton, it'll ride in a specyal vestibule thrain. What was luxuries a few years ago is mere necessities now. Pierpont Morgan calls in wan iv his office boys, th' prisidint iv a naytional bank, an' says he, 'James,' he says, 'take some change out iv th' damper an' r-run out an' buy Europe f'r me,' he says. 'I intind to re-organize it an' put it on a paying basis,' he says. 'Call up th' Czar an' th' Pope an' th' Sultan an' th' Impror Willum, an' tell thim we won't need their sarvices afther nex' week,' he says. 'Give thim a year's salary in advance. An', James,' he says, 'ye betther put that r-red headed book-keeper near th' dure in charge iv th' continent. He doesn't seem to be doin' much,' he says. Ye see, Hinnissy, th' game has got so much bigger since we first made our money that if Jay Gould was to come back to earth with some iv th' plays we used to wondher about, he'd feel like an old clothes man. So, 'tis nawthin' strange whin Jawn D., or Andhrew, or mesilf, buys a string iv universities an' puts in tin millyons to teach th' young idee how to loot. Befure long we'll be racin' thim. I don't know but what 'tis th' finest kind iv spoort th' wurruld has iver heerd about.

"Father Kelly don't think as much iv it as I do. He was in here las' night, an' says he: 'Ye can't buy idjacation f'r people,' he says. 'If ye cud, th' on'y man in th' wurruld that knew annything wud be Jawn D. Rockefeller,' he says. 'Idjacation,' he says, 'is something that a man has to fight f'r an' pull out iv its hole be th' hair iv its head,' he says. 'That's th' reason it's so precious,' he says. 'They'se so little iv it, an' it's so hard to get,' he says. 'They'se anny quantity iv gab that looks like it, but it ain't th' rale thing,' he says. 'Th' wurruld is full iv people wearin' false joolry iv that kind,' he says, 'but afther they've had it f'r a long time, it tur-rns green an' blue, an' some day whin they thry to get something on it, th' pawn-broker throws thim out. No, sir, idjacation means throu-ble an' wurruk an' worry, an' Andhrew Carnaygie himsilf is th' on'y wan I know that's been able to pick it up in th' brief inthervals between wan dollar an' another,' he says. 'Th' smartest man in my day at th' Colledge iv th' Sacred Heart was a la-ad who used to come to school with a half a dozen biled potatoes in an ol' newspaper, an' sawed wood all evenin' to pay f'r his larnin'. Annything that boy larned, he larned, ye bet. Ivry line iv Latin he knew riprisinted a stick iv wood, an' belonged to him. 'Twasn't borrowed at th' back dure iv a millyonaire. He knew more thin anny man I iver see, an' he's now at th' head iv wan iv th' best little wan room schools in Du Page County,' he says. 'Andhrew Carnaygie's tin millyons won't make anny Robert Burns,' he says. 'It may make more Andhrew Carnaygies,' says I. 'They'se enough to go round now,' says he.

"I don't know that he's right. I don't know f'r sure that Father Kelly is r-right, Hinnissy. I don't think it makes anny difference wan way or th' other how free ye make idjacation. Men that wants it 'll have it be hook an' be crook, an' thim that don't ra-aly want it niver will get it. Ye can lade a man up to th' university, but ye can't make him think. But if I had as much money as I said I had a

minyit ago, I'd endow a bar'l iv oatmeal f'r ivry boy in
Scotland that wanted an idjacation, an' lave it go at that.
Idjacation can always be had, but they'se niver enough
oatmeal in Scotland."

"Or Homestead," said Mr. Hennessy.

"Or Homestead," said Mr. Dooley.

THE END OF THINGS

"I'm dead, mind ye, but I can hear a whisper in th'
furthest corner iv th' room. Ivry wan is askin' ivry wan
else why did I die. 'It's a gr-reat loss to th' counthry,' says
Hogan. 'It is,' says Donahue. 'He was a fine man,' says
Clancy. 'As honest a man as iver dhrew th' breath iv life,'
says Schwartzmeister. 'I hope he forgives us all th' harm
we attimpted to do him,' says Donahue. 'I'd give annything to have him back,' says Clancy. 'He was this and
that, th' life iv th' party, th' sowl iv honor, th' frind iv th'
disthressed, th' boolwark iv th' Constitution, a pathrite, a
gintleman, a Christyan an' a scholard.' 'An' such a roguish
way with him,' says th' Widow O'Brien.

"That's what I think, but if I judged fr'm expeeryence
I'd know it'd be, 'It's a nice day f'r a dhrive to th' cimitry.
Did he lave much?' No man is a hero to his undhertaker."

MR. DOOLEY, JOURNALIST

❧

"What's goin' on this week in th' pa-apers?" asked Mr. Hennessy.

"Ivrything," said Mr. Dooley. "It's been a turbylint week. I can hardly sleep iv nights thinkin' iv th' doin's iv people. . . .

"Sure, all that's no news," said Mr. Hennessy, discontentedly. 'Hasn't there annything happened? Hasn't anny wan been—been kilt?"

"There ye ar-re," said Mr. Dooley. "Be news ye mane misfortune. I suppose near ivry wan does. What's wan man's news is another man's throubles. In these hot days, I'd like to see a pa-aper with nawthin' in it but affectionate wives an' loyal husbands an' prosp'rous, smilin' people an' money in th' bank an' three a day. That's what I'm lookin' f'r in th' hot weather."

"Th' newspapers have got to print what happens," said Mr. Hennessy.

"No," said Mr. Dooley, "they've got to print what's diff'rent. Whiniver they begin to put headlines on happiness, contint, varchoo, an' charity, I'll know things is goin' as wrong with this counthry as I think they ar-re ivry naytional campaign."

NEWSPAPER PUBLICITY

"Th' newspa-apers ar-re a gr-reat blessing. I don't know what I'd do without thim. If it wasn't f'r thim I'd have no society fit to assocyate with—on'y people like ye'ersilf an' Hogan. But th' pa-apers opens up life to me an' gives me a speakin' acquaintance with th' whole wurruld. . . . I know more about th' Impror iv Chiny thin me father knew about th' people in th' next parish."

"No wan iver writes to an iditor to say, 'That was a fine article ye had in ye'er vallyable journal on th' Decline iv Greek Art Since th' Time iv Moses.' No, sir, whin an indignant subscriber takes his pen in hand at all it is to says: 'Sir, me attintion has been called to a lyin' article in ye'er scurr'lous sheet called "Is Pro-hibition a Failure?" This is to tell that I will hinceforth niver call f'r ye'er dasthardly handbill at th' readin'-room again. Print this if ye dare in ye'er mendacious organ iv th' Jesuits. Ye'ers very respectfully, Vox Populy an' tin thousand others.'"

♧ ♧ ♧

"WERE YE iver in th' pa-apers?" asked Mr. Dooley.
"Wanst," said Mr. Hennessy. "But it wasn't me. It was another Hinnissy. Was you?"
"Manny times," said Mr. Dooley. "Whin I was prom'-nent socyally, ye cud hardly pick up a pa-aper without seein' me name in it an' th' amount iv th' fine. Ye must lade a very simple life. Th' newspaper is watchin' most iv us fr'm th' cradle to th' grave, an' befure an' afther.

Whin I was a la-ad thrippin' continted over th' bogs iv Roscommon, ne'er an iditor knew iv me existence, nor I iv his. Whin annything was wrote about a man 'twas put this way: 'We undhershtand on good authority that M—l—chi H——y, Esquire, is on thrile before Judge G——n on an accusation iv l——c—ny. But we don't think it's true.' Nowadays th' larceny is discovered be a newspa-aper. Th' lead pipe is dug up in ye'er back yard be a rayporther who knew it was there because he helped ye bury it. A man knocks at ye'er dure arly wan mornin' an' ye answer in ye'er nighty. 'In th' name iv th' law, I arrist ye,' says th' man seizin' ye be th' throat. 'Who ar-re ye?' ye cry. 'I'm a rayporther f'r th' *Daily Slooth*,' says he. 'Phottygrafter, do ye'er jooty!' Ye're hauled off in th' circylation wagon to th' newspaper office, where a con-fission is ready f'r ye to sign; ye're thried be a jury iv th' staff, sintinced be th' iditor-in-chief an' at tin o'clock Friday th' fatal thrap is sprung be th' fatal thrapper iv th' fam'ly journal.

"Th' newspaper does ivrything f'r us. It runs th' polis foorce an' th' banks, commands th' milishy, conthrols th' ligislachure, baptizes th' young, marries th' foolish, comforts th' afflicted, afflicts th' comfortable, buries th' dead an' roasts thim aftherward. They ain't annything it don't turn its hand to fr'm explainin' th' docthrine iv thransubstantiation to composin' saleratus biskit. Ye can get anny kind iv information ye want to in ye'er fav'rite newspaper about ye'ersilf or annywan else. What th' Czar whispered to th' Imp'ror Willum whin they were alone, how to make a silk hat out iv a wire matthress, how to settle th' coal sthrike, who to marry, how to get on with ye'er wife whin ye're marrid, what to feed th' babies, what doctor to call whin ye've fed thim as directed—all iv that ye'll find in th' pa-apers.

"They used to say a man's life was a closed book. So it is but it's an open newspaper. Th' eye iv th' press is on ye befure ye begin to take notice. Th' iditor obsarves th' stork hoverin' over th' roof iv 2978 ½ B Ar-rchey Road an' th' article he writes about it has a wink in it. 'Son an' heir arrives f'r th' Hon'rable Malachi Hinnissy,' says th' pa-aper befure ye've finished th' dhrink with th' doctor. An' afther that th' histhry iv th' offspring's life is found in th' press:

" 'It is undhershtud that there is much excitement in th' Hinnissy fam'ly over namin' th' lates' sign. Misther Hinnissy wishes it called Pathrick McGlue afther an uncle iv his, an' Mrs. Hinnissy is in favor iv namin' it Alfonsonita afther a Pullman car she seen wan day. Th' *Avenin' Fluff* offers a prize iv thirty dollars f'r th' bes' name f'r this projeny. Maiden ladies will limit their letters to three hundherd wurruds.'

" 'Above is a snap shot iv young Alfonsonita McGlue Hinnissy, taken on his sicond birthday with his nurse, Miss Angybel Blim' th' well-known specyal nurse iv th' *Avenin' Fluff*. At th' time th' phottygraft was taken, th' infant was about to bite Miss Blim which accounts f'r th' agynized exprission on that gifted writer's face. Th' *Avenin' Fluff* offers a prize iv four dollars to th' best answer to th' question: "What does th' baby think iv Miss Blim?" '

" 'Young Alf Hinnissy was siven years ol' yisterdah. A

rayporther iv th' *Fluff* sought him out an' indeavored to intherview him on th' Nicaragooan Canal, th' Roomanyan Jews, th' tahriff an' th' thrusts. Th' comin' statesman rayfused to be dhrawn out on these questions, his answer bein' a ready, "Go chase ye'ersilf, ye big stiff!" Afther a daylightful convarsation th' rayporther left, bein' followed to th' gate be his janial young host who hit him smartly in th' back with a brick. He is a chip iv th' ol' block.'

" 'Groton, Conn., April 8. Ye'er rayporther was privileged to see th' oldest son iv th' Hon'rable Malachi Hinnissy started at this siminary f'r th' idjacation iv young Englishmen bor-rn in America. Th' heir iv th' Hinnissys was enthered at th' exclusive school thirty years befure he was bor-rn. Owin' to th' uncertainty iv his ancesthors he was also enthered at Vassar. Th' young fellow took a lively intherest in th' school. Th' above phottygraft riprisints him mathriculatin'. Th' figures at th' foot ar-re Misther an' Mrs. Hinnissy. Those at th' head ar-re Profissor Peabody Plantagenet, prisidint iv th' instichoochion an' Officer Michael H. Rafferty. Young Hinnissy will remain here till he has a good cukkin' idjacation.' . . .

"An' so it goes. We march through life an' behind us marches th' phottygrafter an' th' rayporther. There are no such things as private citizens. No matther how private a man may be, no matther how secretly he steals, some day his pitcher will be in th' pa-aper along with Mark Hanna, Stamboul 2:01 1/2, Fitzsimmons' fightin' face, an' Douglas, Douglas, tin dollar shoe. He can't get away fr'm it. An' I'll say this f'r him, he don't want to. He wants to see what bad th' neighbors are doin' an' he wants thim to see what good he's doin'. He gets fifty per cint iv his wish; niver more. A man keeps his front window shade up so th' pa-apers can come along an' make a pitcher iv him settin' in his iligant furnished parlor readin' th' life iv Dwight L. Moody to his fam'ly. An' th' lad with th' phottygraft happens along at th' moment whin he is batin' his wife. If we wasn't so anxious to see our names among those prisint at th' ball, we wuddn't get into th' pa-apers so often as among those that ought to be prisint in th' dock. A man takes his phottygraft to th' iditor an' says he: 'Me attintion has been called to th' fact that ye'd like to print this mug iv a prom'nent philanthropist'; an' th' iditor don't use it till he's robbed a bank. Ivrybody is inthrested in what ivrybody else is doin' that's wrong. That's what makes th' newspapers. An' as this is a dimmy-cratic counthry where ivrybody was bor-rn akel to ivry-body else, aven if they soon outgrow it, an' where wan man's as good as another an' as bad, all iv us has a good chanst to have his name get in at laste wanst a year. Some goes in at Mrs. Rasther's dinner an' some as victims iv a throlley car, but ivrybody lands at last. They'll get ye afther awhile, Hinnissy. They'll print ye'er pitcher. But on'y wanst. A newspaper is to intertain, not to teach a moral lesson."

"D'ye think people likes th' newspapers iv th' prisint time?" asked Mr. Hennessy.

"D'ye think they're printed f'r fun?" said Mr. Dooley.

"A peeryodical, Hinnissy, is a pa-aper that ye buy a week befure it's out an' that is published a month befure ye buy it."

MR. DOOLEY AND THE
VICISSITUDES OF LIFE

"D'ye think th' wurruld is growin' worse?" Mr. Hennessy asked.
"I do not," said Mr. Dooley.
"D'ye think it's growin' betther?"
"No," said Mr. Dooley. *"If it's doin' annythin' it's just turnin' round as usual."*

"Whin I think what this gob iv arth is like that we live on f'r a few hours, spinnin' around f'r no sinsible raison in th' same foolish, lobsided circle, an' comin' back to th' same place ivry year, without thought or care iv th' poor crathers hangin' onto it, I'm inclined to think a betther race wud be wasted on it. We may be bad, but we're plenty good enough f'r what we get fr'm th' wurruld."

THE GIFT OF ORATORY

♣ ♣ ♣

"I SEE," SAID Mr. Dooley, "that a society has been formed to stop afther-dinner orathry an' I expict ivry day to read that its rooms has been raided by the polis. F'r, iv coorse, this is a murdher society, like th' Mafeeya. Th' on'y way ye can prevint an afther-dinner orator fr'm oratin' afther dinner is to sthrangle him. It wuddn't do anny good not to ask him to th' bankit. He'd go annyhow.

"He'd disguise himsilf as a waiter or concale himsilf behind th' potted palms an' as soon as th' dimmy-tassies came on he'd leap out an' begin: 'Misther Chairman an' gintlemen, I am reminded be this occasion iv a story that I got fr'm me ol' frind Dock Hostetter'—an' so on."

"Ye didn't always feel that way," said Mr. Hennessy.

"I know I didn't," said Mr. Dooley. " 'Twas wanst the hite of me ambition to stand up behind a bank iv flowers, with a good see-gar in wan hand an' a napkin in th' other an' wan minyit have me aujience convulsed with laughter an' another minyit dissolved in tears. I told ye a long time ago what a tur-rble fist I made iv it, how I f'rgot to commit anny part iv the oration to mimry excipt th' parts that ar-re printed in brackets like: applause, loud an' prolonged laughter, cries iv 'No, no. Go on,' an' th' like, an' how without utthrin' a wurrud I sunk to me chair a mute, ingloryous Dan'l Webster. Since thin I go to a bankit iv

235

th' Dimmycratic club on'y to injye mesilf be watchin' th' fellows that expicts to be called on f'r speeches an' obsarve th' wealthy conthractor that has just been ilicted goin' without nourishment because he don't know which fork to use.

"But because I was th' most tur-rble failure as an orator that th' wurruld has iver seen, is no raison why I should want to suppriss th' poor fellows be vi'lence. It's us that encourages them that is to blame. Ivry nation injyes some kind iv a crool spoort an' afther-dinner orathry is th' same with us as bull-fightin' is with the Spanyards.

"Did ye iver go to a bankit? Iv coorse not. Why did I ask ye such a foolish question? Well, ye go into a big room where there's a lot iv little tables occypied be people that ar-re there to injye thimsilves, an' a long, raised table where they stick th' condemned culprits. A man who has been chose because iv his harsh manners an' th' ready flow iv insults at his command sets in th' middle amongst thim. He's th' on'y wan at aise in th' line. An' why shuddn't he be at aise? He's the ixicutioner. Th' others ar-re pale with ambition an' fright. They do not ate or dhrink annything that's passed to thim. They don't speak to each other. Now an' thin they moisten their parched lips with a sip iv wather. But most iv th' time they're wurrukin' away with little stubs iv pencils polishin' up their last dyin' utthrances.

"Manewhile th' la-ads at th' little tables who ar-re not lookin' f'r fame or glory ar-re havin' a gran' time. It's 'Hey, waither, bring another goord iv that Fr-rinch cider,' 'Well, Mike, here's bad luck to ye,' 'Boy, some more dimmy-tassy.' Good stories ar-re goin' round, guests are stealin' each other's souvenirs to take home to th' childher, at a corner table four ol' gintlemen ar-re singin' in clost harmony: 'I was seein' Nelly home.' All at wanst th' chairman gets up, hammers f'r silence, an' inthrajooces th' first speaker in these glowin' terms: 'Gintlemen,' he says, 'th' best iv times must come to an end. We ar-re so unforchnit as to have with us to-night th' Hon'rable E. Lemuel Higgs, who is known to th' polis as th' Big Wind iv th' Sixteenth Ward. I don't know how he got in, but here he is. He has ast me to be allowed to addhress ye, an' owin' to th' prisince iv a few iv me mortal inimies in the aujience I have consinted. Guests ar-re requisted to injye thimsilves as best they can durin' his ballyhoo but I must remind thim that if they applaud him with th' chinyware they will be charged with breakage. Gintlemen, Misther Higgs.'

"At that th' poor fellow leaps to his feet. His face is now a light green in color an' it wears a smile that makes ye think he may have took an overdose iv sthrychnine. Befure he is fairly up he hurls a convivial story at th' aujience. It splutters f'r a minyit an' goes out in th' air like a fire-cracker on a rainy Foorth iv July. He thries another an' th' la-ads down below begin to scrape their feet an' move their chairs. Convarsation starts up again. Th' waiters thrip over chairs. There is a noise iv breakin' dishes in th' panthry. Th' fiddler in th' orchesthry choons his fiddle. An' th' ol' gintlemen in th' corner begin singin' th' sicond verse iv 'Seein' Nelly Home,' which is the same as th' first an' th' twinty-sivinth.

"But Higgs goes right on. He can't stop aven if he wanted to an' now he don't want to. Fin'lly th' brutal chairman hauls him back be th' coattail, yells 'Time' so that it can be heerd above th' hilarity; he murmurs a few wurruds iv thanks an' sets down in his chair, mops his face with a napkin, an' turns to his neighbor an' says: 'How d'ye think it wint?' But th' neighbor's throat is so dry that he can't answer. He's th' nex' victim to be led to th' thrapdure. An' mind ye these ar-re th' first speakers. Th' last orator, if he isn't dead iv fright be th' time he's called, has to compete with a dozen argyments an' close harmony quartets, th' loud laugh that speaks th' vacant bottle, an' maybe a rough-an'-tumble fight or two.

"I wanst knew a man that was a habbitchool afther-dinner speaker. He cuddn't pass a resthrant without composin' a speech, an' afther he'd finished a frugal meal iv wheat cakes an' dhraw-wan in a dairy lunch, he wud rise an', bowin' to the waithress, say, 'Misther Chairman' befure he cud recover himself. He was a pale, thin man because he attinded a bankit every night iv his life an' niver cud ate annything. 'Why d'ye do it, foolish wan?' says I. 'I don't know,' says he. 'I hate it. No wan can imagine th' suffrin' I endure while waitin' to be called on or th' reemorse that follows th' speech,' he says. Something ought to be done to heal these mis'rable brethren iv ours. But I don't believe in harsh methods. Little be little their mind an' body shud be strengthened. They shud be encouraged to shut up. All comic pa-apers shud be kept fr'm thim. Each afther-dinner orator shud be confined to a room be himsilf an' th' nurse shud serve his meals through th' thransom. No meal shud be spoke iv as dinner.

Ye niver heard iv an afther-breakfast orator or an afther-supper orator.

"I can remimber whin afther-dinner orathry was wan iv th' proudest instichoochions iv American life—whin th' sayin' was that hundherds iv people wint to bankits to hear Chansy Depoo talk an' so did Chansy Depoo. But that day has gone by. People ar-re tired iv amachoor orators, an' th' nex' step will be to hire thrained speakers to help us di-gest our vittles just the same as we hire thrained musicians. . . ."

"Ye 're on'y mad because ye failed," said Mr. Hennessey.

"Well," said Mr. Dooley, "what betther reason d'ye want? Besides, I didn't fail as bad as I might. I might iv made th' speech."

"I guess a man niver becomes an orator if he has annything to say, Hinnissy. If a lawyer thinks his client is innocint he talks to th' jury about th' crime. But if he knows where th' pris'ner hid th' plunder, he unfurls th' flag, throws out a few remarks about th' flowers an' th' bur-rds, an' asks th 'twelve good men an' thrue not to break up a happy Christmas, but to sind this man home to his wife an' childher, an' Gawd will bless thim if they ar-re iver caught in th' same perdicymint. Whiniver I go to a polytical meetin', an' th' la-ad with th' open-wurruk face mentions Rome or Athens I grab f'r me hat. I know he's not goin' to say annything that ought to keep me out iv bed. . . . An' be hivins, I don't want anny man to tell me that I'm a mimber iv wan iv th' grandest races th' sun has iver shone on. I know it already. If I wasn't I'd move out."

OLD AGE

"Many a man that cudden't direct ye to th' dhrug store on th' corner whin he was thirty will get a respectful hearin' whin age has further impaired his mind. . . .
"Why," said Mr. Hennessy, "ye'd give annythin' to be twinty-five agin."
"I wuddn't," said Mr. Dooley. "Why shud I want to grow old agin?"

♠ ♠ ♠

"'T IS STHRANGE," said Mr. Hennessy, "how few old people we see nowadays. Whin I was young, it seems to me there were hundherds iv thim in th' ward, tott'rin' around an' mumblin' their foolish ol' stories or spindin' half th' time in church on their shin-bones."

"How old ar-re ye?" Mr. Dooley asked. 'Ye needn't answer. I know to an hour. An' I want to tell ye, Hinnissy, that ye're long passed th' age iv thim decrepit relics.

"I raymimber hearin' ye say something about old Hick Malone wanst on a time. It was a very charitable an' pleasant thing an' dhrew me to ye. What did ye say? Ye said, 'Why don't they take that old derelick back in th' alley, put a bag over his head an' hit him with a sledge?'

"At th' time ye made this kind an' tender recommindation about ye'er aged neighbor, Mickeen was five years younger thin ye ar-re at this minyit. Yes, sir, th' dashin' young bucko that I see befure me in th' red tie is older thin th' man he sought to have threated like a broken down horse.

"There aren't fewer old people in th' ward today thin there were. There are more. There are twict as manny. On'y ye don't recgonize thim. They're disguised. They're disguised with clothes iv youth, but what is betther still, in th' Spirit iv Youth. . . .

"Whin I was a young man, a man iv fifty was given a good shove into th' corner an' told to stay there an' th' undhertaker wud be around in a few minyits. At forty a man was old, at fifty senile, at sixty a dotard an' if he lived to be siventy an' cud make signs with his hands th' fam'ly thought iv takin' him around th' counthry an' exhibitin' him along with th' wild man iv Borneo an' th' iddycated pig. His young frinds see him waltzin' down th' sthreet an' maybe thinkin' to himsilf what a dashin' figure he was cuttin', an' they said to thimsilves: 'Well, I hope th' Lord will take me before I get to be like that old dizzard.' An' whin he sprung his famous story that threw th' convintion iv th' vetherans iv th' Mexican war into convulsions in eighteen siventy-three, th' little childher looked down into their plates in shame an' th' bigger wans gazed at him as much as to say, 'Grampah is failin' fast.'

"An' look at Grampah now. Ye don't see him settin' in no corner waitin' f'r Tim Gavin to measure him f'r a name plate an' a dhress suit an' how wud he like to have th' crate lined. He's not settin' back listenin' f'r th' beatin' iv th' angel's wings that is comin' to get him an' take him where his worth will be betther apprecyated thin it is in th' fam'ly. Not be a damn sight. Th' ol' gazook is down town at th' bank firin' th' payin' teller iv sixty because he's inexpeeryenced or callin' loans in a voice that makes th' walls an' th' borrower quake. Or he's out on th' goluf links pastin' th' ball o'er hill an' dale. An' if th' gran'-childher don't explode over his quips th' nex' day finds him settin' in front iv th' fire with his last will an' testy-mint on his lap an' a blue pencil in his hand.

"Th' raison ye don't see anny old men around is because there aren't anny old men. They won't admit it. They rayfuse to go into th' discard. It's onfashionable to be venerable. Nobody wants th' respict that youth pays to age.

"There niver was such a thing, annyhow. It was on'y a bluff. F'r what respict cud hardy youth feel f'r Doddhr'n ol' Age settin' stingily in a corner an' dhroolin' about th' time he stormed th' heights iv Chupultepec an' captured Santa Anna with his wooden leg? No, sir, th' old boys demand, not respict f'r old age, which means that if ye iver knew annythin' ye've f'rgotten it, but f'r their nachral powers, bedad.

" 'I'm just as young as I used to be,' is th' naytional anthem an' it's a good wan. It's betther annyhow, thin 'Darlin', I am growin' old' or 'Massa's in th' cold, cold ground.' I'd rather see an old lady goin' into a cabaret f'r a whirl thin into a Rethreat F'r th' Aged. She'll last just as long an' she'll have a lot more fun.

"In my time whin a lady approached th' age iv thirty-five she begun to lay out th' white lace cap, th' half-mittens an' th' bombozine skirt an' pick out th' aisy chair in th' corner to prepare f'r a graceful old age in tyranny. Now at that inthrestin' peeryod, she takes a reef in her skirt an' begins to look f'r throuble.

"Th' other day I see little Timmy Cassidy talkin' to a slender crather with a hat shaped like half a mushmelon down over her ears an' a little wisp iv scarlet hair peepin' out in a most fascinatin' manner. 'Who was th' lark I see ye flirtin' with on th' corner?' says I.

" 'Don't ye know?' says he.

" 'I don't,' says I.

" 'She knows ye well,' says he. 'She's crazy about ye.'

" 'Who is it, ye young scapegrace?' says I.

" 'It's gramma,' says he. 'She got lost on her way to her dancin' lesson an' I had to lead her home,' he says. 'I'll tell her she made a hit with ye.'

" 'If ye do I'll murdher ye,' says I.

"But he did, th' imp, an' I got a letter fr'm her th' nex' day, askin' me wud I go to th' Gas Fitters Annyooal Outing with her. An' she's as old as an obelisk. But ye must niver judge a lady's age be her back or her ankles. . . .

"Th' on'y old people I see ar-re undher thirty. They are very old an' wurruld weary. They write old, old sad books. They have penethrated th' illusions iv life. They ar-re without hope. They look for'ard with longin' to th' peace iv th' grave. But, thin, iv coorse, th' oldest thing in th' wurruld is a two-months old baby. . . ."

"Dhress an' paint don't make people younger," said Mr. Hennessy. "Take Monica Casey. Ivrybody knows how old she is. If she's a day, she's——"

"Hol' on," said Mr. Dooley. "I'll have no wan discussin'

a lady's age in this place. Whin a man gets tellin' th' age iv wan iv his female rilitives, ye'd think fr'm th' figures he uses he was describin' th' naytional debt. A woman is as old as she looks to a man that likes to look at her. An' I ain't so sure about dhress an' habits not makin' us younger. What is old age annyhow? It's what Dock Einstein wud call a matther iv relativity. . . .

"Years are no measure iv age—excipt in a gin'ral way. Whin I was twinty a man iv forty was a patriarch to me. Now that I'm—niver mind—I look on a man iv ninety as no more thin machure. . . .

"Me advice to all who ar-re at th' pint iv succumbin' to th' timptation to be ol', is to fight it off. Don't let it git a holt on ye. Th' sooner ye get ol' th' longer ye'll be ol'. If ye get ol' at all, get ol' in modheration. Dhress against it, ate against it, sing against it, dhrink against it an' laugh against it. Thin whin that there disagreeable visitor, th' pa-apers call th' Grim Reaper, pulls th' dure bell ye can have th' hired girl say, 'Th' boss is not in. Ye'll have to call again.' An' if he pursoos ye to th' goluf coorse an' sees ye flayin' a bunker, he'll say: 'I guess this is th' wrong parthy. I'd best not bother him. That's a cross-lookin' niblick he swings. . . .'

"Not, mind ye, Hinnissy, that ol' age be itsilf is a bad companion. It's wise in a way. It knows all ye'er ol' stories an' ol' jokes an' ye cud pass manny a pleasant avenin' with it over a bottle. But th' throuble is, as th' fellow says, ol' age niver comes alone. Wanst ye let it in, it brings around all its poor rilitives to sponge on ye an' ye can't shake thim off.

"It likes low comp'ny such as rhoomatism an' gout an' other nuisances. An' I'm free to say it's a tough frind to shake. Ye keep it off all day but whin ye go home at night an' put th' bicuspids into th' glass iv water an' hang th' wig on th' back iv th' chair, it has a way iv creepin' into bed with ye, an' whin ye wake up there it is; an' sittin' alongside iv th' bed is ol' Uncle Lumbago, waitin' to give ye a kick in th' back th' minyit ye put ye'er feet on th' flure. But ye must go on stallin'. I'll niver admit ol' age till it gets a head-holt on me. I'm as young today as I was fifty years ago. While ye're up, will ye shut that dure. There's a bad dhraft an' I feel th' nooralgy comin' on."

"How long wud you like to live," asked Mr. Hennessy.

"Well," said Mr. Dooley, "I wuddn't want to have me life prolonged till I become a nuisance. I'd like to live as long as life is bearable to me an' as long afther that as I am bearable to life, an' thin I'd like a few years to think it over."

THE PEOPLE OF NEW YORK

"Well," said Mr. Dooley, "nearly all th' most foolish people in th' counthry an' manny iv th' wisest goes to New York. Th' wise people ar-re there because th' foolish went there first. That's th' way th' wise men make a livin'. Th' aisiest thing in th' wurruld is th' crather that's half-on, an' most iv th' people down there are just half-on. They'se no more crooked people there thin annywhere else but they'se enough that wud be ashamed to confiss that they weren't crooked, to give a majority."

THE SERVANT GIRL
PROBLEM

*Two problems, much in the press when this was written,
were the open door in China and the seating of the Mormon
Congressman B. H. Roberts.*

*"How manny wives has this here man Roberts that's try-
ing to break into Congress?" Mr. Dooley asked.*

"I dinnaw," said Mr. Hennessy, "I niver heered iv him."

*"I think it's three," said Mr. Dooley. "No wonder he needs
work and is fighting hard f'r the job. . . . A Morman,
Hinnissey, is a man that has the bad taste and th' rellijion
to do what a good manny other men ar-re restrained fr'm
doin' be conscientious scruples on' th' polis."*

⚜   ⚜   ⚜

"WHIN CONGRESS gets through expellin' mimbers
that believes so much in mathrimony that they carry it
into ivry relation iv life an' opens th' dure iv Chiny so that
an American can go in there as free as a Chinnyman can
come into this refuge iv th' opprissed iv th' wurruld, I
hope 'twill turn its attention to th' gr-reat question now
confrontin' th' nation—th' question iv what we shall do
with our hired help. What shall we do with thim?"

"We haven't anny," said Mr. Hennessy.

"No," said Mr. Dooley. "Ar-rchey Road has no servant girl problem. Th' rule is ivry woman her own cook an'
ivry man his own futman, an' be th' same token we have
no poly-gamy problem an' no open dure problem an' no

Ph'lippeen problem. Th' on'y problem in Ar-rchey Road is how manny times does round steak go into twelve at wan dollar-an-a-half a day. But east iv th' r-red bridge, Hinnissy, wan iv th' most cryin' issues iv th' hour is: 'What shall we do with our hired help?' An' if Congress don't take hold iv it we ar-re a rooned people.

" 'Tis an ol' problem an' I've seen it arise an' shake its gory head ivry few years whiniver th' Swede popylation got wurruk an' begun to get marrid, thus rayjoocin' th' visible supply iv help. But it seems 'tis deeper thin that. I see be letters in th' pa-apers that servants is insolent, an' that they won't go to wurruk onless they like th' looks iv their employers, an' that they rayfuse to live in th' counthry. Why anny servant shud rayfuse to live in th' counthry is more thin I can see. Ye'd think that this dis-reputable class'd give annything to lave th' crowded tinimints iv a large city where they have frinds be th' hundherds an' know th' polisman on th' bate an' can go out to hateful dances an' moonlight picnics—ye'd think these unforchnate slaves'd be delighted to live in Mul-ligan's subdivision, amid th' threes an' flowers an' bur-rds. Gettin' up at four o'clock in th' mornin' th' singin' iv th' full-throated alarm clock is answered be an invisible chorus iv songsters, as Shakespere says, an' ye see th' sun rise over th' hills as ye go out to carry in a ton iv coal. All day long ye meet no wan as ye thrip over th' coal-scuttle, happy in ye'er tile an' ye'er heart is enlivened be th' thought that th' childher in th' front iv th' house ar-re growin' sthrong on th' fr-resh counthry air. Besides they'se always cookin' to do. At night ye can set be th' fire an' improve ye'er mind be r-readin' half th' love story in th' part iv th' pa-aper that th' cheese come home in, an' whin ye-re through with that, all ye have to do is to climb a ladder to th' roof an' fall through th' skylight an' ye're in bed.

"But wud ye believe it, Hinnissy, manny iv these misguided women rayfuse f'r to take a job that ain't in a city. They prefer th' bustle an' roar iv th' busy marts iv thrade, th' sthreet car, th' saloon on three corners an' th' church on wan, th' pa-apers ivry mornin' with pitchers iv th' s'ciety fav'rite that's just thrown up a good job at Armours to elope with th' well-known club-man who used to be yard-masther iv th' three B's, G.L.&N., th' shy peek into th' dhry-goods store, an' other base luxuries, to a free an' healthy life in th' counthry between iliven P.M. an' four A.M. Wensdahs and Sundahs. 'Tis worse thin that, Hinnissy, f'r whin they ar-re in th' city they seem to dislike their wurruk an' manny iv thim ar-re givin' up splindid jobs with good large families where they have no chanst to spind their salaries, if they dhraw thim, an' takin' places in shops, an' gettin' marrid an' adoptin' other devices that will give thim th' chanst f'r to wear out their good clothes. 'Tis a horrible situation. Riley th' conthractor dhropped in here th' other day in his horse an' buggy on his way to the drainage canal an' he was all wurruked up over th' question. 'Why,' he says, ' 'tis scand'lous th' way servants act,' he says. 'Mrs. Riley has hystrics,' he says. 'An' ivry two or three nights whin I come home,' he says, 'I have to win a fight again' a cook with a stove lid befure I can move me family off th' fr-ront stoop,' he says. 'We threat thim well too,' he says. 'I gave th' las' wan we had fifty cints an' a cook book at Chris'mas an' th' next day she left befure breakfast,' he says. 'What naytionalties do ye hire?' says I. 'I've thried thim all,' he says, 'an',' he says, 'I'll say this in shame,' he says, 'that th' Irish ar-re th' worst,' he says. 'Well,' says I, 'ye need have no shame,' I says, 'f'r 'tis on'y th' people that ar-re good servants that'll niver be masthers,' I says. 'Th' Irish ar-re no good as servants because they ar-re too good,' I says. 'Th' Dutch ar-re no good because they ain't good enough. No matther how they start they get th' noodle habit. I had wan, wanst, an' she got so she put noodles in me tay,' I says. 'Th' Swedes ar-re all right but they always get marrid th' sicond day. Ye'll have a polisman at th' dure with a warrant f'r th' arrist iv ye'er cook if ye hire a Boheemyan,' I says. 'Coons'd be all right but they're liable f'r to hand ye ye'er food in ragtime, an' if ye ordher pork-chops f'r dinner an' th' hall is long, 'tis little ye'll have to eat whin the platter's set down,' I says. 'No,' says I, 'they'se no naytionality now livin' in this counthry that're nathral bor-rn servants,' I says. 'If ye want to save throuble,' I says, 'Ye'll import ye'er help. They'se a race iv people livin' in Cinthral Africa that'd be jus' right. They niver sleep, they can carry twice their weight on their backs, they have no frinds, they wear no clothes, they can't read, they can't dance an' they don't dhrink. Th' fact is they're thoroughly oneddycated. If ye cud tache thim to cook an' take care iv childher they'd be th' best servants,' says I. 'An' what d'ye call thim?' says he. 'I f'rget,' says I. An' he wint away mad."

"Sure an' he's a nice man to be talkin' iv servants," said Mr. Hennessy. "He was a gintleman's man in th' ol' counthry an' I used to know his wife whin she wurruked f'r——"

"S-sh," said Mr. Dooley. "They're beyond that now. Besides they speak fr'm experyence. An' mebbe that's th' throuble. We're always harder with our own kind thin with others. 'Tis I that'd be th' fine cinsor iv a bartinder's wurruk. Th' more ye ought to be a servant ye'ersilf th' more difficult 'tis f'r ye to get along with servants. I can holler to anny man fr'm th' top iv a buildin' an' make him tur-rn r-round, but if I come down to th' sthreet where he can see I ain't anny bigger thin he is, an' holler at him, 'tis twinty to wan if he tur-rns r-round he'll hit me in th' eye. We have a servant girl problem because, Hinnissy, it isn't manny years since we first begun to have servant girls. But I hope Congress'll take it up. A smart Congress like th' wan we have now ought to be able to spare a little time fr'm its preparation iv new jims iv speech f'r th' third reader an' rig up a bill that'd make keepin' house a recreation while so softenin' th' spirit iv th' haughty sign iv a noble race in th' kitchen that cookin' buckwheat cakes on a hot day with th' aid iv a bottle iv smokeless powdher'd not cause her f'r to sind a worthy man to his office in slippers an' without a hat."

"Ah," said Mr. Hennessy, the simple democrat. "It wud be all r-right if women'd do their own cookin'."

"Well," said Mr. Dooley. " 'Twud be a return to Jacksonyan simplicity, an' 'twud be a gr-reat thing f'r th' resthrant business."

DRUGS

"Ye niver hear annywan say: 'Hinnissy is great comp'ny whin he begins to talk about his sickness.' I've seen men turn fr'm a poor, helpless, enthusyastic invalid to listen to a man talkin' about th' Nicaragoon canal."

♧ ♧ ♧

"WHAT AILS ye?" asked Mr. Dooley of Mr. Hennessy, who looked dejected.

"I'm a sick man," said Mr. Hennessy.

"Since th' picnic?"

"Now that I come to think iv it, it did begin th' day afther th' picnic," said Mr. Hennessy. "I've been to see Dock O'Leary. He give me this an' these here pills an' some powdhers besides. An' d'ye know, though I haven't taken anny iv thim yet, I feel betther already."

"Well, sir," said Mr. Dooley, " 'tis a grand thing to be a doctor. A man that's a doctor don't have to buy anny funny papers to enjye life. Th' likes iv ye goes to a picnic an' has a pleasant, peaceful day in th' counthry dancin' breakdowns an' kickin' a football in th' sun an' ivry fifteen minyits or so washin' down a couple of dill-pickles with a bottle of white pop. Th' next day ye get what's comin' to ye in th' right place an' bein' a sthrong, hearty man that cudden't be kilt be annything less thin a safe fallin' on ye fr'm a twenty-story buildin', ye know ye ar-re goin' to die. Th' good woman advises a mustard plasther but ye scorn th' suggestion. What good wud a mustard plasther be again this fatal epidemic that is ragin' inside iv ye? Besides a mustard plasther wud hurt. So th' good woman, frivilous crather that she is, goes back to her wurruk singin' a light chune. She knows she's goin' to have to put up with ye f'r some time to come. A mustard plasther, Hinnissy, is th' rale test iv whether a pain is goin' to kill ye or not. If the plasther is onbearable ye can bet th' pain undherneath it is not.

"But ye know ye are goin' to die an' ye're not sure whether ye'll send f'r Father Kelly or th' doctor. Ye finally decide to save up Father Kelly f'r th' last an' ye sind f'r th' Dock. Havin' rescued ye fr'm th' jaws iv death two or three times befure whin ye had a sick headache th' Dock takes his time about comin', but just as ye are beginnin' to throw ye'er boots at th' clock an' show other signs iv what he calls rigem mortar, he rides up in his fine horse an' buggy. He gets out slowly, one foot at a time, hitches his horse an' ties a nose bag on his head. Thin he chats f'r two hundherd years with th' polisman on th' beat. He tells him a good story an' they laugh harshly.

"Whin th' polisman goes his way th' Dock meets th' good woman at th' dure an' they exchange a few wurruds about th' weather, th' bad condition iv th' sthreets, th' health iv Mary Ann since she had th' croup an' ye'ersilf. Ye catch th' wurruds, 'Grape Pie,' 'Canned Salmon,' 'Cast-iron digestion.' Still he doesn't come up. He tells a few stories to th' childher. He weighs th' youngest in his hands an' says: 'That's a fine boy ye have, Mrs. Hinnissy. I make no doubt he'll grow up to be a polisman.' He examines th' phottygraft album an' asks if that isn't so-an'-so. An' all this time ye lay writhin' in mortal agony an' sayin' to ye'ersilf: 'Inhuman monsther, to lave me perish here while he chats with a callous woman that I haven't said annything but "What?" to f'r twenty years.'

"Ye begin to think there's a conspiracy against ye to get ye'er money befure he saunters into th' room an' says in a gay tone: 'Well, what d'ye mane be tyin' up wan iv th' gr-reat industhrees iv our nation be stayin' away fr'm wurruk f'r a day?' 'Dock,' says ye in a feeble voice, 'I have a tur'ble pain in me abdumdum. It reaches fr'm here to here,' makin' a rough sketch iv th' burned disthrict undher th' blanket. 'I felt it comin' on last night but I didn't say annything f'r fear iv alarmin' me wife, so I simply groaned,' says ye.

"While ye ar-re describin' ye'er pangs, he walks around th' room lookin' at th' pictures. Afther ye've got through he comes over an' says: 'Lave me look at ye'er tongue. 'Hum,' he says, holdin' ye'er wrist an' bowin' through th' window to a frind iv his on a sthreet car. 'Does that hurt?' he says, stabbin' ye with his thumbs in th' suburbs iv th' pain. 'Ye know it does,' says ye with a groan. 'Don't do that again. Ye scratched me.' He hurls ye'er wrist back at ye an' stands at th' window lookin' out at th' firemen acrost th' sthreet playin' dominoes. He says nawthin' to ye an' ye feel like th' prisoner while th' foreman iv th' jury is fumblin' in his inside pocket f'r th' verdict. Ye can stand it no longer. 'Dock,' says ye, 'is it annything fatal? I'm not fit to die but tell me th' worst an' I will thry to bear it.' 'Well,' says he, 'ye have a slight interioritis iv th' semi-colon. But this purscription ought to fix ye up all right. Ye'd betther take it over to th' dhrug sthore an' have it filled ye'ersilf. In th' manetime I'd advise ye to be careful iv ye'er dite. I wuddn't ate annything with glass or a large percintage iv plaster iv Paris in it.' An' he goes away to write his bill.

"I wondher why ye can always read a doctor's bill an' ye niver can read his purscription. F'r all ye know, it may be a short note to th' dhruggist askin' him to hit ye on th' head with a pestle. An' it's a good thing ye can't read it. If ye cud, ye'd say: 'I'll not cash this in at no dhrug store. I'll go over to Dooley's an' get th' rale thing.' So, afther thryin' to decipher this here corner iv a dhress patthern, ye climb into ye'er clothes f'r what may be ye'er last walk up Ar-rchy Road. As ye go along ye begin to think that maybe th' Dock knows ye have th' Asiatic cholery an' was on'y thryin' to jolly ye with his manner iv dealin' with ye. As ye get near th' dhrug store ye feel sure iv it, an' 'tis with th' air iv a man without hope that ye hand th' paper to a young pharmycist who is mixin' a two-cent stamp f'r a lady customer. He hands it over to a scientist who is compoundin' an ice-cream soda f'r a child, with th' remark: 'O'Leary's writin' is gettin' worse an' worse. I can't make this out at all.' 'Oh,' says th' chemist, layin' down his spoon, 'that's his old cure f'r th' bellyache. Ye'll find a bucket iv it in th' back room next to th' coal scuttle.' . . .

"Dock O'Leary comes in here often an' talks medicine to me. 'Ye'ers is a very thrying pro-fissyon,' says I. 'It is,' says he. 'I'm tired out,' says he. 'Have ye had a good manny desprit cases to-day?' says I. 'It isn't that,' says he,

'but I'm not a very muscular man,' he says, 'an' some iv
th' windows in these old frame houses are hard to open,'
he says. Th' Dock don't believe much in dhrugs. He says
that if he wasn't afraid iv losin' his practice he wuddn't
give annybody annything but quinine an' he isn't sure
about that. He says th' more he practises medicine th'
more he becomes a janitor with a knowledge iv cookin'. . . .

"Dhrugs, says Dock O'Leary, are a little iv a pizen that
a little more iv wud kill ye. He says that if ye look up
anny poplar dhrug in th' ditchnry ye'll see that it is 'A
very powerful pizen of great use in medicine.' I took
calomel at his hands f'r manny years till he told me that
it was about the same thing they put into Rough on Rats.
Thin I stopped. If I've got to die, I want to die on th'
premises.

"But, as he tells me, ye can't stop people from takin'
dhrugs an' ye might as well give thim something that will
look important enough to be intrajooced to their important an' fatal cold in th' head. If ye don't, they'll leap f'r
the patent medicines. Mind ye, I haven't got annything to
say again patent medicines. If a man wud rather take thim
thin dhrink at a bar or go down to Hop Lung's f'r a long
dhraw, he's within his rights. Manny a man have I known
who was a victim iv th' tortures iv a cigareet cough who
is now livin' comfortable an' happy as an opeem fiend be
takin' Doctor Wheezo's Consumption Cure. I knew a
fellow wanst who suffered fr'm spring fever to that ex-
tent that he niver did a day's wurruk. To-day, afther
dhrinkin' a bottle of Gazooma, he will go home not on'y
with th' strenth but th' desire to beat his wife. There is a

dhrug store on ivry corner àn' they're goin' to dhrive out th' saloons onless th' govermint will let us honest merchants put a little cocaine or chloral in our cough-drops an' advertise that it will cure spinal miningitis. An' it will, too, f'r awhile."

"Don't ye iver take dhrugs?" asked Mr. Hennessy.

"Niver whin I'm well," said Mr. Dooley, "Whin I'm sick, I'm so sick I'd take annything."

WAR

"War is a fine thing. Or, perhaps I'm wrong. Annyhow, it's a sthrange thing. . . . A couple iv stout, middleaged gintlemen get into a conthrovarsy. Instead iv layin' their stove-pipe hats on th' table an' mixin' it up, they hurry home an' invite ivrybody in th' house to go out an' do their war-makin' f'r thim. They set up on th' roof an' encourage th' scrap. 'Go in there, Olaf!' 'Banzai, Hip Lung, ye're doin' well f'r me!' 'There goes wan iv me brave fellows. I'd almost sind somethin' to his widow if I cud larn her name!' "

"But wuddn't ye defind ye'er own fireside?"

"I don't need to," said Mr. Dooley. "If I keep on coals enough, me fireside will make it too hot f'r anny wan that invades it."

THE PROHIBITION ERA

*Joshua Levering, John G. Woolley, and Silas C. Swallow
were the candidates of the Prohibition party for president
in 1896, 1900, and 1904.*
*"What's this Anti-Saloon League, annyhow?" Mr. Hen-
nessy asked.*
*"Well," said Mr. Dooley, "it's like the Anti-Anti-Saloon
League. It's wan way iv makin' a livin'."*

⚜ ⚜ ⚜

"D'YE KNOW, Hinnissy, I niver wanted to be a
liquor dealer. I drifted into th' business because I was
socyable be nature, an' had a joynt's strenth, but didn't
want to use it like a joynt be wurrukin' at a thrade. Besides, it give me a great power an' inflooence. But, at that,
me high position didn't pay me f'r th' kind iv company I
had to face an' inhale day afther day. It give me a great
contimpt f'r human nature to be mixed up with me customers.

"In thim days I was a prohybitionist, an' talked th' good
cause long before Willum Jennings Bryan opened his
noble head about it. Ye niver heerd that great statesman
shoutin' f'r Wooly or Levering or Swallow, did ye? No,
faith. I'm prob'bly th' on'y man now livin' that raymim-
bers their cillybrated names. They were a fine lot iv ol'
fellows, comin' out year afther year, to lead their little
foorces to certain defeat, an' ca'mly carryin' on their campaign with ivrybody laughin' at thim. That was th' hard-

257

est thing f'r th' old heroes. Manny a man can be stopped
be a bullet.

"But they didn't mind, these inthrepid old geezers with
their spectacles an' their throat whiskers. They smiled
serenely, put for'ard argyments that no wan cud answer,
sung 'Where is my wandhrin' boy tonight,' paid out their
own money f'r hall rent, niver held a polytical job an'
were niver heerd about between ilictions.

"Yes, sir, I was with thim at heart, an' I had a hundherd argymints in their favor. You, Hinnissy, were wan
iv me sthrongist. I cud always pint to ye whin language
failed me. Iv coorse I didn't vote f'r these good men. I like
comp'ny whin I go to th' polls. But I was with thim, an'
I am today.

"Thin why do I go on sellin' th' stuff? What is there f'r
a veteran juggler iv bottles to do? I've got to break th'
law or th' law will break me. But whin I look back at th'
old days an' thin cast me eyes around this repulsive candy
an' parfumery store, I wish that Andy Volstead had had
th' heart to provide a Home f'r th' Victims iv his rash act.
Ivry time a fellow comes in here an' ordhers wan iv thim
mixtures iv marble dust an' coal tar producks that some
wag has called soft dhrinks, I reach f'r th' bung-starter.
But it isn't there!

"Th' scepter has gone with th' crown an' excipt that I
have more money I'm no better off thin th' king in Greece.
To see me, that was wanst a free an' law-abidin' citizen
that cud give th' back iv me hand an' th' sole iv me fut to
th' very loot at th' station now keepin' wan eye on th'
customer an' th' other on th' dure, to see ye lurkin' in like

a tom-cat an' me sellin' ye hop that Thomas A. Edison wuddn't handle with rubber gloves an' handin' it to ye as if I was passin' countherfeit money, is grajally breakin' me heart. 'Tis thrue I have more coin thin I iver see befure. But what is money, afther all? As Hogan says, where wealth accumylates man decays. What does it profit me, as th' good book says, if I gain th' whole wurruld be sellin' ye conthraband juice, if th' next I see iv ye a little dog is leadin' ye around at th' end iv a sthring. Oh, th' shame iv it! . . .

"An' there ye ar-re. I've got to go on in th' on'y business I know. Th' saloon desthroyed th' home, but th' home has turned like a rattle snake an' desthroyed th' saloon— th' home an' th' home brew. Where are all th' cheerful saloons ye used to know? Cobwebs hang on th' wall, th' cash registher chimes no more. Where are all me old customers most iv th' time? At home, be dad. Th' fam'ly don't see much iv thim. They're down in th' cellar stewin' hops.

"That's th' throuble us pro-hybitionists are up against. Ye can make alcohol out iv most annything. Ivry German an' most Englishmen know how to make beer. Give an Eyetalyan a bunch iv grapes an' he'll turn out a bottle iv wine. Th' Scotch make it out iv barley; th' Irish out iv potatoes an' th' Mexicans out iv cactus, which is full iv needles an' makes a noble stimylant. Th' Americans, a free, indipindant, injanyous an' law-defyin' people, make it out iv these things an' also corn, wheat, apples, cherries, and pine shavin's.

"Gallagher don't throuble with machinery. He gets his ingrejints at th' dhrug store.

"He was in here last night, so how-come-ye-so that I knew he'd been in th' bosom iv his family. 'Where did ye get it?' says I. 'At home,' says he. 'I've often warned ye again frequentin' that resort,' says I. 'It will be ye'er desthruction.' 'Well, annyhow,' says he, 'me desthruction don't cost me as much as it did,' he says. 'It makes me mad to think iv all th' money I've been robbed iv be th' distillers an' brewers. It amounts to a fortune. If I'd known what it costs thim I'd niver have took a dhrink.'

"I used to think gin was made out iv juniper berries an' I wondhered why all th' farmers in th' counthry raised hay whin they cud be harvestin' gin. Now I know that wan juniper berry will turn a bar'l iv alcohol into th' kind iv gin I used to get. If ye don't want gin stir it around with a piece iv charred wood an' ye have Scotch. Add a little proon juice an' its rye. It cost thim bandits a dollar a bar'l an' most iv that was f'r labels. If I ask him, a little Eyetalyan frind iv mine who used to run a two-dollar-bill facthry before he convarted it, will hand me anny label ye iver see or heerd about. So, when I intertain me frinds, I projooce a bottle iv 'superfin' Sour Mash, nineteen hundhred an' siven, aged in th' wood, McManus an' Comp'ny, Louisville, Ky.' An' whin th' boys choke it down an' with tears in their eyes say 'That's th' rale thing, where did ye get it?' I tell thim I see pro-hybition comin' an' laid in enough to last me th' rest iv me life.

"An' so it goes. I thought f'r awhile th' charackter iv th' dhrink wud stop dhrinkin'. But it seems as if a man that will dhrink annything will take what he can get. It's alcohol he's afther an' all booze is alcohol. If it's wood

alcohol it will dhrop ye in ye'er thracks. If it's made out iv
th' projooce iv our fair westhren farm lands, th' longer ye
keep it th' longer ye'll last. What I have I'm savin' f'r
me wake.

"Do I think pro-hybition is makin' pro-gress? Me boy,
I'm no stasticyan. I hope to die without havin' that to do
pinance f'r that. But if ye want me opinyon, I'll say it
stands to reason that if it's hard to get an' costly th' poor
won't have so much iv it, an' what they'll have will be worse
f'r thim. But it's makin' sad inroads on th' rich.

"Ye see, Hinnissy, th' rich will accumylate annything
that's scarce—pictures, books, postage stamps or money.
Now, whin booze was to be had be high an' low an' Jack
alike, th' low got it an' th' high shunned it. Me frind
Grogan, th' banker, niver wud look at it whin 'twas plinti-
ful. Now he's up an' at it befure he goes to count his
morgedges in th' mornin'. He's got a rare collection iv old
masthers in his basemint. He was showin' thim to me th'
other day, his eye lightin' up as he pinted th' bottles out.
'Here,' he says, 'is a ginooyine ol' Pepper. There ye have
th' Dutch artist Overholt. This wan is atthributed to Mc-
Brayor. That fine spicimen over there is iv th' Maryland
school,' says he. I didn't dare contradict him, Hinnissy.
Him an' me are capytalists an' we've got to stand together. But may th' divvle take me if I didn't see me own
bootlegger puttin' on thim very labels less thin a month
ago. But what was th' use iv ondeceivin' him! They were
as ginooyine, annyhow, as his pictures."

"Don't ye think prohybition has had anny effect?" Mr.
Hennessy asked.

"Sure it has," said Mr. Dooley, "Ivry reform increases th' number iv jobs. Th' more reforms th' more laws, th' more laws th' more polismen, th' more polismen th' more crimes, th' more crimes th' more reformers, an' so on, till fin'lly th' counthry will be akelly divided—fifty per-cint tax payers an' fifty per-cint cops."

"There ain't as much dhrunkenness as there was. I know that," said Mr. Hennessy.

"No," said Mr. Dooley, "but what there is is a much more finished product."

MR. DOOLEY ON SUNDRY
AMERICAN INSTITUTIONS

☘

"Sometimes I look back on th' old days with sorrow, bad as they were. Let us say its a bitther cold Saturdah night. Th' wind is shriekin' down th' sthreet. Th' air is so full iv snow ye can't har'ly see th' sthreet lamps. There's a fut iv it on th' sidewalks. People that have to be out walk sideways an' flail their chests with their arms. Th' few horses blow jets iv steam through their whiskers iv ice. Icicles as long as clothes poles hang fr'm th' roof. There's an inch iv frost on th' window panes.

"But inside it's diff'rent. Th' place is closed tight. Old Boreas niver got into a well-regylated saloon. Women, childher an' fresh air were barred. Th' gas jet burns pink in th' smoke. Th' stove is red hot an' hisses like a sarpint whiniver a gintleman comes in an' spits on it. There's a pleasant odor in th' air iv liquor, nutmeg, lemon peel an' prolitariats. A game iv cards is goin' on in the corner. Hogan is at his accustomed place near th' cheese box makin' a meal iv cheese, crackers, coffee, cloves an' cinnamon, an' spoutin' pothry to an' old intimate frind I've just intrajooced to him. In graceful attichoods with wan elbow on th' bar an' wan fut on th' rail, th' seeryous dhrinkin' men repose. Maybe down at th' end a couple iv auctioneers are singin' 'Annie Rooney.'"

ALCOHOL AS FOOD

*"Ye ra-aly do think dhrink is a nicissry evil?" said Mr.
Hennessy.*
*"Well," said Mr. Dooley, "if it's an evil to a man, it's not
nicissry, an' if it's nicissry it's an evil."*

♣ ♣ ♣

"IF A MAN come into this saloon—" Mr. Hennessy
was saying.

"This ain't no saloon," Mr. Dooley interrupted. "This
is a resthrant."

"A what?" Mr. Hennessy exclaimed.

"A resthrant," said Mr. Dooley. "Ye don't know, Hinnissy, that liquor is food. It is though. Food—an' dhrink.
That's what a doctor says in the pa-apers, an' another doctor wants th' gover'mint to sind tubs iv th' stuff down to
th' Ph'lipeens. He says 'tis almost essintial that people
shud dhrink in thim hot climates. . . .

"Th' idee ought to take, Hinnissy, f'r th' other doctor
la-ad has discovered that liquor is food. 'A man,' says he,
'can live f'r months on a little booze taken fr'm time to
time,' he says. 'They'se a gr-reat dale iv nourishment in
it,' he says. An' I believe him, f'r manny's th' man I
know that don't think iv eatin' whin he can get a dhrink.
I wondher if th' time will iver come whin ye'll see a man
sneakin' out iv th' fam'ly enthrance iv a lunch-room
hurridly bitin' a clove! People may get so they'll carry a

light dinner iv a pint iv rye down to their wurruk, an' a
man'll tell ye he niver takes more thin a bottle iv beer
f'r breakfast. Th' cook'll give way to th' bartinder an' th'
doctor'll ordher people f'r to ate on'y at meals. Ye'll r-read
in th' pa-apers that 'Anton Boozinski, while crazed with
ham an' eggs, thried to kill his wife an' childher.' On
Pathrick's day ye'll see th' Dr. Tanner Anti-Food Fife
an' Drum corpse out at th' head iv th' procession instead
iv th' Father Macchews, an' they'll be places where a man
can be took whin he gets th' monkeys fr'm immodhrate
eatin'. Th' sojers'll complain that th' liquor was unfit to
dhrink an' they'll be inquiries to find out who sold em-
bammin' flood to th' ar-rmy. Poor people'll have simple
meals—p'raps a bucket iv beer an' a little crame de mint,
an' ye'll r-read in th' pa-apers about a family found starvin' on the North side, with nawthin' to sustain life but wan
small bottle iv gin, while th' head iv th' family, a man
well known to th' polis, spinds his wages in a low doggery
or bakeshop fuddlin' his brains with custard pie. Th'
r-rich'll intrajooce novelties. P'raps they'll top off a fine
dinner with a little hasheesh or proosic acid. Th' time'll
come whin ye'll see me in a white cap fryin' a cocktail
over a cooksthove, while a nigger hollers to me: 'Dhraw
a stack iv Scotch,' an' I holler back: 'On th' fire.' Ye will
not."

"That's what I thought," said Mr. Hennessy.

"No," said Mr. Dooley. "Whisky wudn't be so much
iv a luxury if 'twas more iv a necissity. I don't believe 'tis
a food, though whin me frind Schwartzmeister makes a
cocktail all it needs is a few noodles to look like a biled

dinner. No, whisky ain't food. I think betther iv it thin that. I wudden't insult it be placin' it on th' same low plane as a lobster salad. Father Kelly puts it r-right, and years go by without him lookin' on it even at Hallowe'en. 'Whisky,' says he, 'is called th' divvle, because,' he says, ' 'tis wan iv th' fallen angels,' he says. 'It has its place,' he says, 'but its place is not in a man's head,' says he. 'It ought to be th' reward iv action, not th' cause iv it,' he says. 'It's f'r th' end iv th' day, not th' beginnin',' he says. 'Hot whisky is good f'r a cold heart, an' no whisky's good f'r a hot head,' he says. 'Th' minyit a man relies on it f'r a crutch he loses th' use iv his legs. 'Tis a bad thing to stand on, a good thing to sleep on, a good thing to talk on, a bad thing to think on. If it's in th' head in th' mornin' it ought not to be in th' mouth at night. If it laughs in ye, dhrink; if it weeps, swear off. It makes some men talk like good women, an' some women talk like bad men. It is a livin' f'r orators an' th' death iv bookkeepers. It doesn't sustain life, but, whin taken hot with wather, a lump iv sugar, a piece iv lemon peel, and just th' dustin' iv a nutmeg-grater, it makes life sustainable.' "

"D'ye think ye-ersilf it sustains life?" asked Mr. Hennessy.

"It has sustained mine f'r manny years," said Mr. Dooley.

"Ye'll niver find Father Kelly openin' a saloon. He hates me business, but he likes me. He says dhrink is an evil, but I'm a nicissity. If I moved out a worse man might come in me place."

DIVORCE

*"In me heart I think if people marry it ought to be f'r life.
The laws ar-re altogether too lenient with thim."*

♣   ♣   ♣

"WELL, SIR," said Mr. Dooley, "I see they've been
holdin' a Divoorce Congress."

"What's that?" asked Mr. Hennessy.

"Ye wuddn't know," said Mr. Dooley. "Divoorce is
th' on'y luxury supplied be th' law that we don't injye in
Ar-rchey Road. Up here whin a marrid couple get to th'
pint where 'tis impossible f'r thim to go on livin' together
they go on livin' together. They feel that way some mornin' in ivry month, but th' next day finds thim still glarin'
at each other over th' ham an' eggs. No wife iver laves
her husband while he has th' breath iv life in him, an'
anny gintleman that took a thrip to Reno in ordher to
saw off th' housekeepin' expinses on a rash successor
wud find throuble ready f'r him whin he come back to
Ar-rchey Road.

"No, sir, whin our people grab hands at th' altar,
they're hooked up f'river. There's on'y wan decree iv divoorce that th' neighbors will recognize, an' that's th'
wan that entitles ye to a ride just behind th' pall bearers.
That's why I'm a batch. 'Tis th' fine skylark iv a tim-
prary husband I'd make, bringin' home a new wife ivry
Foorth iv July an' dischargin' th' old wan without a
charackter. But th' customs iv th' neighbors are again it.

"But 'tis diff'rent with others, Hinnissy. Down be

268

Mitchigan Avnoo marredge is no more bindin' thin a dhream. A short marrid life an' an onhappy wan is their motto. Off with th' old love an' on with th' new an' off with that. 'Till death us do part,' says th' preacher. 'Or th' jury,' whispers th' blushin' bride.

"Th' Divoorce Congress, Hinnissy, that I'm tellin' ye about was assembled to make th' divoorce laws iv all th' States th' same. It's a tur-rble scandal as it is now. A man shakes his wife in wan State on'y to be grabbed be her an' led home th' minyit he crosses th' border. There's no safety f'r anny wan. In some places it's almost impossible f'r a man to get rid iv his fam'ly onless he has a good raison. There's no regularity at all about it. In Kentucky baldness is grounds f'r divoorce; in Ohio th' inclemency iv th' weather. In Illinye a woman can be freed fr'm th' gallin' bonds iv mathrimony because her husband wears Congress gaiters; in Wisconsin th' old man can get his maiden name back because his wife tells fortunes in th' taycup.

"In Nebrasky th' shackles ar-re busted because father forgot to wipe his boots; in New York because mother knows a judge in South Dakota. Ye can be divoorced f'r annything if ye know where to lodge th' complaint. Among th' grounds ar-re snorin', deefness, because wan iv th' parties dhrinks an' th' other doesn't, because wan don't dhrink an' th' other does, because they both dhrink, because th' wife is addicted to sick headaches, because he asked her what she did with that last $10 he give her, because he knows some wan else, because she injyes th' society iv th' young, because he f'rgot to wind th' clock.

A husband can get a divoorce because he has more money thin he had; a wife because he has less. Ye can always get a divoorce f'r what Hogan calls incompatibility iv temper. That's whin husband an' wife ar-re both cross at th' same time. Ye'd call it a tiff in ye'er fam'ly, Hinnissy.

"But, mind ye, none iv these raisons go in anny two States. A man that wants to be properly divoorced will have to start out an' do a tour iv our gr-reat Republic. An' be th' time he's thurly released he may want to do it all over agin with th' second choice iv his wild, glad heart.

"It wud be a grand thing if it cud be straightened out. Th' laws ought to be th' same ivrywhere. In anny part iv this fair land iv ours it shud be th' right iv anny man to get a divoorce, with alimony, simply be goin' befure a Justice iv th' Peace an' makin' an affydavit that th' lady's face had grown too bleak f'r his taste. Be Hivens, I'd go farther. Rather than have people endure this sarvichood I'd let anny man escape be jumpin' th' conthract. All he'd have to do if I was r-runnin' this Govarnmint wud be to put some clothes in th' grip, write a note to his wife that afther thinkin' it over f'r forty years he had made up his mind that his warm nature was not suited to marredge with th' mother iv so manny iv his childher, an' go out to return no more. . . ."

"I dare ye to come down to my house an' say thim things," said Mr. Hennessy.

"Oh, I know ye don't agree with me," said Mr. Dooley. "Nayether does th' parish priest. He's got it into his head that whin a man's marrid he's marrid, an' that's all there is to it. He puts his hand in th' grab-bag an' pulls out a blank an' he don't get his money back. . . . He says:

" 'If people knew they cuddn't get away fr'm each other they'd settle down to life, just as I detarmined to like coal smoke whin I found th' collection wasn't big enough to put a new chimbley in th' parish house. I've acchally got to like it,' he says. 'There ain't anny condition iv human life that's not endurable if ye make up ye'er mind that ye've got to endure it,' he says. 'Th' throuble with th' rich,' he says, 'is this, that whin a rich man has a perfectly nachral scrap with his beloved over breakfast, she stays at home an' does nawthin' but think about it, an' he goes out an' does nawthin but think about it, an' that afthernoon they're in their lawyers' office,' he says. 'But whin a poor gintleman an' a poor lady fall out, the poor lady puts all her anger into rubbin' th' zinc off th' washboord an' th' poor gintleman aises his be murdhrin' a slag pile with a shovel, an' be th' time night comes ar-round he says to himself: "Well, I've got to go home annyhow, an' it's no use I shud be onhappy because I'm misjudged," an' he puts a pound iv candy into his coat pocket an' goes home an' finds her standin' at th' dure with a white apron on an' some new ruching ar-round her neck,' he says.

"An' there ye ar-re. Two opinions."

"I see on'y wan," said Mr. Hennessy. "What do ye ra-aly think?"

"I think," said Mr. Dooley, "if people wanted to be divoorced I'd let thim, but I'd give th' parents into th' custody iv th' childher. They'd larn thim to behave."

FIREMEN

⚜ ⚜ ⚜

"I KNOWED A MAN be th' name iv clancy wanst,
Jawn. He was fr'm th' County May-o, but a good man
f'r all that; an' whin he'd growed to be a big, sthrappin'
fellow, he wint on to th' fire departmint. They'se an
Irishman 'r two on th' fire departmint an' in th' army,
too, Jawn, though ye'd think be hearin' some talk they
was all runnin' prim'ries an' thryin' to be cinthral comity-
men. So ye wud. Ye niver hear iv thim on'y whin they
die; an' thin, murther, what funerals they have!

"Well, this Clancy wint on th' fire department, an' they
give him a place in thruck twenty-three. All th' r-road
was proud iv him, an' faith he was proud iv himsilf. He
r-rode free on th' sthreet ca-ars, an' was th' champeen
hand-ball player f'r miles around. Ye shud see him goin'
down th' sthreet, with his blue shirt an' his blue coat with
th' buttons on it, an' his cap on his ear. But ne'er a cap or
coat'd he wear whin they was a fire. He might be shiv'rin'
be th' stove in th' ingine house with a buffalo robe over
his head; but, whin th' gong sthruck, 'twas off with coat
an' cap an' buffalo robe, an' out come me brave Clancy,
bare-headed an' bare hand, dhrivin' with wan line an'
spillin' th' hose cart on wan wheel at ivry jump iv th' horse.
Did anny wan iver see a fireman with his coat on or a
polisman with his off? Why, wanst, whin Clancy was

272

standin' up f'r Grogan's eighth, his son come runnin' in to tell him they was a fire in Vogel's packin' house. He dhropped th' kid at Father Kelley's feet, an' whipped off his long coat an' wint tearin' f'r th' dure, kickin' over th' poorbox an' buttin' ol' Mis' O'Neill that'd come in to say th' stations. . . .

"Well, Clancy wint to fires an' fires. Whin th' big organ facthry burnt, he carrid th' hose up to th' fourth story an' was squirtin' whin th' walls fell. They dug him out with pick an' shovel, an' he come up fr'm th' brick an' boards an' saluted th' chief. 'Clancy,' says th' chief, 'ye betther go over an' get a dhrink.' He did so, Jawn. I heerd it. An' Clancy was that proud!

"Whin th' Hogan flats on Halsted Sthreet took fire, they got all th' people out but wan; an' she was a woman asleep on th' fourth flure. 'Who'll go up?' says Bill Musham. 'Sure, sir,' says Clancy, 'I'll go'; an' up he wint. His captain was a man be th' name iv O'Connell, fr'm th' County Kerry; an' he had his fut on th' ladder whin Clancy started. Well, th' good man wint into th' smoke, with his wife faintin' down below. 'He'll be kilt,' says his brother. 'Ye don't know him,' says Bill Musham. An' sure enough, whin ivry wan'd give him up, out comes me brave Clancy, as black as a Turk, with th' girl in his arms. Th' others wint up like monkeys, but he shtud wavin' thim off, an' come down th' ladder face forward. 'Where'd ye larn that?' says Bill Musham. 'I seen a man do it at th' Lyceem whin I was a kid,' says Clancy. 'Was it all right?' 'I'll have ye up before th' ol' man,' says Bill Musham. 'I'll teach ye to come down a laddher as if ye

was in a quadhrille, ye horse-stealin', ham-sthringin'
May-o man,' he says. But he didn't. Clancy wint over to
see his wife. 'O Mike,' says she, ' 'twas fine,' she says.
'But why d'ye take th' risk?' she says. 'Did ye see th'
captain?' he says with a scowl. 'He wanted to go. Did ye
think I'd follow a Kerry man with all th' ward lukkin'
on?' he says.

"Well, so he wint dhrivin' th' hose-cart on wan wheel,
an' jumpin' whin he heerd a man so much as hit a glass to
make it ring. All th' people looked up to him, an' th' kids
followed him down th' sthreet; an' 'twas th' gr-reatest
priv'lige f'r anny wan f'r to play dominos with him near
th' joker.

"But about a year ago he come in to see me, an' says he,
'Well, I'm goin' to quit.' 'Why,' says I, 'ye-re a young
man yet,' I says. 'Faith,' he says, 'look at me hair,' he says
—'young heart, ol' head. I've been at it these twenty year,
an' th' good woman's wantin' to see more iv me thin
blowin' into a saucer iv coffee,' he says. 'I'm goin' to quit,'
he says, 'on'y I want to see wan more good fire,' he says.
'A rale good ol' hot wan,' he says, 'with th' wind blowin'
f'r it an' a good dhraft in th' ilivator-shaft, an' about two
stories, with pitcher-frames an' gasoline an' excelsior,
an' to hear th' chief yellin': "Play 'way sivinteen. What
th' hell an' damnation are ye standin' aroun' with that
pipe f'r? Is this a fire 'r a dam livin' pitcher? I'll break
ivry man iv eighteen, four, six, an' chem'cal five to-morrah
mornin' befure breakfast." Oh,' he says, bringin' his fist
down, 'wan more, an' I'll quit.'

"An' he did, Jawn. Th' day th' Carpenter Brothers'

box factory burnt. 'Twas wan iv thim big, fine-lookin' buildings that pious men built out iv celluloid an' plasther iv Paris. An' Clancy was wan iv th' men undher whin th' wall fell. I seen thim bringin' him home; an' th' little woman met him at th' dure, rumplin' her apron in her hands."

THE GAME OF CARDS

"WHO D'YE suppose iver invinted cards?" Mr. Hennessy asked.

"Faith," said Mr. Dooley, "ye'll have to ask some wan older thin me. Wan iv me arliest ricollections was seein' me father pull a pack out iv his coat-tail pocket, wet his thumb, and dale a hand to th' village smith. I know they're that old annyhow. Hogan says th' origin iv cards is lost in antikity, an' be th' dim light iv th' dawn iv civilization, primitive man, says he, took a peek at his neighbor's hand an' hauled an ace out iv his boot. He says all games iv cards ar-re as old as th' hills. Like as not Moses could bate ye at siven up, an' Joolyus Cayzar make a hare iv ye at forty-fives.

"I don't suppose there's anny game iv cards I haven't played, or anny wan that I know. Th' style iv thim changes too quick f'r me. I study thim all as they come along, an' about th' time me idjacation is finished and payed f'r an' I'm at th' pint where I can prolong th' struggle f'r me money till midnight, all me frinds stop playin' th' game I've larned an' start somethin' new, an' I have to begin all over an' take another expinsive coorse. . . .

"In hundherds iv thousands iv homes in this fair land four good frinds are glarin' murdherously at each other over th' tops iv th' cards. Millyons iv beautiful ladies ar-re ladin' out iv th' wrong hand an' thrumpin' their pardner's thrick. In me day a lady wud as soon've thought iv votin' or turnin' a handspring as iv gamblin'. They played cards it is thrue, but it was f'r fun—or betther f'r indignation an' anger. Th' game started pleasantly enough afther supper, but at nine-five it had become a deadly feud; at nine-thirty, sarcastic insults were passin' freely, an' just as th' clock sthruck ten, mother fired th' pack at father's head or into th' fire.

"But now-a-days it is no oncommon sight to see th' fond parent poundin' th' mantelpiece with baby's bank befure goin' out to rassle with th' Demon Chance. It is estimated that th' deposits in these little institutions has decreased ten millyon pennies since mother took to th' cards, an' no one is surprised to see a lady feedin' th' baby with wan hand an' revokin' with th' other. Though I will say this that most gamblin' ladies don't have fam'lies. Childher ar-re not their long suit, ye might say. No, I don't play th' game, especyally with ladies. If I did I'd have me head out iv th' window half th' time callin' f'r th' polis. A game iv auction among perfect ladies wud make a cynic out iv th' Oregon Jew, who cud mark all th' face-cards be shufflin' th' deck wanst. Th' things he use to do to a party iv retired grocers in a hotel game iv a Saturdah night was effeminate compared with what a lady will do in an auction game. A man's idee in a card game is war—crool, devastatin', an' pitiless. A lady's idee iv it is a combynation iv larceny, embezzlement, an' burglary. In auction th' fair sect has ivry opporchunity to show th' qualities that endear thim as card players to th' sect that is sthronger but is cursed with fear iv th' handcuffs.

"No, I niver played auction with th' fair sect, but I wanst lost a watch to a lady gambler in a sthreet-car. But I've seen a gintleman's game, an' if, as Hogan says, th' ladies' game keeps up th' same ratio it must be about as square as an egg. I dhropped into Gallagher's house th' other night. Gallagher is a simple soul. He used to wurruk in the claim department iv a sthreet-railroad. Him and Larkin and Grady were playin' with Hogan. Hogan is wan iv the most larned card players in th' wurruld. He's what ye might call a card-sharp. He wanst wrote a book on games iv chanst, and th' same week morgedged his house an' deposited th' proceeds in a ladin' faro-bank. I told him he ought to write another book on games iv skill an' endurance which was th' kind he was up against.

"Annyhow, there he was sortin' th' cards carefully, puttin' th' dimons among th' hearts an' th' clubs among th' spades. 'Won't ye cut in?' says Gallagher with a pleasant but hurried smile. 'No, Willum,' says I. 'Ye may get me money, but 'twill not be through dalin' me an armful iv dooses an' thrays. Ye'll have to go down to th' hardware store an' buy ye'ersilf a brace an' bit an' a pound iv joynt powdher,' says I. 'Go an' administher th' anæsthetic to Hogan,' says I. So they begins. 'I make it two clubs,' says Hogan. 'Why, ye mamalook,' says I in a whisper, 'ye haven't got a club in ye'er hand.' 'Hush up,' says he. 'That's to tell me pardner I'm short iv dimons,' he says. 'Thin why don't ye kick him undher th' table an' pint to ye'er shirt-front?' says I. 'That wud be cheatin','

says he. 'An' what's this?' says I. ' 'Tis givin' information,' says he. 'It's what makes th' game th' most scientific in th' wurruld,' he says.

"Well, Hinnissy, I ain't goin' to thry to describe this
here gr-reat sthruggle. It didn't last long annyhow, an' I
didn't understand most iv it. But Hogan explained afther
I'd paid his sthreet-car fare home. 'Ye see,' he said, 'th'
idee is to give ye'er pardner as much information as ye
can be ye'er biddin' an' ye'er signals,' he says. 'F'r in-
stance,' says he, 'I bid a club. That tells me pardner I'm
weak in dimons but have th' ace, king, ten, an' doose iv
hearts an' th' queen, twice garded in spades. If I make
it three spades it manes that I have no spades but a long
club suit, three little hearts an' th' ace, queen, six, an'
four iv dimons. If I make it a heart I tell me pardner I
can help a no thrump if he's sthrong in clubs. If I make
it——'

" 'That's enough,' says I. 'It's a fine game, a fine gintlemanly game. But why don't ye simplify it? What's th'
use iv painin' ye'er intelleck with all these calklations?'
'What cud I do?' says he. 'Why,' says I, 'ye might write
a little note to ye'er pardner describin' ye'er hand an' slip
it to him undher th' table.' 'That wud be cheatin',' says he.
'This is givin' legitimate information,' says he. 'Well,'
says I, 'I noticed that Gallagher didn't bother his pardner
with any such inthricate system. His way iv givin' information is more nachral an' simple. I don't undherstand
this gintlemanly pastime but wan time whin ye made it a
heart I watched that innocent fellow. He studied his hand
f'r two minyits. Thin he counted his suits with his finger

while ye were gazin' into ye'er beautiful hand as if 'twas a mirror. Thin he said: "Hearts, eh?" Thin he laid down his cards and looked over at Grady an' up at th' ceilin'. Thin he picked up th' hand again an' studied it with a frown an' said: "Pass." If Grady didn't know what to do afther that, Grady oughtn't to be at large in a gr-reat city. But he did.'

"No, sir, I niver will play auction. I'm not avarse to a game iv poker, an' I'm willin' to concede a percintage to th' readiest cheater. That's on'y fair. I've played that old-fashioned pastime with fellow mimbers iv th' County Democracy whin there was on'y thirty-six cards left in th' deck afther th' first round. I've played in a game where if a man was called to th' tillyphone he took his cards and checks with him, an' whin he came back passed six times without lookin'. But to be pleasant an' romantic, cheatin' ought to be secret. It loses all its flavor when practised in th' open. To make it accordin' to rule is like licensin' burglary. Who wud come to be a burglar if 'twas lawful?

"But ye'll never cure Hogan iv gamblin'. 'Why does he do it?' says ye. Faith, I don't know. If Hogan could bate the game he wuddn't enjy it. He'd go on batin' it but he wudden't be happy. Ye don't see anny profissyonal gambler singin' at his wurruk anny more thin a bank prisident. Ivry night whin he has finished his breakfast, he kisses his wife at th' onyx dure iv their home an'· hurries down-town in his autymobill to his labors. Thin with a weary sigh he takes off his coat, puts th' elastic band around his sleeves, an' th' sthraw hat without a top on

his head, shuffles th' cards, tests th' dice, sees that th'
springs ar-re wurrukin' in th' roulette-wheel, lays out th'
knock-out dhrops on th' side-boord, and waits f'r Hogan.

"In due time he comes, iv coorse, an' goes through the
usual formalities befure passin' over his week's wages to
th' banker. But if ye watch th' two faces, which is th'
happier? Is it our frind Hogan who is losin', or our frind
Mose who is winnin'? Th' pro-fissyonal has a weary,
pained look, but in th' amachoor's eyes there is a bright
light iv hopeless but happy avarice. He thinks he may
win, but he doubts it. But Mose knows he can't, an' that
takes all th' flavor out iv Mose's life. In his mind he is
wondhering why Hogan should come so far whin he cud
just as well sind th' money be mail. Fin'lly he can stand
th' sthrain no longer. He gives a kick undher th' table,
calls out: 'Double O on th' green' an' hauls in th' last iv
a wanst proud fortune."

"I don't see anny objiction to a game iv cards among
frinds," said Mr. Hennessy.

"Nor me either," said Mr. Dooley, "if 'twas possible.
I've seen a game iv cards start among frinds, but I niver
see frinds in a game iv cards. It don't stand to raison
that ye can love annywan that's tuggin' at ye'er watch-
chain."

*"I see a fellow says in th' pa-aper that th' brokers all
has yachts an' th' customers hasn't," said Mr. Hennessy.*

*"It is not thrue," said Mr. Dooley. "Both if thim has
yachts, but th' broker has thim longer. Th' way it is, is
th' customer has th' yacht first, thin th' broker has it f'r a
while an' thin th' banker is stuck with it f'r keeps."*

CRIMINAL TRIALS

"I WAS R-READIN' in th' pa-aper a hard kick again th' delay between th' time a criminal bumps some wan an' th' time he gets th' bump that is comin' to him accoordin' to th' law. This iditor feels bad because there's a dif-f'rence between this counthry an' England. Th' sentences like th' language ar-re th' same in th' two counthries, but they're pronounced diff'rent. In England a man is pre-soomed to be innocent till he's proved guilty an' they take it f'r granted he's guilty. In this counthry a man is pre-soomed to be guilty ontil he's proved guilty an' afther that he's presoomed to be innocent.

"In th' oldher civilization th' judge reads th' news iv th' crime in th' mornin' pa-aper an' stops in at a hat shop on his way to coort an' buys a black cap to wear at th' approachin' fistivities. Whin he gets up on th' bench he calls th' shuriff to his side an' says he: 'Cap, go out an' grab a jury iv cross-lookin' marrid men to thry th' condimned.' The shuriff dhrags twelve indignant grocers fr'm their stores an' they come into coort protestin' be-cause they will be bankrupted be sarvin' their counthry. But they ar-re soon restored to good humor be th' jovyal remarks iv th' coort, who makes thim laugh heartily at wanst be askin' thim if they ar-re opposed to capital punishmint.

"Th' pris'ner is thin hauled in in chains, an' th' judge, afther exprissin' his dislike iv his face with a look iv scorn, says: 'Murdherer, ye ar-re entitled to a fair thrile. Ar-re ye guilty or not guilty? Not guilty, ye say? I thought ye wud. That's what th' likes iv ye always say. Well, let's have this disagreeable business over with in a hurry. I'll allow th' prosecution three hours to show ye up an' th' definse can have th' rest iv th' mornin'. Wake me up whin th' ividince is all in.'

"About noon his honor is woke be a note fr'm th' jury askin' how long they ar-re goin' to be kept fr'm their dinner. He hauls th' black cap out iv th' bandbox an' puttin' it on over his wig, says: 'Pris'ner at th' bar, it is now me awful jooty to lave ye'er fate to a British jury. I will not attimpt to infloonce thim in anny way. I will not take th' time to brush away th' foolish ividence put in in ye'er definse. Ye'er lawyers have done as well as they cud with nawthin' to go on. If anny iv th' jury believe ye innocent let thim retire to their room an' discuss th' matther over a meal iv bread an' wather while th' chops burn on th' kitchen stove an' their clerks ar-re disthributin' groceries free to th' neighborhood.'

"But it's betther in this home iv th' free, mind ye. Afther th' polis have made up their mind that none iv th' polis foorce did it, they may or may not grab th' criminal. It depinds on th' weather. But supposin' it's a pleasant summer's day an' th' fugitive is in th' saloon nex' dure showin' th' revolver an' thryin' to thrade in a silver candlestick f'r a dhrink, an' th' polis foorce ar-re bendin' ivry effort to apprehind him an' ar-re combin' th' whole counthry f'r him, an' he doesn't know where to turn, but goes into th' station an' registhers an' gets his key an' ordhers his breakfast in th' cell an' gives a pair iv sugar tongs, a dimon necklace, a dozen knives an' forks, his autymatic an' other vallyables to th' sergeant to lock up in th' safe, an' laves wurrud not to be called, that's on'y th' beginnin' iv th' exercises.

"Th' first year or two he passes away delightfully, havin' his pitchers took an' put in th' pa-apers an' bein' intherviewed while th' iditor iv th' sob section sinds beautiful ladies out to talk with his wife an' describe his pretty little flat full iv keepsakes. But wan mornin' he wakes up an' gets th' pa-apers an' there's har'ly anny more mintion iv him thin if he was a meetin' iv th' Epworth league, or a debate in congress, or a speech iv th' prisidint, or a war in th' Ph'lipeens, an' that disturbs him. He fires his press agent, sinds f'r his lawyer an' demands a thrile. If th' fish ar-re not bitin' th' lawyer coaxes a judge to come into town, an' wanst more th' mallyfacther becomes a prom'nint citizen an' can read th' pa-apers without bein' disgusted at th' way they fill their colyums with news about nobodies.

"Th' first six months iv th' thrile ar-re usually taken in gettin' a jury that will be fair to both sides, but more fair to wan side thin th' other. Th' state's attorney makes an effort to get twelve men who have no prejudices excipt a gin'ral opinyon that th' pris'ner is guilty. Th' lawyer f'r th' definse on'y asks that his client shall be thried be a jury iv his peers or worse, but wud compromise if all twelve were mimbers iv th' same lodge as himself. In due

time twelve men iv intilligence who have r-read th' pa-
apers an' can't remimber what they've r-read, or who
can't r-read, or ar-re out iv wurruk, ar-re injooced to
sarve, an' th' awful wheels iv justice begins to go round.

"Th' scene in th' coort is very beautiful an' touchin'.
Th' pris'ner's wife rents a baby f'r th' winter an' sets
where th' jury can see her whin her husband kicks her
undher th' table an' she weeps. Th' table in front iv th'
culprit is banked with flowers an' he comes into th' coort
wearin' a geeranyum in his button-hole. Afther a flash-
light iv th' august thribunal iv justice has been exploded
an' th' masheen f'r takin' th' movies has been put up, th'
dhread proceedure pro-ceeds. On th' first iv August th'
prosecution succeeds in gettin' into th' record th' fact that
such a person as th' victim iver lived in spite iv th' objictions iv th' definse on th' ground that it is immateeryal.
Th' lawyer f'r th' definse objicts to all th' questions an'
whin th' coort overrules him he takes an exciption. That
is as much as to say to th' judge: 'I'll make a jack iv ye in
th' supreme coort.' On th' twintieth iv Decimber afther
a severe cross-examination iv th' principal witness th'
jury asks th' coort f'r a recess so they can lynch him.

"On th' fifteenth iv th' followin' April th' tistymony iv
th' definse is submitted. It is, first, that th' pris'ner is
insane an' five profissors fr'm th' infirmary swear that he
was looney whin he done th' deed. Besides, he shot in self-
definse, to protict his home an' th' honor iv American
womanhood, while sthrugglin' with th' victim to keep
him fr'm committin' suicide because th' pris'ner wuddn't take his watch as a presint, th' gun accidintally wint

off, a long an' a short man were seen leavin' th' premises afther th' crime, an' th' pris'ner was in Mitchigan City on that night, an' while on his way to see his sick child was stopped be an old lady who he rescued fr'm drownin' in th' park, who gave him all she had in her purse, a forty-four, a jimmy, a brace an' bit, an' a quantity iv silverware, clothing, curtains, an' joolry.

"So th' years roll brightly by an' day by day th' pris'-ner sees his face on th' front page, th' fam'ly iv th' deceased is dhrove fr'm town be th' facts that has come out about his private life, an' most iv th' vallyable real estate in th' county is sold f'r taxes to pay th' bills iv th' short-hand writers f'r takin' down th' tistymony an' th' objictions iv th' definse.

"But though slow, American justice, Hinnissy, is sure an' will overtake th' crim'nal if he'll on'y be patient an' not die, an' wan day all th' ividince is in. Th' disthrict attorney, who's a candydate f'r mayor, makes his closin' argymint, addhressin' th' jury as 'fellow Republicans.' Th' lawyer f'r th' pris'ner asks th' jury on'y to consider th' law an' th' ividince an' to sind this innocent man home to his wife an' his starvin' childher. Afther th' judge has insthructed th' jury that he's all up in th' air about th' case an' doesn't know what he ought to say to thim, th' jury retires, charges its last meal to you an' me, an' discusses whether it ought to sind th' pris'ner home or some-wheres else. Afther askin' an' gettin' a description iv his home they decide on temperin' justice with mercy an' find him guilty. Th' pris'ner is brought into coort, smilin' an' cheerful, th' flashlights boom, th' cameras click, th' ladies swoon, an' th' judge says with a pleasant smile: 'It is me dhread jooty to sintince ye to th' Supreme Coort. Long life to ye.'

"Thin there's a lull in th' proceedin's. Th' seasons go swiftly by. Other things happen an' I can't remimber whether th' pris'ner was th' victim iv th' crime, th' witness f'r th' prosecution, or th' disthrict attorney. Manny times has blithe spring turned to mellow summer. Manny times has autumn reddened th' threes in th' parks. Men that were old durin' th' thrile ar-re dead. Men that were young ar-re old. Wan mornin' with decrepit fingers I open th' pa-aper an' r-read: 'Supreme Coort revarses th' Bill Sikes case. Th' coort yisterdah afthernoon held a long session fr'm two to a quarther to three an' cleared th' calendar up to eighteen sivinty-five be revarsin' th' lower coort f'r errors an' ign'rance iv th' law in all th' cases appealed. In th' Sikes case th' decision is that while th' pris'ner was undoubtedly guilty, th' lower coort made a bone-head play be allowin' th' disthrict attorney to open th' window an' expose th' pris'ner to a dhraft, be not askin' Juryman Number Two whether he had iver been in th' dhry goods business, an' be omittin' a comma afther th' wurrud "so" on page fifty-three thousan' sivin hunderd an' eighty in th' record.'

"An' th' pris'ner is brought back f'r a new thrile. Th' new thrile is always hurrid. Th' iditors refuse a requist fr'm th' pris'ner to sind around annywan to report it, th' iliventh assistant disthrict attorney appears f'r th' state in spite iv th' law on child labor, th' witnesses ar-re all dead an' burrid, an' th' onforchnit crim'nal is turned out on a wurruld that has f'rgotten him so completely that he can't aven get a job as an actor on th' vodyville stage."

"What happens to him if he hasn't got anny money?" asked Mr. Hennessy.

"He might as well be in England," said Mr. Dooley.

THANKSGIVING

"I'm thankful I ain't Prisidint Tiddy, f'r whin me day's wurruk is done, I can close up th' shop, wind th' clock an' go to sleep. If th' stars an' moon don't shine, if th' sun don't come up, if th' weather is bad, if th' crops fail or th' banks bust or Hinnissy ain't illicted director iv th' rollin' mills, no wan can blame me. I done me jooty. Ye can't come to me an say: 'Look here, Dooley, what ails ye sindin' rainy weather befure th' hay is cut?' 'No sir,' says I. 'I promised ye nawthin' but five cints worth iv flude exthract iv hell f'r fifteen cints an' ye got it. . . . But th' Prisidint can't escape it. He has to set up at night steerin' th' stars sthraight, hist th' sun at th' r-right moment, turn on th' hot an' cold fassit, have rain wan place, an' fr-rost another, salt mines with a four years' supply iv goold, thrap th' mickrobes as they fly through th' air an' see that tin dollars is akelly divided among wan hundherd men so that each man gits thirty dollars more thin anny other. If he can't do that he's lible to be arrested th' first pay day f'r obtainin' money be false pretences."

THE IDLE APPRENTICE

♣ ♣ ♣

"THEY HANGED a man today," said Mr. Dooley.

"They did so," said Mr. McKenna.

"Did he die game?"

"They say he did."

"Well, he did," said Mr. Dooley. "I read it all in th' pa-apers. He died as game as if he was wan iv th' Christyan martyrs instead iv a thief that'd hit his man wan crack too much. Saint or murdherer, 'tis little difference whin death comes up face front.

"I read th' story iv this man through, Jawn; an', barrin' th' hangin', 'tis th' story iv tin thousan' like him. D'ye raymimber th' Carey kid? Ye do. Well, I knowed his grandfather; an' a dacinter ol' man niver wint to his jooty wanst a month. Whin he come over to live down be th' slip, 'twas as good a place as iver ye see. Th' honest men an' honest women wint as they pleased, an' laid hands on no wan. His boy Jim was as straight as th' r-roads in Kildare, but he took to dhrink; an', whin Jack Carey was born, he was a thramp on th' sthreets an' th' good woman was wurrukin' down-town, scrubbin' away at th' flures in th' city hall, where Dennehy got her.

"Be that time around th' slip was rough-an'-tumble. It was dhrink an' fight ivry night an' all day Sundah. Th' little la-ads come together under sidewalks, an' rushed th' can over to Burke's on th' corner an' listened to what th' big lads tol' thim. Th' first instruction that Jack Carey had was how to take a man's pocket handkerchief without his feelin' it, an' th' nex' he had was larnin' how to get over th' fence iv th' Reform School at Halsted Sthreet in his stockin' feet.

"He was a thief at tin year, an' th' polis 'd run f'r him if he'd showed his head. At twelve they sint him to th' bridewell f'r breakin' into a freight car. He come out, up to anny game. I see him whin he was a lad hardly to me waist stand on th' roof iv Finucane's Hall an' throw bricks at th' polisman.

"He hated th' polis, an' good reason he had f'r it. They pulled him out iv bed be night to search him. If he turned a corner, they ran him f'r blocks down th' sthreet. Whin he got older, they begun shootin' at him; an' it wasn't manny years befure he begun to shoot back. He was right enough whin he was in here. I cud conthrol him. But manny th' night whin he had his full iv liquor I've see him go out with his gun in his outside pocket; an' thin I'd hear shot after shot down th' sthreet, an' I'd know him an' his ol' inimy Clancy 'd met an' was exchangin' compliments. He put wan man on th' polis pension fund with a bullet through his thigh.

"They got him afther a while. He'd kept undher cover f'r months, livin' in freight cars an' hidin' undher viadocks with th' pistol in his hand. Wan night he come out, an' broke into Schwartzmeister's place. He sneaked through th' alley with th' German man's damper in his arms, an' Clancy leaped on him fr'm th' fence. Th' kid was tough, but Clancy played fut-ball with th' Finertys on Sundah, an' was tougher; an', whin th' men on th' other beats come up, Carey was hammered so they had to carry him to th' station an' nurse him f'r thrile.

"He wint over th' road, an' come back gray an' stooped. I was afraid iv th' boy with his black eyes; an' wan night he see me watchin' him, an' he says: 'Ye needn't be afraid,' he says. 'I won't hurt ye. Ye're not Clancy,' he says.

"I tol' Clancy about it, but he was a brave man; an' says he: ' 'Tis wan an' wan, an' a thief again an' honest man. If he gets me he must get me quick.' Th' nex' night about dusk he come saunterin' up th' sthreet, swingin' his club an' jokin' with his frind, whin some wan shouted, 'Look out, Clancy.' He was not quick enough. He died face forward, with his hands on his belt; an' befure all th' wurruld Jack Carey come across th' sthreet, an' put another ball in his head.

"They got him within twinty yards iv me store. He was down in th' shadow iv th' house, an' they was shootin' at him fr'm roofs an' behind barns. Whin he see it was all up, he come out with his eyes closed, firin' straight ahead; an' they filled him so full iv lead he broke th' hub iv th' pathrol wagon takin' him to th' morgue."

"It served him right," said Mr. McKenna.

"Who?" said Mr. Dooley. "Carey or Clancy?"

❧